Sticky Kisses

Sticky Kisses

A novel
by Greg Johnson

 alyson books
los angeles | new york

© 2001 BY GREG JOHNSON. ALL RIGHTS RESERVED.

MANUFACTURED IN THE UNITED STATES OF AMERICA.

THIS HARDCOVER ORIGINAL IS PUBLISHED BY ALYSON PUBLICATIONS,
P.O. BOX 4371, LOS ANGELES, CA 90078-4371.
DISTRIBUTION IN THE UNITED KINGDOM BY TURNAROUND PUBLISHER SERVICES LTD.,
UNIT 3, OLYMPIA TRADING ESTATE, COBURG ROAD, WOOD GREEN,
LONDON N22 6TZ ENGLAND.

FIRST EDITION: OCTOBER 2001

01 02 03 04 05 **a** 10 9 8 7 6 5 4 3 2 1

ISBN 1-55583-637-2

LIBRARY OF CONGRESS CATALOGING-IN-PUBLICATION DATA
JOHNSON, GREG.
    STICKY KISSES : A NOVEL / BY GREG JOHNSON.—1ST ED.
    ISBN 1-55583-637-2
    I. TITLE.
PS3560.O3775 S75 2001
813'.54—DC21   2001031595

CREDITS
PORTIONS OF THIS NOVEL APPEARED PREVIOUSLY IN *ONTARIO REVIEW, PRAIRIE
SCHOONER, SOUTHERN HUMANITIES REVIEW, TRIQUARTERLY,* AND *MEN ON MEN 7: BEST
NEW GAY FICTION.*

For Terry Simmons

Love's not Time's fool, though rosy lips and cheeks
Within his bending sickle's compass come;
Love alters not with his brief hours and weeks,
But bears it out even to the edge of doom.

—Shakespeare, "Sonnet 116"

We had often kissed before but not like that. That was
the life and death kiss and you only know a long time
afterwards what it is, the life and death kiss...

—Jean Rhys, *Wide Sargasso Sea*

Chapter 1

Outside her window, a young man in shirtsleeves ascended through the whirling snow.

Long-haired and slender, he looked like an angel, Abby thought. She blinked, frowning, as she always did when something failed to make sense. Along with the other passengers on this side of the plane, she watched as the man lifted a silver wand and began spreading a foamy pink substance along the wing. Now she understood, or thought she did. He must have arrived at work expecting a warm day, wearing his faded blue jeans and oversize white shirt that now flapped along his arms like wings of his own. No jacket, no hat or gloves. Abby leaned forward and pressed her nose to the blurry little window. Far below, the service truck looked snug and protected, while the metal tentacle it had sent upward—a small platform bobbing at its tip, the lone shivering workman inside it—bounced and swayed in the frigid wind.

She and her mother, Lucille, had heard a weather bulletin on their way to the airport. The temperature outside was fourteen above, the sky darkening. The temperature had plunged fifty degrees in advance of a winter storm. By lunchtime the snow had begun.

Abby's mother, after exulting for several days that her daughter was going, had abruptly decided she shouldn't.

"Not only is the weather bad *here,* but it's raining in Atlanta," Lucille had moaned, hovering at the bedroom door while her daughter packed.

Abby didn't answer; long ago she had learned not to acknowledge her mother's fickleness. You simply had to wait it out, sticking with a decision once you had made it.

"Thunderstorms," her mother said forlornly. "I was just watching the Weather Channel, honey, and what if it's a sign? Bad weather here, bad weather there, and you know how Thom drives. What if..."

Abby told her mother that she didn't believe in signs. She started zipping the garment bag, making more noise than necessary, and by the time she turned around Lucille had vanished.

She didn't believe in angels, either, yet that's exactly what she'd imagined—or hallucinated—when she saw the man outside the airplane. An angel who resembled her brother, wafting upward through the snow as if to prove he was fine, fine, they needn't worry; as if echoing the words Thom had whispered over the phone, during his surprise call on Thanksgiving day. *Listen, Abby, I'm so glad you answered. Mom isn't in the room, is she? Good. Listen, honey, I've got something to tell you....* Watching the workman de-icing the plane's wing, Abby felt her mouth cementing in a grim line even as her heart began throbbing, glowing. It was Thom; it was her lost brother Thom.... But she quelled these emotions at once.

Steeling herself to face Thom, to "let him have it" in a way that even her mother, had she known her daughter's plans, might have approved, she had no business giving way to sentimental whimsies. And now, as the man turned his head briefly in her direction, eyes clenched to slits, mouth contorted in a pained grimace against the bitter cold, Abby saw that in fact he didn't resemble her brother at all. Abby felt an annoying flush creeping up her throat, as sometimes happened in class when she misspoke, or inadvertently said something that made the students laugh. Her susceptibility to blushing (Lucille insisted it was her thin, delicate skin, inherited from Abby's father's side of the family) was one of the minor plagues of her life, but only recently had she suffered these attacks of red-facedness when alone. Quickly her chagrin would turn to anger, which brought an even hotter blood into her cheeks. Sometimes she would stare at her flushed face in a mirror, frustrated and angry, not understanding herself.

As she vowed to banish these pointless, pestering thoughts, she felt movement at her side: a petite, well-dressed woman had settled into the next seat.

"I hope you don't mind," the woman said, leaning to whisper in Abby's ear. "But they put me two rows back, next to this *awful* man."

The woman, in her late forties, genteel and perfumed, reminded Abby of the friends her mother had made since they'd moved to Philadelphia four years ago. Ladies who lived on the Main Line, or in one of the grand old apartments on Rittenhouse Square: her aunt Millicent's friends, actually, but they'd become her mother's, too. They tended to be snobbish, shallow, vain; they liked to ask Abby why on earth she wasn't married. To keep the peace at home, Abby was usually polite to them, but today she wasn't in the mood. Already the blood had drained from her face, leaving her skin feeling cool, slightly damp.

"What was so awful about him?" she said, more coldly than she'd intended.

Unfazed, the woman smiled confidingly and touched Abby's forearm. "Look for yourself," she said. "Two rows behind us, on the other side. The aisle seat."

Abby glanced back and saw a young, very obese black man. She'd noticed him boarding the plane and had tensed at the possibility of his sitting beside her. He must have weighed close to four hundred pounds. Instead of carry-on bags he'd brought two boxes of Dunkin' Donuts on board, and had rammed one into an overhead bin before maneuvering into his seat with the other. In the seats across the aisle from Abby, a pair of teenage boys wearing Braves caps turned backwards had snickered as the man trundled past.

The woman whispered to Abby, "People like that should have to buy two seats, don't you agree?"

Abby didn't agree, but gave the woman a thin smile and made a pointed gesture of opening the book she'd brought on board—a paperback of *Wide Sargasso Sea*, recommended by one of her colleagues at West Chester Academy, the girls' school where Abby taught. A rather bad, sexually explicit film had been made of the book, so the paperback featured a near-pornographic still shot: Abby made sure the woman saw the illustration before she started reading. Maybe she'd think that Abby was "awful," too, and would change her seat again.

Instead the woman said, extending a tiny suede-gloved hand, "I'm Valerie Patten. It's terrible weather we're having, isn't it? And this is still November!"

Abby shook the woman's hand, murmuring her own name. She tried to resume her reading, but the man working on the plane had come within a few feet of Abby's window. The snow had lightened, the flakes were smaller now, but the wind had strengthened, blowing the man's white shirt into a kind of balloon around his chest.

Next to her, Valerie Patten clucked her tongue. "Young men think they're invulnerable, don't they? They think they'll live forever."

Abby turned her head, startled, but before she could answer the captain's voice came over the loudspeaker.

"Sorry for the delay, folks," he said, in an airline pilot's offhand, avuncular tone, "but this little storm kind of took us by surprise. We're in the process of de-icing the wings, just as a safety precaution, and when that's done we'll be preparing for our departure to..." The voice faltered. "To, uh...to, let's see..." The microphone clicked off—there were nervous titters from the seats around Abby—and clicked on again. "To Atlanta!" the captain said brightly, like a schoolboy giving the correct answer.

Laughter rippled through the plane.

Valerie Patten touched Abby's arm and said, "Did his voice sound a little...*slurred*?" But she was smiling.

"Let's hope not," Abby said shortly. She didn't want to be rude, but she hated making small talk in airplanes, preferring to read a book or think her own thoughts.

"A surprise snowstorm, and a drunken pilot," Valerie Patten said. "Sounds like we're in for a delightful trip."

Despite herself, Abby laughed. The woman's exterior seemed so conventional, even fussy—this playful drollery came as a surprise. Valerie Patten wore an oatmeal-colored wool suit, heart-shaped gold ear clips, a matching gold necklace of imbricated heart-shaped links that caught the light whenever she turned or gestured. As if responding to Abby's curiosity the woman began tugging at her gloves, one tiny finger at a time, revealing exquisitely slender hands tipped with bright crimson nails. A manicure within the past three days, Abby judged, and it didn't surprise her that the ring finger was bare. Not that Valerie wasn't attractive or, as Lucille would say, well-preserved. Dark, wavy hair, expensively coiffed; an oval, powdered face, placed into the fragile triangle of brittle cheekbones and pointed chin like an opal gentled into its setting. The kind of pampered, self-conscious woman Abby normally disliked, but something about Valerie Patten had snagged her interest. The woman's throaty, surprisingly deep voice had an edge, as if roughened by cigarettes and alcohol, and she wore her clinging, heavily floral perfume like a mantle of desperation. Inside the mascara-spiked lashes a pair of pale-blue eyes peered out, girlish and forlorn.

Abby felt a tug of curiosity. "Are you from Philly?" she asked. "I don't hear an accent."

She was thinking of her mother's speech rhythms, clipped and somewhat abrading to Abby's ears. Since moving north, Lucille had mentioned often how happy she was that people no longer made fun of the way she talked, as they'd done in Atlanta; it was so nice to be *normal* again. Abby honestly couldn't remember anyone "making fun" of Lucille's speech—the city attracted so many newcomers, from so many parts of the country, that you rarely met a native Atlantan, and even they didn't sound particularly Southern—but it was like her mother to claim that people did. Lucille had lived in Atlanta for three decades but now claimed she'd never felt at home there.

"Oh, I'm from all over, really," Valerie Patten said. "I've got family here, but my husband lives in Atlanta." She paused, her lip curling. "My ex-husband, I mean. We've just gotten divorced."

"I'm sorry."

"Don't be." She gave a mirthless laugh. "He's number four, I'm afraid. Or was." She laughed again. "I'm training myself to use the past tense when I talk about him, but it's hard."

She gave Abby a quick, assessing look, as if seeking permission to keep talking. Abby tried to smile, but the strain must have shown, since the woman said nothing more. Abby didn't want conversation of a personal nature, not today of all days. She could imagine a string of queries from the woman's crimson-glossed lips: *Why are you traveling to Atlanta? And your husband couldn't join you? Oh, I see. You're divorced, then? No? But you're so attractive, why on earth...?* If necessary, Abby thought, she too could change her seat.

A sudden small jolt, and the plane began to move. Abby turned to her window but of course the young man, the angel, had vanished, leaving only a shimmer of windblown snow obscuring the dim grayish outline of the airport buildings.

Young men think they're invulnerable, don't they?

"Oh well," Valerie Patten said, clicking her seat belt in place. "Time to say our prayers."

Abby breathed deeply and considered doing exactly that. Although she hadn't, to her mother's dismay, attended mass in years, she knew well enough that a docile Catholic schoolgirl lodged deeply in that element of herself she may as well call, for lack of a better word, her "soul." This child wore the white veil from her First Holy Communion ceremony and still felt, at the vaguest throb of sexual desire, a responding and considerably stronger prod of censure, like a stick poked rudely into her side. A resigned agnostic—even to her adult ears, the word "atheist" sounded uncivil—Abby still felt herself reduced, in moments of seeming peril, to that desperate nine-year-old whose bony knees had ached against the cold black marble edging the side altar devoted to the Blessed Virgin. Standing with her plaster arms outstretched and her pleasant but mysterious gaze trained on the far distance, the Virgin had answered few of her childhood prayers. Yet she lingered in Abby's awareness as a benevolent tribunal, an opportunity for special pleading. A few nights ago, after she'd gotten the heart-numbing phone call from her brother, the statue's pallid features had come to her mind's eye for the first time in years, a taunting chimera floating out from an improbable past.

Her first impulse had been to flee, which she might have accomplished by remaining where she was. She'd felt a little breathless at the thought of putting down the phone and simply resuming her life, exactly as if Thom hadn't called. Her school, half of whose students were boarders from far-flung parts of the country, closed between Thanksgiving and New Year's. She had no excuse for hanging around the office, but she'd agreed to go house-hunting this week with two of her colleagues, Jane and Ted Mickelson, who were looking at several farmhouses in Bucks County; she'd planned to spend a couple of days in the library at Penn, doing some research for an honors seminar in the English novel she would teach next fall; and she'd offered to drive her mother into Center City for one of her dreaded gynecological exams, which made Lucille so nervous that she had fantasies of plunging her car over the guardrail and into the Schuylkill River, if she tried to drive herself. All these things Abby could accomplish, and would have, with the sort of even-tempered pragmatism that dominated this phase of her life, an efficiency in accomplishing tasks focused on others that had always come naturally to her. (That bony-kneed girl of nine had longed to become either a teacher or a nurse, and Abby had often thought if she'd chosen the latter option, she might have done equally well.) Within five minutes of answering her phone, Abby had said, "All right, I'll come. I'll call you back when I've made the flight arrangements." But she might have pushed her brother's raw, anxious voice into the same cluttered mental closet where the plaster Virgin Mary had long resided, knowing Thom would never call back.

He'd be too proud—and too angry. More than four years had passed since Abby or their mother had last spoken to him, and she'd sensed Thom's mix of anguish and excitement passing through the phone wires like an electric current, so much more powerful than their relatively pallid exchange of words. Just before they hung up, Abby did say, "I'm glad you called. We've got a lot to talk about, and now *this*," in a queer toneless voice that had silenced them both for a moment. Despite her self-indulgent, cold meditation that she need not go to Atlanta, after all, and could let her brother suffer there, angry and alone, she knew that she'd meant those unlikely words (*I'm glad you called*—who was that?) even if she couldn't feel whatever ancient emotions had prompted them.

Abby and Thom had agreed not to share his bad news with their mother, at least for now, since that conversation required a good deal of thought and planning. "Maybe she won't have to know," Thom had said quickly, guiltily. "She's almost seventy, isn't she? And I'm feeling fine, basically. I've lost a few pounds, but otherwise I'm OK, so why throw a bombshell into her life? When she's doing so well?"

Abby had felt like asking bitterly why Thom supposed she was doing well—she wasn't, particularly—but she'd let it pass. She knew Thom was right, and between them they plotted, in a quick rush of words, the carefully distorted version of the truth Abby would pass along to Lucille. She would announce that the prodigal son, at long last, felt ashamed by his past behavior and wanted to make amends. He'd spoken to Abby first in the hope she would intercede for him, and Abby had suggested he shouldn't come to Philly—not yet; instead, she would go to Atlanta, as though to test his sincerity, help pave the way for the grand reconciliation between Lucille and her son. (The more complicated, baroque, and unlikely the scenario, they both knew, the better the chance that Lucille would believe it.) Thom had always claimed their mother was a "drama queen." She loved intrigue, controversy, operatic emotions, and she'd made the most of the few opportunities her fairly conventional life had yielded—her grandmother's death of lung cancer in 1962, her sister Grace's stormy marriage to an alcoholic, and her son's violation of the family code of denial, which had caused this four-year breach between them. Otherwise, she pursued her addiction to hand-wringing in vicarious ways. These days Lucille spent much of her time watching television soap operas and talk shows featuring extremes of personal behavior never encountered in her own experience; she particularly enjoyed family squabbles—the messier, the better.

Abby had felt amazed that she and Thom could resume, so quickly, the effortless rapport and bemused daring of their childhood conspiracies. Despite herself, as they talked her pulse had quickened with pleasure, an almost discomforting surge of happiness, giddiness, relief—a reaction linked inextricably with early memories of her brother, emotions she hadn't felt in many years and didn't pause to examine until she hung up the phone.

And then, the possibility entering her soul like a cool sliver of glass: *It didn't happen, he didn't call. I could simply ignore him.* How furious she was with him, after all; how deeply, coldly angry to a degree she could not quite fathom.

But the idea of ignoring his call was pure fantasy, she knew. Pure self-indulgence of the kind Abby didn't allow herself these days. Within minutes Abby had come out into the den, and Lucille had looked up from her needlepoint (a six-inch-square portrait of a red-nosed reindeer, one of five she was making as Christmas presents for her canasta club) to ask in her plaintive way, "Who was *that*?"

This was probably a good time, Abby had thought. Earlier that afternoon they'd endured a grim Thanksgiving meal with Aunt Millicent and several of her widowed, lonely friends; for Abby, this annual ritual could not end soon enough, but she'd been aware that Lucille had enjoyed the outing. Holiday get-togethers, no matter how dismal, always cheered her. If she were liable ever to think indulgently about Thom, Abby supposed, the hours when she sat digesting Millicent's dry turkey breast and sugary yams might be the time. Yet when Abby told her, Lucille's hands gave an involuntary spasm, the needlepoint frame fell to her lap, and in a guilty rush Abby thought of her mother's last, rancorous encounter with Thom, and all the horror and disruption that had followed. Helplessly she thought, *Not again. It won't happen again....* So she said into her mother's blank, startled face, as if they might have been discussing what to cook for dinner, "He sounded fine, really—and sort of apologetic. He wants me to fly down there."

"You? Fly down there?"

"He asked about speaking to you," Abby said carefully, "but I told him you might not be ready."

Lucille had nodded, licking her lips. "That was good, honey. Yes." She clutched the arms of her chair. "*Then* what did he say?"

"He said...um, he said he understood," Abby said, groping. "He probably should have written first, he admitted, instead of calling out of the blue. That's what he said."

She lied so poorly!—but of course her mother didn't notice.

Lucille stared into the spotless brick-bordered fireplace—they hadn't used it once—as though mesmerized by writhing flames. "He was never much of one for writing," she said.

"No, I guess not. Anyway, he seems to want a reconciliation. He asked if he could come visit, but I said no."

Lucille gave her a startled look, but then her eyes narrowed, as if her daughter's refusal masked some shrewd maneuver Lucille couldn't fathom but was prepared to admire. "You did?" she said, nodding. "And *then* what did he say?"

"That's when he asked if I'd fly down there. I said I'd think about it."

"But what are you going to do?" Lucille said, exasperated. Her voice had turned shrill; in this same tone she often complained she got tired of "dragging" information out of Abby.

Abby had taken a chair opposite her mother's. Normally she avoided sitting here, and not only because the matching silk-upholstered wing-backs, angled cozily before the fireplace, suggested the kind of tête-à-tête they never had. She was tired generally of feeling paired with her mother, in all sorts of unlikely contexts. It was bad enough they'd bought this sub-urban town house together with its roommate floor plan—identical bed-room suites on either side of the living area—and that her mother had recently gotten her hair cut short and fluffy about her head, a much younger style than her daughter's demure little pageboy. Even worse, she'd had it tinted a flame-like reddish-orange, several shades brighter than Abby's. Why didn't Abby change her hair after breaking up with Graham? one of her friends at school had suggested, but this idea held no appeal. Shortly after moving to Philadelphia she'd gotten the pageboy cut, impul-sively, after thumbing a newsstand copy of *Harper's Bazaar* and seeing it on a pouting, soigné model in a sequin-collared tuxedo. She'd never felt com-fortable with the haircut but had not wanted to resume the shiny, bouncy, popular-high-school-girl style she'd kept into her thirties. Her mother had urged Abby to copy her new "Shirley MacLaine bob," as she called it, but to resemble her mother's younger-looking twin was the last thing Abby wanted. On Lucille the haircut had a pixie-like flair, at least, for someone in her sixties, but on the taller, thinner Abby it would resemble, she knew, a mere shapeless cap stuck onto her head.

Abby had spent little time thinking about her appearance these past few years, as though stubbornly taking a different path from Lucille. (Her mother had also started dressing "younger," as she admitted freely, now and then buying a blouse or piece of jewelry gaudier than anything Abby would wear.) Lucille crowed with delight whenever one of her friends, or sometimes a perfect stranger—a checkout lady at the A & P, most recent-ly—insisted they looked "like sisters." Lucille was almost seventy and looked it, and Abby was thirty-six: how could they look like sisters? Since ending her long engagement several months earlier, Abby was hardly prone to vanity, but she bristled at the assumption that she and her mother, because they lived together and seemed to get along, must have a great deal in common. "You're so lucky," Abby had heard her Aunt Millicent tell Lucille one day, "to have your daughter as your best friend. I hardly *ever* hear from Evelyn or Sandra, either one." The thought of Lucille being mistaken for her best friend had chilled Abby's heart. She and her mother were no more alike than two women randomly thrown together in a college dormitory.

During their awkward conversation after Thom's phone call, Abby had grown tired of the pretense that they were in cahoots against him. She said, "I'm going to do exactly what I told him I'd do. Think about it."

"What? You've *got* to go," her mother said. "This was what we were waiting for, the first year or two, wasn't it?—until we sort of gave up. I thought it was over, really. I thought he'd never call."

Abby hadn't given up, but saw no point in telling her mother that.

"I guess you're right," she said. She paused, feeling a childish intransigence. "But I'll have to think about it."

"What for? You can go down, spend a few days, and then you can both come back here. You gave your last exams on Tuesday, didn't you?—so this is perfect timing. And we've still got several weeks to work everything out before Christmas. We'll have Millicent and her girls over, of course, and the kids. We'll have a little reunion on Christmas eve."

Abby knew better than to feel surprised at her mother's mind racing ahead, the reconciliation all but accomplished, the past forgotten; in another few seconds Lucille would be planning Thom's homecoming party, thinking about the food and the color of the napkins. Abby's need to stop her, to apply the brakes, induced a perilous, quicksilver moment when she longed to blurt out the truth. The force of this yearning pulled her forward in her chair, made her take a deep breath. She said in the calm, even tone her mother would interpret as stubbornness, "I said I have to think about it, Mom. Please try to relax. Please don't get carried away."

She stood and left the room, affecting a brisk decidedness though her hands were shaking. Whether this was anger or simple terror she couldn't have said.

She went to the phone on her bedside table and made the reservation, discussing fares and seating arrangements in the mild, businesslike voice in which she taught her classes and made small talk with colleagues in the faculty lounge. There was no point in waiting or thinking. There was no way to keep Lucille's fantasies in check, no matter that her children, as she said often, had never failed to disappoint her. But a few days later, strapped into her seat as the plane lumbered into the air, Abby wondered if perhaps their lives shouldn't remain as they were. As Thom had said, there was surely a good chance that Lucille, who had grown querulous and irrational with age, would interpret his illness as yet another betrayal. Abby could return from Atlanta and say ruefully that she and Thom had quarreled: it was likely, in fact it was certain, that neither of them would hear from him again. No, he hadn't apologized. He hadn't sent along any message to his mother. This would bring a few tears, perhaps, but it would also bring closure. (This was a word Lucille had picked up from the talk shows she watched; she only wanted *closure* with Thom, she would say wistfully.) After a while, Lucille would begin wondering why her children had quarreled, and what Abby had done or said to provoke him, but that was something Abby would refuse to let her mother drag out of her. So Lucille would never suffer the truth, and she could blame her vague unhappiness on her two inconsiderate children for the rest of her life.

But that was fantasy too. Abby took a deep breath and opened the paperback she'd brought, but within seconds Valerie Patten, that pert little made-up woman she'd all but forgotten, interrupted her.

"Is anything wrong?" the woman asked.

"Wrong?" Abby said.

"That book you're reading—are you enjoying it?"

"Yes, it's—" Then she saw: she was holding the book upside down.

Valerie Patten laughed brightly. "Sorry," she said, touching Abby's wrist. "I couldn't help but notice."

Abby closed the book and put it aside. "I'm a little preoccupied," she admitted. "And flying makes me nervous."

"Me, too. I can't even pretend to read." She laughed again, her tiny palms held upward in comic resignation. Abby smiled. There was something sad but sympathetic in the dogged effort implied by the woman's clothes, jewelry, make-up. Almost everyone on this flight wore ordinary jeans and jackets, or sweatshirts. (Abby had already tugged one sleeve of her old blue sweater down over the cuff with the missing button, which she'd fastened with a safety pin this morning; and she wished she'd at least bothered with some lipstick—and some polish for her bitten-down nails.) Perhaps Valerie had imagined being paired at random with some handsome stranger who would become helplessly smitten and take her to lunch at the Ritz-Carlton when they reached Atlanta. Ten years ago, Abby herself might have entertained such a fantasy.

"Speaking of reading," Valerie said, "I went to a fortune teller yesterday down on South Street. That's what they call it, you know—a reading. She used the Tarot cards, she stared at my palms for a while, and guess what. A new man is about to enter my life! I thought to myself, four husbands and you're telling me there's going to be another man? Why not remind me, too, that after Tuesday comes Wednesday? Anyway, for this I paid $60. The woman claimed to be Jamaican, she wore some sort of native costume and talked about voodoo for a while, but she didn't fool me. I know she was just a little black girl from North Philly. She sounded about as Jamaican as I do. It was fun, I guess, but really—a new man!"

Abby nodded. "My brother and I did that once, when we were in college. It was my birthday, and he took me to an old woman in Little Five Points. I think her name was Sister Amelia—a spiritual reader and adviser, she called herself. She assumed Thom was my boyfriend, and in the first five minutes she told us we should go ahead and get married."

"Oh, you're kidding. How hilarious!" Valerie cried. When she laughed, her eyes crinkled agreeably. Abby noticed that some of the glossy lipstick had rubbed onto her front teeth. "Then what happened, did you tell her the truth?" she asked.

Before Abby could reply, a male flight attendant appeared in the aisle, tugging at his beverage cart and asking what they'd like to drink. Valerie quickly turned to him, asking questions, prolonging the transaction with some flirtatious banter, even though the attendant, a handsome, dimpled man with curly blond hair, looked no older than twenty-five. Abby ordered a diet cola, but to her surprise Valerie asked for a glass of red wine though it wasn't yet eleven o'clock. After serving their drinks the attendant handed them each a foil-wrapped bag of peanuts and moved to the next row.

Valerie sipped gingerly at her wine. "This should help," she murmured, then amended: "This should help a lot."

Abby didn't ask her to explain, and wondered if that fruity odor might be more than just perfume. She wondered, too, if it would be rude to pick up her book again, since Valerie Patten was clearly in the mood to talk.

"Do you live in Atlanta?" Valerie asked. "You don't sound like you're from Philly, either."

"We moved north a few years ago, my mother and I," Abby said quickly, "but my brother stayed behind. We grew up in Atlanta."

"So you're going to visit him? That's nice," Valerie said vaguely. "I haven't seen either one of my brothers in years. They disapproved of my second husband, thinking I shouldn't have divorced the first one. They were probably right, as it turned out. They never even met number three or four! And now I've gone back to 'Patten,' my maiden name. What about you, hon? You married?"

Valerie had slipped the question in so swiftly that Abby answered without thinking, "No, I just broke off a long engagement." She bit her lip. Normally, she was skilled at evading such queries. Even the other day on the phone, she'd managed to sidestep certain oblique questions from Thom, disguised as casual conversation: What was she doing with herself lately? How was the nightlife in Philly? Abby had said she stayed very busy with her work and then changed the subject.

"Oh, sorry to hear that," the woman said, and the sympathy in her voice did sound genuine. "But you're younger than I am and probably smarter too." She touched two fingers to her lips and hiccuped briefly. "Better you broke it off than to be stuck in a bad marriage," she added. "Believe you me."

Abby allowed the image of Graham's face—tense, anguished in disbelief—to drift into her mind's eye. She felt a bit light-headed, as if she were the one drinking a glass of wine. The altitude, she supposed. Valerie Patten, after all, was a woman she didn't know and would never see again. So she said the words she hadn't said to her mother or her friends, or even to Graham. "I didn't love him. Simple as that." She knew her voice sounded cool and unconcerned—again, her schoolteacher's voice—but she supposed it didn't matter. "I don't know why I ever agreed to marry him."

"God, do I know *that* feeling," Valerie laughed. She sipped her wine, her necklace of tiny, tilted gold hearts winking brightly. "Especially with Marty, the guy I married two years ago. In fact," and now Valerie leaned close, her voice husky and conspiratorial, "that's why I'm going to Atlanta. To try and get things settled, once and for all."

Abby had tensed, resisting the urge to draw back in her seat. The blend of the woman's cloying perfume and wine-soaked breath was faintly repellent.

"Do you mean...are you reconciling?" Abby said.

Valerie shook her head. "No, no. That's what he wants, but—" She paused. "Well, I hope you don't mind listening to this, but Marty sent me a letter. It came just yesterday." She stopped again, giving Abby a sideways look. "I'm just wondering," she added, "how *you* would handle this. You seem like such a sensible girl. Not a sentimental fool like me."

But Valerie said "fuel," not "fool"; Abby wondered how much the woman had drunk before boarding the plane.

"I don't mind," Abby said doubtfully. "He sent you a letter? Your ex-husband?"

Valerie nodded. She'd nestled her small leather handbag between her hip and the armrest, and now she undid the clasp and extracted a small, folded-over envelope.

"It's just a note, really." She held it in the air between them, turning it over as though displaying evidence. "See, I've been staying with my sister for a while. She's divorced, too, but she's still got her big place in Society Hill. Anyway, Marty doesn't have Andrea's address or phone number, so he sends letters to my mom's house—*she* lives in Miami Beach—and begs her to forward them. I've gotten two, three letters a week, sometimes more, all pleading with me to come back, let's give it another try. Never mind that we've already given it thirty-five tries. Andrea thought I should return the letters unopened, but I didn't have the heart. The letters were so *sweet*, in a way. Marty always wrote very well. In fact, he works for an ad firm."

She laughed, as if recalling some private joke.

"I guess he figured I wasn't buying, since the letters stopped coming about a month ago. I hadn't answered a single one, you see. Andrea insisted I shouldn't. She was afraid he'd turn into a psycho stalker and come murder us in our beds or something. If I ignored him, she said, he'd eventually give up, and for awhile I really thought he had. I was *so* relieved. I thought he'd finally gotten on with his life, you know? But then yesterday, out of the blue"—she flicked the envelope with one of her crimson nails—"comes this."

She paused; her face had sagged a little.

"I—I just wondered what you would do, if you got a letter like this." Again she stopped. To Abby's surprise, the woman's pale-blue eyes glistened with tears.

"But what's in it?" Abby said, trying not to sound too eager. "What did he write?"

Valerie said, sniffling, "I shouldn't bother you with this. You'd rather be reading your book." Again she rooted in her purse. She brought out a wrinkled blue Kleenex and dabbed at her eyes.

"I really don't mind—"

"Nope, I've got to stop acting this way. It's so foolish and irrational."

Valerie dropped the envelope back in her purse, then fastened the clasp with a decisive twist of her fingers. Again she brought the Kleenex to her eyes.

Abby said, her gaze fixed on the purse, "Are you OK?"

Valerie gave a brief, pained-looking smile. She'd begun fiddling with her seat belt.

"Sure, I'm fine—thanks for asking." She patted Abby's hand. "I'd better get to the little girls' room. This wine is going right through me."

Valerie fastened the tray table, neatly depositing the empty bottle in the seat pocket and cradling the plastic cup of wine in her hand. As she stood, steadying herself against the seatback, Abby's attention stayed on the purse, which Valerie had casually dropped onto her seat.

A small, vanilla-suede clutch purse, expensive-looking but soiled around the edges.

Abby took a breath. She recalled guiltily the time when she was about fourteen and Lucille had scolded her. Aunt Millicent had come to visit, and one morning when Millicent had gone out Lucille had caught Abby and Thom in the guest room, systematically rifling through their aunt's private things. Abby had just held up one of Millicent's ancient corsets— an impossibly complicated, heavy contraption, faded from its original white to a pale ivory—for Thom's inspection. Both had been giggling, joking back and forth, tugging at the corset between them, when Lucille appeared at the doorway, hands on her hips: "Abigail! Thomas!" She'd given them a predictable lecture about respecting the privacy of others, about the ignominious character of people who descended to "snooping." Twelve-year-old Thom had hurried off, snickering under his breath and leaving Abby to another volley of scolding. "I might have expected this of Thom," Lucille fumed. "He's still a boy, after all, and he's always been prankish. But *you*, Abigail."

Her mother's eyes had narrowed. This had marked the moment, as Lucille would say throughout Abby's teenage years, when she had "seen the light" about her daughter.

After that morning, Lucille enjoyed pointing out that Abby could surely fool her Grandma Sadler, who was so sweet and trusting; or Daddy, who was always preoccupied with his job or his woodworking or whatever he did during his long evenings in the basement; or even the eagle-eyed nuns at school, who were forever sending Abby home with report cards studded with A's and glowing written comments (bordered with shiny gold-foil crosses) on Abby's "docile and cooperative" nature, her status as "one of the best-behaved girls in the school." But, her mother said, Abby couldn't fool *her* any longer.

"Once a snoop, always a snoop," Lucille had pronounced, turning smartly away and leaving her daughter to think about that.

It was true. Never mind that Lucille shared the trait, going through her children's possessions routinely while they were at school. Once or twice she'd even read the pink-leatherette five-year diary Abby had gotten from Grandma Sadler for her tenth birthday, and she hadn't troubled to hide the evidence of her tampering, leaving the diary's metal clasp undone. But yes, it was true that even at age nine or ten, when Thom was too young to take an interest, Abby had gone through her parents' drawers regularly, whenever she knew they were in the backyard or busy with company out in the den. She'd dug to the bottom of her mother's stack of nylon underwear and lingerie, she'd pawed through her father's drawer of boxer shorts and socks, looking for...for what? She hadn't quite known, and as an adult she hadn't cared to think about it. Even now, teaching her classes, she felt stray but oddly intense impulses of curiosity toward certain of her students. Once a troubled girl in Abby's first-year English class had left her notebook behind in Abby's office, and without hesitation Abby had paged through it, pondering each drawing and doodle, reading all the random girlish sentiments—"I luv luv *luv* L.C."—scattered through the pages.

She no longer told herself, as she'd done in college when snooping in her roommate's desk drawers, that she felt an "innocent curiosity" about other people, wanting to know much more than Abby Sadler in person, with her traits of Southern courtesy and reserve, could ever have found out directly. She was not the kind of girl in whom other girls readily confided, a realization that had helped her decide in her junior year to change her major from psychology (she'd had fantasies of becoming a school counselor) to English. As a teacher of literature, at least, she could dissect the private lives of fictional characters and even their authors with impunity—and without having to reveal anything of herself. Yet she'd stayed intensely curious about the bright-eyed teenage girls in her classes, who hung on Abby's every word with such absurd expressions of deference and admiration; and about her faculty colleagues, whom she liked but had not really befriended; and above all, and endlessly, about her brother Thom with whom, until last week, she hadn't spoken for an impossible four and a half years, yet about whom she thought daily, sometimes hourly, telling herself she ought to try and forget him, since he clearly had no further interest in *her* life.

Yet it was true that her curiosity was seldom "innocent," as her mother had perceived. Lucille would be the last one to use the word, but Abby was closeted, she thought. A closeted snoop.

While Valerie Patten made her way down the aisle, Abby kept watch on the teenage boys across from her, the only passengers in a position to see what she was doing. Both were fast asleep, their arms folded tightly across their chests. Abby's hand felt for the purse, fingered the clasp, and extracted the envelope. Quickly she unfolded the note and read:

Thurs.

Val:

You know I'm not the type to write, "By the time you read this,"
etc. I don't want to sound melodramatic. But I'm tired of fighting it.
Val—all of it. Nothing is worthwhile without you.
 Enclosed is my lawyer's card. He has a copy of my will, darling,
and of course everything is for you. I mention this because Mom and
"Big Steve" may try to contest it and I want you to fight, if necessary,
for what's rightfully yours.
 God knows, I tried to.
 Please don't feel bad or guilty. I know that you tried as well. It's
better this way.

All my love,
Marty

Abby stared at the note, stricken. She felt a sudden chill, especially in her hands: her fingertips had numbed with cold. Fumbling, she refolded the sheet and stuffed it back inside the envelope. She had already reached for the purse when she heard, from behind her, that unmistakable husky, good-humored voice: "Oops, I'm sorry, hon. Didn't mean to sideswipe you!"

A moment later Valerie had settled back in her seat, clutching the purse in both hands. She was laughing. "I guess we're getting into some rough air," she told Abby. "I practically fell into that poor woman's lap a couple of rows back."

Abby had quickly rerouted her outstretched hand and started fiddling with the air control above her seat. Just in time, she'd managed to slide the envelope beneath her hip.

"It's getting chilly in here, too," Abby said awkwardly. She was thinking: how long had she sat there, staring at that alarming note? It seemed that Valerie had been gone for less than a minute. Abby added, casually,

"That was a quick trip. Did you find the restroom?"

"Yeah, but there are half a dozen people in line," Valerie said. "I'll wait a few minutes, I guess."

Abby felt the light skittering of her heartbeat; her breath came in brief, shallow lunges.

"Let's see, what were we talking about?" Valerie said. Then, in a subdued voice, "Oh, I remember. You wanted to read Marty's letter."

"Oh no, that's all right," Abby said quickly. "It's really none of my business."

She watched nervously as Valerie fingered the clasp of her purse.

"It's not that," Valerie said. "I just didn't want to impose, I guess. But I haven't told anyone about—about his letter, or why I'm flying to Atlanta. I guess I *would* like your opinion, if you're sure you don't mind."

Abby took a deep breath. What had her mother said, whenever she suspected Abby or Thom had misbehaved? *Confession is good for the soul, you know.* Her mother was a never-ending source of clichés, which she pronounced in a lilting, prideful voice, as if her words had been particularly clever. At such moments, Thom usually had confessed; Abby, almost never.

But Valerie didn't open her handbag. From the speakers above their seats, the captain's voice had crackled into life. Simultaneously, a gong had sounded, illuminating the FASTEN YOUR SEAT BELT warning.

Saved by the bell, Lucille might say. *You're one lucky young lady, Abigail Sadler.*

"Ladies and gentlemen, we've begun our descent into Atlanta, but we're encountering some rough air. It's nothing to worry about, but the city is getting hammered with some pretty strong thunderstorms at the moment. So just hang on, and please keep your seat belt securely fastened. We'll have to suspend cabin service at this point, but we hope to have you on the ground in about half an hour."

"Half an hour!" Valerie wailed. She gave Abby a sheepish look. "Why didn't I use that darned restroom when I had the chance?"

"Oh, I'm sure they wouldn't mind if you went back," Abby said.

"You think not?" Valerie craned her head into the aisle. "All the others have sat back down," she said doubtfully. "I don't want to get chewed out by a stewardess half my age." She sighed. "Oh, I can wait. I guess this is my punishment."

"Your punishment?" Abby said faintly.

"Yeah, for indulging myself with that glass of wine. Before lunch." She gave a small, saddened laugh, then settled back into her seat. Abby noticed with relief that she'd inserted the purse into the seat pocket, next to the empty wine bottle. Evidently she had forgotten about the letter.

Abby took up her copy of *Wide Sargasso Sea* and pretended to read. She could replace the letter when they landed, she thought. She'd offer to hold Valerie's purse while she retrieved her coat from the overhead rack, presuming she'd brought one on board, or else seize a moment's opportunity while Valerie was looking the other way. It would take a couple of seconds, no more. *I hope you've learned a lesson from this,* Lucille's self-satisfied voice whispered into her ear.

Abby held the book open, turning a page every minute or two, but she could not pay attention. Outside her window, the clouds had darkened steadily; the plane pitched and swayed as it descended through the heavy wind, leaving a queasy sensation in Abby's stomach. She remembered the young guy she'd seen de-icing the wings at the Philly airport. Lacking a coat or hat, seeming angelic in his rippling white shirt as he ascended through the eddying snow. The man hadn't really resembled her brother. Even after four years, of course, she would recognize Thom at once, anytime and anywhere. He could never elude her.

Or rather, she could never escape *him*. Thom had insisted he was all right, that he felt fine, but still her mind's eye suffered those long-familiar images from the TV news and occasional magazine reports she'd paged through. Men in their twenties or thirties, in the prime of life, yet their faces sunken and deathly pale, skeletal arms hanging useless at their sides. Their skin ravaged, some of them, by those awful raspberry-colored lesions—*scarlet lesions,* she'd thought. Nothing to do with her, she must have imagined back then. Idly watching the TV reports in her smug innocence. No connection to *her* life, she must have assumed as she skimmed through the magazine stories, staring briefly at each gruesome photograph before turning the page.

Even if she'd known about Thom, she might have done the same thing, closing her heart against him. "Serves them right," she'd heard her bigoted cousin Sandra mutter one day. Abby tasted the syllables: *Serves him right.* Only now had he summoned her, after all this time. Wanting help. Wanting sympathy. Like the pathetic husband who'd written that suicide note to Valerie Patten, pretending love while thinking only of himself.

Brothers, husbands. Loved ones. Even as her heart churned, Abby felt a vile sensation in her throat, the tingling of nausea.

The plane ride had gotten bumpier; she heard something from Valerie Patten—a little exclamation that sounded like "Goodness!"—but Abby turned in the opposite direction, facing the rain-streaked window. Tears of frustration had filled her eyes and she touched at them quickly, then wiped her fingertips along the side of her skirt. If Valerie noticed, she reasoned, she could say something about the book she was reading. A poignant scene, she could say. A tragic story.

Her blood jumped: a loud cracking of thunder had jarred the plane, like a mighty clap of hands in the unsettled lead-colored air outside her window.

"My goodness!" Valerie said again. Laughing nervously, she glanced at Abby. Valerie opened her mouth to say something else, but she stopped. She must have seen.

"Don't worry, hon." She slipped an arm around Abby's shoulder. "I've flown in weather much worse than this, believe it or not."

"I'm all right," Abby lied. "This book I'm reading—"

Another crack of thunder, jolting Abby and everyone else into silence. None of the flight attendants had been visible for several minutes. Evidently they'd retreated, strapped themselves into their seats. This time, even Valerie Patten didn't cry out or give one of her throaty, nervous laughs. An eerie silence overtook the plane. The storm clouds hugging the windows filled the cabin with a sickish half-light. After each blast of thunder, sheets of lightning turned the clouds a ghastly silver, a neon shriek of tin-colored light Abby saw reflected pitifully on Valerie's pale, damp-looking forehead and cheeks. Across the aisle the two teenage boys sat forward, their heads swiveling between their window and Abby's. They elbowed each other as though trying to joke themselves out of being afraid. One of the boys had removed his cap, pulling his thick hair upward in dark, surprised-looking tufts.

Valerie leaned close, her hand gripping Abby's shoulder. "Now *I'm* getting a little worried," she said, abashed. "Those clouds, they're so—"

Again the loudspeaker roared to life. "Ladies and gentlemen, we're encountering some very rough weather." Just as abruptly, the speaker went dead.

"Thanks for the update, Captain," Valerie said. She sounded almost angry. "My God, does he think we're all morons?"

Abby glanced over, trying to smile. As the plane bucked left and right, as thunder boomed and lightning blazed and rain clattered like slanted knives around them, she'd grown strangely calm. Minutes ago she'd felt so anxious, her breath coming fast, but now she felt she could endure or even enjoy whatever might happen. She gave herself up to the violent lurching of the plane like one of the Victorian heroines in the novels she taught, abandoning themselves in torrents of passion to the embraces of tempestuous, dark-browed lovers.

Another crackling of the speakers.

"Sorry for the interruption, folks," the captain said, "but we were getting some advice from the tower at Hartsfield. Just wanted to assure you that everything's under control. It's one of those situations that looks much worse than it is." He chuckled briefly. "The weather is pretty crabby out there, I know, but—"

A deafening crack of thunder drowned him out.

A few seconds later, as the thunder rumbled off, Valerie whispered in Abby's ear, "'Crabby?' Is that what he said? This guy's crazy!"

Though Valerie was trying for sarcasm, Abby could hear the terror in her voice.

"Don't worry," she said. "I think he's just trying to—"

Then came a glare of lightning so intense that Abby broke off, blinking. In the same instant the cabin lights blinked off, and the plane tilted wildly to the left, accompanied by a loud *Badoom!* as though the left wing had been struck by the fist of God.

Somewhere behind Abby, a girl screamed; a man several rows ahead stood abruptly, hitting his head on the luggage bin. "What the hell?" he cried, confused. He bent at the waist, as though readying himself to vomit. "Sit back down!" a woman yelled. "And for God's sake, fasten your seat belt!" Abby saw the woman's arm grab at the man and jerk him back down to his seat.

Inside the cabin there was only the dusky light emitted by the pewter-colored storm and occasional sickly-bright flashes of lightning that glittered off the swaying wings. Abby sat numbed, feeling nothing. Valerie Patten's arm still clutched her shoulder, and when the lights went out she'd pressed her head against Abby's breast, like a child in need of solace. Abby worried the passengers might panic and rush chaotically into the aisles, but within a few seconds that unearthly silence had filled the plane again.

"Don't worry," Abby murmured, though she couldn't be sure if Valerie Patten heard. The woman had begun to sob, her body shaking in rhythmic spasms. Yet the plane seemed to have righted itself, and unless Abby was imagining it, the clouds had turned a lighter, paler gray. Had the rain stopped? Again came the familiar crackling of the captain's microphone.

"Folks, we're just a few minutes from landing. Sorry for that rough patch—and for the loss of the cabin lights. We had a lightning strike on the wing, and sometimes the power gets knocked out when that happens. But it's nothing to worry about—happens all the time. The worst is behind us, so just sit tight. We'll be on the ground in a few minutes."

And they were. The moment the gong sounded, the passengers shambled into the aisles. They hauled down their luggage from the overhead bins and chatted back and forth as if nothing extraordinary had happened. Even Valerie seemed unfazed: she raised her head and shook herself briefly as though waking from a dream and, in the same instant, forgetting it. She said to Abby, "It was fun talking with you, hon. Hope you and your brother have a nice visit." She smiled briefly, not quite meeting Abby's eyes; by now her front teeth were liberally smeared with lipstick.

"Yes, thanks," Abby said awkwardly.

She sat there, stunned, as the other passengers waited in the aisle. What was she doing here? Why had she come? She felt a wild longing for her life back in Philadelphia, its calm and safety. Only one phone call from her prodigal brother and here she was, risking everything.

The other passengers, including those behind her, were shuffling toward the exit, but Abby waited, her heart chilled at the thought of Thom standing somewhere beyond the gate. She did not know what would happen or what she felt, thinking only that she must compose herself. Her lips had made a small, frozen smile. By now the other passengers had filed off the plane, Valerie among them, but only when Abby felt reasonably sure she could hold the smile in place, no matter what, did she stand and begin feeling around for the purse and book she'd brought on board. Her movements were stiff and preoccupied, as though she'd been temporarily blinded. Only after she exited the plane did she understand that, in her numbed left hand, she held in a tight clutch the letter she had stolen from Valerie Patten.

Chapter 2 . . . .

"Do I look *that* bad?" she asked him.

So Thom understood that his face had fallen. He tried to compensate by grinning, and hugging her extra-tight. For an extra-long moment.

But my God, it was true: she looked terrible. For four years he'd been staring at the photo on his bedside table, which he'd snapped during the little party their mother had given to celebrate Abby's getting her master's at Emory. Her hair had been longer then, pulled taut and tied in back but nonetheless full and luxuriant, her best feature. That burnished auburn shade he loved with a few lighter, almost-blond streaks, especially the pale tendrils curling at her temples and all but concealing her tiny, elegant ears. She'd stared forthrightly into the camera, with a fixed smile he recognized as a little strained but others would not, and she'd worn a fancy red blouse their mother had bought for the occasion.

"Your sister is so pretty!" his friends said whenever he showed them the picture. The droll, slow-talking Carter, who lived in the same section of their condominium complex and who had become, Thom supposed, his best friend, had been the first to crack "Yes, she's really attractive. She doesn't look a thing like *you*."

Thom wondered what Carter would say now—or rather, what he would think, for Carter's old-guard Southern courtesy would have precluded any critical comment on a friend's sister, even in jest—if he'd seen Abby emerge confusedly from the gate. Thom had sprung forward, singing out her name, but yes, his face had fallen, and after they hugged, and he thought to himself that she felt lighter than a rag doll, they separated and stared for a long, hungry moment.

"No, you don't look bad at all," he said, with deliberate lightness. "I was starting to worry, that's all. You were the last one off the plane."

"Well, I—I just waited," Abby said, briskly running splayed fingers through her short, helmet-like hair. The haircut was awful, he thought. Her clothes were a little grim, too. She wore an ordinary cotton blouse under a pale-blue sweater, both tucked inside her tightly cinched jeans, an unflattering emphasis of her gaunt, boyish figure. Her face was denuded of makeup, and her skin looked drawn and pale, with faint bruise-like shadows beneath her eyes; the eyes themselves were reddened as if from eyestrain or simple exhaustion.

Thom hadn't planned to mention this until later—much later, in fact— but as they began the long trek toward baggage claim he said, "I was sorry to hear about you and that guy you'd been seeing—Graham, was that his name?"

Abby looked over, more annoyed than surprised. "Have you talked to Mom? When did—"

"No, not Mom," he said quickly. Damn, he shouldn't have popped off like that, but at once he'd assumed that Graham—whoever he was—must be the reason for his sister's weary, forlorn appearance. "I've been talking on the phone with Ginger once in a while," he explained. "She's been keep-ing me posted."

Instantly he regretted that, too. Abby and their youngest cousin had never really gotten along; or rather, they simply had nothing in common. Ginger got the family news from her mother, Lucille and Millicent's younger sister, and then passed it along to Thom.

"She hasn't kept *me* posted. I haven't seen Ginger or Aunt Grace in years." She glanced away. "Not since Daddy's funeral."

For a few seconds, they trudged along in silence.

"OK," Thom said, chagrined. "I guess I deserved that."

Abby looked over, with a ghost of the childlike conspirator's smile they'd exchanged so often when they were growing up. It was all the encouragement Thom needed.

"My God, Abby, you can't imagine how I wanted to call, to try and explain, but the timing was so awkward...I was *so* damned furious at some of the things Mom had said and...and I guess at you too, because you didn't say much to contradict her. I don't think you said a word, did you?"

He didn't wait for an answer. It felt so good, after all this time, to unleash the torrent of words that had swirled madly in his head for so long—explanations and accusations, justifications and denials, all the sheer pent-up emotion he'd experienced after the rift with his mother and sister. He loped along, then saw that Abby was trotting to keep up with him; he forced himself to slow down, adjust to her pace, but the words kept rushing out.

"By the time I did call," he said, "the phone had been cut off. I don't know why that was such a shock—you'd told me which day the movers were coming. You left the news on my answering machine, remember? But my God, that same phone number we'd had since we were kids, somehow the idea of its being disconnected…"

He stopped, gulping; an unexpected surge of emotion had choked off his words. He remembered that he'd sat on the side of his bed in a kind of stupor, his prepared little speech dissolving in the wake of that brisk, record-ed announcement: "The number you have reached…" (It was the same number their mother had drilled into his and Abby's memory when they were tiny preschoolers: in case they ever got lost, Mom had explained, or in some kind of trouble.) Though he should have known better, he'd dialed the number again, and again had gotten the recording; he'd dialed another time, and another. It was a moment etched forever in his memory.

"Then I started calling Information in Philly—you know, to get the new listing, but they never had anything, not in Mom's name and not in yours. I had Aunt Millie's number, of course, but at some point I thought—well, I figured Mom would call *me* once she calmed down. Or you would. You know, after you'd gotten moved in and settled. So I went into this waiting mode, I guess, and after a while I got upset and angry all over again. I kept remembering some of the things Mom had said, which I thought were *so* unfair, and how you hadn't backed me up. And *my* phone number hadn't changed, after all. After a while I thought, well, if that's the way they want it…"

They'd reached baggage claim, and Thom found the carousel where Abby's bags would arrive; he realized they were both out of breath. The familiar airport noises eddied around them—garbled announcements over the loudspeaker, the laughing and chattering of other passengers—but an awkward circle of quiet descended on Thom and Abby. They half-turned toward each other, and Thom used the uncomfortable moment to notice again how gaunt she looked, her cheekbones and chin too prominent and her rib cage curved sharply inward, like the sides of a frail violin, under her plain blue sweater. Her cheeks had turned a faint pink from the exertion of their long walk but her eyes seemed unfocused, looking off beyond his shoulder. Maybe she hadn't listened to a word he'd said.

Then she startled him, reaching in a slow, deliberate gesture to touch his forearm, with a smile that seemed rueful and conciliatory. Or so it looked to his hopeful, hungry stare.

He was wrong. She said quietly, but firmly, "It's unforgivable, what you did. I knew you were upset about the funeral, and she shouldn't have done that, but not to call before we left, to just ignore what was happening..."

His stomach turned to lead. "Why didn't you call me, then?" he said awkwardly.

She gave him the same look, he thought in misery, she might give to one of her students who claimed the dog had eaten her homework. But when she did speak, he was relieved by the mildness of her voice.

"Come on, we're all grown-ups now. You can't assume everything will be done *for* you. Not any more."

"Look, I'm not expecting sympathy," he said, "or forgiveness or whatever you think—"

"Don't expect anything," she said. "I'm here because Mom wanted me to come, and because we've got to figure out how to deal with this...this new situation. In a way that's best for *her*."

He stared down at his shoes. "All right, then. We'll do that."

"And in a few days, we'll fly back up there together, and you can work it out with her. But that's your job. I'm bringing you home, but then I'm staying out of it."

He didn't answer. Her resolution, and the way she had coldly thought everything out, startled him. Was this Abby?

He said slowly, "Well, we have a few days to...to think about it. Like you said..."

He had no intention of flying to Philadelphia. He stood there taking in the fact he'd asked her to come for one reason, and she'd come for a different reason, and the two motives were irreconcilable. How could they avoid, once again, disappointing each other? What had he hoped this would accomplish?

Now she offered him a weary smile, and he tried to let that comfort him.

"We'll work it out," he said doubtfully.

"Yes. OK," she said.

Relieved, Thom let out a sudden gush of air, only now aware that he'd been holding his breath. "Great," he added.

Beside them, the carousel had begun revolving, suitcases and boxes blundering through the little curtain of black rubber strips, then down the narrow chute to the conveyor belt. One of the packages was wrapped in bright red paper, but its wide green ribbon had come undone, the half-crushed bow flapping dismally against one side of the box.

"Oh," Thom said, "and one more thing. Merry Christmas."

Impulsively, he bent to give Abby a peck on the cheek, but at that moment she turned to him, startled. As nearby travelers watched idly, Thom's fleeting kiss alighted—accidentally, but firmly—on his sister's vaguely parted lips.

After he'd loaded her two bags into his Accord and navigated the expressway in his strenuous do-or-die manner—weaving impatiently among slower cars, cursing softly whenever the traffic slowed—they finally reached his condominium complex, a buff-colored brick structure off Rock Springs Road. Pulling into the lot, Thom saw the place through Abby's eyes: cracking sidewalks, doorways and trim that needed paint, flower beds thinly planted with a ragged-looking assortment of purple and yellow pansies. Like most real estate agents, Thom frequently suffered these objective, appraising looks at his own home. Until he'd gotten the bad news last month—the date *October 19, 1998,* was seared into his memory, his private doomsday—he'd been planning to put his unit on the market, but now those plans were stalled. He'd had a couple of good years and could afford a nicer place, but he knew he should conserve his cash. He and Carter had decided they'd try to dress up the complex themselves (their homeowners' board of directors was notoriously indifferent to routine maintenance, much less permanent improvements) and they'd started one Saturday by cleaning out the flower beds and, at their own expense, putting in the pansies. But within a week the flowers had started to wilt. Carter, who unlike Thom had some gardening expertise, said the soil was poor, and they'd probably done the planting too early in the season. They decided to replace the pansies with monkey grass but then Carter had suffered a bout of pneumonia. He'd been hospitalized for three days, on a respirator, and since coming home he'd been depressed and out of sorts, finding a reason to decline any new projects or outings Thom proposed. Lately, when he arrived home Thom simply glanced away from the sad-looking flower beds. He didn't have the heart to replace them on his own.

"Sorry," he told Abby, as he hauled her bags out of the trunk, making a rueful gesture toward the complex and grounds, "but it *does* look better in the springtime, when the trees have budded out, and the grass—" Hearing himself, he broke off.

Abby smiled faintly. "Born salesman," she said.

Thom led her along the bumpy sidewalk toward his corner unit. "About a third of them are on the market," he admitted, "including the one next to mine."

"Hmm. But you have more privacy that way, don't you?" In Abby's words Thom could hear something of their mother's lilting, reasonable tone, the voice she used when trying consciously to be pleasant. Through their childhood, Lucille had insisted both Thom and Abby made insufficient efforts to be, as she termed it, "agreeable." She didn't mean they were disagreeable children, she'd add quickly—not at all. But they were not particularly agreeable, either. Not like John and Caroline, for instance. Lucille had compared her children so often to the Kennedys' offspring (she'd been pregnant with Thom at the time of the assassination, as she'd reminded him constantly as if he were somehow responsible) that for a while, in their early teens, Thom and Abby had started calling each other "John-John" and "Caro" when their mother was in earshot. Lucille found nothing more disagreeable than her children's unaccountable habit of ironic behavior.

"Yeah," Thom said, "but it's an ominous kind of privacy. It's the silence of property values going steadily down and down."

The moment he put his key in the door, he heard the dogs' frantic yipping.

"Oh, Thom, I almost forgot," Abby said, with what sounded like genuine pleasure. "How are they, Mitzi and...and Callie?"

"Chloe," he said. "They're thriving, as usual."

The two miniature dachshunds leapt onto Thom the moment he came inside, one dog attaching herself to each leg, as usual. The moment Abby bent down to them, they transferred their ecstatic attentions to her.

Thom laughed. "They've never met a stranger, these two," he said. "If a burglar broke in, they'd lick him to death." The plump, red-haired Mitzi, eight years old and showing white around her muzzle, quickly calmed and began administering a series of tidy, dignified kisses to Abby's bent cheek; five-year-old Chloe, more rambunctious and mischievous, snapped playfully at the wiggling fingers Abby held out.

"They're so adorable...," Abby murmured.

Though the phone started ringing, Thom lingered a moment: he'd forgotten how much Abby had loved the dogs. Mitzi had been a gift from Roy, and after he died Thom had gotten Chloe to keep Mitzi company. Thom had noticed before how well the dogs served as a buffer against awkward moments, diverting attention from human quandaries. Now Abby had squatted to their level, using both hands to stroke their heads, their elegant snouts; instantly the dogs had stilled, eyes closed in bliss.

Thom hurried to the kitchen, catching the phone just as his machine clicked on.

"Home for Wayward Boys," he said, loud enough for Abby to overhear.

His old friend Pace was calling, reminding him of the fund-raiser on Friday night at Pace's house, for an organization focused on violence against gays. Though Thom had heard the spiel before, there was no stopping Pace, whose manic energies were often fueled by good causes. Pace was a tall, slender man in his mid forties, the heir to a South Carolina banking fortune. He spent his weekdays managing his investments, sending and receiving E-mails and faxes, having incessant phone conversations with his brokers, lawyers, business partners. Pace had recently bought a million-dollar showplace in Ansley Park and loved hosting fund-raisers, cocktail parties, random gatherings organized on the spur of the moment.

"So Mitch and Angela will get on my case if I don't produce a crowd on Friday," Pace was saying. "Did you see their picture in *Southern Voice* last week? The article said they'd get matching funds from some endowment or other, if they can raise—"

"Hold on," Thom said, laughing. "Like I said before, I'll come if I can, but my sister's in town. She just got here."

"Great, then bring her along!" Pace barked, with his deep-voiced exuberance. He paused, then added mischievously, "Is she philanthropically inclined? Does she have lots and lots of money?"

"Yeah," Thom said. "She's one of those overpaid high school teachers. I'll make sure she brings her checkbook."

"You'd better bring her, goddamn it," Pace said, with playful belligerence. "I've known you for—how long is it, half a century?—and you've never introduced me to any member of your family. Not a single *one*. So who are you ashamed of, them or me?"

"Pace, you know they moved to Philly," Thom said quickly. They'd had this jokey conversation before. "We'll try to—"

"Then let's go to Philly, goddamn it!" Pace cried, good-naturedly. "I need a vacation!"

Thom heard a clicking in the receiver: Pace was getting another call.

"Thom, sweetie, I've got to go," he said. "But you bring along that darling sister of yours—I *have* seen her picture, at least. It must be me you're ashamed of, come to think of it. Gotta run. See you Friday night!"

After hanging up, Thom found Abby in the guest room, her two bags opened on the bed. While she unpacked, Mitzi and Chloe sat attentively next to the closet door, their tails wagging as if keeping time with inaudible music.

"That was my friend Pace," Thom said, "he wants us to—" but he stopped when Abby turned from the closet and he glimpsed her face, which wore that tired, absent look he'd glimpsed at the airport. Just before he left to meet her flight, Thom had spent half an hour in here, vacuuming and dusting, putting fresh linens on the bed, stacking magazines on the night table next to the half-dozen iris he'd bought at Kroger's last night and arranged in the Waterford vase Abby gave him for Christmas in 1993, the last time they'd exchanged gifts. Thom felt that she hadn't noticed any of this.

"Are you OK?" he asked. At once Abby's gaze focused intently on her brother, as though the question startled her.

"What? Yes, but—is there a phone I can use?"

"Not in here—this room is hardly ever used. There's one back in the kitchen." He paused. "Or in my room, if you want some privacy. I keep meaning to buy a cordless, but..."

She gave a vague smile. "The kitchen's fine. I'll just be a minute." She glanced behind her, snatching up her purse from the dresser. Halfway to the door she stopped, turning to face him.

"But I should be asking you. If you're all right, I mean."

"Me?" Thom held his arms out, palms up, in a casual gesture. "Sure, I'm feeling great."

"I didn't mean to sound callous, back at the airport. I *have* been worried, but...I don't want to be intrusive. It's hard to know what questions to ask—or not to ask."

"You shouldn't worry," Thom said, touched. He'd heard versions of this speech from several of his friends, too. This might be the second decade of the epidemic, but still there was no established "AIDS etiquette," as Carter had observed. Do you ask about an infected friend's condition every time you see him, or every other time? Or do you wait for *him* to bring up the subject? Some people complained their friends now thought of them as "guys with AIDS," rather than the people they'd always been, and became annoyed if you inquired about their health; others were angry or hurt if you failed to inquire.

"We have plenty of time to talk about that, too," Thom said, "don't we?"

"I'll be right back," Abby said, turning. "It's just one phone call—it'll only take a minute."

Thom stood next to the bed, feeling unmoored and vaguely depressed. He felt so out of touch with Abby, after all this time, and didn't know what she might be whispering to Lucille in the other room. He had a brief, ignoble fantasy of creeping out into the hall and straining to overhear what he could. There wouldn't be much, he decided. Lucille would be peppering her daughter with questions and allowing time for only the briefest replies. He remembered when they were kids, their ears pressed to the closed door of their parents' bedroom, their eyes fixed on one another in mingled excitement and dread as they heard Lucille haranguing their father about some misdeed or other: his late arrival home from the office the night before, for no good reason; his absence from a family gathering, causing Lucille such "humiliation"—a word she used often—that she had no idea how she'd ever face her relatives again. Sometimes Thom and Abby clamped their palms over their mouths if a fit of giggling threatened, but just as often they listened pale and wide-eyed, particularly on those rare occasions when their father tried to fight back. He didn't get a word in, usually, and Thom had imagined him sitting on the side of their bed, rubbing a hand across his face or through his hair while Lucille ranted, waiting it out the way you waited out a thunderstorm or the sudden headache after downing a greedy mouthful of ice cream.

On rare occasions her complaints or accusations did nettle him into speech. "For God's sake, Loo, get off my goddamn back, would you?" Hearing that, Thom had felt a queer sense of elation.

For all their eavesdropping Thom and Abby had never heard anything really upsetting. His parents probably hadn't argued more frequently or viciously than other long-married couples. And always behind closed doors. Never in front of the children. Yet these overheard quarrels had haunted him, particularly when he thought guiltily that family tensions must have increased after he'd left for college. Abby had continued living with their parents, but Thom, after finishing school in Macon, had moved back to Atlanta but not back to the teenage boy's room his mother had preserved carefully for his return. Instead, he'd rented an apartment, claiming with youthful bravado that he had *his own life to lead*. Another eight years passed before, at age twenty-nine, he'd told his parents quietly that he was gay.

Lucille's alternately furious and tearful protests over "that life"—as she scornfully termed it, not daring to utter the current platitude "lifestyle," much less speak its name in plain English—had only confirmed his decision to keep his distance, even though he and his family lived in the same city. He'd argued to Abby that she deserved her own life, too, but in her mid-twenties she'd begun exhibiting signs of the weary resignation that today showed so plainly in her face and voice, even in the slow, deliberate way she gestured and walked, as if weighted with invisible burdens.

While they were still at the airport, the thought had slipped into his mind, swift as a knife through water: *She's not going back. I'm going to keep her here, somehow.* In the 1950s, a young Catholic woman might willingly stay home and care for a widowed parent, a pious mother or strong-willed, possessive father, taking on spinsterhood the way other healthy young women took the veil—and in the same quiet and almost thoughtless gesture of self-immolation. But he hated to think of Abby, the bright-voiced witty older sister he'd known as a boy, obediently making this phone call to Lucille. Was Abby still prey, after all these years, to their mother's querulous complaints and caprices? It occurred to him now that their conversation itself was so predictable he need not bother to eavesdrop. He knew his sister in that bone-deep way siblings always know one another. He could imagine easily what she and Lucille were saying.

Frustrated, he stalked back to the bed and unfolded a handful of Abby's clothes from her garment bag. Followed by Mitzi and Chloe who, watching him, had grown suddenly grave and quiet—they knew *him* so well—he took the outfits into the small walk-in closet and with exaggerated care arranged them along the metal rod. Her clothes were attractive enough, but plain and functional: a gray pleated skirt with a burgundy silk blouse, a large and bedraggled-looking bow at its throat; several polyester-and-cotton blouses in neutral colors; a sweater decorated modestly with tiny seed-pearls; a navy skirt with a vaguely nautical-looking jacket, striped navy and white; and a black wool dress and matching cardigan with two roomy pockets that reminded him of the big shapeless sweaters the nuns had worn at St. Jude's. Thom stood inside the closet, pointlessly adjusting the hangers, smoothing out imaginary wrinkles in his sister's clothes, wondering at the hot salty tears that had filled his eyes. Pawing them away, he looked down and saw Mitzi and Chloe in the doorway, parked on their haunches and watching him dolefully. Despite himself, he laughed.

"I know what you're thinking, you two," he said. "What's Daddy doing *in the closet*?"

The dogs cocked their heads, as if eager for the answer. But at that moment the doorbell rang, and they raced off in an ecstatic frenzy of barking.

When Thom opened the door, there Carter stood in his shy, vaguely apprehensive slouch, as if he regretted having rung the bell at all. Thom had told him countless times that if he saw the Accord in the lot, he could simply come in—"*Mi casa, su casa,*" Thom liked to say—but Carter was a stringent observer of the Southern proprieties. A tall, gaunt man with a shadowy handsomeness many of Thom's friends found appealing, Carter was the only son of a bluff, well-connected bank president who'd attended the Citadel and served in Vietnam as a Green Beret, and his even more socially impeccable wife, a former Miss South Carolina from a blue-blooded Charleston family. Carter's mother now spent her time doing volunteer work for a local historic preservation society, and attending luncheons and teas with her expensively coiffed and similarly face-lifted friends. Both of Carter's grandmothers had been lifelong members of the DAR, and it was their photographs as fetching young belles that graced his fireplace mantel, not those of his lovers or friends. Today, Thom thought, he looked tired: his glinting brown eyes embedded deep in their sockets, cast into shadow beneath his bony, prominent forehead and straight dark brows.

"Hey," Thom said, swinging the door open. As Carter shuffled in, he bent to acknowledge the yipping dogs, feebly patting each of their heads. Long familiar with Carter, they quieted at once. After they'd trotted off through the dining nook, Carter threw a few quick glances around the room.

"She's in the kitchen," Thom said. "On the phone. Are you feeling OK? You look a little tired."

"No, I'm fine," Carter said. He'd folded his arms across his sunken chest, hands clamped beneath his armpits. He wore a navy sweater over his button-down shirt and jeans, but he seemed to be shivering. "It's getting colder out, I think."

Last week, Thom and a few other friends had taken Carter to dinner at the Prince George to celebrate his thirty-eighth birthday, and he'd complained several times that the restaurant was too cold, although everyone else was comfortable. Thom found it difficult to judge, since he saw Carter almost every day, but he guessed that his friend, who'd always been slim, had lost twenty pounds in the last year.

"Come on back," Thom said. "I'll make us some coffee and introduce you to Abby. I stopped at Starbucks and picked up some of those chocolate scones you like—you can eat one, can't you?"

Halfway across the room, Thom sensed that Carter wasn't following. He turned back and saw that his friend lingered near the doorway, studying the Dali print hanging in the tiny foyer.

"Hey, why don't you come *all the way* in?" Thom laughed.

Carter looked over, startled. "What? Oh, listen, I just got a call from Pace about that benefit, or whatever it is. Do you think he'd mind if Connie came along?"

"Didn't you ask him?"

"About Connie? Well...no."

They'd known Constantine Lefcourt—all his friends called him "Connie"—for years, but although Thom and Carter both adored him, some of their friends found him obnoxious. Too flamboyant, too opinionated. Too inclined to call attention to himself. Pace, who called him "Queenie" behind his back, particularly disliked him, since Connie had borrowed some money from Pace a couple of years back—either $250 or $750, depending on whose story you believed—and had never repaid him. Connie's mother had died when he was a kid, leaving him almost as well off as Pace himself. Connie was coming into his trust fund just this year, and Thom couldn't understand why he wouldn't repay the loan.

"Of course he won't," Thom said, though he knew that Pace probably would mind, a little.

"Connie sort of invited himself, after I told him we were going," Carter said. "He said he's planning to donate $250, so maybe Pace won't hate him any more."

"Pace doesn't hate him," Thom said. "But Connie ought to make it $750, if he really wants to mend fences. Anyway, you know how Pace's parties are. There'll be so many people...."

Carter smiled at him, wanly. "That Connie might get lost in the crowd? You think so?"

Now Carter did shamble into the living room; he sat on the edge of Thom's couch, hands still clamped beneath his arms.

"There isn't a crowd big enough for Connie to get lost in," Thom said. He gestured back toward the kitchen. "Hey, don't you want to meet my sister?"

"What? Of course, I—"

Carter's gaze had drifted past Thom's shoulder. Behind him, Thom heard the frantic, familiar clattering of Mitzi and Chloe's toenails as they raced out from the kitchen and across the dining room hardwoods. Abby followed them into the living room; her face wore a guarded smile.

"Here I am," she said. "Ready or not."

A Southern gentleman to the marrow, Carter struggled to his feet. He took several steps forward, one hand extended. "Nice to meet you, Abby. I've been hearing about you for years."

Thom waited while they exchanged small talk, Carter flashing his wide, white smile—his best feature. It occurred to Thom how seldom he'd seen it recently. Abby responded politely to Carter's queries about her teaching, her flight to Atlanta, her plans for Christmas and New Year's. On the way home from the airport, Thom had wondered anxiously if Abby would warm to his friends or whether she might resist meeting them, staying focused on her mission to bring him "home." Since phoning her, he'd resolved to introduce her to everyone and to hide nothing, or almost nothing. Throughout his twenties, he'd shielded his family from anything that might distress them, or so he'd rationalized his cowardice in neglecting, year after year, to talk about his life. Abby had known, of course, but even they hadn't really *talked*. During those years there were two Thom Sadlers—one for his parents' house and a second for everywhere else. Though sharing the same name and body, these Thoms had become two distinct people and wore two quite different faces.

Yes, he thought, remembering that era with a shudder of distaste. Two faces.

Those days were over, he'd promised himself. Within minutes of his phone conversation with Abby last week, he'd vowed that since he'd told her about his infection he might as well be honest about everything else. Nowadays there was only one Thom Sadler. Otherwise their reunion had no real point.

It had begun well, he thought. His sister seemed genuinely to like Carter Wilson Dawes III and to show no signs of the tactics their mother would deploy if thrown into this same situation. On the few occasions Thom had visited his parents with Roy or with one of his friends, his mother had studiously avoided eye contact; she'd either chatted with them in the chilly, high-pitched tone she used with door-to-door solicitors or had resorted to her impression of a Southern matron, affecting a shrill, semi-hysterical politeness that frightened everyone present. But Abby chatted pleasantly with Carter, asking about his work, his background, and Thom remembered she was a teacher, after all, who interacted with people every day. Her manner suggested no alarm at Carter's pale, emaciated appearance, though he'd sat back down after shaking Abby's hand, resuming his old-mannish slouch, hands tucked beneath his arms.

"I'm not really sure," Abby said now, glancing at Thom. "Am I?"

He hadn't been paying attention. "Sorry. Are you what?"

Carter laughed abruptly, but the laugh turned into a hacking cough: this had been happening quite a bit, since Carter's recent hospitalization with pneumocystis. He bent over, coughing strenuously for several long seconds, while Thom and Abby watched with the same pained, helpless expressions.

"Some water?" Thom asked, as he always did, and Carter shook his head, as he always did. He stayed bent almost double, his face reddened with strain. When the coughing subsided he stood up, shakily. He tried to smile.

"I—I asked whether Abby was coming to the party," he said, taking deep breaths. "The one at Pace's house."

"Oh, sure," Thom said quickly. "If she wants to come. Are you all right, Carter?"

"Good, maybe we can all go together," Carter said, studying his scuffed moccasins. He was taking slow, deep breaths. "Connie and Warren, too." Carter glanced sideways at Abby. "Connie is excited about meeting you. Very excited, in fact."

"Connie?" she said, looking from Carter back to Thom. "Who is she?"

This time, it was Thom who laughed. "A friend of ours—a male friend," he said, thinking that Connie exceeded his descriptive powers. "Warren is his roommate."

"I see." Abby looked confused, as though she didn't see, but she smiled at Carter. "Do you have a roommate?"

He glanced at her, startled. "No, I did have a partner but...but he's deceased. Two years ago."

"Oh. I'm sorry," Abby said.

"That's all right. Thanks for asking. Well, Thom, it's time for my afternoon meds. I'll have one of those scones tomorrow, OK?" Carter smiled morosely, edging away from the sofa. "I'm a slave to doctor's orders," he told Abby.

Thom and Abby escorted him to the door. As they watched him hurry down the sidewalk, arms folded and head bent against the damp wind, Thom slipped his arm around Abby's waist and gave a brief squeeze.

"Thanks for being nice to Carter," he said. "He's having a tough time."

"Is he—is he going to make it?"

Thom closed the door and gestured her back to the sofa; when they sat, Mitzi jumped into Thom's lap, nosed into the space between him and Abby and shut her eyes. Off in another room, he could hear the squeak of a toy and the muffled stampede of Chloe's paws along the carpet as she lunged and played.

"Honey," Thom said, taking her hand, "I don't know. His new drugs haven't worked too well, but he could certainly rebound. He's done it before. A few months ago, he was in the hospital with some intestinal thing, plus a high fever, and they called his family into town. Said he had a day or two at most. But he battled back."

Abby was staring down at their linked hands. She seemed so girlish and vulnerable, he thought, her hair mussed on one side—from the phone receiver, he supposed—and her fingers so limp and cool. And so tiny. How long since he'd held a woman's hand? he wondered. He couldn't recall.

"Did Mom upset you?" he murmured.

"Mom?" She looked up, and her confusion appeared childlike, too. Her eyes were damp, a milder blue than he remembered.

"On the phone," he said.

"Oh, that wasn't Mom," she said quickly. "I wasn't calling Mom."

A catch in her voice, as though she were about to say more but thought better of it. He decided not to pry.

"You want to rest for a while?" he asked. "You could use a nap, it looks like. Then later, we'll go someplace nice and quiet for dinner. We'll catch up on a few things."

She nodded, glancing around the room as if lost.

"OK then," he said, smiling. "Alley-oop!" And he pulled her up from the couch, his arm circling her waist as they went back to the guest room. Mitzi trotted beside them, but as they approached the door she lunged ahead and leapt onto the bed. Chloe was already there, curled inside one half of Abby's opened suitcase and methodically ripping her newest toy, a latex fire hydrant, into tiny pieces.

"Chloe," Thom scolded her, gently. He clapped his hands. "Out of there."

She jumped out of the suitcase and snuggled next to Mitzi, who had nestled into one of the pillows. The dogs stared at Thom and Abby as if awaiting an explanation.

"This is your Aunt Abby's room now," Thom told them. He folded the suitcase and placed it against the wall, then hung the empty garment bag in the closet. He turned back the bedclothes on one side, allowing Mitzi and Chloe to stay curled on their pillow. Second only to eating, they loved napping; they had sensed what was about to happen.

"Now, if you don't want the girls to sleep with you," Thom said, "just chase them out and shut the door. But I can promise the second you lie down, they'll shut their eyes and sleep as long as you do. They won't bother you."

He folded the bedspread and placed it on top of the dresser. The blinds were already drawn, so there was nothing left to do.

"OK, then," he said. "I guess I'll—"

But before he had quite turned to her, she hurried forward into his arms.

"Oh, Thom," she said, pressing her cool cheek against his throat. "It's so—so awful."

At first he'd been too startled to react; his arms hung uselessly at his sides. But then he wrapped them around her trembling shoulders.

"What's so awful, honey?" he murmured.

"Your being sick, and your friend," she said. "And—and all of it."

"I know, but really I'm OK," he whispered urgently. "The new drugs I mentioned—protease inhibitors, have you heard of them?—they work well, for most people. I mean, Carter was diagnosed long before me, so you shouldn't assume—I mean—"

At such times, he wasn't too good with words; his salesman's glibness abandoned him. Gently, he urged Abby down onto the bed. While she wiped at her eyes with one edge of the pillowcase, he removed her scuffed low-heeled black shoes—her teacher's shoes, he supposed—and eased her legs under the sheet. He paused, watching her. She had one palm over her eyes as if in embarrassment, or some new extreme of exhaustion. He decided to follow his instinct and not think about it. He quickly removed his own shoes.

"Move over, honey," he said thickly. His throat had tightened, but he knew he would not cry. These days, he rarely cried. Abby shifted to make room for him, and he cuddled against her, wrapping her snugly in his arms. She had stopped trembling. Her entire body went limp, yielding to his.

She said something—a long, drawn-out "Oh...," scarcely audible. He pulled her closer.

The dogs, who had watched all this with an alert, puzzled look, understood that Thom and Abby had settled, and they began their ritual circling into napping position, Mitzi squeezing between Thom and Abby while

Chloe burrowed, with a little sigh, into the crook of Thom's bent legs. Then everything was quiet. He hadn't felt Abby's slender arms circling his waist, but now he was aware of them and of the gentle rise and fall of her chest against his. Though fully clothed, they must have resembled, from a distance, spent lovers, or else victims of some accidental catastrophe that had flung their lifeless bodies indissolubly together. Thom opened his mouth to speak, to reassure her of something, but his mind seemed to darken with exhaustion, or capitulation, thinking groggily that he was content simply to lie here with Abby, their bodies entwined, the top of her head nestled just beneath his chin. The thought soothed him, and finally they fell asleep that way.

The next morning, they fought bitterly.

Since he had no appointments until one o'clock, he'd suggested they take the dogs for a walk through Piedmont Park. Perfect fall weather had arrived—a crisp blue vault of sky; brisk, bracing air; crunching leaves underfoot along the snaking paths through the park. Last night they'd had a quiet dinner at Nino's, one of his favorite Italian places, and had talked of stray, safe subjects. The Atlanta real estate market. The city's insanity over the Olympics in '96. Abby's thoughts about applying to Penn and getting her doctorate, moving into university teaching. They'd come home and retired early, and this morning he'd wakened optimistic and full of energy. Abby had seemed receptive to his plans, but once they'd gotten to the park—both of them led along straight-armed as Mitzi and Chloe raced ahead—Thom had sensed that same fatigue edged with sullenness he'd noticed when Abby exited the plane. Running out of things to talk about, he'd started reminiscing about the past. Later he supposed that was his big mistake.

They'd stopped to rest on a bench near the bandstand. They were far enough from the street that Thom unfastened the dogs' leashes and let them cavort among the leaves—they never strayed far—and while Thom and Abby sat watching them, he told his sister more about Carter, whom she had so clearly liked. Before coming to the park, Thom had driven her around a bit, showing her some of the new lofts and condo conversions in midtown. Cruising along Peachtree, talking busily, he'd suddenly confronted Crawford Long Hospital, where Carter had stayed recently and where Roy had died. Usually he detoured around it, or glanced the other way, but this morning it had sneaked up on him. Briefly he'd felt that old, familiar caving sensation in his chest, his stomach. So Thom told his sister about the hospital and the times Carter had been there. Sitting on this park bench with the leaves swirling about their feet Thom found the thought of the hospital, which was one of the undeniable landmarks in his emotional universe, a bit easier to handle.

"I hope he gets past this rough spot," Thom said, "without having to go back. Each time he goes in, we all wonder if it's the last time."

Abby shook her head, sadly; her gaze was focused on the other side of the path, where Mitzi and Chloe had been diverted by something underneath a laurel shrub. They resembled a pair of whispering conspirators.

"Poor guy," Abby said. "I hope so, too."

"A few of my friends have died there—including Roy, of course. You remember him."

She glanced aside, but didn't quite meet his eyes. "Roy. Of course, I remember…"

Thom laughed, self-consciously. "He really liked you, did you know that? Said if he were straight, he'd date you instead, so he was bound to marry into the family. One way or the other."

Abby gave a small, polite smile, but it vanished quickly.

"He always felt Mom didn't like him, though. It's funny, the first time we visited, on the way home he said, 'Thom, your mother is *so* Southern.' You know how she would get when she was uncomfortable with someone—so ultra-polite. I think she even affected a Georgia drawl, without quite realizing it."

"Did she?" Abby said, vaguely.

"Anyway, I told him she wasn't a Southerner, but she could have played one on TV."

He laughed again. The dogs had started digging frantically underneath the bush, so Thom called out to them. "Mitzi, Chloe, stop that! You're not supposed to dig up the park!"

Mitzi glanced over her shoulder briefly, but they both ignored him and kept digging.

He said, "I guess she never really came to terms with it, did she?"

A short pause. "It?"

"You know. Having a queer son."

He saw a small flinching movement in her face.

She said, "I wouldn't know, Thom. We just don't talk about that." He detected a note of sadness in her voice; or imagined he did.

He tried his casual laugh, but this time it sounded more like a hiccup.

"I guess that was our problem. We were such typical, white-bread Southerners. Incessant talking, but never about anything significant. Like who we were. Like what we felt."

Abby fixed him with a brief, pointed look. "It's interesting that you keep using the past tense."

He smiled. "Force of habit, I guess. It *has* been a long while."

Abby bent forward and clapped her hands. "Mitzi, Chloe!" To Thom's surprise, the dogs looked up, both with reddish dirt on their noses, and after a second's hesitation first Mitzi, then Chloe came racing back to the bench. Resting on their haunches, they sat patiently while Abby extracted a tissue from her pocket, wetted it with her tongue, and bent down to wipe the dirt off their noses. "Good girls," she cooed, "such *good* little girls…"

"I guess my friends have become like family in a way," Thom said, watching fondly. "What about you? Have you made any close friends there? The people you teach with, or—"

"You still *have* a family, you know," she said. "Whether you acknowledge us or not."

She had straightened, her backbone stiff as a rod, while the dogs stared upward with longing in their eyes.

"Hey, I wasn't denying that. I just meant, in everyday life…" He broke off, not sure what he meant.

She brushed at her knees, wearily. "Since you and I ended up not having kids, our little threesome is all we've got, Thom. Do you ever think about that?"

The note of contempt in her voice angered him.

"Now who's talking in the past tense? We're still in our thirties, so how have we 'ended up' without kids? You could still have them, and I've thought about—about adopting. I'm not in a relationship right now, but—"

"Adopt a child? You?" She laughed angrily.

"A lot of gay couples adopt," he said. "Even single people. In fact, there's a very nice lesbian, right in my complex—"

"Why are you changing the subject?" she said. "You're not comfortable with family matters, are you?"

He tasted that odd phrase on his tongue, *family matters*; the taste wasn't pleasant. Neither was the dull throb of anger in his chest.

"I might have expected this from Mom," he muttered. "But not from you."

"Mom is almost seventy," Abby said, sharply. "She's not likely to change. But we—"

"She never acknowledged that I was a separate person, with my own life," he said. "Never."

Thom hated the whining sound of his voice, but at once he felt better. He hadn't said these simple words aloud to another person, and he understood he'd needed to say them.

"You should take that up with her," Abby said.

"That would be a productive conversation, wouldn't it?" He allowed himself a brief, skeptical laugh.

Abby stood, brushing her hands as though ridding herself of him. Thom struggled to his feet, feeling vague and out of focus in the face of her taut fury. Her skin had flushed in the brisk wind, but the tip of her nose looked waxen, an unhealthy white. Her eyes had narrowed in disdain, fixing him as if patiently awaiting the next childish thing he might say.

"Abby—"

"Listen, I want to visit your friends, I want to know about your life," she said. "That's one reason I'm here. But when we get back to your place, I also want you to call and make your flight reservation for next Sunday, because when that plane lands, Mom is expecting to see both of us, not just me. You owe her that."

He tried to smile. "I've thought about this a lot, really. Please give me some credit. I've played out the whole scenario in my mind a hundred times. I know I'd get up there, and she'd start talking not to *me* but to some fantasy son she still has lodged inside her head. I can't play that role anymore, Abby. I can't be dishonest about my life just to please somebody. I don't owe her that."

"All right, try this. You owe *me* that. I'm the one who consoles her every Mother's day when you don't call. And on her birthday and Daddy's birthday. And their anniversary. I'm the one who drives her to mass and sits through those deadly-dull Sunday dinners at Aunt Millie's. You can't imagine what Thanksgiving is like, and don't ask about Christmas."

He sat there, his stomach roiling with guilt and resentment, knowing he couldn't fight back. After all, he was the evil child who had been banished from his own father's funeral, the child who hadn't phoned his mother in over four years. He said pettishly, "You've done a lot for Mom, I'm sure she appreciates it. But really, Abby, your halo is showing."

She went pale; she turned and stalked off. Taken off guard, he glanced around for the dogs, but at that moment a hopping bird had caught their attention, and they'd raced in the opposite direction toward the street. He lunged toward them, but the need to placate Abby made him stop and rush back the other way. After a few strides he stopped altogether, feeling absurd, as if performing some comic routine from a silent movie. He cupped both hands to his mouth and shouted the dogs' names at the top of his voice. Hearing its note of urgency, they stopped in their tracks, turned and stared with their heads cocked, then tore back toward him. Or rather they chased him, as he chased after Abby. He caught up with her near the gate on Piedmont Avenue, where it appeared she was about to take off down the sidewalk, though they'd left Thom's car on tenth Street on the other side of the park. He took hold of her wrist, and she stopped, her frail arm tense as a bowstring.

"Come on, I'm sorry," he said.

The dogs had reached him and were clawing at his pants legs for attention; he reached down to them with vague petting motions but kept his desperate gaze fixed on Abby.

He added, "I'll think about it, OK? About flying to Philly with you, I mean. I just hate the idea of going back and—and pretending. Doing the whole prodigal son routine when I don't feel it...." He paused. "I hate being dishonest."

She turned to face him, eyes brimming with tears. "I need help with her, Thom. You don't know how—how difficult she's gotten. She'll get this obsessive focus on something, usually something so stupid and minor, and talk about it day after day. I feel...sometimes it's like I'm choking, suffocating..."

She stopped, taking deep, wheezing gulps of air. He had the sudden memory of Carter on the sofa yesterday, bent double in the effort to breathe.

He thought clearly: *I'm not going back. And you're not either. You're not getting on that plane.*

But he said, "Don't worry. Just try to relax, OK? Here's this beautiful fall morning, so why don't we just enjoy it and talk about all this in a couple of days? Tell you what, I'll cancel my appointments for this afternoon and we'll..."

He came up with a litany of suggestions, his mind racing in the hope of pleasing her, soothing her, and to his relief she nodded. They walked for another half hour, their pace brisker as they returned to safe topics, their cheeks glowing in the chilly air. A couple of times Mitzi, always the first to tire when Thom brought the dogs to the park, stopped in the middle of the path, refusing to take another step. Thom bent to pick her up, carrying her for a few minutes until a cawing blue jay or a squirrel scuttling through the leaves caught her attention, and she'd squirm to get down again. Abby's mood had lightened, and every few minutes she would banter with the dogs as they trotted along, using baby talk with them, which touched and amused Thom. As they neared the car, she seemed not only willing but excited about Thom's improvised plans for the rest of the day, the rest of the week.

Thom's relief was short-lived. By the time they drove home, he'd begun affecting a lightheartedness he didn't feel. Her accusations had stung, and his heart writhed in guilt as he recalled those horrible last months of their father's dying. These past few years he'd indulged in so much self-flagellation over that brief, chaotic period in his life that he'd finally decided enough was enough; he'd declared himself purged and had become reasonably comfortable with the self-serving conviction that he'd suffered as much as anyone. But that hardly laid the memories to rest, or the guilt, or the lingering resentment that could start churning so quickly if he allowed himself to think, to remember.

Though he tried to joke about the matter with his friends, he'd never forgiven his mother for suggesting that he had hastened his father's death. Of course, she'd seized on the coincidence: only a few weeks after Thom's coming out, his father began experiencing vertigo and uncharacteristic mood swings and eerie, intermittent headaches at the base of his skull. Thom had wanted to protest to his mother that he had in fact put off telling his parents throughout his twenties—he had come out to himself in high school, to Abby the night before he went off to college—but that it was her own volatile temperament and his disinclination to make waves that had kept him quiet.

As he'd tried to explain to Abby, he'd endured years of chafing at the sense of confinement, the awkwardness and dishonesty of the old-fashioned "double life" that had never suited him. By the time he'd stumbled out of the closet, he was no longer in sync with the times. Clinton was president, gay movies were box office hits, the talk shows Lucille watched religiously every morning decried homophobia with a shrill self-righteousness that Thom found almost unpleasant. Yet he'd lingered in the closet, hesitating. During the aftermath of Roy's death, he'd vowed that he'd come out to his parents before his thirtieth birthday—it had then seemed comfortably distant—and he'd finally told them almost matter-of-factly, on the Sunday after Thanksgiving, as they were digesting their leftover turkey and dressing out in the den.

They were watching a Falcons game, and during a commercial Thom had reached shakily for the remote control, pressed the mute button, and asked for their attention. His parents sat on their overstuffed floral-print sofa, and from the other side of the room Thom had felt as though he were gazing at them across the Sahara. He and Abby were sitting together on a love seat that matched the sofa; afraid he might chicken out, he hadn't told his sister today was the day, but it was obvious she knew. He'd felt her body stiffen, seeming to retreat to her side of the love seat.

From their usual positions on the sofa, Thom's parents had stared at him: his lanky father half-sitting, half-reclining, his head propped by cushions, Lucille prim and erect on the other end. Lucille had paused in her needlepoint, a hobby that soothed her nerves.

"Yes, honey?" she said blankly. Thom's father had offered the same polite, unreadable look he gave to anyone who requested his attention; he'd worked as a loan officer at a downtown bank for more than 30 years. Five or six seconds passed—easily the longest silence Thom had ever lived through—and then in a creaky, closeted voice, he told them.

It was over before the commercial had ended. (He would never forget: a Budweiser ad featuring male athletes flanked by bosomy blond models, three or four women for each man.) There was another silence, and Thom wondered whether he should press the mute button again, whether they might simply continue watching football as though nothing had happened.

His mother's reaction was predictable enough. She stood, white-faced; fled into the kitchen; returned immediately and dropped onto the sofa; burst into tears. What had affected Thom far more keenly than Lucille's histrionics was his father's reaction. As Thom delivered the news, his father had bravely maintained the open, nonjudgmental facial expression he must have used every day at the bank. The reserved Southern gentleman in George Sadler forbade so much as a creased brow, or a dubious shake of his head. Yet Thom had glimpsed something in his father's gray, placid gaze. A clouding of the eyes, a look of closure that put Thom in mind of a bank vault, its massive gray steel door soundlessly and irrevocably sliding shut.

Before Lucille, gape-mouthed in shock after Thom's announcement, had uttered a word, his father said quietly, "Thanks for telling us, Son," his lips forming a brief, rueful smile. Then Lucille had started in, and for the next few minutes Thom's father had stared silently at the silent TV screen. The game had been scoreless, but Thom, his own eyes grazing the screen, noted that Detroit had just scored a touchdown. Atlanta was losing.

• • •

Shortly after New Year's his father had fallen ill, diagnosed with an inoperable brain tumor, and Thom had started spending more time around the house. His parents bought their place in 1965, the year after Thom was born, and until he left for college it was the only home he knew. A comfortable four-bedroom ranch in Sherwood Forest, an in-town neighborhood that had become unexpectedly trendy in the late '80s and '90s, his parents' house was one of the few that had not changed hands, suffered a "complete renovation," and been resold for an unbelievable sum. Thom's father had often insisted he would never sell; he remodeled only as needed—an updated kitchen when Thom was a teenager, a new roof several years later—and he liked to remark that when he left this house, it would be feet first.

Driving slowly through the neighborhood during his frequent visits that winter, Thom had experienced sudden throes of nostalgia. As a boy, he'd loved the storied names of the neighborhood streets—Robin Hood Road, Little John Trail, Nottingham Way—and had raced with his friends along the untrafficked pavement and through the flat, enormous lawns that were never again so green as in his childhood memories. When he was seven or eight, he'd played Robin Hood to his sister's Maid Marian, wearing a green chintz cape his mother had fashioned from leftover drapery fabric, loping ecstatically among the towering backyard pines and water oaks on a stick horse his father had made at his worktable in the basement. As an adult, Thom seldom saw kids playing outside: most of the renovated places were bought by affluent, childless couples or gay men. The elaborately landscaped front lawns were now dotted with placards warning of security systems, and the lawns themselves were tended not by white-legged dads jauntily riding their mowers, but by professional crews arriving in large trailer-trucks with three or four men who cut, clipped, trimmed, blew, and departed after less than an hour.

When Thom left for college, his mother insisted that he'd chosen Mercer only as an excuse to move out of the house. There were plenty of good schools right here in Atlanta, after all; he could have gone to Emory, as Abby had done. For once, Lucille's paranoid suspicions were correct. But Thom knew better than to tell his mother that, and once he'd moved back to the city after graduation, he evaded her petulant queries: what was the point of renting an apartment, instead of reclaiming his perfectly good boyhood room? He did intend to *visit* his family once in a while, didn't he, since he lived just a few miles away? Though Thom came to dinner every Sunday night and often stopped by on weekdays, his visits were never frequent enough or long enough to suit Lucille. "Thanks for granting us an audience!" she would call out, as he hurried down the sidewalk to his car.

Once his father had become bedridden, however, Lucille grew strangely silent. Thom visited every day for several hours, giving Abby a breather so she could have a date or study in the university library, and at times his mother sent him long, sad-eyed looks that seemed to suggest— if only for a moment—some measure of gratitude. Through January and February his father's condition deteriorated steadily, though in their mother's presence Thom and Abby maintained the fiction that he might eventually recover.

Not surprisingly, neither of his parents had referred again to their son's announcement a few months earlier. After Lucille's fit of lamenting and lambasting had gone on for half an hour, Thom's father had given her a quick, sharp look and said, "That's enough, Loo," and turned back to the football game. Thom later supposed that he shouldn't have made the announcement in the first place. Like his friends Carter and Pace, he should have allowed the matter to remain an open but undiscussed fact of his life, like a wart on his nose that no one in a good Southern family would be rude enough to mention. Even Lucille, with her limitless capac- ity for denying the obvious, had years ago stopped inquiring whether Thom was "dating anyone," or thinking about "settling down"; and when he moved in with Roy in the spring of 1989 and began bringing him along to family dinners, she behaved with the same effusive politeness a moth- er often adopts toward her son's unacknowledged lover.

In private, though, her complaints about her children—she hauled them both into the same net—grew equally shrill. Outside her earshot, Thom and Abby coped with the stress of their father's illness by reverting to the nicknames, John-John and Caro, they'd used during their teenage years. Thom would murmur in his sister's ear, "You're looking very *well groomed* this evening, Caro," when she came downstairs after primping for one of her dates. Or Abby would catch Thom as he paused before the oval mahogany-framed mirror in the foyer. "Don't worry, John-John, you're still the sexiest man alive," she'd say smartly, passing by. They seized what- ever scant opportunities for humor came their way, falling easily into the banter of their adolescence, as if their father were laboring at one of his woodworking projects downstairs—a bluebird house for Lucille, another bookshelf for the Civil War collection he kept in the den—instead of veg-etating in his bed; as if their mother were handling all this with maturity and good humor instead of alternating between outright denial and the occasional outbursts of self-pitying emotion that were rendering a painful situation almost unbearable.

As the doctors predicted, George Sadler had deteriorated slowly. March passed, and April; by the middle of May, he was semi-comatose but still at home, attended in his last days by several home-care nurses, mid-dle-aged women who came and went in regular shifts. Abby arranged everything, did the hiring, spoke with the doctors and pharmacists and insurance people. Dropping by the house several times each day, Thom spoke politely to the various nurses but couldn't keep their names straight, much less their constantly changing schedules. For Thom, the only real constant was his father lying motionless in bed, surrounded by flower arrangements sent by his friends from church and from the bank. Making his way toward the bed, Thom felt himself struggling through the over-sweet stench of the roses, gladioli, and chrysanthemums that multiplied daily in the room, their sensual and riotous life seeming to crowd out his father's, like bright and unruly children. Or so Thom imagined, feeling a vague sickness to his stomach that he blamed on the flowers. He'd have liked to take them all outside and toss them into the trash barrel.

Sitting quietly next to the bed while his father slept, Thom kept push-ing away his recurrent *déjà vu*: all the rituals of the sickbed, the pragmat-ic details surrounding fatal illness, and even his emotions were essentially the same as during Roy's final bout with AIDS. Roy had died of a brain disease, too, a rampaging viral infection that overtook him with such mer-ciful swiftness, he'd lived only a few days in the same twilight state Thom's father had inhabited for months. Roy had been hospitalized once with a case of pneumocystis so virulent he almost choked to death, and once with a stomach virus that had ravaged his entire system. On that Friday in spring 1991 when he'd complained of a dull but persistent headache, they hadn't thought much about it. In his logical, decisive way, Roy had decided to wait until Monday before calling his doctor; he'd begun to feel that he bothered her too often, complaining of ailments that turned out to be minor or even—it *was* possible—imaginary. Thom's lover had a CPA's methodical, almost grave tendency to figure the odds and act accordingly, distrusting mere impulse, and as usual, Thom had kidded him: "I thought you had no imagination. I thought you were proud of that." Roy had performed one of his dry smiles, then he leaned across—

they were sitting on the den sofa, Mitzi snuggled between them—and gave Thom a peck on the cheek. "But I can't discount the possibility," he said. He cupped his hands and raised them, doing his dead-on impression of President Bush. "That wouldn't be prudent. *Wouldn't be prudent."*

Thom laughed, but by Saturday night Roy's headache had reached migraine proportions, and Thom had called the doctor himself. On Sunday, in his hospital bed, Roy complained that his vision was wavering— "It's like I'm seeing you through water"—and that night he developed a fever that reached 104, causing even the eminently sane Roy to talk out of his head. Or so Thom had thought.

"I need the Baxter file, the Baxter file," Roy kept saying, raising up on one elbow with a wild, unfocused look in Thom's direction. Roy died two days later, but it was months before Thom accidentally learned, in a conversation with one of Roy's coworkers, that the "Baxter file" was one of Roy's most important and problematic business accounts. Roy had fallen sick and died in early April, in the raging heart of tax season.

The shell-shocked aftermath of Roy's death: a period of numbed, thoughtless routine during which Thom showed and sold houses during the day, watched television and saw his friends after work, and visited his parents and Abby on weekends, imagining he'd stumbled accidentally into someone else's life and didn't quite know what he was doing. The pain he took in small doses (alone at night, or driving in his car), like a bottle of hateful medicine he must sip and sip over months, years, until every drop was gone. When he'd told his parents about the pneumonia and the viruses, he hadn't spoken the word *AIDS* and neither had they. He knew they must be worried about his own health, and when Abby had asked quietly, one afternoon when they were driving somewhere together, if he'd been "tested," he'd needed only to say "Yeah, I'm negative" to know that she'd pass along the good news and that the subject need never be mentioned again. At Roy's funeral, Lucille had embraced Roy's mother tearfully, and Thom's father had shaken Roy's father's hand for a long, solemn moment, as befitted this wordless and puzzled bond between two men whose sons had loved one another. And that was all. No one in his family spoke Roy's name again, and it began to seem that Thom had loved, married, and been widowed in some dimension that could not be acknowledged, so that his memories of Roy took on a slightly surreal, dreamlike quality, as though he'd existed only in Thom's imagination.

During his father's last days, Thom had spent almost all his free time with Abby and Lucille, doing what he could to help care for him. The nurses did most of the grunt work, but he could see that his mother and sister needed moral support. Abby looked drawn, pale, underfed; the spring term was ending, and she was teaching almost daily at an Episcopal school where she was a substitute—one of the regular teachers had resigned abruptly—in the midst of her father's dying. Both she and Thom were worried about their mother, who did indeed seem to be breaking down, though in an unexpectedly quiet way. After her husband became incontinent, Lucille began sleeping in the guest room, and during the day she escaped almost wholly into television, not even entering their father's room for days at a time, frowning briefly whenever one of the nurses passed through the den on her way to the kitchen, as though the woman were a stranger wandered in from the street. When Abby and Thom discussed their father's condition over dinner, careful to make only encouraging remarks—he seemed to be resting more comfortably; he'd gained a little weight—Lucille did not bother to accuse her children of lying, though plainly they were. After dinner, they sat with her in the den and watched more television, one program after another, the sitcoms and cop shows and TV movies all passing before their glazed, undiscriminating vision like a version of life itself they accepted gratefully, since they were not included.

One night they sat watching a hospital drama, in which emergency room doctors and nurses rushed around with the ceaseless frantic motion of an ant colony busily working its small mound of earth, when the program was interrupted to report some "breaking news." Lucille had been laboring over a newspaper crossword puzzle, but now she stopped, frowning at the screen. Thom and Abby glanced at one another, alarmed. Thom had seen an article in today's newspaper and had shown it to Abby, who had quietly crumpled the page and thrown it away. They knew the article would upset Lucille. But now they watched helplessly as Tom Brokaw, in deep and mournful tones, announced "the impending death of Jacqueline Kennedy Onassis in her Manhattan apartment." According to family sources, the end was "very near." Immediately, Thom suspected that Mrs. Onassis was receiving euthanasia, though the television report did not hint at that. Neither had the newspaper article, which had noted that all treatment had been suspended and that the former first lady was "gravely ill." Last week, Thom had seen a tabloid newspaper his mother brought home from Kroger's, its front page showing a frail-looking Jackie on the arm of her male companion, walking through Central Park, and of course there had been earlier articles in the daily paper; but

Thom and Abby had known better than to mention the stories to Lucille. As usual, a tacit silence had reigned in the house, making their lives still bearable day by day, hour by hour, but now Tom Brokaw had ruined all that.

Thom glanced fearfully at his mother, who had slumped in her chair. Although Lucille, unlike Abby, had looked remarkably the same through their recent ordeal, keeping her hairdresser's appointment every Friday and seldom missing a meal, Thom saw now that her skin had paled, making her look older, grayer. Her facial muscles seemed to sag. Although the news bulletin had ended and the hospital show had resumed, she'd kept her pale bluish eyes fixed on the television set.

"Mom, are you OK?" Abby asked.

Lucille didn't answer. She stared at the set, unblinking.

Thom felt dully, unaccountably angry. "There's no point in getting upset, you know. We have our own troubles."

His mother said nothing, as though he and Abby were beneath her notice. Thom had the helpless idea that if Caroline and John-John were in this situation, they'd know exactly what to do. Kennedys always knew, didn't they? They *acted*. They wouldn't have sat here gaping, their hearts pounding queerly.

Now Tom Brokaw reappeared on the screen. *God out of a machine*, Thom thought. *Save us*. In a reverential, almost inhumanly deep voice, he reported that Jacqueline Kennedy Onassis had, as expected, died. The family would issue a statement in the morning, he told them, and the funeral arrangements would be announced. There was no further information at the moment, but yes, Jackie Kennedy was dead. "Please stay tuned for further details. Good night."

The hospital drama resumed. Not knowing what else to do, Thom had grabbed the remote control and flicked off the set.

Lucille stood, her eyes a little wild. Her expression reminded Thom of something, but he couldn't remember what. His mother's unfinished crossword puzzle fell to the floor.

"Mom?" Abby said, leaning forward. "Are you—"

"I'm going," Lucille announced. She looked briefly at each of her children, as though daring them to argue. "I'm *going*."

"That's a good idea," Thom said. "It's been a tough day. I'll make you some hot chocolate, I'll bring it back when it's…"

But Lucille had stalked back toward the bedroom. Abby sat there next to Thom, shaking her head. She didn't look at him, either.

"That's not what she meant, Thom," she said, in an older sister's gentle, explanatory tone. "Going to bed—that's not what she meant, at all."

What she had meant, evidently, was that she was going to Jackie Kennedy's funeral. She stayed up late in the guest room, packing and repacking her overnight bag, making reservations for her hotel accommodations and her flight to New York. Thom and Abby took turns venturing into her room, trying to reason with her, insisting that she get a good night's sleep before making any plans. At first Lucille ignored them, and then she became hostile. "You don't understand, *you*!" she said to Thom, the last time he'd tried. He stood in the doorway, staring dully. What did she mean, *you*? Her tone was accusatory, almost hateful.

He escaped to the den and told Abby he'd given up. The earliest flight reservation their mother had been able to secure was for eleven o'clock tomorrow; if she still wanted to visit the Kennedys in the morning, he would drive her to the airport himself. Abby told him to calm down. He'd been sitting perched on the edge of the sofa, methodically cracking the knuckles of one hand, then the other—a habit from his teenage years. He heard the echo of his voice and knew he must have sounded like a teenager. He hadn't felt this jumpy and out of sorts in years, and his sister's standing there in the middle of the room with her air of saintly forbearance didn't help.

"Thanks so much, Caroline," he said. "I'll certainly try."

"Good," she said, then turned and left the room.

It was official, he'd thought. Everybody was mad at everybody. He went back to check on his father, expecting to find Abby in there, but evidently she'd retreated to her room. The nurse, a crabby-looking woman in her fifties who was Thom's least favorite of the three, glanced up briefly from the dark corner of the room where she sat with a paperback romance novel, a portable reading light clipped to the cover. He'd never seen her do much of anything. Thom stood for a minute next to the bed, gazing at his father's comatose form with a pang of something like envy. No anger for him, and no pain, either. He'd already reached the end of his journey, Thom thought, and now lay here with his usual patience and quietness, simply waiting for his body to catch up.

The next morning, Thom had returned before ten o'clock, fully expecting to cooperate with his mother's lunatic wishes. He went first to the kitchen, where he found Abby preparing a tray of sliced cantaloupe, frosted pastries, a cup of cinnamon-scented tea. Their mother's favorites.

"I talked her into spending the day in bed," Abby said, shortly. She hadn't quite met his eyes.

"Look, I'm sorry I snapped at you last night." Thom leaned back against the counter, his palms turned upward in a gesture of appeal. "It's starting to get to me, I guess," he said, though he couldn't have said what "it" was, exactly.

A brief pause, and then she looked at him. She'd pulled her hair back and tied it carelessly on one side, but a few limp reddish strands had escaped, hanging along her slender throat; her normally clear, fine skin had a waxen pallor. She'd thrown on a wrinkled plaid blouse and blue-jean skirt, and Thom felt shamefacedly fresh and well-groomed in his starched khakis and polo shirt, the scent of his cologne and hair gel invading the room.

"Well," she said, smiling slightly. "I guess I forgive you."

"Honey," he murmured, "you're the one who needs a day in bed."

Abby rolled her eyes in her old, girlish way, reassuring him. "Sure. Like I have time for that."

He offered to help, and after returning from Lucille's room with the empty tray—Thom still didn't dare to go in there—and hurrying off to grade a few more papers, Thom cleaned up the kitchen and then made a "to do" list for the rest of the day. The yard needed mowing, and last night he'd noticed a stack of unopened bills on his mother's rolltop desk in the den; he could sort through those, write out the checks, and have Abby take them in for Lucille's signature. Then he'd go to Kroger's and buy groceries. He added a few more items to the list, aware that he'd begun feeling better. The list looked so neat and orderly; it would guide him through the day. But before starting the first chore, he went back to check on his father.

The room was dark and close-smelling, the blinds drawn. To Thom's surprise, his father was sitting up, propped by pillows, glancing around the room with the mechanical alertness of a bird. His sleep-mussed whitish hair and purse-lipped mouth seemed oddly birdlike, too, and Thom edged into the room, not wanting to startle him.

"Hey, Daddy," he said.

On the other side of the bed, the day nurse—a stocky, unsmiling woman whose thick glasses cruelly magnified her dark, popping eyes—stood fiddling with some items on a tray table. She was lifting the foil wrapper off a container of ready-made pudding. Neither she nor Thom's father had even acknowledged his presence. The nurse kept her dark gaze lowered as his father's glance flitted about the room.

"Why don't you take a break?" Thom said. "I can feed him."

He joined the nurse on the other side of the bed; she hesitated a moment, then handed him the pudding and spoon.

"Just a tiny bit each time," she said. "Otherwise he'll spit it out." Her huge eyes blinked behind her glasses, seeming to focus just past his shoulder. "I guess I should check on your mother. Abby said she's not feeling well."

"She's fine, she's just resting," Thom said quickly. "Why don't you take an hour off? Go have some lunch."

The nurse looked offended. "He'll probably eat a third of that, if you're lucky." She hesitated. "Well, I'll be back," she said.

Despite the constant movement of his father's head, Thom managed little by little to feed him. He would hold out the spoon with its dab of vanilla pudding, his hand trembling, and his father's head would swivel in that direction, his lips parted like a communicant's—just enough for Thom to slip the spoon inside. His father's stubbled jaws made a chewing motion, and Thom was ready with a napkin, touching at the tiny spots of pudding that oozed from each side of his father's mouth. Then he put down the napkin and took up the spoon again. A kind of rhythm was established, soothing Thom's nerves. Clearly, his father no longer had the capacity to recognize him or anyone, but somehow that didn't matter. Thom felt how his shoulders and arms had relaxed, as though someone had massaged them. He took deep, slow breaths, in rhythm with his father's feeding. The surrounding room was so dim and quiet, Thom thought, they might be anywhere—disembodied, out of time. Thom's eyes had grown moist; they stung pleasantly. He dabbed at them with the same pudding-stained napkin he'd used for his father. That's when he heard the ruckus starting up, somewhere behind him: his mother, followed by the nurse and a bewildered-looking Abby, had blundered into the room.

"What are you doing?" Lucille cried. She'd just woken up, Thom saw. Her eyes were puffy, and her dark-tinted reddish hair stood in angry tufts about her head. "Mrs. Phillips is supposed to do that."

Lucille grabbed the pudding cup and spoon out of Thom's hand and dropped them onto the tray.

She stood there, breathing fast. Abby and the nurse appeared too shocked to speak, and Thom had nothing to say. Did his mother want him to wait here, docile on the edge of the bed, while she screamed at him?

Did she still want him to drive her to the airport, so she could catch the plane for Jackie Kennedy's funeral? Whatever she wanted, he thought calmly, he would oblige.

Now she looked shame-faced; she went to the opposite side of the bed and fiddled with the blanket, bunching it around her husband's waist.

She said, "You can't feed him too much—the doctor told us that. He throws up all the time, just like a little baby...." Her face had started to crumple.

"It's just some pudding," Thom said. "He seems to like it." He added, "He seems happy, in fact."

He glanced at his father who was, indeed, happily oblivious to the scene playing out before him.

Lucille had put the tips of her fingers against her forehead, in an attitude of woe. Tears slid freely out both sides of her eyes, but when she looked up, her voice was amazingly steady and her eyes held a malevolent glare.

"What do *you* know about it? Happy? You think he's happy? Are *you* happy now, Thomas Sadler. Are you?"

"Mommy, stop it." Abby had stepped forward and clamped one arm around her mother's shoulders. "Be quiet," she said sternly. "There's no point in blaming Thom."

But Lucille kept glaring at him—there *was* a point, and she would not relinquish it—while Thom stared back with his new calmness, which must have struck the others as defiance, or simple indifference.

"*Are* you happy?" Lucille repeated.

Thom stood, sighing. He gave Abby a rueful smile. He was always doing this—leaving his sister to clean up. "Guess I'd better shove off," he said, to no one in particular.

And no one answered. The nurse had looked around at all of them, her eyes like blurry dark wounds behind her glasses.

"Should I feed him the rest of that pudding?" she asked.

And so it happened that Thomas Jefferson Sadler did not attend his father's funeral. The morning after his mother's outburst, Abby called him at 7:12; he would always remember the time, for he'd awakened to the shrilling phone. The blaring red numerals on his digital clock had seared the moment into his memory. Abby told her brother in a subdued, almost apologetic voice that their father had died in his sleep.

Thom blinked, staring at the clock. Now it was 7:13. "OK, I'll be right over."

"Thom?" Abby said. She'd sounded fearful. "Thom, could you wait a little while?"

That's when he knew: Lucille was determined to blame him. After an awkward pause, Abby acknowledged that his mother, for the moment, had forbidden him from the house, adding quickly that she was being "irrational," that she would certainly "come around." But Abby's voice held little conviction: its fearful, girlish apprehension was something else he would never forget.

They talked for a few more minutes, and Thom insisted that he could make phone calls, at least, so that Abby could cope with Lucille. "Oh Thom, thanks so much," Abby breathed out. "That's a great idea."

Another long, awkward silence. Thom felt the question hovering between them. "*You* don't blame me, do you? Abby?"

But he didn't dare ask. He didn't want the answer.

So Thom made phone calls: the funeral home, his mother's favorite priest from Christ the King, a handful of far-flung relatives around the country. Only to Father Reilly—a bluff, barrel-chested man he'd met a few times and disliked—did Thom mention that he might not be attending the funeral. Family conflicts, he muttered. The priest said he'd spoken to Lucille often in the past few months and that he understood. He seemed eager to get off the phone.

You understand? Understand what? Thom didn't ask.

"During the eulogy, I could say that you're indisposed," Father Reilly said awkwardly.

"Thanks," Thom said, feeling a pang of sympathy for the man. "That's probably for the best."

Early on the morning of the service, which was scheduled for two o'clock, Thom slipped into the funeral home. He'd hurried into the same jeans and pullover he'd worn the previous day; he hadn't bathed or shaved. Although Lucille had not "come around," Abby told Thom that an early-morning visit would be safe: she and Lucille had stayed with the body late the night before, receiving a steady stream of visitors. Whenever anyone had inquired after Thom, Abby reported, Lucille told them Thom was sick and then pointedly changed the subject.

Now a sleepy-looking man appeared in the dim, high-ceilinged hall and stared at Thom, blinking.

"Sadler?" Thom said. The man gestured quickly to a door on his left and wandered off. Thom went inside. He saw the opened visitors' book with its long list of signatures, but of course he didn't sign. The casket was opened, and his father, dressed in one of his gray banker's suits, looked no different from the sleeping man Thom had watched over these past few weeks. Standing here, Thom felt a little sleepy, himself. The night before, he'd drifted off while watching one of the endless documentaries about the Kennedy family that had been broadcast since Jackie Kennedy's death the previous week. The familiar clips from JFK's funeral had been replayed, and Thom had stared balefully at Jackie in her black veil, holding her children's hands—Caroline and little John-John in their tailored woolen coats. He'd seen the film countless times, of course, but despite his exhaustion he forced himself to watch it again, his eyes aching as that little boy, urged gently by his mother, stepped forward the moment his father's coffin passed by. Thom had closed his eyes when the scene shifted, or had a commercial come on?—he couldn't remember. And this morning, raffish and inconsequent above his own father, he felt that same drowsiness, almost a numbness, spreading through him like a drug. He waited a minute or two before knowing that he couldn't shed a proper tear, much less imagine some noble gesture—Thom Sadler's belated version of that tiny, perfect salute.

Chapter 3

Abby had almost backed out of attending the party that forever changed her life.

This perhaps melodramatic thought would haunt her in the months to come, and the more she lectured herself, in her brisk schoolteacher's voice, and in clichéd terms she would have marked in red on a student's paper— *What's done is done; hindsight is 20/20*—the more her thoughts wound back to that night, to the benefit for that organization whose name she could never keep straight.

Gays against violence, stopping violence against gays—something like that.

Nor had she wanted, that same day, to have lunch with Thom and his friend Connie Lefcourt; she claimed she had phone calls to make. Their mother started to fret, Abby told her brother, if she hadn't called by noon with a "progress report" on Thom and a few minutes of repetitive chatter about their plans for Sunday afternoon. Lucille had decided not to meet them at the airport, after all, but to make a brunch reservation at the Four Seasons hotel. The hotel provided shuttle service from the airport, so she would meet her children in the pretentious gilt-decorated lobby with its gargantuan chandeliers and its majestic staircase sweeping upward into the realm of thousand-dollar-a-night suites. And, though Abby didn't mention this, she needed to call Valerie Patten, too. The carefully worded suicide note from Valerie's husband had worried her all week, like a pebble in her shoe. Logically considered, the letter had no value to anyone: Valerie had already read the contents, and of course Marty, if he were still alive, had no need of it. Abby wondered at her own motives: was she simply prying? Of course, she wanted to know what had happened. Valerie's husband had gone through with his threat, or he was not dead but had injured himself critically (with a gunshot, with a car rammed into a tree), or he had used emotional blackmail to persuade Valerie to come back to him...or did the story have some other, unimaginable outcome? The letter seemed a lingering token of her own deceit and uncertainty, the cloud of unexamined emotion in which she'd returned to Atlanta.

She wanted clarity. She wanted knowledge. A couple of days ago, while Thom was out showing one of his listings, she'd opened the top drawer of her brother's night table, lugged out one of the phone books, and found a listing—thankfully, there was only one—for "Luttrell, Martin," with an address in Druid Hills. Of course, she should simply copy down the address and return the letter, as she'd originally planned, but instead she'd lifted the receiver and dialed.

To her dismay, a woman had answered on the first ring. "Hello? Hello?" The voice was unmistakable. Abby hung up.

Panicked, she took a few deep breaths. It was 11:30 in the morning, a weekday; she'd expected no one would be home. She would hear Marty Luttrell's recorded greeting and know that all was well. Since then, the pebble in her shoe had seemed larger, sharper. *Yes*, as her mother would say, *confession is good for the soul* and she'd decided to call again, tell Valerie she had taken the letter, apologize, and ask if she wanted it returned. If Valerie's husband had carried out his threat, which Abby doubted, then of course she would offer to talk with the woman, even to visit her; she remembered Valerie saying she had no real friends in Atlanta. Given what Abby had done, she was perhaps the last person Valerie would want to see, but nonetheless she'd make the call. When she left Atlanta this time—for the last time?—she wanted to feel that she'd met her obligations, snipped every loose thread.

Once Thom had returned from walking the dogs, rubbing his hands together briskly, and reminded her about lunch with Connie, she closed the newspaper—she'd been sitting at the dining room table, paging through the paper but not reading it—and told him she'd decided not to go.

"What?" Thom said, with the boyish frown he used when something impeded him. "Why not?"

When she told him, in a deliberately vague, offhand way, that she had phone calls to make, Thom said, "Come on, honey, can't they wait until we get back? Connie will be *so* disappointed."

"Thom, I—"

"He called the other night, you know, after you'd gone to bed, and was raving about how nice and smart and pretty you are. He was an only child, you know, and he's always wanted a sister. Or so he claims. He'd probably like to spirit you away."

Earlier in the week Thom had cooked dinner for Abby, Connie, and Carter; he'd also invited Warren, Connie's roommate. Thom wore an apron that read "Kiss the Cook"—everyone did, of course—and had exercised his natural flair as a host. Carter had seemed to feel better than on that first afternoon, and had eaten generous portions of Thom's Caesar salad and crab cakes, and the apple-raspberry pie Thom had made from scratch. Warren was a slender, boyish-looking psychologist, with a Kennedy-like shock of thick auburn hair and a shy but ready smile; and the much-heralded Connie, after introducing himself a bit pompously as "Constantine Lefcourt, Jr.," had relaxed during his first minutes of intensive chatting with Abby and had become, after his second glass of Merlot, quite witty and garrulous. He dominated the talk but not offensively, occasionally bringing Carter or Warren into his monologue while staying focused on Abby, insisting he wanted to hear *everything* about her and Thom's life when they were growing up, yet never really giving her the chance: he was too busy talking about his own life.

Connie was a tall, imposing man, blond and fair-skinned, dressed exquisitely in a turquoise silk shirt (turquoise being Connie's "trademark color," Thom had said), slacks of pale gray wool, a glossy-black pair of tasseled loafers. He had referred, with a roll of his eyes, to his upcoming "dreaded fortieth birthday," but his face was unlined, almost cherubic, and his cheeks flushed with pleasure as he chatted and sipped his wine. Though perhaps ten pounds overweight, he had vivid blue-green eyes, a strong nose, lips of an almost womanly thickness. Abby supposed he must have been spectacularly good-looking as a younger man. In fact, Thom had mentioned that Connie once "did some modeling" and was always, in the opinion of some, overdressed. Abby didn't agree. She'd thought he looked wonderful, and he'd been quite entertaining. He'd talked virtually nonstop during their cocktails, and right through dinner, and then coffee and dessert in the living room; he was still talking as Thom and Abby accompanied him to the door. No one had seemed to mind.

Abby gazed down at the closed newspaper. She took a breath. "I liked him too, Thom. It isn't that."

"And you're leaving day after tomorrow, right?"

He tried to turn the boyish, grumpy frown into a smile, but it was a pained and pleading smile.

"Thom, I—"

"And it seems like we haven't done much of anything."

Yesterday, as she'd accompanied Thom to show one of his listings, he'd apologized for his laxness as a host, insisting that when people visited from out of town he liked to "entertain" them. He took them to the Botanical Gardens, or the Cyclorama. They'd visit the Margaret Mitchell house. They'd take the CNN tour. But since Abby had grown up here, he'd said with a grin, she posed a special challenge. She'd assured him that going around with Thom to visit his friends, show his listings, even tag along on his everyday errands, was all she wanted; she enjoyed learning what his life was like. He'd agreed, nodding vigorously, claiming he'd like to spend a few days with her in Philadelphia, too, sitting in on her classes, driving into Center City on weekends to visit the bookshops and art galleries she favored. As if fulfilling her half of their bargain, she'd gone with him yesterday to show a listing in Morningside, meeting another agent who insisted her client was close to making an offer. Abby's eye had caught on the Remax "For Sale" sign in front of the house, with its white strip along the bottom that read THOMAS J. SADLER, AGENT, with his office and home phone numbers under that. Thom had mentioned that he'd "done well" these past couple of years, and Abby supposed it must be true. He had more than a dozen listings in the trendiest Atlanta neighborhoods, he'd said, with a boyish pride that Abby found touching. His listings—renovated houses, mostly, plus a few condos—were in Morningside, Virginia-Highland, Ansley Park. Most of the owners were gay men or lesbians, he'd said, but not all; he'd developed a substantial reputation throughout the in-town real estate community.

Abby had trouble picturing Thom as a salesman. He'd always been so brash and outspoken. Patience had never been one of his virtues. She couldn't imagine him giving tactful or evasive answers to skeptical queries about his listings (didn't all real estate agents have to do this?) or negotiating detailed, fussy contracts with other brokers, real estate lawyers, temperamental clients. But only last night he'd insisted that he "loved real estate" because every day was a challenge and completely unpredictable.

Abby had nodded, not quite understanding.

Thom had asked about her life in Philadelphia, too, though they talked less often and less freely about that. Since their argument in the park, they'd carefully avoided the topic of his flying back with her, and more generally she'd felt a lingering tension in their elaborate mutual deference over petty things: where they would go for dinner, which movie they would see. Though they'd tried to catch up on each other's lives, talking incessantly, Abby felt they'd achieved only an approximation, even an impersonation, of their high school camaraderie. She'd given a brief, selective rendition of her six-month engagement to Graham Northwood, and of their sudden breakup this past August; Thom reciprocated with details about the handsome University of Georgia graduate student he'd met recently at Hoedown's (a gay country and western bar, he explained) and with whom he'd had a handful of promising dates. He didn't like the idea of a long-distance relationship, he told Abby, but Athens was only an hour away, after all, so they could see each other virtually every weekend. In fact, Chip was driving over this afternoon and would be coming along with them to Pace's party. Thom hoped she would like Chip, he'd said nervously, more than once, and Abby had responded each time that he "sounded nice" and she looked forward to meeting him. Each time they had quickly changed the subject.

They'd carefully avoided talking about their mother, dancing around any references to the immediate future. Of course, she had heard his slip of the tongue a minute ago—*you're* leaving day after tomorrow, not *we're* leaving—but she'd decided that if they had to endure the same fight all over again, it could wait until Saturday night, or even Sunday morning. She didn't intend to leave without him, and she decided that having won the war, she could afford to yield another skirmish.

"All right, then," she said. "I'll call Mom and...I'll make the other calls later. I am getting hungry, come to think of it."

"Great! Connie is meeting us, so we'd better get going. You'll love this place, I promise."

He stepped forward and—catching her off guard—gave her an impulsive peck on the cheek.

Half an hour later they occupied a window table at Agnes & Muriel's, a restaurant whose theme was 1950s nostalgia. Abby didn't care for the place but pretended she did. The dominant colors were hot pink and bright aqua, the ice water came in jelly glasses, the plates and cups Abby glimpsed on the other tables were Fiesta Ware, cheerfully mismatched. Thom kept craning his head toward the window.

"Connie is *always* late," he said, annoyed. "I don't know why I can't remember that, and arrive late myself."

Abby checked her watch. "He said twelve, didn't he? It's only five after."

The restaurant was bustling, the crowd mostly young and professional-looking, the atmosphere casual and even festive. Abby noticed a few tables occupied by men, two or three per table, and her eye lingered a moment at each of these. If it mattered, she supposed she could pick out which were gay men; today, she thought, virtually all of them were, with the possible exception of two harassed-looking young men in dark business suits, striped ties. For one thing, Abby thought, the gay men tended to dress more carefully, their shirts and khakis crisply starched, their sweaters colorful and expensive-looking (though she supposed Thom's habitually rumpled appearance argued against this theory). Not long ago, on a TV sitcom, Abby heard a joke about "gaydar," and it had stuck in her memory, because she hadn't been sure if the line had meant to acknowledge such a notion or to satirize it. She had a graduate degree in literature, and it annoyed her that she hadn't been able to interpret a line from a TV comedy. She'd now spent nearly a week in her brother's world, and so far she'd kept her foot a comfortable distance, or so she hoped, from her mouth; but she felt the need to keep sharpening her awareness, to notice and absorb certain subtleties that her brother and his friends would take for granted, not wanting to embarrass herself. Her years living with her mother in Philadelphia had dulled her senses; so had teaching in a girls' school, where the students were bright and high-spirited but rather naive, being children of privilege; and so, for that matter, had dating Graham, a man approaching his thirtieth birthday who still attended law school and lived at home. Graham would never have brought her to a place like this. They'd usually dined in restaurants with white tablecloths and big chandeliers, where most of the patrons were their parents' ages. This was Graham's idea of a classy date. Unlike most of the women he'd dated, Abby had a lot of "class"; he'd told her this more than once, without irony.

Thom was complaining in general terms about people who were habitually late. "It's my pet peeve, I guess. People like that, they're assuming their time is more important than yours. I know they don't think of it that way, but…" He smiled. "I'll stop griping now."

Abby's gaze had drifted to the restaurant foyer where Connie loomed in the doorway, glancing around.

"There he is," Abby said.

Thom waved, and Connie approached them breathlessly. "Sorry I'm late," he said, settling his considerable frame onto the small, wobbling chair. (All the tables and chairs were "dinette sets," with vinyl upholstery and chrome legs.) He unfolded his napkin and dabbed his forehead. "This is my day to deliver for Open Hand, and it took longer than usual."

He patted Abby's forearm. "How are you, sweetheart? Are you warm enough? It's drafty in here sometimes, especially by the window, and it's getting colder out. Did you hear it's supposed to snow?"

Even in this nicely groomed crowd, Connie stood out. He wore charcoal twill slacks and a lush, deep-turquoise sweater that must have been cashmere; Abby glimpsed a wafer-thin silver watch beneath his sleeve and on one of his pinkies a diamond solitaire set in white gold, or platinum. The brisk, lemony scent of Connie's cologne had instantly cut through the aromas of the meat loaf, deep-fried shrimp, and steamed greens borne on trays by waiters endlessly crisscrossing past their table.

"Your deliveries took longer?" Thom said shortly. "Why is that?"

"Now don't be skeptical," Connie said, wiggling the fingers of one hand toward Thom while keeping his glittering blue-green eyes on Abby. "He always fusses at me for being late."

Thom said, "You always *are* late."

"They added some new stops to my route," Connie said airily, "and one of the new clients—ahem—invited me in. He has a condo in Colony Square. Sort of cramped and poorly decorated, it must be said, but the man was *very* sweet. He kept saying how guilty he felt, with people like me bringing his meals every day. Isn't that sweet? He *did* look perfectly healthy, but he said he'd gone on disability from his job, selling insurance or something, and I told him, hey, that's what Open Hand is for, so don't worry about it. Plus, he's cute. He had the heat turned up to about eighty-five, just so he could wear this little tank top. Isn't that sweet? Biceps to die for, too. I was burning up in this sweater. His name is Chuck."

Connie breathed deeply, then took a sip of ice water. He glanced around the restaurant, waved vaguely at someone, and then gave an audible sigh, as though his narrative had exhausted him.

Thom said, "Have you and Chuck set a wedding date?"

Connie gave Thom a long, pensive look. "We're not supposed to date the clients, are we? Warren said something about that."

"It was a joke," Thom said.

"Oh. Then maybe I'll ask him out." He turned to Abby. "Sweetie, have you and your mean old brother ordered yet? I could kill for a glass of wine, but I'm dieting. I've had the most hectic morning imaginable, and my reward is a glass of unsweetened iced tea. Life is decidedly unfair."

Thom laughed. "Poor thing. I'm sure you'll make up for it tonight."

"Tonight? Oh, you mean at Pace's. I'll have you know that I declined *three* Christmas parties to attend this little 'benefit,' and of course, the only one benefiting will be Dr. Dracula, who'll probably bore us silly with one of his earnest, eye-glazing speeches. When all we *want* to do is flirt with the bartender. Pace does hire cute bartenders, I'll give him that, though his caterer leaves something to be desired. Did you try those cheese puffs at his Halloween party? The next day, I called and told him frankly that—"

Connie was interrupted by the waiter, and after Abby and Thom ordered, Connie made a show of requesting *un*sweetened tea—"unlike my svelte friends here, I have to watch my sugar"—and then ordered the butterflied shrimp with french fries and cornbread.

After the waiter left, Abby asked, "Dr. Dracula?"

"His name is Mitchell Drake," Thom said quickly. "A dentist. He's a friend of Pace's who's sort of—well, 'prominent' in the gay community here, though quite a few people don't like him. He's the president of—what's it called, Connie? Gays Against Violence?"

Connie gave a twisty little smile. "Gay People Stopping Violence—or GPSV, as the clever acronym has it. Sounds like a TV station, doesn't it? Or some dreaded new disease."

"Anyway, he organized this benefit tonight," Thom said. "The one at which Connie is happily going to donate $750."

Connie fluttered his eyelids briefly. "Two-fifty, you mean. Yes," he said, turning back to Abby, "Dr. Dracula is tireless on behalf of so many good causes. Stop the violence, save the whales, stamp out the heartbreak of psoriasis—you name it."

Thom said, "Come on. Don't be mean."

"And he's called Dr. Dracula because he has these huge molars, which he shows constantly during his speeches," Connie added. "They represent his desire to suck the blood out of your checking account."

"He really *does* do a lot of good," Thom said, giving Abby an anxious look.

She said guiltily, "Dr. Dracula sounds intriguing, but I think I'm staying home tonight."

"What, you're not coming?" Connie cried. "But why not? We were going to have so much fun!"

He sounded like a small boy whose birthday party had been canceled.

"Don't worry," Thom told her, "Mitch won't talk all that long, and there's no real pressure to contribute. They pass around some envelopes and suggest you can mail something in. After that, there *will* be a party."

"Yes, Virginia, there will," Connie said. "Please say you'll come. I wish I hadn't said that about Mitch. And Thom's right, he isn't *that* bad. I tend to exaggerate, sometimes."

In the pearly gray light from the window, Connie's widened eyes were a brilliant turquoise, the color of a David Hockney pool. Abby hadn't anticipated that Connie would react so strongly. Why should it matter whether she came to the party or not?

Thom said, mimicking Connie's whispered, frank admission, "'I tend to exaggerate sometimes.' I'd like that in writing, Connie."

"Funny. Now, *talk* to your sister, would you?"

Within minutes, she had relented. Another small battle she considered it a good idea, a strategic idea, to yield to Thom. She supposed the prospect of this party intimidated her, somewhat; she might be one of the few women in a crowd of dozens, if not hundreds. ("Pace's house is *huge*," Thom had said. "Wait till you see it.") But Connie insisted she would have a wonderful time, no matter what.

"If Mitch or Angela comes anywhere near you, sniffing out money, I promise a swift rescue," he said. "So *please* don't worry."

The food arrived, and they talked of other things. As he'd done during his dinner party, Thom stayed quieter than usual, as if to let Abby and Connie get acquainted. Connie asked about Abby's teaching, saying he hoped she liked Philadelphia but she really ought to move back to Atlanta, so they could see more of each other; and Abby, choosing her words with care, asked Connie about his life. She already knew, from Thom, that he came from a prominent Oklahoma City family and had taken the scenic route through Emory, finally earning an undergraduate degree in journalism after eight or nine years. His father was an oil executive who clashed frequently with his son over money, and over Connie's lack of a career. Soon, Connie would come into the trust fund his mother, who died when Connie was ten, had set up after her cancer diagnosis. It was Connie's mother, whose father had been a locally famous oil man, who had gotten her husband into the business, and it was her own enormous fortune that Connie had inherited, much to his father's chagrin. (Thom knew few other details; Connie seldom talked about his mother, whose loss had been the great trauma of his early life.) For years Connie had drifted from job to job, working off and on, Thom had said, "but mostly off." He had dabbled for a while in furniture sales, but argued with the designers; he'd edited newsletters for a consulting firm, but found the work "meaningless"; he shelved books in a branch library for more than a year—his lowest-paying job, and also his favorite—but had been dismissed, he insisted, because the branch manager, a woman in her sixties, envied Connie's expensive clothes and his late-model Seville.

So Abby asked about his home (he loved redecorating his penthouse condominium in Buckhead, Thom had told her) and about the vacation he'd taken recently to Hawaii. On their way to the restaurant, Thom had mentioned that, too, and said Connie loved to talk about it.

"It probably isn't polite lunch conversation," Connie said as he buttered a hunk of cornbread, "but Warren and I had booked this little place in Maui, supposedly the only gay bed-and-breakfast on the island. The brochure looked lovely and the rates were sky-high, which is usually a good sign. Imagine our surprise when we got there and discovered the place is run by *nudists!* Yes, here we are, innocent young boys from Atlanta, and we ring the front bell, and there stands this skinny, aging little man wearing nothing but his black-rimmed glasses! And that's just the beginning. I won't go into the gory details, but—"

"Since when!" Thom laughed. "You haven't spared anyone else."

"OK," Connie said, ignoring him, "let's just say that not everyone should be a nudist. Not if you're pushing sixty and have just a little fringe of hair around your ears and look like Allen Ginsberg's younger brother. I mean, really. We thought it was *very* unprofessional. He stands there explaining to you about the house and when breakfast is served and so forth, and you're trying to look firmly into his eyes or off into space—anywhere but at *that*. Fortunately, the island of Maui does have its charms. We avoided the house as much as possible. But you can't imagine how traumatizing it is to have some ugly little man serve you breakfast in the *nude*. I mean, if they'd hired cute staff people, it might have been a different sort of experience, you know? But every time we looked up, here came junior Ginsberg, his little whoozit flapping from side to side."

Connie shivered, clearly enjoying the laughter he'd elicited from Thom and Abby.

"Tell Abby about your first trip to Hawaii, the one with your parents," Thom said.

"Not my parents—my father and my stepmother," Connie said, shaking a forefinger at Thom.

"Right, sorry," Thom muttered.

"No prob, a common mistake." Connie turned to Abby. "Let's just say that my father's second wife—her name is Wilma, poor thing—is not the most brilliant woman. Until she married him, less than a year after my darling mother died, Wilma had never left central Oklahoma. I think she grew up in a trailer park or something. She's sweet in her way, and very naive, and has six kids from her own first marriage, and then she lucks into marrying my father and wants to start seeing the world. The first summer she lived with us, I was eleven, and guess who got dragged along on their trip to Hawaii? We did all the fun tourist things: suffered through a luau at our hotel, took a boring guided tour of some extinct volcano, got third-degree sunburn on the beach, and listened to that whiney Hawaiian music from morning till night." Connie gave one of his small shudders, throwing his eyes upward. "And one day, we're driving along in our rented Town Car, and guess what my stepmother says? She tells my father, 'Honey, this is such a popular tourist spot, but isn't it amazing?—I haven't seen a single out-of-state license plate!' And I promise you, she was not joking."

Thom looked at Abby, his eyes crinkled in amusement. "I'm never sure if he's made that one up."

"I don't need to make things up!" Connie said, in mock indignation. "These pearls just issue from the woman's mouth. When she was little and her family would go driving on the highway, they had this game where they would look for out-of-state license plates, see how many they could find...oh, I'm not going to try and convince you."

"And the time you went to Myrtle Beach?" Thom prompted him.

"Oh, yes, I got hauled along on another beach vacation, later that same summer." Connie had lifted his hands, palms toward Abby, fingers outspread—a gesture he performed often, Abby noticed, conveying his helpless martyrdom to a world of folly. His fingertips were smeared with butter, like a child's. "We were driving down the South Carolina coast from Myrtle Beach, and for some reason we stopped at a big hardware store, right on the highway. I remember this gigantic sign: SCHOFIELD'S HARDWARE. Anyway, as we were coming out in the parking lot, Miss Wilma bends over and picks up something. Then she turns to my father and says—I swear to almighty God and all the saints, these were her exact words—'Honey, do you need a good screw?' I even caught my father snickering at that one, but of course, Wilma went along blithely, and dropped the little treasure in her purse. I think the poor woman must be used to people laughing in her presence, so she ignores it."

"Connie has bad luck on his vacations," Thom said, clearly enjoying

Connie's bubbly narratives. "Tell Abby about the gay cruise you and Warren took. The one with the overweight stripper."

"Thom, your darling sister wouldn't care about *that*," Connie said, cutting his eyes in Abby's direction. He must have glimpsed something in her face, for he bit his lower lip, primly, and reached for another piece of cornbread. Abby noticed the way her brother had leaned in toward the table, with his eager, boyish smile and glinting blue eyes. His irritation with Connie had vanished.

Connie shook his head, giving a mock shudder. "No, I dare not reopen those wounds. Such a trauma, that was." He gave them a quick grin. "My shrink got a lot of mileage out of that one," he added with an impish tilt of his head. "The overweight stripper was a stand-in for my father, or some such thing, and when he sat on my lap, nearly *pul*verizing my poor thighbones in the process, it gave rise to a castration anxiety of operatic proportions. God knows, it didn't give rise to anything else."

Thom laughed; Connie was cackling softly.

"Connie loves to make fun of his therapist," Thom said, "but he couldn't live without him."

Connie pressed his lips together. "That's probably true. But Lord, how I'd love to try."

Between them, Thom and Connie narrated the history of Connie's "adventures in therapy"; Connie arched an eyebrow when pronouncing that phrase. Six or seven years ago, Connie told Abby, he'd sunk into a clinical depression for no particular reason and had first visited a woman recommended by his internist.

"She was a darling little Chinese lesbian with a Buster Brown haircut—I mean, it was *exactly* as if her butch lover put a soup bowl over her head and did the job—and she wore the usual dyke uniform of flannel shirt and jeans. And Hush Puppies. Delia Dong, I swear that's her real name. It's on her diplomas and everything. Well, Delia seemed to think my depression could be cured by *hugging*."

"Come on, Connie," Thom said.

"I'm serious! We would hug, she informed me, at the beginning of each session and at the end of each session. Sometimes she would come over and hug me in the *middle* of a session. Pretty soon, everything I said in therapy was designed *not* to inspire a hugging fit from Miss Delia! Most of the time I was sitting there, sweating in my clothes, saying to myself, 'Please don't hug me, woman. *Please*.' If I hadn't known she was a dyke, I'd swear she had a thing for me. And her hugs were not charming. She'd simply wrap her arms around and hang on, like I was a giant redwood or something. What was worse, she wore Old Spice cologne, which was sort of cute but way too butch for me. And she told *me* I have a hang-up about my father!"

"Delia Dong does not wear Old Spice, and you know it," Thom laughed.

"She *does*," Connie insisted. "Extra-strength, I believe. Your brother always encourages me to talk," he told Abby, "and then he contradicts me. But I'm sure you're familiar with that trick."

Abby smiled. "So you stopped seeing Delia?"

"Yes, I had to. I'm just *not* a hugger, I'm sorry. When did that vogue for hugging start, anyway, around the mid '80s? Now it's running amok, in my opinion. People hug perfect strangers on the street. On TV, Clinton hugs everybody. He hugs senators, even Republicans. He hugs that dyke attorney general—what's her name, with the Hitler haircut? He'd probably hug Saddam Hussein if he had the chance."

The waiter arrived to ask about dessert: Thom and Abby ordered coffee, but Connie couldn't resist the blueberry cobbler.

"I've been good all morning," he said, glancing off.

When the waiter had left, Abby said: "You forgot to tell me about your therapist. The newer one."

"Oops, he must have slipped my mind! Does that count as a Freudian slip? Well, Abby"—he patted her forearm again in his intimate, confiding way—"we all have our addictions, don't we? And mine happens to be therapy. I've been going to this pretentious fellow named Michael Purvis for several years now, and after the first few months all we've done is have the same five or six conversations over and over about my five or six most fascinating problems. Once a month, Dr. Purvis sends me a bill for $480— that's $120 per session, if you please, and of course a 'therapeutic hour' is forty-five minutes—and I send him a check. Sometimes he gets lucky and there are five Mondays in a month, so he gets $600. Getting checks in the mail from unwell people—that's *his* addiction."

"Tell her about the letter he sent you," Thom said. He grinned at Abby. "This just kills me. It tells you everything you need to know about Michael Purvis."

Connie gave a mild, faraway smile. "Yes, poor Dr. Purvis sent me a letter one time, because evidently I'd neglected to send his monthly check. It had just slipped my mind, you know? So he sends me this polite letter about the bill, and he signs it, 'Dr. Michael Purvis, Ph.D.' Well, Abby, I was a journalism major, and I have this bad habit of correcting people. So, the next week I told Michael that he could sign his name, 'Michael Purvis, Ph.D.,' or 'Dr. Michael Purvis,' but that 'Dr. Michael Purvis, Ph.D.' was redundant. I thought he'd appreciate the tip, you know? But no, he stiffens in his chair and says he's been told that before, but he *prefers* signing his name that way. 'I worked hard to become a doctor,' he said. And I said, 'But you're not a doctor. An MD is a doctor—you're a psychologist.' And he turns red in the face and asks if I'm envious of his 'achievement'—yes, that's the word he used. I mean, the man got a doctorate from Georgia State, for God's sake, and you don't have to be a rocket scientist for that."

Abby blinked; the psychologist did sound awful. "But you've kept on seeing him?" she asked.

"Michael? Oh, yes," Connie said, dismissing the matter with a wave of his hand. "We're just like an old married couple. But listen, Abby, enough about me! I want to hear all about *you*!"

Thom laughed. "Too late," he said. "I've got an appointment. Besides, I think we've overstayed our welcome."

Abby and Connie glanced toward the entrance, where a throng of people huddled in small groups, waiting.

"I guess you're right," Connie said, glancing down as he pushed away from the table. "Oh, I didn't realize the bill had come."

The waiter had placed the check near Connie's arm at least ten minutes earlier, and Abby was sure he *had* seen. She took up her purse, but as he'd been doing all week, Thom put his hand over hers.

"Connie and I are splitting this," he said, laying a twenty down on the table.

"For heaven's sake, yes," Connie said breathlessly. "We're taking *you* out for lunch." After frowning at the check Connie took some bills from his wallet, handed them to Thom, and the three of them made their way out of the restaurant. Both Thom and Connie spoke to the hostess as they left. "The cobbler was *fabulous!*" Connie called out, blowing an elaborate gourmet's kiss with his fingertips.

Outside, the air seemed colder; the clouds overhead had turned a darker gray, like tufts of soiled cotton.

"My goodness," Connie exclaimed, shivering. "Do you think it really *will* snow?"

As Thom and Abby turned toward the parking lot, Connie abruptly reached out his hand. "The lot was full when I got here," he said, taking Abby's extended fingertips and giving an affectionate squeeze, "so I had to

park on Cumberland. By the way, Thom, congratulations—I saw that
UNDER CONTRACT sign on Jim and Randy's house."

"Thanks," Thom said, crossing his fingers. "Let's hope it goes through.
See you tonight, Connie."

"Bye now," Connie called over his shoulder, already hurrying down the
driveway toward the street with his arms crossed against the cold.

"Thanks so much for lunch!" Abby called back.

They'd arrived at Thom's Accord, and Abby stood there waiting for him
to unlock the doors; she gazed idly down to the street where Connie was
hurrying along, a bright turquoise beacon among the passing traffic and
the freezing wind, and that's when she noticed the tiny flakes swirling
through the air.

Inside the car, Thom bent over the ignition, gunning the engine and
muttering, "Damn, it's cold."

Within seconds the flakes had grown larger, and now Abby, feeling a
sudden childlike exultation, reached across and tapped her brother's
shoulder.

"Look, honey, it's snowing!" she cried.

Disbelieving, Thom looked up, squinted out the windshield, a smile of
delight already creasing his face as instinctively he leaned sideways to
receive the quick, impulsive kiss Abby planted on his cheek.

The snowfall had lasted for less than an hour, and none of it stuck. The
temperature hovered in the middle thirties all day. That evening Abby stood
in the kitchen, shaking her head as she watched the six o'clock news on
the small set perched on the counter beside the refrigerator. This special
one-hour report called "Snow Jam '98" featured the same group of stories
the local channels reported (even when Abby was a small child, hoping for
a day free from school) whenever there was a chance of snow in Atlanta.
One reporter interviewed A & P customers, who were "flooding the aisles"
and "stocking up" in case a significant snowfall materialized. Shots of
empty racks where the bread had been; empty dairy cases where the milk
had been; live interviews with customers in checkout lines who invariably
grinned sheepishly into the camera and mumbled that they "didn't want to
take any chances." Then came interviews with city officials, claiming they
were "prepared for the worst," and with truck drivers who had spent the
day covering area bridges with sand and salt. There were videotapes of the
last major Atlanta snowfall, two years ago, that showed a car fishtailing on

Interstate 20 and a MARTA bus careening into a ditch along Northside Drive. Then a series of "live shots"—one from Interstate 85, one from Midtown, one from Buckhead—in which bundled-up reporters excitedly informed the public what the public already knew: some big, slushy flakes had fallen for an hour that afternoon, there were no driving problems "yet," and only "time would tell" whether Atlanta would wake up to a "winter wonderland" in the morning.

Thom strolled into the kitchen, whistling, fresh from his shower. Mitzi and Chloe raced behind him, lunging at his heels. "What are you snickering about?"

"These weather reports," Abby said.

Now the weatherman and his map filled the screen; he was solemnly calibrating the likelihood of more snow that evening. There was a fifty percent chance the city could get several inches of "the white stuff," the weatherman said. Everything depended on the temperature, he said slowly, with a long, searching look into the camera.

"The gist of the story," Abby told her brother, "is that it might snow tonight. Or it might not."

Thom squeezed past her, briefly grasping her waist. "Excuse *me*," he said smartly, a phrase Abby remembered from their high school days. He bent over, opened the oven door, peered inside; he'd put together some leftovers from the dinner Abby had cooked the night before. They'd decided to have a quick bite before Pace's party and not bother with another restaurant meal. Straightening, Thom said: "Now stop making fun. Just because you've become a sophisticated Easterner."

"Someone visiting from Minneapolis must be in stitches, watching this," Abby said.

She turned, feeling self-conscious as her brother looked her up and down, appraisingly. While he was showering, she'd changed into the nicest clothes she'd brought on this trip; in fact, the only really nice outfit she owned, a black velvet jacket and skirt over a dressy white silk blouse with frilly collar and sleeves. The skirt fit a little tighter than she liked, and was a little shorter than she liked, but she'd bought the outfit despite herself, the week after her first date with Graham Northwood last January. For Valentine's Day, her mother had given her jewelry specifically for the dress: necklace and earrings of red and black enamel trimmed in gold. Though she knew the outfit was attractive, it felt more like a costume than something the real Abigail Sadler—whoever that was—would wear. She'd dabbed some lipstick and mascara onto her face (since arriving, she hadn't bothered with makeup) and had brushed her hair vigorously in the attempt, probably futile, to give her tired pageboy a bit more shine and energy. She was conscious of a mild blush rising along her throat as her brother stared, assessing.

"You look nice tonight," he said. "The cutest date I've had in years."

That reminded her: Thom *did* have a date.

She said, "What about your friend from Athens? Isn't he driving over?"

Thom glanced away. "Chip? He left a message on my machine. Held up by some graduate-student function at school. He might come tomorrow."

"Oh. Sorry." She glimpsed the disappointment in his eyes.

"No problem." He turned back to the oven. "I'd rather take you."

While Thom finished preparing dinner, Abby went back into her room to fetch her purse, and that was when she thought again about Marty Luttrell. She dug out the bit of paper where she'd scrawled his number, then edged quietly into her brother's room. Mentally she rehearsed once again the apology she would deliver to Valerie Patten. Punching the numbers, she saw that her fingers were shaking.

This time, after several rings, an answering machine did pick up. The message, delivered in a man's voice, was perfunctory, the tone as monotonous as if read from a card: "You have reached the Luttrell residence. No one can take your call. Leave a message at the beep." When it sounded, Abby took a breath and opened her mouth, but didn't quite know what to say. She hung up.

An hour later, heading down Piedmont Avenue on their way to Pace's, Thom said: "So, did you call Mom?"

They'd been silent for several minutes, and her eye had drifted out to the damp, darkened street, where the traffic moved with a bewildered slowness through the moisture-thickened air; the lighted buildings, the streetlamps, the headlights of other cars blurred and wavered in the foggy darkness. More of the oversized snowflakes were falling, and Thom's windshield wipers batted them in a lazy, monotonous rhythm. The flakes melted the instant they hit the street and were not even sticking on the grassy strips along the sidewalks.

"Mom?" Abby said blankly.

"I noticed you went in my room, so I figured you must be calling Mom again."

His tone was so casual, it seemed almost affected, she thought. As if he'd run the words through his mind before saying them.

She shook her head, relieved that he couldn't see her face in the darkened car.

"No, I—I was calling someone else."

In fact, this was the first day she'd neglected to call Lucille. After returning from their lunch with Connie, she'd thought about her mother but reasoned that she had all afternoon. She'd drifted into Thom's cozy living room with her now-raggedy copy of *Wide Sargasso Sea*, which she'd been reading unusually slowly, ten or twenty pages each day. Mitzi and Chloe had curled up with her on Thom's bedraggled sofa with its faint, pleasant smells of hair oil and men's cologne, and soon she'd gotten drowsy and napped for a while. Thom was home by four o'clock and woke her— "Hey, lazy"—and her mother's scowling face popped at once into Abby's mind. Just as quickly she banished it. She tried not to blame her mother for the enervating awareness that she must return to Philadelphia on Sunday, resume her stale, accustomed life, endure her mother's litany of stored-up complaints. With Thom there, Abby reasoned, she might get a breather, though she could imagine that her function as a buffer between Thom and Lucille, if not as a referee, might sap her energy even more than her role as the child who lived at home, the child who listened patiently. She was so accustomed to listening, she thought, that she could no longer hear her own voice.

She supposed she was avoiding today's call to Lucille because yesterday, when Abby had waited until after lunch, her mother had been more truculent than usual.

"What took you so long, honey?" she had demanded. "I've been worried to death all morning."

Abby had explained about going with Thom to show one of his listings. "We've been staying really busy," she said airily, as if this were an ordinary vacation. "I've enjoyed being with Thom—it's been a good time."

"A good time?" She heard her mother's quick expulsion of smoke. Shortly after they'd left Atlanta, her mother had taken up the habit she'd abandoned when she got married (George Sadler had detested the smell of cigarette smoke) but now practiced avidly, two to three packs of Salem Lights each day. She claimed that because they were "Lights" they did no real harm, and in any case she insisted—with the wry twist of her mouth she used when trying to be witty—that she didn't inhale. She'd even done a needlepoint cigarette-and-lighter case decorated with pink rosebuds, as if facilitating one harmless habit with another. Abby could now imagine her sitting by the silent phone, twisting the ends of her newly tinted cinnamon-red cap of hair, smoking fiercely. Her makeup, recently updated to coordinate with the hair, would be freshly applied, as would her nail polish. Around the time she'd gotten her new haircut Lucille had started dressing younger, too, favoring sleeveless silk or linen shifts in bright stripes and paisleys, outfits that showed off her still-slim figure. Sometimes she wore these at home, even when she had no plans to go out, claiming they cheered her up. Abby favored anything that cheered her mother up, and often complimented Lucille on her appearance, especially when her feathers needed smoothing. Yesterday that hadn't been an option, and in fact she'd heard herself blurt out, "Yes, do you mind? If I have a good time while I'm here?"

Her mother had paused. Abby heard the long, contemplative drag on her cigarette.

"Of course not, honey. You know I'm just—I'm just anxious, I guess, with both of you there and me stuck here by myself."

Relieved they weren't going to argue, Abby had reminded her that Sunday was a few days away, after all. Improvising, she added that Thom was looking forward to the trip and at that point she'd stopped herself, confused and vaguely embarrassed. She wasn't good at lying, but fortunately her mother veered onto another topic—something about Aunt Millicent, who had invited Lucille to join her and several other women for a Caribbean cruise shortly after New Year's, but of course Lucille couldn't go, now that…. Abby had stopped listening. She stood there in Thom's bedroom—for some reason, she'd wandered in here instead of using the kitchen phone—and her eye caught on the framed photograph of herself on her brother's bedside table. It dated from the party celebrating her master's, but the woman in the snapshot looked like a high-school girl playing dress-up. She'd worn a crimson blouse her mother had given her, and her eyes (normally a milder blue than her brother's, but somehow brightened in this photo) were spiked with more mascara than she'd probably worn since, even for her dates with Graham Northwood. A three-quarters shot, with her shining auburn hair looking so ample and healthy—what a contrast, she thought, to the meek little pageboy she'd worn the past few years. And how frank and forthright, her too-bright smile for the camera! That girl seemed ready for anything, and she wondered if Thom, with the photograph there beside the bed, still thought of her that way.

"I'd better go," she'd told her mother. "Thom will be here any minute, and I want to make his dinner."

Lucille laughed sharply. "He's got you doing the housework, does he?"

No, her brother had been taking her out most days to expensive restaurants, lunch and dinner, gallantly deflecting her attempts to pay her share. She'd barely lifted a finger since she arrived. So she'd decided to surprise him. Shortly after Thom left for work, Carter had stopped by, saying he was headed to Kroger's. She'd made out a quick list, and half an hour later Carter returned with the makings for baked pesto lasagna and sweet-potato pie, two of Thom's favorite dishes. She was grateful when Carter declined her invitation to join them. "No, you guys need some time together, just the two of you," he said. He looked drawn and pale, though his wan handsomeness and ghostly smile heightened his appeal, as though he were on the verge of disappearing altogether; even the brief trip to the grocery store had exhausted him. He added, "But thanks, Abby." So he'd left, and Abby hoped to have everything in the oven by the time her brother got home. But there was no point in explaining to Lucille.

"I'll call you tomorrow," Abby had said.

"First thing in the morning, OK, honey? And if he happens to be there, maybe you can put him on, too. But don't say I asked you to."

Lucille continued referring to Thom as "he," as though it were a point of pride not to use his name.

"OK, Mom," Abby had said. "We'll see."

As Thom slowed for the turn onto Montgomery Ferry Road, Abby vowed that she would call Lucille in the morning, get the apologies over with, discuss the flight home; and yes, she would put Thom on the phone, and let him explain how much he was looking forward to their visit.

That would settle the matter, she thought. Tomorrow.

While Thom struggled to parallel park, cursing softly, Abby understood that she'd become excited about this evening out. She saw other cars lining the street, brake lights glowing in the damp air; people bundled in jackets and scarves rushed along the sidewalk, heads bowed under the cascade of wet flakes. At the corner of Montgomery Ferry and Beverly Drive, Thom had pointed to an imposing, brightly lit, multilevel contemporary structure of stucco and glass looming into the snow-strewn night.

"That's Pace's house," he said.

They hurried along the damp sidewalks, heads ducked against the snowflakes. Entering through Pace's big double doors, Abby saw the front rooms were thronged with people, their chattering softened by the mildly plaintive jazz muffling the room like invisible gauze, the air spiced with the guests' eager talk and the aroma of warm hors d'oeuvre trays borne by young men in white dress shirts and black trousers. The guests were dressed more colorfully. On the second-floor loft, Abby glimpsed Connie leaning against the rail, wearing a diagonally striped white-and-aqua sweater and sipping from a glass of white wine, chatting and laughing with several men. Other such groups clustered through the living and dining areas, a bobbing, gesturing sea of brightly hued sweaters. There were a few women, too, some with short haircuts and wearing jeans but more of them, Abby noted with relief, in dressy outfits not too different from her own. Thom had mentioned that Pace had a number of straight friends who would be attending, too, no matter that the benefit was for "Gay People Stopping Violence." None of Pace's friends liked to miss one of his parties, Thom had observed.

"Come on," Thom said eagerly. He'd shrugged out of his leather jacket and now reached out to help Abby with her coat. "Let me dump these down in the guest room, then I'll introduce you around."

Before she could answer, he'd taken the coats, maneuvered through the crowded living room, and begun descending some stairs, calling out to several people along the way. Feeling stranded, Abby glanced around for the bar. Near the kitchen, a handsome young man with curly auburn hair stood vigorously shaking a pitcher of amber-colored liquid and cubed ice. Among the ceaselessly roving guests, she saw a small line of four or five men waiting patiently as the bartender poured two Manhattans and handed them to a dark-haired man, very handsome, in a red cashmere sweater. Abby wandered toward the end of the line. She'd been standing there a few seconds, craning her neck toward the stairway and looking for Thom, when she felt a stirring of warm breath against her ear.

A male voice said, "…What you're thinking? I can tell."

She looked around, startled; a slender olive-skinned man with thick, glossy-black hair waited beside her, smiling.

"Excuse me?" she said. She'd put one hand to her throat, an instinctive gesture when anyone caught her by surprise. The man's gaze fell briefly to her hand (her left, she would later recall, pondering this moment: her ringless left) and he blinked slowly, and smiled slowly, then held her startled glance with his placid dark eyes. They must have been a deep brown, but they looked black, all pupil. The same glossy black as his hair, his collarless silk shirt.

She must have misheard, she thought, the man's words distorted by the ceaseless buzzing of the guests and by the music, an esoteric arrangement of random blips and caroming, dipping wails from a plaintive horn.

The man bent close to her ear; this time he enunciated more clearly, and she detected a posh-sounding British accent.

"I was trying to guess what you're drinking," he repeated. "White Zinfandel? My name is Philip, by the way. Philip DeMunn."

Abby smiled, relieved, and shook his extended hand. It was slender but strong-looking, the fingers exquisitely long, like a pianist's; the nails appeared recently manicured, gleaming with a transparent lacquer. Abby offered her name and said that she'd just arrived.

"I know. I saw you come in." He reached out, dabbed at something on her collar. "A bit of snow. Melted," he added with a smile, touching the edge of his forefinger to his lips.

"Yes, it's started again," she said, awkwardly. When he'd touched her sleeve, she became aware that alone among the guests, or so it seemed, she and Philip were dressed in black. Yet she felt self-conscious in her outfit, whereas he appeared so sleek and well-groomed that she supposed him a performer of some kind. An actor, perhaps; or a classical musician. His good looks were almost alarming. Even his skin had a waxen gloss, as though he'd just stepped from the shower, and she detected the faint but musky-sweet odor of his cologne, which reminded her of incense: that heavy, sweetish incense from the endless masses she'd endured as a young girl. It had a pleasant, faintly ashen smell. Strong but alluring, the scent had mingled with his warm breath from the moment he'd bent to whisper in Abby's ear.

Now they'd reached the front of the line, and the bartender looked up inquiringly. She started to speak, but Philip DeMunn made a quick V with his fingers. "Two champagnes, please."

Abby watched the bartender pour the foaming liquid into flutes. She disliked champagne, but Philip's gesture intrigued her. From nowhere the image of Graham Northwood's earnest, concerned expression floated through her mind. "Is the wine all right, honey? And how about the food? We can send it back if it's not." From their first date, he'd been so attentive and solicitous and smothering that she'd often longed to get up and rush out of the restaurant.

"I think you'll like the champagne," Philip said, taking the flutes from the bartender and offering her one. "It's Moët, my favorite."

"I do, thanks," Abby lied. She sipped at the champagne, oddly pleased with herself. She supposed she should be looking around for Thom, but she reasoned he would find her, eventually. She glanced toward the stairway and saw the guests drifting incessantly up and down, but Thom was not among them. She kept being distracted by the spare but elegant design of the house's interior, all white walls and pale hardwoods and tall rectangles of glass. The floors were bleached oak or pine, their gleaming expanses broken occasionally by dark rugs in geometrical designs that looked vaguely Indian, or Oriental; the vaulted ceiling had matching beams on one side and slanted panes of glass on the other. The furniture was dark and plain. An occasional sofa, a simple table, a row of straight-backed chairs, so the eye kept moving toward the abstract paintings and sculptures—most of them, like the rugs, in monochromatic dark red or brown—that were placed with a kind of impersonal deliberateness through the open, high-ceilinged rooms.

There were few personal touches, Abby thought. Perhaps there were no personal touches. She'd noticed there was no Christmas tree, no deco-ration of any kind. Along one wall of the upstairs loft, near a white lami-nate computer station, she glimpsed a row of bookshelves and, she thought, a grouping of photographs, though it might simply have been another artwork, a collage meant to suggest photographs. The house had the feel of a contemporary museum, one normally hushed but tonight, for this special occasion, enlivened by the piping, enveloping jazz, the cease-less laughter and hilarity of the sipping, chattering guests.

A sudden chill ran through Abby. Briefly she closed her eyes.

"Have you seen the upstairs?" Philip asked.

"The upstairs?"

"Pace's playroom, as he calls it." He grinned, showing a row of even, perfectly white teeth. "It's quite something."

He'd grasped the crook of her arm and was leading her toward the steps.

"But my brother—"

"He ran into some old friends, downstairs. I just left him there."

So he knew Thom, then. Guided up the weightless-looking stairway by Philip DeMunn—the steps were pale slats of wood suspended in air, extending two more floors above Abby's head—she felt an unpleasant sense of vertigo. She knew this had nothing to do with climbing stairs. Immediately, she'd recognized the same emotion she felt whenever she pondered her brother's private life, as she'd done so often during the years of their separation. Like some harsh, unnameable force striking her abdomen, a brief but decisive twist of her insides. She knew Thom, but she did not know him. Had she supposed that Philip DeMunn was not gay, then? And what did it matter, really? He was merely being considerate and kind, like all of Thom's friends. When they reached the next floor, Abby paused and glanced around, disoriented, glimpsing a large bedroom with a stone fireplace near which another cluster of men in colorful sweaters stood drinking and chatting. When she glanced back, she saw that Philip was halfway up the last flight of steps, casting a tilted smile over his shoulder.

"Come on up," he said, crooking one finger. "We're almost there."

She followed. The top floor consisted of an enormous mirrored room with another vaulted glass ceiling above which she saw, amid beams of the outdoor lights, great coils of snow eddying through the bare, forked trees. In two of the room's upper corners were speakers piping in the unpredictable, slightly unnerving piece of jazz she'd heard downstairs. She stood with Philip near the center of the room, catching her breath after their hurried climb, glancing around her. The room did suggest, in fact, a "playroom": along one wall she saw a wet bar, a glass-doored sauna, a walk-in tiled shower large enough for several people. Dominating another corner was an enormous, raised hot tub of cream-colored marble, and ranged along a nearby wall was a daybed covered with overstuffed Indian-print pillows of earthy browns and deep reds, the color of dried blood. The only other furniture was a scattering of gym equipment looking isolated and unused, placed in odd corners of the room like eccentric pieces of sculpture. A stationary bike, a treadmill. A huge contraption of white metal and silver that featured a padded seat and dozens of weights, metal cords, pulleys. With a quiet, ironic smile Philip watched her surveying the room, as if reading her thoughts.

"I don't think the equipment gets much use. But the hot tub does."

Abby smiled, shaking her head. "It's amazing. I didn't expect—" but Philip interrupted by grasping her hand and, with that gentle but insistent tug he'd used to urge her upstairs, pulling her into one corner of the room, near the daybed. Abby heard voices ascending toward them, and she understood that Philip wanted privacy. A group of seven or eight people had thundered up the stairs, one a shrill-voiced woman who began exclaiming histrionically over the room. The others laughed, scarcely glancing at Philip and Abby.

His back to them, Philip took a sip of champagne and said, "This is better, isn't it?"

He'd braced himself with one hand against the wall, his black-sleeved arm isolating her in this far corner of the room, preventing her escape if she had wanted to escape. She did not. She found his gesture oddly incongruous and charming, for he was standing in the same posture the high school boys had always used when talking to a girl back in the corridors of St. Jude's High School, the boy keeping one arm braced firmly against a wall or a row of lockers, as in some atavistic display of physical size, dominance; the girl smiling and nodding with her arms around the books she clasped to her breast. Through such whispered "private" conversations (for when a boy and girl were standing that way, not even their most boisterous classmates would dare to interrupt them) had the complicated high school romances at St. Jude's been conducted. All at once the image had struck Abby as funny and she laughed aloud, one hand fluttering to her mouth. She must have looked as giggly and surprised as any high school girl.

"What?" Philip asked, with a pleased-looking grin.

Again she sipped the champagne. She shook her head. "I'm sorry, I was just thinking of…I don't know what I was thinking. It must be the champagne."

From across the room came a raucous burst of laughter from the other guests, who had clustered near the stationary bicycle. At first it seemed to Abby they'd laughed at her remark, but of course they were paying no attention to her and Philip, and she quickly gathered they were exchanging jokes. There were two women in the group, a heavy-set blonde with frizzy-permed hair who wore a clinging Chinese-red silk dress and laughed constantly—it was her shrill, grating laugh that Abby had first heard when the group came up the stairs—and a quiet, spidery-thin woman with a pale pocked face and thin but carefully painted red lips. The others were men in their thirties and forties, all well-dressed, one of them rather short, his back to Abby. She saw a bald spot the size of a silver dollar gleaming underneath the track-lighting as he bent forward, with a conspiratorial hunching of his shoulders, to offer his own joke: "The rallying cry at the million-man march?" he asked, then pursed his lips and emitted a parody of black dialect. "Fried chicken, watah-melon, Cadillac cah! We ain't as dumb as you *thinks* we is!"

"Oh, Brock, that's *aw*ful!" the blond woman cried, shivering with laughter.

Abby glanced back at Philip, who had paused to listen, too. "Charming, isn't it?" he murmured, with a rueful twist of his mouth.

She decided to change the subject and began asking Philip the usual questions one asked at parties—what he did, where he lived, how long he had known Thom and Pace. Abby listened to the answers but not closely;

she kept thinking about Thom, who must be wondering where she was. She supposed it was inconsiderate to indulge herself with this handsome man and a glass of champagne, which she'd decided she liked, after all. She did listen vaguely to Philip. He was a securities analyst and worked mostly from home on his computer, and he lived near Emory, and he'd known her brother and other people here for more years than he cared to recall. His avocation was theater, however, and he'd acted in plays locally for quite a while. Abby smiled but did not say she'd guessed he might be an actor; somehow the remark would have sounded rude. Instead, she encouraged him to talk about his background, quietly enjoying his urbane-sounding British accent, the ironic lilt of his voice. In his early twenties, he told her, he'd come to Atlanta from London for college and had liked the city so well that he'd stayed on for his MBA. He'd met Pace at Emory, in fact, and after "a brief misunderstanding" they'd become friends.

"A misunderstanding?" she said. He'd left the phrase dangling, clearly waiting for her to ask.

Lowering his voice Philip said, "I'm not gay, you know. Though obviously, I've got no problem with it."

And Abby, not knowing what to say, said quickly, "Or you wouldn't be here, would you?"

Flustered, she took another sip of champagne, surprised to find that she'd almost emptied the flute. She'd begun to feel the alcohol, which gave her a pleasant swirling lightness not unlike the circling gusts of snowflakes she kept glimpsing outside, through the glass roof above her head.

"I wanted to make that clear, right away," Philip said. Again he had that oddly solemn look, his arm braced against the wall, but this time he seemed nothing like a high school kid. He was older than she'd first thought, perhaps in his late thirties, but he had the smooth olive-pale skin of a younger man, and his dark eyes were clear and shining as a boy's. He'd spoken earnestly, bending toward her, his voice lowered to a whisper. Briefly she closed her eyes, again enveloped by that pungent musk-like scent of his cologne, and she found the moment unexpectedly pleasurable, savoring his deep-toned voice with its British intonation. But when she opened her eyes she thought firmly that enough was enough. She'd make her excuses to Philip and go find her brother.

Before she could speak, Philip said, "Wait here, won't you?" His voice held a pleasing sort of urgency. "I'll refill this." She felt the empty cool glass slipping from her fingers.

"But I—"

"I'll be back," Philip said. "You've heard about my life. Now I want to hear about yours."

As he descended the steps, Abby noticed the short balding man had craned his neck to watch Philip, gazing after him with a lingering, appreciative look. Then, coming back to himself, he glanced at Abby with a nervous grin. She smiled vaguely at the man. Then she heard the blonde in the red dress say to him, "Brock, pay attention. You have to listen to *my* joke!"

Abby turned away, focusing on the music in the effort not to hear. The jazz piece had given way to a folksy, long-familiar voice singing plaintively, "It's all *oh*–ver now..." and she tried not to hear that, either. She drifted to one of the windows and stood there gazing out at the cascading torrents of snow. Now that she'd drunk the champagne the snowfall seemed reckless and exhilarating, an image of her sudden bold elation. The snow, she thought lightly, was a storm of confetti thrown by numberless revelers...or a blaze of demented white butterflies overtaking the night...or heaven's cold manna flung to earth in ceaseless handfuls by a drunken God. She smiled at these silly ideas, and why not? How long since she'd felt even mildly intoxicated? A decade, at least. Perhaps not since college. When she and Graham had dated, she'd always ordered white wine but had sipped at the glass so slowly through their long, formal meals that she'd felt nothing. She'd wanted to feel nothing. More than once they'd left a restaurant or a theater to be greeted by an unexpected fall of snow not unlike this one, but up north Abby had considered the snow a mere annoyance.

Though Abby kept her back to the group of joke-tellers across the room, their snide, boisterous laughter pestered the edges of her awareness, dissipating the vague foggy cloud of her euphoria. Annoyed, she glanced at her watch. Difficult to know, in this mood, how much time had passed since Philip went downstairs. Surely no more than five minutes. Ten at the outside. Probably he'd found a long line at the bar. Again she remembered Thom and felt a twinge of guilt. But just as quickly she had a distinct, selfish thought, released by the alcohol but no less pleasurable for that: her brother could wait. How many years had she waited for him, after all?

Outside, the snow had lightened. The flakes were smaller, the wind less intense. All at once the sight seemed ordinary and depressed her, so she turned away. The little group across the room had begun disbanding, and Abby's gaze settled on the smaller, emaciated woman who stood detached from the others, glancing around. Abby saw how unhealthy she looked: her skin parchment-pale, her frizzed hair thin and patchy. She'd been taking small but determined sips from her highball glass, as if dosing herself; the drink was the color of iced tea but Abby supposed it was straight bourbon. As though drawn by Abby's stare, the woman gave her a brief, wan smile. She said in a throaty but surprisingly loud voice, "You coming downstairs? I think it's time for the sermon."

Her words were slurred and from her colorless, unfocused eyes Abby could tell she was drunk. She took another sip of the bourbon. The blonde and her friend Brock had looked over, too.

"Yeah," the blonde said. "Time to pay the piper." She laughed brightly as though she had said something witty. The man called Brock was smiling at Abby politely, his forearm still clutched in the blonde's plump, red-nailed hand.

Abby said, "Thanks, but I'm waiting for someone. We'll be down in a minute."

Alone, Abby spent another minute looking out at the snow, which had almost stopped, and then she wandered through the room, running her hand absently along the seat of the exercise bike. She turned idly and faced the mirrored wall spanning one length of the room. She felt so lightly, whimsically happy that her reflection in the mirror came as a shock, like a sudden punch in the stomach. Alone in this vast well-lit room Abby looked pale, lost, frightened. She had thought she must be smiling, but her lips were vaguely parted in an expression she now saw as foolish, distended as though she had glanced into a fun-house mirror. But of course it was an ordinary mirror and could not be blamed. More than anything, she looked stranded. Her arms hung awkwardly, and her hair seemed mussed on one side. How had that happened? Had Philip touched her hair? She couldn't remember. As her mind cleared, Abby had mercy on herself and turned away from the mirror. At the same moment she forced herself to swallow the bleak nugget of awareness that Philip DeMunn was not coming back.

He had left her here deliberately, or he'd been waylaid, or he'd forgotten her—what did it matter? She should know better than to feel humiliated since she was not a high school girl, after all, but nonetheless humiliation hugged her like a damp cloak as she made the long walk back across the room and down the stairs and into the living area where everyone else had gathered, listening to the tall, perspiring man giving a speech. Fortunately, the crowd was looking away from the staircase, and no one noticed Abby as she slipped into the room. She took a deep breath, then another. After a moment she felt the familiar, fond slide of an arm around her waist.

Startled, she drew back, her body tensing, but of course it wasn't Philip DeMunn but Thom, grinning down at her. He whispered, "I've been looking all over, where have you been?" A mischievous pause. "Or should I ask?"

Her flip response came from nowhere, "Up in the orgy room, where else?" and Thom laughed aloud, clamping one hand over his mouth as several people near them glanced around. He gave an affectionate tug to Abby's waist and turned his attention back to the speaker, evidently not noticing that his sister's body had stayed tense, ungiving, and that her throat and cheeks had turned a feverish red, flushed uncomfortably with some emotion she could not have named.

"Yes, we've done a great deal, but there's so much more to be done," the man was saying.

Abby tried to listen; she half-listened; but her eye kept straying from the speaker—he had a toothy tic-like smile, a perspiring round face, and a gleaming bald pate that made Abby think of a lobster, a talking lobster—and out to the crowd of still sipping but muted guests jammed into Pace's living room. Some had been pushed back into the foyer and stood alongside the double front doors as though poised for escape; some sat on the stairs and watched through the railings; others had stayed upstairs and gazed down from the loft. Near the front of this gathering was Connie, one hand on the rail and the other holding a half-empty glass of wine; he caught her glance and, grinning, rolled his eyes as if the man's speech were a torment he could scarcely endure much longer. Abby smiled and looked away, surveying the crowd with a methodical, grim slowness. Clearly, Philip DeMunn was no longer here; wanting to avoid the speech he'd slipped out the front door in his dark clothes into the dark night. She could hardly blame him. She thought with longing of the frigid wind outside; in here the air was overwarm and stale, heavy with the mingled scents of spicy food and liquor and cologne.

"In the coming year," the man was saying, flashing his overbright smile to the crowd, "we've planned a number of interactive events with the community. Male violence is pervasive, and we have to band together. In January we're taking part in the MLK Week symposium on domestic violence; in March we're doing a walkathon with the Buckhead Optimist

Club—they're going to close a section of Peachtree for us, isn't that great?—and of course we're going to have a float in the Gay Pride march in June and an informational booth in Piedmont Park. Then in September we're sponsoring a nonviolent gamesmanship event at the Arts Festival, and we're very excited about that because the U.S. badminton champion will be giving a talk on sports and nonviolent behavior *not* being mutually exclusive." At this point the man grinned, dropped his eyes, and waited, but instead of the big laugh he clearly expected, there were a few courteous titters. "And we're already talking about Christmas," he went on, faltering, "I mean *next* Christmas, believe it or not, with the Atlanta Gay Men's Chorus, since we couldn't get them this year. We're planning a candlelight memorial vigil in memory of women and gay men killed by batterers, and of course the Chorus will perform and do carols, and we'll have a sing-along. We haven't got a location confirmed yet, but..."

Beside her, Abby noticed that Thom had put one hand over his mouth, this time to hide a yawn; he looked at her sideways and smiled. Despite Thom's promises, the speaker had been talking for twenty minutes and still seemed to be warming up. Yet the crowd listened quietly. Politely. Only now did Abby glimpse a tall, scowling young man who'd been leaning by himself against one wall, uneasily shifting his weight from side to side. He looked Scandinavian, blond and smooth-skinned, no older than twenty-five, yet he was powerfully built and had a somewhat raffish look amid this polished, well-dressed crowd. His hair was cut brutally short—a "buzz cut," Abby thought they called it—and he wore tight, faded blue jeans and a bright-orange T-shirt, the sleeves pushed up to the shoulders to emphasize his opulent biceps. His face was bony and angular, handsome in a cruel way; or so it seemed at the moment to Abby, as he kept scowling at the speaker, his mouth curled in a derisive sneer, the sculpted arms folded bluntly across his chest.

The leader of Gay People Stopping Violence kept talking, his toothy smile no less evident as he discussed a recent incident in Cobb County, where a gay math teacher had come out to his tenth-grade class at eleven in the morning and had been beaten savagely by a group of high school boys at four that afternoon—arm and collarbone broken; ribs kicked into splinters; stomach repeatedly kicked, causing massive internal bleeding; groin "stomped" to the degree that major reconstructive surgery would be required. The following day, as the man lay comatose in Kennestone Hospital, he was fired by the school superintendent on grounds of moral turpitude.

"But we shouldn't assume," the perspiring man said, as the crowd shifted uncomfortably, and Abby felt a hollowed-out sensation in her stomach as if she too had been kicked, "that being gay means being virtuous and nonviolent. In Midtown two men were recently killed by their lovers, one shot and one stabbed. And you remember the case of the lesbian, a couple of years back, who stalked and killed *her* former lover. Violence cuts across both genders and all sexual orientations..."

Again Thom bent to Abby's ear: "This is cheery, isn't it?" He gave a rueful smile, but his face looked pale and strained. She didn't answer.

"Nor should we think of violence as something 'other people' do. No, we've got to 'own'—if I may indulge in a bit of psychobabble—the contributions we make to a cultural mindset that *permits* violent behavior, even though we don't intend it. How many times have you gay men referred in a derogatory way to gay women—we know all the words, I don't need to repeat them here—or to each other, for that matter? If we call each other 'fag,' even in jest, then we're promoting gay bashing, whether we want to admit it or not. And how many of us..."

Abby's attention had strayed back to the muscular young man against the far wall, who alone among the crowd did not keep still: he shifted his weight from one foot to the other, he glanced around with his contemptuous sneer. Abby alone seemed to have noticed him, and somehow she wasn't surprised when he unfolded his arms and jabbed one hand bluntly in the air.

The speaker failed to notice, or chose to ignore him. He was clearly near the climactic point of his spiel, discussing specific ways in which GPSV intended to combat violence against women, gay people, and people of color. Though instinctively, Abby had not liked the man—there was something a bit shrill and self-righteous in his manner—she had to admit that he was an effective speaker. She imagined the crowd would open their checkbooks and give generously; she'd already seen several guests reaching into their pockets and handbags. Near the speaker, a small dour-looking woman who also faced the crowd and seemed to be an assistant of some kind was counting out envelopes onto a small wooden table. The muscular young man in the back of the room now cleared his throat loudly, jerking his upraised arm back and forth. The speaker clearly had seen him—Abby thought she detected a glimmer of panic in the man's eyes—but now kept his gaze fixed in another direction and continued talking, his face a damp brick-red and his smile even brighter and more desperate than before.

Around the scowling young man, several of the guests began edging away, discomfited, exchanging whispers and worried glances. The longer he was ignored, the angrier he became. Yet when he finally spoke, his sharp voice cutting easily through the speaker's, he sounded calm and reasonable, even friendly.

"Mitch?" he called out. "Could I ask a question?"

Startled, the speaker's head jerked aside as though pulled by a string. "Excuse me? Oh, Ricky, hello. Didn't see you there. You had a question?"

The younger man had paused, rhetorically, aware that everyone in the room had turned in his direction; the small space that had formed around him as people moved away had given him an aura, as though a stage light had been trained on him.

"Yes, Mitch," Ricky said with a brief, mocking smile. "I do have a question."

Mitch said, awkwardly, "I was going to do a Q & A later, but if it's something urgent—"

"Just a point of clarification," Ricky said, mocking the speaker's pompous tone. He scratched one side of his nose, then shoved his hands in the pockets of his jeans. "Since you mentioned gay people, and women. And people of color."

"That's right," Mitch said, nodding. Out of habit he glanced around the room with his toothy smile. "The primary victims of violence, certainly."

Ricky nodded, his expression turning solemn—or mock-solemn, Abby thought—as if they were parsing some subtle philosophical point. Then he said, "But what about children, Mitch? What about kids?"

Mitch nodded violently. "Oh, of course—children, too. They're the most helpless victims of all, and certainly we must—"

"And what about pedophiles, Mitch? Gay men who abuse young kids, for their own sexual gratification? What about child pornography, and the gay men who perpetuate the victimization by buying it?"

Mitch continued his vigorous nodding; he couldn't agree more. "Oh, of course. Certainly. Now, it must be pointed out that statistically, heterosexual men are more likely to abuse children than gay men—"

"But what about this organization called NAMBLA, Mitch? North American Man-Boy Love Association, I believe it is. Do you think anyone in this room belongs to that group, Mitch? Do you think anyone in this room buys child pornography, Mitch? What do you think?"

Ricky's voice had sharpened with contempt. He glared around the room, as if daring anyone to contradict him. "Yes, yes, clearly it's a problem,"

Mitch said quickly. His face had paled, and he'd reached a hand toward his assistant. Abby saw that the hand was shaking badly. "Well, I guess I've done enough speechifying for one night," he said, laughing weakly, "so Angela, why don't you pass out the envelopes? Of course, contributions are strictly voluntary...."

Ricky had turned and stalked off toward the door; people edged aside to make way for him. As he went, he called over his shoulder, "I guess a nonviolent child abuser would be a conflict in terms, wouldn't it?" he asked. "What's that fancy word? Oh yeah, an oxymoron."

Mitch ignored him. He'd stepped away from the area where he'd given his speech as if retreating, willing himself to disappear; he was visibly trembling, his eyes looked panicked and desperate. "Yes, it's not necessary to... You can mail them in..."

Another man rushed forward: it was Pace. He, too, looked uncomfortable; after all, the young man called Ricky, who had just slammed the front door behind him, had ruined his party.

"Please stay as long as you like. Feel free," Pace said. He gestured to the opposite wall, where the bartender had resumed his station. "Drinks are once again being served. Don't let good liquor go to waste!"

Several people laughed, including Thom. Groggily, as if shaking off a collective bad dream, the crowd began fidgeting, dispersing. Scattered whispers rose in volume until people were conversing again, normally; someone had turned on the stereo, which now played a muted classical piano piece. Chopin, Abby thought. Soothing lovely Chopin. She took a deep breath and turned toward Thom.

"Should we leave?" she murmured. "Are you ready...?"

Thom looked uncertain. Other guests had begun heading toward the door. He whispered, "Let's stay a few minutes, OK? If there's a mass exodus now, it's going to be even more embarrassing for Pace. And I'd like to speak with him. Do you mind?"

"No, of course not," Abby said.

"Come on, let's have one more drink." Thom took her arm and they crossed to the bar, had their drinks refilled; it was clear that no one else was staying. The room was half empty and had taken on that dismal look of a concluded party, crumpled napkins and half-empty glasses littering the tables, a stale odor of food and perspiration hanging in the air.

A few others had gathered around Thom and Abby. One by one, Thom introduced them to his sister. All smiled and spoke politely, but she could see the strain at the edges of their smiling eyes and lips as they made small talk and glanced nervously around at the swiftly departing guests. Abby had noticed that Mitch and his assistant, Angela, had been among the first to leave. For several minutes Pace stood at the door, receiving the thanks of each hurrying guest; he had taken over Angela's job and was quietly putting envelopes into his friends' hands as they left.

In their determined little cluster near the bar, no one had referred to the incident, as if none wanted to be first to acknowledge what had happened, but now Abby heard a familiar voice.

"Well, did you girls *ever,*" Connie exclaimed, hurrying up to join them. He turned to wave off some of his friends, then eased himself in between Thom and Abby. "That Ricky Devine—he really got his shorts in a wad, didn't he? Do you suppose it's PMS, or have those steroids finally done something to his *brain?*"

Relieved, everyone laughed. Pace had joined them, too; with a grim smile he held out the leftover envelopes.

He said, "Don't everybody lunge for these at once."

They laughed again, and for a while they chatted excitedly about Ricky and Mitch and the "scene" that had taken place. Abby learned that Ricky had a housecleaning business, and that Mitch had been one of his clients for several years; not long ago, Ricky had quit. It was Connie, of course, who alone in their group knew why, and he told them breathlessly that he'd run into Ricky at the Metro late one night—Ricky was not above doing a little hustling, Connie added—and Ricky had told him that he'd opened a drawer of Mitch's nightstand, just looking innocently for a Kleenex ("Yeah, right," said a slender, fair-haired man who stood next to Connie, and who'd been introduced to Abby as "Edwin") and inside the drawer, guess what Ricky had found? Here, of course, Connie paused for dramatic effect, glancing over his shoulder as if he feared being overheard.

"It was a pile of magazines," he said. "Kiddie porn, believe it or not—yes, a big messy stack of magazines, right there in the nightstand of our virtuous, nonviolent Mitch!"

Connie took a deep breath, his eyes damp with excitement.

"Then, fueled by moral indignation, heroic Ricky started ransacking the house and evidently found a few dozen videos with titles like *Hot Tots* and *Little Weenies*—I'm *not* kidding, you guys!—and even some mailings from NAMBLA, too, that suggested Mitch is a card-carrying member. Ricky claimed that later he phoned Mitch and confronted him. He said Mitch started bawling and swearing he'd throw everything out, he knew he needed help and was going to get it, he was begging Ricky please not to call the police, please don't ruin my reputation—that whole routine. And Ricky didn't. He just quit cleaning at Mitch's, that's all. But obviously if he told me about it, he's told other people, and after tonight it's bound to get around to Mitch's patients, or their parents..."

That's right, Connie told Abby after a suitable pause: many of Mitch's dental patients were children. He was renowned, in fact, for how well he worked with them, allayed their fears, made them laugh.

So there they stood, Abby and Thom and Connie, with two or three other close friends of Pace's, and finally the subject had been closed when Pace said, in his deep booming voice, "Oh the hell with it, what can you do? Mitch is a close friend, and he'll stay a close friend. As for Ricky, he doesn't clean houses worth a shit—I hired him once and never asked him back. But I guess he needed to do that, for his own conscience or whatever. The hell with it—he's a friend of mine, too."

Shaking his head, Connie said in marveling voice, "Pace, you're so wonderfully *tolerant*."

"That's why he has so many friends," Thom said, smiling.

"That, and his fabulous parties!" Edwin said, giving Pace a friendly poke in the ribs.

"You bastard," Pace told Edwin, cheerfully. "Why haven't you gotten another drink?"

But Edwin had to leave, and the others took that as permission to say their goodbyes as well. At the door, Thom said to Pace, "Really, don't worry. This time next week, no one will even be talking about it."

"Hell, let 'em talk!" Pace said, smiling. "I don't give a good goddamn."

At the door, they discovered the wet snow had turned to rain, so Pace loaned them an umbrella and, huddling close together, they jogged out to the car. Abby's head was swirling, as though filled even now with that image of wild coiling snowflakes she'd seen from Pace's upstairs room; but she felt strangely calm. A dreamlike aura had descended, cloaking these past few hours. Had she really met an impossibly handsome, black-clad stranger, whose warm breath had mingled with the thrilling cold of expensive champagne to give her an intoxicated sense, however short-lived, of a wild new life, a wild new self, as unpredictable and exciting as those torrents of snow that had blown against the ceiling? Now as she and her brother drove through the drizzling familiar streets of Ansley Park, enveloped in a companionable silence, she doubted it, and felt she could forget what had happened as easily as she would shrug off any dream. Yes, she was forgetting already.

As they pulled into Thom's complex she saw that her brother was shaking his head. "I still can't believe it," he said. "Poor Pace."

Abby blinked, then glanced over. "Believe what?" she said.

Chapter 4

During the week before Christmas, an unbroken string of drizzly, cold days, Thom navigated traffic-clogged Peachtree Street each morning with Abby, Connie, and Warren, on their way to visit Carter in Crawford Long Hospital.

After a brief period during which he'd seemed to improve with a new drug "cocktail" that had brought his T-cell count into triple digits, he'd gotten worse just as abruptly, suffering a fainting spell one evening during a mild workout at the gym. Later that night, he'd blacked out while having dinner with some friends at the Colonnade (someone made the inevitable joke: "Maybe it was the food") and the next morning his doctor had him in the hospital undergoing a battery of tests that were still inconclusive. Other problems followed: violent headaches, incessant vomiting and diarrhea, intermittent fevers that reached such dangerous levels his doctor firmly refused Carter's repeated pleas that he wanted to go home and spend his "last days" with a bit of dignity.

These were not his last days, she told him.

Dr. McIlhaney was a petite, serious-minded woman highly admired in the local gay community; she'd been known as an "AIDS doctor" long before it was fashionable. Yet she had a stubborn, authoritarian streak that reminded Thom uncomfortably of the nuns from school. Thom had been in the room that day, an awkward bystander, listening as the doctor spoke to Carter in a tone that closed off any argument. There were more tests to do, she said, and he should remember that he'd suffered bouts of grave illness before and had pulled through. These were *not* his last days, she repeated.

Thom understood that she'd been hurt by Carter's request. Her tone had changed slightly; there was an edge of little-girl's plaintiveness in her voice that pulled at Thom's heart. Yet during endless conversations since that day it became clear that no one believed her, this time—not Thom or Connie or Warren, Carter's closest friends, and certainly not Carter himself, who had kept his moist fevered eyes fixed on the muted TV screen during his doctor's pep talk.

That had been Sunday; now it was Wednesday morning and little had changed. When Thom stopped for a light at Tenth Street, Connie's voice—atypically somber and irony-free—complained from the backseat.

"I hate to say this, but these daily visits are getting to me. I don't know how long I can keep it up."

Thom glanced into the rear-view mirror, just in time to see Warren reach across and give Connie a hug.

"You shouldn't feel obligated," Thom said. "You could visit on alternate days, or you could just call him. I don't think Carter's keeping track of the visits."

"That's right," Warren said. "Don't be so hard on yourself, honey."

Thom glanced sideways at Abby, and they exchanged a brief smile. Just the night before, he'd told her the long, tangled history of Connie and Warren, who had dated for several months until Warren, Connie said, became too "clingy" and Connie broke it off in favor of a Platonic friendship. They'd lived together now for six years in Connie's large, expensively furnished condominium off Pharr Road, and everyone knew that Warren was still madly in love with Connie. Outsiders meeting them for the first time usually assumed they *were* lovers. They shopped, cooked, took semiannual vacations; they spent holidays, including Christmas, with each other instead of with their families.

Thom thought Connie was lucky to have sweet, baby-faced Warren, with his shining mop of light-brown hair ("an altar boy's haircut," Connie once observed) and his damp, deep-brown eyes Thom could not help silently comparing to the worshipful eyes of his own uncritical admirers, Mitzi and Chloe. Sometimes Connie did treat Warren shabbily, canceling long-standing plans in deference to one of Connie's gorgeous, temporary boyfriends; or, after a few glasses of wine, making a cutting remark when other people were present, embarrassing Warren and, Thom knew, hurting him deeply. They had one of those strange, intense loves that often

develop between two gay men: less than a marriage but more than a friendship, a unique relation crafted slowly through years of wily bargaining and
crazy need, funded by shared experience and mutual knowledge and an
awareness on each man's part that the other knew him thoroughly and still
loved him, and you thought long and hard before tossing that away.

Warren reached across and patted Connie's hand. "Carter knows how
sensitive you are. He wouldn't mind if you skipped a day."

Connie looked unconvinced. "But we've been going every morning,
this same little group. We're like the four musketeers or something. If you
guys keep going and I stop, it'll look like I don't care. I *do* care, but seeing
Carter like that makes me depressed for the rest of the day."

Abby smiled back at Connie. "I think Warren's right," she said.
"Tomorrow, why don't you and I both stay home? Thom and Warren can
go. Would that make you feel better?"

Connie said, "Oh, sweetheart, *thank you*. Maybe we can go to lunch or
something, just the two of us." He nodded, clearly relieved. "I'll take you
to the Peasant Uptown, where all the ladies who lunch go. I need to pop
into Saks anyway."

The others laughed, even Warren, though Connie had not intended to
be funny.

"What's so amusing about Saks?" he demanded.

As they turned into the hospital parking lot, Thom began steeling himself for the sight of Carter's gaunt, near-skeletal face and arms, the glaze
of deadened hopelessness in his eyes. These past few days, everyone but
Dr. McIlhaney seemed aware that Carter had given up; the whole story was
in his eyes, for anyone to read.

Those first couple of days, upon entering the impersonal, bustling corridors of Crawford Long, one of them would make the obligatory remark
about hating hospitals, and the others would agree, and they'd giggle
uncomfortably during the elevator ride and the long march down to
Carter's room. In this way they had immunized themselves, or tried to,
against the inevitably depressing hospital aura of brisk white-clad industry
overlaying the pulsing silence of animal decay and human sorrow leaking
from the rooms they hurried past. Today, jammed in an elevator with two
orderlies, a patient in a wheelchair, and a corpulent nun in an old-fashioned habit of black veil and white wimple, all four of them stayed silent.
By rote, they veered to the left when the doors shuddered open. The west
corridor of Carter's floor was the so-called "AIDS wing" where, Thom and
the others had informed Abby, they'd visited—and lost—other friends in

recent years. It might have been Thom's imagination, but it seemed to him now that their pace had slowed, as though they were avoiding the inevitable moment of entering the room and donning their masks of fake cheerfulness for Carter.

"Do you think he'll be asleep?" Connie whispered outside the half-open door. "Maybe we shouldn't have come this early."

Thom glanced at his watch: five past eleven.

"Really, you don't have to go in," Warren said, putting one hand to his hip in mild exasperation. "Why don't you go downstairs and wait in the coffee shop?"

Connie shook his head. "Nope," he said, "I've made it this far. I'm not going to be a pussy about it."

"It's a little late for that resolution," Thom said, annoyed. "Come on, then."

As they entered, Thom was surprised to see that Carter was sitting up. His head was turned vaguely in the direction of the TV screen where Sally Jessy Raphaël was interviewing a weeping, overweight woman.

"I know this is hard," Sally was saying.

Thom grabbed the remote and pressed the mute button.

"Hey, Carter," Thom said, as the others shuffled in behind him. "You're looking better this morning."

Why did he tell such extravagant lies? Carter looked exactly the same: exhausted, spiritless, a bag of sticks in his hospital-issue nightgown. Thom had offered to bring pajamas, but Carter said the gown was more comfortable.

"Hey, guys," Carter said, his voice croaky from disuse. Slowly, he licked his lips. He reached a shaky hand toward the night table, grasped a plastic cup, and brought it to his mouth. But it was empty. Thom sprang forward, took the water pitcher, slowly filled the cup. It was always a relief to do something, at such times. Carter's hand was still trembling, so Thom helped him hold the cup while he took a few sips.

"Thanks," Carter whispered. A drop of water meandered down the side of his whisker-stubbled jaw. During the weekend Thom had asked if he wanted a shave, but Carter declined. His skin hurt, he said.

Now Connie bolted forward, energetic as a windup doll. For all his bellyaching, Thom often thought Connie was better than any of them at navigating these awkward visits.

"Hi, sweetie," he said, planting a kiss on Carter's forehead. "What's in that pitcher—vodka? We should have brought olives and hors d'oeuvres. For that matter, we should have brought dancing boys!"

Carter smiled, vaguely. "Hey, Connie," he said.

Now Warren came forward and greeted him, followed by Abby, and for several minutes they chatted about general, safe topics, carefully avoiding direct questions to Carter, who clearly lacked the energy to say more than a few words. Thom's heart had become a sore lump in his chest. He, too, would be depressed for the rest of the day, but unlike Connie he had a busy schedule to distract him: half a dozen phone calls to return, a client who wanted to see some houses in Peachtree Hills, an inspection for one of his contracted listings at four o'clock. During the ride over, his pager had buzzed twice at his side, but he hadn't bothered to check the numbers. The callers could wait.

In recent years, it seemed to Thom that his life came more and more to be ruled by the telephone. (He was the only agent in his office who did not yet have a cell phone; he needed his drives around town as a breather from the pressures of clients, lawyers, other agents. The pager was bad enough.) Over the phone, he'd learned that he was HIV-positive: he'd been in the process of switching health insurance, and a doctor in California had called him. During a closing, he'd gotten the news that Roy had died: he'd been summoned by the lawyer's secretary to take an "urgent" call and had heard the dreaded words alone, in an empty conference room. Almost all his boyfriends, during his four or five years of frenetic dating after Roy's death, had broken up with him that way, too cowardly or too indifferent to tell him in person. There was one exception: Edward, the man who had infected him, had taken him to dinner at the Food Studio and abruptly ended the relationship as they shared a chocolate torte. (Months later, in a Christmas card to his lawyer-friend Andrew in San Francisco, he'd called this the night of the "chocolate tort.") At the time, Thom hadn't known Edward was positive, much less that he'd infected Thom, and because Edward had been the most glamorous of Thom's boyfriends, and the one, excepting Roy, he'd loved the most, he'd been grateful that Edward at least had told him in person.

It embarrassed Thom now to remember that, on the verge of tears, he'd thanked Edward for the "courtesy" of breaking the news so gently, and in person. Startled, Edward had simply said, "You're welcome."

Thom hadn't told him that Steven, the twenty-something blond stockbroker with rippling abs Thom had dated the year before Edward, had left the bad news on Thom's answering machine.

Standing here with his sister and several of his closest friends, one of whom was dying, he saw that era of semi-desperate searching as remote, even vaguely comical. If he hadn't come away from those years with HIV infection, it might now seem merely amusing, an antic period that in retrospect was clearly his way of dealing with Roy's death. Maybe there *had* been a kind of death wish there, after all, since with a couple of the boyfriends he hadn't been "safe," whatever that term really meant. One time a condom had broken, and although his boyfriend Trent (a two-month fling he'd had after Steven, but before Edward) could have withdrawn in time, he did not; an hour later, the heat of their wild intimacy worn off, he'd apologized profusely and sworn to Thom that he was negative, that he'd just been tested the previous month, specifically because he'd decided to sleep with Thom. Perhaps Trent, who at twenty was the youngest man Thom had dated in a long while, had glimpsed the skeptical light in Thom's eyes, for Trent's own eyes had filled with tears, and his protestations had grown even more intense. But later, when Thom's frenzy of dating was over and he'd gotten his bad news from that California doctor, he'd dutifully called each man. All claimed to be negative, all got tested again, and all phoned Thom back and told him, to his great relief, that they were still negative.

All except for Edward. Their final conversation, too, had taken place over the phone and had upset Thom deeply. Edward's voice, his tone, were almost unrecognizable, as though Thom were speaking to a different person. Dour and resentful, even a bit sarcastic: "You might want to get tested, Thom dear, I've gotten a bit of bad news. I'm positive for the dreaded plague, isn't that fun?" No sympathy for Thom's bewilderment, though Edward had claimed he was negative—and monogamous—when they were together.

"Come on, Miss Innocent," he'd added, that day on the phone, "I can hardly believe—"

Shocked, Thom had simply hung up. They never spoke again.

Thom hadn't told Abby any of this. Except for Chip, the guy he'd been dating casually, and irregularly, for the past few months and from whom he expected a "dear John" phone call (or answering machine message?) any day now, Thom hadn't said much to Abby about the men he'd known, partly because she had seemed uncomfortable when Thom mentioned her own recent boyfriend. Was it Gary, or Graham?—he'd already forgotten the name. Thom supposed they ought to be discussing such things, but for now it seemed easier to avoid them. He and Abby were still trying to relearn each other, he reasoned, after their four-year estrangement; they picked their way slowly and carefully, shadowed by the unspoken but powerful awareness of their mother, hundreds of miles away but hovering invisibly over their every conversation, their every reference to the past or the future.

The morning after Pace's party, once he'd talked Abby into extending her visit, they'd gotten on the telephone—Thom in the kitchen, Abby in his bedroom—and broken the news to Lucille. She'd been so taken aback to hear Thom's voice at all (or so he imagined) that she hadn't been prepared for what came next. As he'd promised Abby he would, he'd spoken first when Lucille answered.

"Mom? Hi, Mom. It's good to hear your voice."

Silence.

"Mom, are you there?"

"I'm here. I'm just trying to think what to say."

Thom laughed, and Abby said quickly, "I'm here too, Mom. On the extension."

Another pause. "Are you still in Atlanta? Both of you?"

"We're at my place," Thom said. "We just thought we'd give you a call, and…but how are you doing? You sound good."

It wasn't true. She sounded faraway and vulnerable, and already he knew it had been a mistake for him and Abby to call together; later, their mother would claim her children had blindsided her, two against one.

But first came a touching surprise. Lucille said, "I guess I'm the one who should be asking that. How are you feeling, Son?"

He said at once, "Oh, I'm feeling great, I have a terrific doctor and the medications don't give me any problems. I'm totally asymptomatic and I—" He stopped. Why this rushing, urgent flood of words? He was protesting too much. He continued, in a chastened voice, "I'm fine. Really."

"He looks well, too," Abby said. "He looks wonderful, in fact."

It was unusual for their mother to pause before speaking; he supposed these long silences were the measure of her confusion, her lack of a strategy. When she spoke, she sounded almost timid.

"Abby has lost some weight, don't you think?"

"Maybe, but I'm fattening her up," Thom said. "We've been eating out almost every night."

"That's good. We have brunch reservations, you know"—this time, there'd been no pause—"at the Four Seasons for tomorrow. Your plane lands around one, doesn't it? So I made the reservation for two o'clock."

This time, Thom and Abby were silent. After a moment, Abby said: "Thom?"

"Oh, OK. Um, Mom, I hope you'll understand, but I've sort of talked

Abby into staying down here a while longer. So we won't be flying up tomorrow."

He spoke slowly, deliberately, expecting she'd interrupt with a squawk of protest. But there was silence on the other end.

"In fact, we've decided to stay down here through the holidays. A friend of mine is sick, you see, and we thought it would be better—" He broke off, not sure himself what he meant. Better for whom?

Lucille said, hoarsely, "You're not coming home? Not even for Christmas?"

Abby broke in, "But Thom has promised to come back with me, a day or two after New Year's. My classes start on the fourth, you know, and he's going to block out his calendar for the first half of January. He can make a nice long visit, and while I'm at school—"

"We've always spent Christmas together, honey," Lucille said. "What would I tell Millicent? *Her* girls are coming, of course."

Thom said abruptly, "Why don't you fly down here, Mom?"

A rash, impulsive idea, he thought, wincing, knowing his mistake before the words were out; he should have discussed it with Abby first, of course. He paused, but she didn't second his proposal. She stayed silent.

"Fly down there?" Lucille said, her tone vaguely puzzled as if this were a foreign phrase.

Abby said, "I don't know if that would work. I'm not sure you'd like it here. Thom's condo is kind of small, and we spend most of the day visiting his friend in the hospital, and doing errands for him."

Since this was not true, Thom understood that Abby didn't want—very much didn't want—their mother to visit; her vehemence surprised him even more than the white lie.

His mother and Abby chatted back and forth, debating the idea, finally deciding that Lucille should stay in Philadelphia, after all, while Thom stood there feeling useless, his shoulders slumped. Once they'd said their goodbyes, he sat on the bed for a few minutes, recovering. His mother hadn't seemed angry, at least; she hadn't exploded into rage, or burst into tears, as he'd feared she might. More than anything she'd seemed bewildered, unable to react.

Family relations were like a minefield, he'd thought. One misstep and your entire sense of self, the place you had found livable in your emotional universe, could explode off its axis, leaving you stranded in some airless, alien place. It was ten in the morning, a Saturday, yet he felt as if he'd just worked a twelve-hour day.

He felt a similar tiredness now, in Carter's crowded hospital room. Chatting with Carter, the others had drawn closer to the bed, but Thom stayed back, leaning against a windowsill crammed with flower arrangements and balloons. As usual, Connie peppered the conversation with his well-turned quips and comic monologues, keeping everything light, making the others laugh—including Carter, who lacked the strength to laugh aloud but who squinched his eyes shut with pleasure at each joke—and Thom, enjoying his mood of morose self-pity, didn't want to hinder them but didn't quite want to join in, either. He kept an eye on Abby, who stood next to Connie on the far side of Carter's bed, her eyes bright and smiling, her skin glowing, a different woman from the pale, shaken girl who'd come off the plane from Philadelphia three weeks ago. Since deciding to prolong her visit, she'd become more relaxed and buoyant, as though some private, pestering anxiety had dissolved, restoring the girl he remembered from high school—so smart and energetic, so attractive with her pert smile and shining eyes.

The "real" Abby, as he liked to think. She'd come back to him.

"And when you get out," Connie was saying, "you're coming to Key West with us, Carter Dawes. You *are*. We've made our plans at the last minute, to be sure, but I've been staying at Lighthouse Court once or twice a year for eons, and the manager—a lovely man who has a bit of a crush on me, I think—is bumping us to the head of the waiting list. He says there are always a few cancellations at the last minute. So we'll get three of their little efficiencies, one for Warren and me, one for Thom and Abby, and one for you, Carter, and whoever you'd like to bring." Connie's hands went to his hips, elbows flung outward. "Now stop shaking your head. You *are* coming with us."

Amused, Thom stayed silent. During yesterday's ride to the hospital, the four of them had vaguely discussed going to Key West for Christmas, but in Connie's imagination the trip had become a fait accompli. Thom doubted that Connie had phoned the Lighthouse Court; when Connie planned to do something, he often announced to others that the thing was done, which could cause complications if it could not be done, or if Connie later changed his mind. The others knew this, except for Abby. Thom saw the look of confusion in her face as Connie spoke confidently of the trip. Thom imagined how much more confused, and perhaps alarmed, she would be if she knew that Lighthouse Court was a guesthouse exclusively for gay men, who often lounged and cavorted nude on the sundecks and around the pool. The idea of Abby staying there was preposterous, but of course that hadn't occurred to Connie.

Carter raised his head from the pillow, lifted his bony chin. His voice was a croaky whisper: "Won't be up to it, but you guys send me a postcard, OK?" His head sagged back.

"Oh, by next week you'll gadding about like one of Santa's dwarves," Connie insisted.

The others laughed. "Santa's *elves*," Warren said.

Connie wiggled the fingers of one hand in the air; the other held onto Carter's. "Dwarves, elves, what's the difference. They're gay little creatures who get very busy and full of themselves at Christmas time, just like Carter's going to."

Carter, resting his eyes, tried to smile.

Connie was glancing around the room. "Everyone *is* still up for Key West, right? I don't want anybody flaking out on me. Thom, since I'm doing the rooms, why don't you make the plane reservations, OK? I mean, we *are* talking about Christmas here, so we'd better get cracking." Keeping hold of Carter's hand, he glanced toward Abby. "You do want to come, don't you? Have you ever been to Key West?"

Abby said, "No, but I've always wanted to. I've heard the sunsets are wonderful."

Thom smiled at his sister, perplexed. If she'd "always wanted" to visit Key West, it was certainly news to him.

"The sunsets are the least of it, believe me," Connie said. "Some of my snobby friends say Key West has gotten overrun with tourists, but I think it's still the most fabulous place on earth. People just *enjoy* themselves there, you know? Believe me, the Puritan work ethic never made it to Key West! Praise be."

"You really would enjoy it, Abby," Warren said. He often assumed the role as confirmer, or gentle denier, of Connie's emphatic and sometimes outlandish assertions.

"I'm looking forward to it," Abby said. "We *are* going, aren't we, Thom?"

Startled, Thom looked up. He'd been watching the silent, unexpectedly moving tableau of Carter lying there with his eyes closed, his hand gripped in Connie's; he'd been listening to the chatter about Key West only vaguely.

"What? Oh, sure, why not?" he said. "Our office is closed all next week, so there's nothing keeping me here."

"And Miss Dawes *is* coming with us, whether she believes it or not," Connie said, looking back to Carter.

A brief silence as, Thom thought, they all paused at this touching sight: Carter with his purplish eyelids closed and wearing that strained half-smile, listening as his friends' conversation washed around him. Thom was the last, it seemed, to know anything was wrong, for his memory of the next few seconds included his vague awareness of Connie's elbow pumping gently, then frantically, as he tried to extricate his hand from Carter's, and Abby's barely audible cry (a small, girlish "Oh!") and an instinctive retreat by Warren, who edged back toward the sill where Thom was leaning, his arms complacently folded.

The truth shuddered into Thom's awareness, his seeing, with the force of a thunderclap: his dear friend Carter wasn't resting his eyes but had quietly, all but unnoticeably, died.

In the pandemonium that ensued—Connie, his hand freed, crying out, putting both palms over his eyes, then a couple of nurses rushing in— Thom felt enveloped in a sudden wave of nausea that caused him to turn away, back toward the window, the wild thought caroming through his mind that if the window couldn't be opened, which it couldn't, he might simply vomit into one of the potted plants. But he took a deep breath instead, then rushed over to Abby who stood there stricken, staring, as a nurse bent down and thumbed Carter's eyelids rudely to peer inside. Thom drew Abby into the hall, vaguely aware that Connie and Warren had followed. Thom's first deep breath had spawned several more, and his chest had flooded with urgent raw emotion like a hot fluid that needed release. His throat had gone scratchy, sore. *Carter, no, how could you....* He felt Abby's arm circling his waist, and then Connie was hugging him from the other side, weeping profusely against Thom's throat, and Warren was holding onto Connie.

Thom, noting the glances from other visitors in the hall, said thickly, "The four of us are quite a sight, aren't we."

The others didn't laugh, but his words calmed them a little. The nurse came outside and told them what they already knew, asked a few questions, said she would be paging the doctor and they could wait down the hall if they liked.

As she turned away, Connie grabbed her arm. "But we were all chatting, talking back and forth, and he just closed his eyes for a minute—just for a minute! That's very strange, isn't it?" he cried. "Isn't that unusual?"

His voice had turned shrill, disorderly.

The nurse, a sturdy middle-aged Hispanic woman whose weary expression suggested she'd answered such questions many times, responded in a surprisingly gentle, measured voice.

"Really, no," she told Connie, extricating herself from his grip. "It isn't that unusual, at all."

Throughout the afternoon, friends of Carter's gathered in his condo, comforting one another and exchanging memories and exclaiming over the awful "suddenness" of his death, a sentiment that Thom, though he'd experienced the awfulness firsthand, didn't quite understand. They'd all known Carter probably wouldn't win this latest battle; he'd simply lost heart. Thom canceled his appointments and spent much of the day on the phone, going through Carter's address book and calling people from out of town. Of course, he'd called Carter's parents first: as Carter's closest friend, that obligation fell to him. Thom supposed it was fortunate they were both home for lunch, having a "quick bowl of soup," Carter's mother said, and it didn't surprise Thom that once he got them on separate extensions and gave them the news in a quiet, quickened voice, it was Carter's father the Citadel graduate who broke down, and his mother the Southern beauty queen who, though her voice quavered a bit, took things in hand. Mrs. Dawes with her cultured Charleston drawl was the epitome of the velvet steamroller, the steel magnolia, whatever cliché you preferred, while Carter's father, like many bluff, hyper-masculine men, was a walking time-bomb of powerful, repressed emotion.

"Oh, God. My God," Mr. Dawes rasped into the phone.

While her husband wept, Carter's mother thanked Thom for calling—"I know this wasn't easy for you," she said huskily—and said they'd get to the airport and take the first flight down to Atlanta.

Thom felt guilty for putting Abby through the long, tumultuous afternoon in Carter's living room. He kept glimpsing her as she stood off to the side while the others, strangers to her, emoted and hugged and broke into fresh tears each time a new friend arrived. For a while Abby stayed in the kitchen, making coffee and hot tea, serving the others efficiently, quietly. Around three o'clock Thom drew her aside and said, "Honey, you can go home if you want to. Don't feel obligated to wait around…" But she shrugged and gave a wan smile, saying she might as well stay. "I liked Carter," she said simply. "Besides—" She stopped herself, and Thom glimpsed a pained look in her eyes. He thought, *My God, she's practicing. She's practicing for me.*

"We'll talk later," he said, ignoring her puzzled look. "We should have talked before this, but…now we will."

Then someone interrupted them, and Abby drifted back to the kitchen.

Shortly before Carter's parents arrived, as Connie was holding forth in the living room about the first time he'd met Carter and how he'd known instantly what a sweet, special person he was, Thom slipped back into Carter's bedroom, carrying a garbage bag he'd found in the kitchen pantry, for a little ritual he'd performed already for two or three other friends. Bending to the storage cabinet under the TV set, he pawed through Carter's videotapes and took out any that looked even vaguely suspicious; he proceeded to the nightstand, where he removed the packets of condoms and the bottle of lube, and then to the bathroom, where he found more condoms in the cabinet under the sink. He rifled through Carter's dresser but found nothing more exotic than a pair of black bikini briefs, which he left alone. The tapes, condoms, and lube he stuffed into the garbage bag, and then he slipped into the kitchen and dropped the package into the trash. Abby, who was making more tea, saw him come in, and she glanced at the bag. She avoided his eyes and asked no questions, continuing briskly with her work.

Around six o'clock Carter's parents arrived. They'd called from the airport, and when the group of eight or ten people still chatting in the living room heard the Dawes' plane had landed, they rose quickly and began saying their goodbyes. Thom and Abby stood near the front door, receiving hugs and handshakes like the hosts of an impromptu party. Throughout the afternoon dozens of friends had come and gone, asking the same questions of Thom, Connie, and Warren, having the same conversation about the obituary that should be written for *Southern Voice* and the memorial service that should be planned. Inevitably, the conversation then would drift away from Carter onto safe, everyday topics, as if this were some ordinary party, after all. These people were all friends or at least acquaintances of Thom, but he was glad to see them go. As the door closed on the last of them, Thom exchanged glances with his sister, Connie, and Warren, all of whom were gazing expectantly at him.

"Here we are again," Connie said, wearily. Once or twice Thom had told Connie too that he needn't stay, that he would wait here for Carter's parents, but Connie insisted he wanted to stick it out. "I feel too guilty that I almost didn't come to the hospital today," he said. "What if I hadn't? I'd have hated myself the rest of my life for losing those last few minutes with Carter."

None of them were hungry, but they were talking idly about going somewhere for dinner when the doorbell rang.

Carter's parents looked surprisingly composed, Thom thought. Mrs. Dawes wore a long cashmere coat with a fur collar, and as usual her frosted dark-blond hair, careful makeup, and glossy dark-orange nails looked as though she'd just stepped from a salon. Her heavy perfume instantly filled the room. The ruddy, square-jawed Mr. Dawes was dressed more casually, in jeans and a blue pullover sweater that drew attention to his sky-blue eyes, exactly the color of his son's; but the eyelids were reddened and swollen, and his jaw was clenched as though he were purchasing his controlled, civil demeanor with immense effort. Yet he too gave a forced smile, shaking hands gingerly with his son's friends, and then he stepped back a foot or two, as though gladly relinquishing social duties to his wife. Mrs. Dawes exchanged a few words with each of them, thanking them profusely for visiting her son that morning.

"Will and I were talking about that on the plane," she said. "It's such a consolation that he was among friends, instead of lying there alone. Of course, if we'd had any idea of his condition..."

"We didn't know, either," Thom said. "When they admitted him on Sunday, he wasn't nearly as ill as the last time you were here. The other times, remember, he was in Intensive Care."

Thom stopped, hoping this didn't sound rude; of course Carter's mother would remember.

"This time, he just had a regular room," he added lamely.

Connie came forward as if on cue, voicing yet another time in a still-puzzled, petulant tone the complaint he'd expressed to the nurse and to each of Carter's friends who visited that day.

"He just closed his eyes for a minute, that's what we thought. Just for a minute!"

Even the gregarious, socially practiced Mrs. Dawes didn't know how to reply. Thom broke the awkward silence by saying they should be going.

The goodbyes were polite but swift. Thom offered, for the third or fourth time, to take care of the condo, the packing, the shipping, and Mrs. Dawes thanked him with a fervent press of Thom's hand. She assured him she would call when they'd decided about "the arrangements," and Thom thanked her for that.

Finally, there was a pause. There was nothing left to say.

In Thom's car there was an awkward silence, too, broken only by random words, observations.

"His parents seem nice," Abby said. "Now I see where Carter got his good looks."

Connie sighed. "This has been *one* exhausting afternoon. I don't want any dinner, really. I just want a big, stiff drink."

"I didn't know what to say," Warren said. "I'm not sure they remembered me..."

"I guess we could eat at Indigo," Thom said. "This early, there shouldn't be a wait."

They were all talking to themselves, Thom thought, rather than to each other.

Once they'd been seated and ordered cocktails—even Abby, who usually sipped white wine, had requested a vodka martini—their mood began to lighten.

"It's weird," Warren observed. "It already seems like it happened a week ago."

"A month ago," Connie said. "Last year."

Abby said, "It *was* a long day, but I think his parents appreciated our being there. Don't you, Thom?"

Thom glanced at her, startled. She'd spoken as though trying to wake him.

"Sure," he said.

He glanced around: this trendy, noisy restaurant with vaguely Cuban decor was one of his favorites, but it was fairly expensive and usually so crowded that he didn't come here often. Tonight, they deserved a decent meal: that must have been his reasoning. He felt befuddled, a bit numbed, as though someone else had driven them here. Too much had happened; he'd had to chat with too many people; somewhere during the long afternoon, he'd lost himself. Normally he didn't drink much, but now he reached for the Absolut and tonic he'd ordered and took a long, greedy swallow. From the corner of his eye, he saw Connie dig inside his pocket and then pop something into his mouth.

"Are you taking something?" Thom said.

Connie raised his eyebrows. "Just a Darvon, honey," he said. "I've got a slight headache, and this Whiskey Sour isn't helping."

"You're not supposed to mix those with alcohol," Warren said. But he spoke wearily, as though he'd repeated this warning often and knew Connie wouldn't listen.

"Darvon? Oh, piddle," Connie said. He smiled impishly, shrugging his shoulders. "It's just a light analgesic—you know, for daytime."

"You don't have a headache," Warren said grumpily. "You take them for the high, why don't you just admit it."

"I take them for *pain*," Connie said, shaking his finger at Warren. "Whether it's headache or heartache, pain is pain. And the pills *work*, goddamn it."

Warren looked away. "Whatever," he said.

"Now, later tonight," Connie said sweetly, turning to Abby, "when this whole day comes crashing on my head, I can haul out my cookie jar full of Percocet and get down to business."

"Yeah, and why don't we rent *The Boys in the Band?*" Warren said. "You can get hysterical and climb the draperies."

Startled, Connie laughed. "Warren, doll, you actually said something mildly witty. I'm so impressed."

Thom said, "Come on, Connie. Let's just relax, OK?"

"Relax? I just lost my best friend, and I'm supposed to relax?"

Thom saw Warren's jaw stiffen: of course, Warren was Connie's best friend, not Carter. Thom didn't think Connie had intended to be mean, this time. Not after a single cocktail.

The waiter approached to take their order.

"Not yet," Connie said, waving him off. "But you can bring us another round."

Abby, who looked confused and vaguely unhappy, made an awkward attempt at changing the subject. "Connie," she said, "tell me more about your family—your father and his wife, I mean. Do they visit Atlanta often?"

Connie drew back in his chair. To anyone observing from another table, he must have looked formidable: this tall, imperious-looking blond man with his alert blue-green eyes and startling good looks. As usual, he was dressed impeccably. Black sleeveless sweater over a white-on-white silk shirt; crisply tailored black wool slacks. No matter how much he drank tonight, he wasn't capable of rudeness to Abby, but nonetheless Thom, who knew Connie's miserable family history, tensed at his sister's naive, unexpected question. Occasionally Connie joked about his family life, but Thom and his other friends knew better than to bring up the subject themselves.

After a few seconds' pause, Connie said, "Family, family—let's see, I'm sure Oscar Wilde must have said something witty about the family, but I can't recall what it was. Let's just say that my family lives quietly among their own kind in Oklahoma City. That probably tells you all you need to know."

"I knew that," Abby said quickly, "I just—I just wondered if they would come to town. You know, to support you. To attend Connie's funeral, maybe."

Connie gave an abrupt laugh. "Is that a Freudian slip, honey? A buried longing?"

"Carter's funeral, I meant," Abby said, blushing.

"They don't visit often," Warren told Abby, gently. "Connie doesn't—I mean, Connie and his father don't have much in common."

Abby looked contrite. "Sorry," she said. She sipped her martini. "I didn't mean to pry."

Connie said, patting her hand, "Don't worry, doll. It's just that my father is a temperamental man, and since the day my mother died we've never gotten along. During my teenage years I was something of a rebel, and a bit flamboyant—believe it or not! In no uncertain terms, I was told that my father didn't approve of what he and his church members like to call my 'lifestyle.' All these years later, he feels the same way, of course. It's such an old, stale story that I'm a bit embarrassed to tell it! But there it is."

Thom knew there was more to the story he wasn't telling and was pleased when Warren, craning his head to look past Thom's shoulder, waved to someone.

"Look, there's Alex and Randy," he said.

Connie reached for his drink and rolled his eyes. "Oh, goodie," he muttered.

Thom glanced over his shoulder and saw Alex Fletcher approaching their table. He and Randy, his reserved and sometimes unfriendly lover, were internists who owned a busy Midtown clinic. Alex, a ruddy-faced man in his late thirties, was quite gregarious, though almost as widely disliked as his boyfriend. Tonight, as usual, Alex looked as though he'd stepped from a magazine ad: khaki slacks with a razor-sharp crease, a Tommy Hilfiger shirt so heavily starched it might have been sculpted onto him. Everyone Thom knew considered Alex and Randy the epitome of pretentious Atlanta queens—members of the so-called "A-list." (Whispering about this at one of Alex and Randy's parties, Connie had murmured, "Well, we may not be A-list queens, but we're close, aren't we? I give us a B, maybe a B+.") The couple had spent two years redesigning and decorating their Buckhead mansion on West Paces Ferry Road—a house which, Thom knew, since he was friends with the listing agent, they'd barely been able to afford. Recently they'd thrown a huge costume party, using some lavish ball given in Newport in the 1890s as their model, and both Randy and Alex had sat on gilded antique chairs in their grand entrance foyer, like members of royalty deigning to greet their subjects. The party had been the source of bitchy gossip for months.

Now Alex greeted Thom, Connie, and Warren, and said a few polite words to Abby after Thom introduced them. Out of some collective tact, or mere apprehension, no one mentioned to Alex that Carter had died that morning.

"So what have you and Randy been up to, Alex?" Connie asked, in the innocently "sweet" tone Thom could interpret but Alex could not.

"Oh, we bought a summer place up in Highlands, did you know?" Alex glanced at each of them, as if to gauge how impressed they were. "I was asking Randy just last night, can we really stand another round of designers and architects? The pool alone is a huge headache—we're razing that whole area and starting from scratch."

"Sounds like another showplace in the making," Thom said, with a grim smile.

Alex waved his hand as though fanning imaginary smoke. "Oh, no, it's just a summer cottage," he said. "But we want to do it right, of course."

"Goodness, it's a wonder you two find time to practice medicine," Connie observed.

Alex laughed. "Sometimes, we wonder the same thing. We're leaving for a week in Paris on Friday, and we're stopping in Manhattan for a couple of days beforehand to catch a few plays."

Alex was backing away: he'd seen someone else he knew at another table. "Well, great to see you guys. There's Tim Taber over there, so I'd better go say hello. Nice to meet you, Abby."

"You, too," Abby said.

"Have fun on your trip!" Connie called out, sweetly. "Tell Randy hello for me, OK? And call me for lunch."

"Will do," Alex called over his shoulder, hurrying across the room.

Connie bent immediately toward the center of the table, glancing around at the other three. "Did you ever meet such a shit?" he said gleefully.

They laughed. After a pause Warren said, still smiling, "I can't let you get away with that, Connie. You stole that line from Dorothy Parker."

"Of course!" Connie cried. "I steal most of my good lines from Dorothy—I'm a friend of Dorothy's, remember?"

Thom said, "Come on, Alex isn't that bad. He does a lot of good in the community, you know."

"Yeah?" Connie said. "Well, he'd feel a lot better if he'd pull that two-by-four out of his ass."

Connie was getting drunk, Thom thought. This was the first crude remark he'd made in Abby's presence. Now Connie turned toward her, and Thom expected that he would apologize, but he merely added, "You should see those two at the gym. They both wear designer gym clothes, including matching sweat suits—white with lavender piping, and I'm not making this up! They parade around for a while, chatting, while the rest of us are huffing and puffing on our favorite instruments of torture, and then they wander into the locker room. When they come out, of course, they're in matching gym shorts and tops; I swear, their tank tops look *starched*. I think they take them to the cleaners."

"Come on, Connie," Warren said.

"They *do*," Connie insisted. "And you should see them on the StairMaster, side by side, making a spectacle of keeping their arms up in the air, to show how fit they are. Randy actually folds his hands on top of his head! I swear, he ought to bring his crochet bag and knit a doily or something up there, if he's so determined to show off. Of course, the rest of us are hanging onto the handles for dear life."

"He isn't exaggerating that part," Warren said. "I've seen them. The rest of us are snickering, but Alex and Randy don't even notice."

"Of course not, their gaze is trained upon the mirrors!" Connie said. "Narcissus had nothing on those boys."

Thom tried to change the subject, but as the salads arrived Connie said, "What about you, Thom? Haven't seen you at the gym lately."

"He doesn't need to," Warren said. (Warren was so sweet!)

"Sometimes I go in the early morning," Thom said, "when you're still getting your beauty sleep. But I've been slacking off, I confess."

"Oh, you Catholics!" Connie said, chewing energetically. There was a dab of honey mustard on his cheek, but Thom decided not to tell him. "Bless me, Father, for I have sinned. It's been two weeks since my last workout!"

Abby laughed. "Well, Connie," she said, "I guess I'm going straight to hell. I haven't set foot inside a gym since high school."

"You don't need to, either," Warren said, smiling. He had caught Connie's eye, dabbing at his own face with one corner of his napkin; Connie grabbed his napkin and swabbed his cheek vigorously.

"We're both Sadlers," Thom said. "We worry the fat away."

Connie said, "It's all such folly, anyhow. I don't know why I go. I have the same little roll above my belt I had ten years ago, and I have it whether I work out every day for six months or don't work out at all. What's the point?"

"Have you ever worked out every day for six months?" Thom asked, smiling.

"Besides," Connie said, "the music they play in those gyms is intolerable. The place is full of middle-aged white guys, and half the time they're playing rap!"

Thom's last memory of the gym was Carter standing on a treadmill, his mouth sagged open with effort, his T-shirt drenched with sweat against his thin, heaving chest. Since then, Thom hadn't had much interest in going back.

After their dinners arrived, the conversation became more boisterous, with Abby holding her own, taking the cue from Warren and teasing Connie for his more outlandish remarks. Again Thom was surprised at how well she looked, her cheeks flushed as she ate, her eyes shining with amusement. He didn't quite understand. Though she'd seemed to shrug off the melancholy he'd sensed that day he met her flight, at the same time she'd become secretive, spending more time on the telephone in Thom's room, the door firmly closed. (There had been several hang-up calls, too, when Thom had answered. Was that Lucille? Hanging up on her son, after all these years?) Abby had seemed shy and remote at the small dinner party he'd given during her first week back in town, but now she seemed to enjoy his friends. She bantered with them tonight as though she'd known them for years. Thom had the morose thought that the other three had forgotten about Carter, but he knew it was the liquor and the need for a respite after their long, grueling day. He couldn't blame them.

Somehow the conversation had wound back around to Connie's childhood.

"I won't say I was *abused*, exactly, though some hysterical counselor on Sally Jessy would probably disagree. But my father had a violent temper, and I guess you could say he bashed me a few times. Once, the year before my mother died—I would have been nine—I came in from school and for some reason he was home. I chatted with my mother in the kitchen for awhile, and he was sitting at the breakfast bar, just watching us. I have no idea what I said, or the tone of voice I'd used, but as I went back to my room he followed me, screaming that I was acting 'prissy' and ought to go put on a dress. Now I'm sure that I *was* acting prissy, but I certainly didn't know it—not at the tender age of nine! So he gets out his belt and whacks me a few times around the shoulders, screaming something about wanting to 'toughen me up'—some goofy dialogue he must have gotten out of a John Wayne movie. But the damn belt *hurt*, and I remember crying afterward. Then Mother came back to comfort me, after Daddy had left the house, and I felt—"

He stopped abruptly, an unexpected surge of emotion choking off his words. He cleared his throat and reached for his whiskey sour.

"But I wouldn't say I was abused, exactly," he repeated.

"That's awful," Abby said. "Our father was so gentle—he didn't believe in corporal punishment."

Thom looked at her, surprised. It was true that their father never raised his hand to them, but Thom hadn't heard him speak about any "belief" on the matter.

"You're lucky," Connie said. He cocked his head slightly, glancing at Thom. "But Thom, you were 'bashed' once, weren't you? In high school or something? Did you ever tell Abby about it?"

Thom gave a nervous grin; he didn't want to talk about that. "In college," he said. "And yes, Abby knows about it. In fact, she was there."

Connie gave a theatrical gasp, turning to Abby. "You were *there*? That must have been awful for you!"

Thom and Abby exchanged a pained look; this was a memory they shared but didn't talk about.

"Let's change the subject, OK?" Thom said.

Connie looked confused, and a bit displeased. "But—"

Thom reached across the table and squeezed Connie's forearm, hard. "I mean it," he said. There was no other way of getting through to Connie.

And so Warren, dependable sweet Warren, chimed in with a long, rather tiresome story about his own childhood—something about his father chasing him up into a tree, Thom couldn't quite pay attention—and that was that.

They continued eating and drinking, and for the rest of the evening they talked of harmless things.

It could be said that Thom had never told anyone about the time he'd been bashed, not even Abby. She'd been there, she'd witnessed it, but that was a different thing.

They'd never spoken about that night, and he imagined they never would.

Each was alone with what had happened.

It was 1983, Reagan was president, and Thom was cruising through his sophomore year at Mercer. Unlike his first year, when homesickness had prompted trips to Atlanta every weekend, by then he stayed in Macon for weeks at a time, studying or hanging out with his straight roommates. A couple of times that fall, he'd gone out with a girl from his accounting class named Lisa who seemed neither surprised nor offended that he didn't try anything before taking her home. Thom had known he was gay at least since eighth grade, but no one else knew—not even Abby—and that was fine with him. Even telling Abby would be a mistake, he'd decided, since the recent firestorm of publicity about AIDS. Thom knew he couldn't talk about that: he couldn't have found the words, not then, to say he'd done nothing to put himself "at risk," so naturally she would worry.

And she would worry alone, with no one to talk to, and he knew what that was like.

So the night in mid-October when his sister called and asked him to come home for the weekend, to help celebrate her friend Chrissie's birthday with Chrissie and her new boyfriend, he couldn't disappoint her. He'd heard an unaccustomed note of pleading in her voice. During high school, she'd dated regularly; for more than a year, a period encompassing her senior prom and her first few months as a college freshman, she'd even had a steady boyfriend, a handsome but clunky boy named Justin who had attended the same Catholic schools with Thom and Abby since first grade. Thom guessed he was a boyfriend of convenience, and he hadn't been surprised when they broke up during Abby's first semester at Emory. Since then, the number of her dates seemed to have tapered off, which Thom attributed to her involvement with her studies—she was a wildly enthusiastic English major—and with new friends she'd made at school. At the same time, she seemed to have difficulty letting Thom establish his own life: she couldn't quite let him go. All this went unspoken but he'd felt it in the urgency of her voice as she described all the fun they would have with Chrissie and her boyfriend, someone named "Jim" whom Thom had never met, and in the obvious relief she'd expressed when he agreed to come.

"Oh great, Thom. That's just *great!*" she cried.

He'd stood in the little hallway of the tumbledown frame house he shared with Derek and Shane, shifting his weight back and forth, hunched over the old-fashioned telephone stand they all used, since there were no phone connections in any of the three tiny bedrooms. While using this hall telephone he tended to whisper, even when Derek and Shane weren't home. That night they'd gone out for a pizza, but still Thom glanced over his shoulder, made uneasy by his sister's voice but not understanding why.

"Yeah, I'm looking forward to it," he said, awkwardly. "Great."

When they hung up, he pulled a folded-over scrap of paper from his wallet and dialed Lisa's number and broke the date he'd made with her for Saturday night. He explained the situation, and she didn't seem upset.

"OK, Thom, you have a good weekend," she said. "Call me next week, if you want."

"Sure, I will," Thom said, feeling his own warm breath against the receiver. "Monday or Tuesday, all right? I'll call you then."

(But after he'd recuperated and returned to campus, he would drop his accounting class, though he was making an A, and would never see or speak with Lisa Spradlin again.)

Driving home that Friday morning in his ancient black Firebird, he'd felt enlivened by the brisk autumn weather. Fall had been his favorite season, always; he loved the blazing reds and oranges of the huge trees in the neighborhood where he'd grown up, and he associated the brisk gray weather with the energy and excitement he felt when returning to school after the heat-heavy doldrums of summer. He'd been one of the few kids he'd ever known who preferred the regimented life of school to the formless, ever-shifting summertime intrigues among the neighborhood kids—a sentiment that even Abby, herself an excellent student, had never quite understood.

In high school, among the black-veiled nuns and the half-dozen, equally strict lay teachers, as they were called, Thom had been one of the popular boys, liked by everyone for his energy and high spirits, his ability to be "good" without being nerdy or antisocial. Though he hadn't played sports, he'd been elected president of his junior class, vice-president of the student council all three years, and had belonged to the drama club, the French club, the Honor Society. St. Jude's was the city's most "elite" Catholic school, and the year Thom graduated, there had been only thirty students in the senior class. During his time there, he'd dated virtually every pretty girl in the school at least once (but no one girl for more than a month or two), and even one of the homely girls, occasionally, if he found her interesting, or when the stifling conformity of St. Jude's, an excellent but not very progressive school, made him feel rebellious. Popular, "cute" boys did not go out with despised, "ugly" girls, but sometimes Thom Sadler did, and he enjoyed those evenings more than the obligatory movies and proms with bouncy cheerleader types people expected him to date.

One obese and pimply girl named Janie Pridgen, in particular, had a wicked, hilarious wit that she revealed only when they were alone, never at school. During his first year at college, feeling bored and acutely lonesome, he'd been tempted to call Janie in Atlanta, just to talk, to hear her dishy gossip about the current goings-on at St. Jude's, and yet he wanted the kind of long, giggly conversation you had lying in bed, propped against several pillows with the phone cradled between ear and shoulder, not standing in a drafty hallway where your roommates might overhear. Anyway, he reasoned, high school was over, and he couldn't go back; he was too sensible not to accept this dismal fact.

His freshman year at college had been the loneliest of his life. No one on the Mercer campus knew Thom Sadler or seemed interested in knowing him. He'd gone through rush, attending one party after another, but he'd been turned off by the fraternities and their boisterous, self-conscious bonhomie, their jeering scorn of professors and classes, their immersion in alcohol. His being gay, in fact, was the least of it; those yearnings he was accustomed to suppressing, and pondering in solitude. But he'd had little in common with the other students he met, including his roommates (Derek and Shane were best friends, leaving him the odd man out), and it was only this year he'd begun to feel a sort of pleasure in his isolation, the promise and excitement of a new start. He'd always had the ability to sit back, like someone viewing a movie of his own life, and watch eagerly for what might happen.

He'd begun looking around inquisitively at other guys in his classes. He found it exciting rather than frustrating that he couldn't guess which of them might be gay (except for the flamboyant ones, who didn't interest him) and when he came across arch references to "gaydar" in a magazine he'd started buying, *The Advocate*, hoarding copies in an old canvas bag stowed in the trunk of his car, he smiled but didn't quite understand. Operating much of the time on automatic pilot, Thom still noticed girls— their smiles, their shining hair, their plain or pretty features—as though imagining he might wake one morning and find that all his emotional longings toward men had only been a phase, after all. The distinction between what he felt and what he'd been taught to feel seemed graspable but now wavered in his vision, as a solid object submerged in water will start to ripple and change its shape, confusing the eye. In someone less patient or thoughtful, such confusion might have led to experimentation, the full-scale sexual abandon about which he read and sometimes heard whispered about among his new acquaintances at Mercer; but instead Thom stayed idle, in a kind of bewildered chastity that he found not only bearable but pleasant, since it demanded so little of him.

That October day when he turned onto Friar Tuck Road and saw his father out front raking leaves, he was pleased and relieved, the same emotion he felt when he called home and his father, rather than his mother, answered the phone. Sometimes when Thom arrived for a weekend visit, his mother glimpsed his car from the kitchen window and came running out, already complaining how seldom he visited or called.

His father propped his rake against the side of the house and shook Thom's hand. Southern propriety demanded that father and son shake hands rather than hug, which was fine with Thom. His mother's histrionic greetings usually embarrassed him.

"How was the drive?"

"Fine. I love this weather."

"School going OK?"

"Not too bad. Haven't flunked out yet."

"You doing all right for money? If not, just let me know."

"Thanks, Dad. I'm fine."

They had essentially the same conversation each time Thom came home, speaking in a familiar, slow-paced rhythm he found soothing: it was this rhythm, along with the smiles and crinkled, friendly glances they exchanged, that mattered, not the forgettable words they spoke.

Thom and his father went inside. His mother, bearing a small stack of towels out of the laundry room, gave a small cry of surprise, dropped the towels, rushed over to hug him.

"Abby said you were coming, but I didn't think you'd get here *this* early! Come sit down and I'll fix you some lunch—you must be starving." She stepped back, looking him up and down. "Honey, you've gotten thinner since the last time. Aren't you eating right?"

"I'm fine, Mom. I ate just before I left."

He and Lucille likewise conducted the same conversation when he came home, but with her the exchanges were *not* soothing.

He crossed to where she had dropped the towels and bent to retrieve them.

"Never mind that!" Lucille cried. She hurried over, wrested the towels from his arms. "Come sit down, honey. Is tuna salad all right? I just finished making it."

Thom stared after her, balefully, as she carried the towels back toward the kitchen, accompanied by the brisk slapping noise of her fluffy pink flip-flops. His mother dressed casually at home—an ordinary cotton house dress with deep pockets in the skirt where she kept wadded-up Kleenexes and the TV remote control; flesh-colored panty hose; and always a pair of flip-flops in her favored colors of red, pink, or white, supplemented in cold weather with a pair of thick white socks. Yet her wispy reddish hair was always carefully done (that year in a short, teased style similar to Nancy Reagan's), her lipstick and mascara freshly applied, and for years her routine had included a manicure once a week, a pedicure once a month. Although she mostly stayed home, with only a few minutes' notice Lucille Sadler could change her clothes and be instantly presentable as a reasonably attractive Atlanta matron. She kept the house (working especially hard when her twice-a-week maid, Latonya, was there), read magazines, watched television, took care of her husband, and monitored as closely as possible the lives of her adult children.

His mother had passed out of view, but her voice was clearly audible: "Thom, are you coming? Do you want milk or sweet tea?"

Thom and his father exchanged a smile, and to Thom's surprise his father touched his shoulder. "Abby's in her room, working on a paper. Why don't you go back and say hello?"

"What about—"

"I'll take care of things in the kitchen. As long as *somebody's* eating, she'll be happy."

"Thanks, Daddy," Thom said.

Before turning away, George Sadler paused in surprise. Usually, Thom called him "Dad." For some reason the "Daddy" had slipped out.

When Abby opened her door in response to Thom's knock, she gave out a brief cry of pleasure and hugged him.

"I'm so glad you're here," she whispered.

"Me too," he said.

He stepped back, taking in her pastel-blue angora sweater and beige wool slacks; she wore pink lipstick and had done something to heighten her pallid complexion, which seemed to glow with health. Her wavy auburn hair fell freely to her shoulders, the style she'd worn throughout her high school years. Though less outgoing than Thom, she'd been equally popular, known as a girl who "got along with everybody." She was pretty, but not pretty enough to inspire jealousy from the cheerleaders or prom queens; she was intelligent, but didn't retreat into the snobbery affected by the plain, insecure girls who joined the math or chess clubs and spent their free time talking earnestly with teachers instead of their peers. Thom most admired Abby for treating all the other kids at St. Jude's with a cheerful friendliness, which contained a reserve that Thom could see but others could not. She gave the same eager smile and bright greeting to the school pariahs as she gave to the adored football players and social arbiters at St. Jude's. She had many girlfriends, but no best friend; many dates, but rarely a steady boyfriend. Only in the last year had Thom worried that she'd begun to isolate herself; that she'd had far more trouble than Thom in adjusting to college life.

Yet today she looked radiant.

Cocking her head to one side in a mock-critical look, she said, "So, I hope you brought some other clothes? It turns out Chrissie's having this big party at Ginger's house, and you're going to be my date." She added, quickly, "We don't have to stay long..."

She must have glimpsed the disappointment in his eyes; he didn't feel like a big, boisterous party. He glanced down at his stained sweatshirt and corrupt blue jeans. "I didn't bring anything fancy," he said. "I guess I could run over to Rich's, get a shirt or something..."

Abby leapt forward and hugged him again. "Don't bother," she said. "You look fine the way you are. I'll tell everybody you're in a Jack Kerouac phase—that you've been on the road for three weeks, stopping every few hours to jot down a poem or something, and you can't remember the last time you had a bath."

"Yeah, very funny. I'm sure they'll buy that, won't they?" He paused. "By the way, who's going to be there tonight?"

"Everybody who's in town, I imagine. Why, is there someone you—"

"Including your great love, the brilliant Lawton?" he asked, with affected slyness. It was an old joke between them—initiated and kept alive by Thom—that Abby nourished a hopeless infatuation for Lawton Williams, a gorgeous blond hunk from one of Atlanta's oldest families. Of course, it was Thom who had endured this intense attraction throughout his junior and senior years.

"Lawton? Honestly, Thom, when will you give that up. No, he won't be there. He has a new girlfriend—she goes to Vanderbilt. I heard he drives up to Nashville every weekend."

"In his beloved Porsche," Thom laughed.

"But of course," Abby said, smiling. Yet she looked a bit puzzled, too.

"Poor Abby," Thom said, with a small downturn of his lips. "No Lawton

Williams to ogle tonight."

He felt such vast relief that his spirits lightened at once, and the rest of the afternoon they chatted and reminisced, going back and forth between their rooms as they got ready for the party, doing their best to avoid Lucille's constant efforts to "help" them. She offered to style Abby's hair, to choose Abby's dress, to iron a shirt for Thom (he'd found an almost-new one in his closet), to have dinner ready at six o'clock instead of seven, so they wouldn't be late.... "Are you going to drive, Abby?" she asked. "You're a much better driver than Thom, you know, and if he has something to drink at the party—"

"Mom, Thom *has* to drive," Abby said, tartly. "The boy always drives."

"I'm not going to drink anything, Mom," Thom lied. "Don't worry about it, OK?"

"What time will the two of you be home, do you think? You'll probably want a snack or something, won't you?"

"Please don't wait up," Abby said, mechanically. The request was futile, of course; never in all their high school years had Abby or Thom returned from a date and not found Lucille hovering near the front door. Their father always went to bed at 11:30, after watching the news, but on the nights her children had dates Lucille stayed up no matter how late, sometimes until one or two A.M., saying with fake nonchalance to her children as they came in, "Oh, I can't believe how late it is! I just had a little housework to catch up on."

Finally, after rushing through Lucille's dinner of meat loaf and twice-baked potatoes, and hurrying back to their rooms to brush their teeth, Thom and Abby escaped out the front door. Lucille followed them onto the porch, not ready to let them go. "Didn't you want some ice cream or something? What's the rush, you two?"

"Thanks, the dinner was great!" Thom called over his shoulder. Abby, always more annoyed by their mother's nagging than Thom, didn't turn around; she lifted one hand and wiggled her fingers in the air.

Half an hour after he'd arrived at the party, Thom found to his surprise that he was enjoying himself. He drank a couple of beers, he chatted with old pals from St. Jude's (even Janie Pridgen was there; she'd come with one of her girlfriends), and he danced with Abby, and with Janie, and with Chrissie, and with a couple of other girls. The kids were a mix of recent graduates now dispersed among colleges across the state and others still at St. Jude's; it occurred to Thom that each group probably wasted a good deal of time envying the other. The party was at Ginger Bishop's house in

Ansley Park, a big two-story colonial on Beverly Drive. Since Ginger was the "rich kid" at St. Jude's and her parents were often out of town, this huge high-ceilinged house with its thick moldings and dully gleaming antique furniture had been the setting for many of their high school parties.

Around ten o'clock a few of Chrissie's girlfriends brought some brightly wrapped packages out of a closet, and Ginger came in from the kitchen carrying a lighted birthday cake, and they all sang "Happy Birthday" and watched Chrissie open her presents. There were pieces of jewelry, mostly earrings, and tiny glass decanters of perfume; from several of the boys there were bottles of champagne, which were brandished gleefully amid cries of "Open it! Let's have a toast!" But Chrissie, a petite but strong-willed blonde who tended to get her way, made a little wry movement with her lips and shook her head.

"You guys are already drunk," she said smartly. "I'm not wasting good champagne on *you*. Just have another beer."

And there were gag gifts, also from Chrissie's male friends: a packet of flavored condoms; a "French" dildo, heavily ribbed, which Chrissie stuck playfully in her mouth, letting her eyes close in mock-bliss; and a year's subscription to *Playgirl* magazine, the current issue nestled inside the box. Chrissie snatched up the magazine, opened it to the centerfold, and panned it around the room for all to see. The girls giggled, the boys whooped and yelled.

"Yeah, like you guys have anything like *this*," Chrissie said.

Then a boy named Brad, whom Chrissie had dated in their sophomore and junior years, cleared his throat and asked for everyone's attention.

Brad was a tall slender good-looking basketball player with reddish hair and big, boyish blue eyes: during their senior year at St. Jude's, he and Thom had been good friends, and Thom had something of a crush on him. One day in the locker room after Phys. Ed. he'd caught Brad staring at him as he toweled off, or so he'd thought. He'd supposed it was wishful thinking. Now Brad said, jerking his thumb toward the ornate winding staircase in the foyer, "OK, it's time for you to come upstairs, Chrissie honey, and get *my* present."

There were a few awkward giggles; for a moment, Chrissie went pale, for not only was the remark inappropriate (Chrissie's new boyfriend, a big scowling boy from Georgia Tech who knew hardly anyone here, was standing next to her), but there had been a snide, unfriendly tone in the way Brad spoke the words. Thom, who'd always found Brad a good-natured, friendly guy, was startled; next to him, he could feel that Abby had stiffened, too.

Chrissie was the first to recover. She gave Brad a brief smirk and said, "Sorry, hon, but I've graduated, didn't you hear?" She took hold of her boyfriend's massive bicep. "From boys, that is. To *men.*"

Everyone broke into laughter; a few of the girls even clapped. Brad took a final swig of his beer (Thom supposed he'd had too much to drink), slammed it down on the table, and stalked from the room and out the front door.

"God, what brought that on?" somebody asked.

"He's been having some problems," Ginger said quickly. Her face wore a stricken look; she'd always taken her "hostess" role very seriously. She tried to smile, shrugging her shoulders.

"Let's forget about it," one guy said, lifting his beer bottle. "Here's a toast to Chrissie's birthday!"

Several voices shouted in unison: "Yeah!" "Right on!"

Then a girl named Amber, who had dated Brad for a while after he'd broken up with Chrissie, touched one finger to her cheek and glanced behind her, as if there were someone who might overhear. "But you know what, you guys?" she said, in a loud whisper. "I heard Brad is *gay.*"

A brief, stunned silence. Thom felt the blood draining from his face.

"Come on, Amber," one guy said, dismissively. He'd been one of Brad's basketball teammates. "You don't know that. He dated girls all through high school."

"That doesn't mean anything," Amber said pertly. "That's the way they cover it up, sometimes."

"God, can't you see it?" said one of the drunker boys, drawing a line in the air with his beer bottle. "The headline in the school paper? 'St. Jude's basketball star'"—he paused for effect—"'revealed as man-hungry fruit!'"

"Oh my God, Tim, that's terrible!" one girl shrieked, above the general laughter.

Chrissie took a step backward, clearly upset at the turn the conversation had taken. Thom supposed everyone would be talking in the next few days about the way Brad Chalmers had "ruined" poor Chrissie's birthday party.

"Listen, I dated Brad for two years," Chrissie said. "He may be a lot of things, but he isn't *queer.*"

For the first time, Chrissie's burly new boyfriend spoke: "God, I hope not," he said. Grinning, he stepped away from Chrissie in mock alarm. "I'm too goddamn young to die of AIDS!"

There were a few nervous titters as Chrissie, enraged, turned to him. "Are you implying I have AIDS?" she cried. "Just because I dated Brad?"

Jim's expression quickly turned contrite; he put his arm around Chrissie and squeezed, whispering something in her ear. Then he said, for all to hear, "Sorry, you guys. Just wasn't thinking."

Chrissie, who seemed mollified, shrugged her shoulders and said, "Oh, the hell with all this. Let's party!"

Again there were whoops and cheers. Everyone turned from the dining room table with its heap of opened gifts, wadded-up paper, scattered ribbons, and broke again into chattering groups. Ginger had disappeared briefly, and Thom noticed that the stereo had been cranked a few notches higher, Olivia Newton-John chanting "Let's get *physical!*" at high volume. He and Abby, left to themselves, exchanged a quick look. Thom couldn't tell if Abby was embarrassed or merely annoyed. Something in the look she gave Thom troubled him: had she expected him to intervene, somehow? Lately he'd suffered a single, generalized emotion no matter where he was, or with whom: if something unpleasant happened, no matter how unrelated to him, Thom felt guilty. Irrational, but he felt it. *His* fault.

By midnight the party was breaking up. Chrissie had cornered Thom and Abby in the big domed foyer, where a clutch of forlorn, half-deflated pink balloons bobbed dismally above their heads.

"Listen, you guys," Chrissie was saying, "this was supposed to be a double date, remember? Let's go somewhere, just the four of us. Where should we go?"

"What happened to Jim?" Thom asked, stalling. He'd hoped to slip out the front door with Abby and go home. The beers he'd drunk earlier had worn off and now he felt groggy, ready for bed. Nor was he particularly fond of Chrissie.

"God, who knows," Chrissie said, rolling her eyes. "Upstairs banging one of my dearest friends, probably."

She gave a bright, ribald laugh and took a long pull on her beer. Thom had noticed that both Chrissie and her boyfriend had drunk a great deal tonight—another reason he'd hoped to elude them.

"Um, I don't know," Abby said. "What do you think, Thom? Want to go somewhere, maybe get a bite to eat?"

Abby looked as fresh and cheerful as when they'd first arrived. She'd been nursing the same beer for two hours, and Thom saw that it still wasn't empty. He knew his sister well: he could see that she wasn't ready to go home.

"OK, I guess you're the designated driver," Thom said, smiling.

"Yeah, aren't you ashamed?" Chrissie told Abby. "You're supposed to be celebrating. You hardly drink at *all*, do you?"

"Well, it usually gives me a headache—" Abby began, but Chrissie turned to Jim, who had sidled over and slipped an arm around her waist. "So where have *you* been?" she asked.

Jim smiled, a bit sheepishly. "Just back in the kitchen, having a cold one," he said. "Didn't want good beer to go to waste."

Chrissie laughed shrilly as though he'd said something witty. "God, you must have a hollow leg or something," she said.

Or maybe a hollow head, Thom thought. He had met Jim's eyes a few times and saw nothing much in them. Jim had the flat, pale-blue gaze of the typical muscle-bound football player who didn't shine in the classroom. He was brawny and square-jawed, his blond hair cut short as a military recruit's; Thom supposed most women, and maybe most gay men, would consider him a hunk, but he definitely wasn't Thom's type. If he and Jim had to sit in a restaurant together, he had no idea what they would talk about. So he was relieved when Chrissie broke off her chattering and said to Abby: "Listen, why don't we just go over to my house? My parents will be in bed, and they sleep like rocks. We can make some sandwiches in the kitchen or something. Maybe have a nightcap, too. My dad always has some Jack Daniels."

"Good idea, babe," Jim said, giving Chrissie a hug. Thom could imagine what he was thinking: they'd have a sandwich and a drink, then Thom and Abby would go home and he'd have the inebriated Chrissie to himself.

"Sure, great!" Abby said, and together they drifted out into the brisk night air, heading for their cars.

"Don't you want us to drive you?" Thom asked. "Abby hardly drank anything tonight."

Under the streetlights Jim stared at him, offended. "I'm fine, don't worry about it," he said. "We'll meet you there."

Driving, Abby had said she hoped Thom didn't mind: "We'll just stay a few minutes. I didn't know Chrissie and Jim had gotten so drunk."

Thom shrugged. "It doesn't matter. High school revisited." Impulsively he leaned across, gave his sister a peck on the cheek. "And why not?"

As they pulled into Chrissie's driveway, Thom was surprised to see that Chrissie and Jim were leaning against the hood of Jim's Honda, talking, as though they'd arrived long ago. Chrissie's house was in Buckhead, off West Wesley Road; Abby and Thom had taken Peachtree Road up from Ansley Park, forgetting that Peachtree was always clogged with traffic on Friday night. Jim must have used the side streets.

Thom called out, smiling, "You guys observed all the speed limits, I presume?" But as they got closer, under the whitish illumination cast by the floodlights over the driveway, he could see that neither Chrissie nor Jim had paid any attention. Chrissie's elbows jutted out from her sides; Jim was glaring past her shoulder, shaking his head.

"You asshole!" Chrissie was saying. "You apologize right this second, Jim Driggers!"

Jim had folded his big, beefy arms, defiant. "What, are you riding the rag or something?" he said. He turned aside and spat; the little wet glob landed only a couple of feet from where Thom and Abby had stopped, not knowing if they should come any further.

"Chrissie?" Abby said in a mild, apprehensive voice. "Is everything OK?"

Chrissie glanced over, briefly. "Hi, you guys. Everything's OK except that Jim here is being a *total* asshole!"

Abby touched Thom's arm, saying in a voice loud enough for Chrissie to hear: "Maybe we should go. I'm not really hungry, anyway..."

At that, Chrissie came running over. She threw her arms around Abby's shoulders. "Oh, no, I want you guys to stay. I *never* get to see you anymore. God, I wish I could have gotten into Emory. I just *hate* going to a state school."

She glanced over her shoulder, and Thom understood she'd intended this as an affront to Jim, who had gotten into Tech with a football scholarship. Yet Thom had heard that Chrissie was close to flunking out at West Georgia, a school that admitted practically anybody.

Jim had stepped away from his car and was digging in the pocket of his jeans. He pulled out his keys and pointed one of them at Chrissie. "No, you stay here with your nice, polite friends," he said, his voice pitched low and mean. "I'm outta here."

Thom saw the flicker of panic in Chrissie's eyes. She said, looking around at all of them, "Oh, let's everybody just calm down. I was just mad," she added, glancing at Abby, "because on the way over here, *of course* this jealous lunatic had to bring up Brad. I'm so sick of all these rumors about Brad, aren't you?"

Neither Thom nor Abby knew how to answer that.

"If you want to date fags," Jim said, "go right ahead. I'm sure there were quite a few back at that party, from your fancy-ass private school."

"There were *no* queers at my birthday party!" Chrissie cried. "What the hell's wrong with you?"

Under her breath, Abby whispered to Thom: "Oh God, let's get out of here."

Chrissie had started sobbing. "I didn't *know* Brad was gay," she said. "It's not my fault." Then an idea seemed to strike her. She looked over at Thom; her face had crumpled with self-pity, like a small child's. "Thom, you were his best friend in high school," she said, "did you ever hear anything? Did he ever tell *you*?"

Thom had that sudden, blood-draining sensation he'd felt at the party. He said quickly, "We weren't best friends. Just friends."

Abby looked at him and their eyes met, briefly. He glanced away.

Jim, next to his car door with the keys out, gave a brief snarl of a smile. "Oh, so you and sweet little Brad were *best* friends, were you?"

"Oh my God," Chrissie cried, "would everybody please be *nice*?" She'd placed one palm flat against her forehead, as though stricken with a sudden headache.

Thom glared at Jim, and Jim glared back, and the look in Jim's smug, mean little eyes—they had narrowed to slits—ignited something in Thom's chest. Within seconds the tiny pinprick of resentment had ballooned into rage. He felt the blood throbbing in his throat where the flame of anger had surged, aching for release. He heard himself say, in a hard, measured voice: "Yeah, Brad and I *were* friends, but so what? He never said anything about it, but it wouldn't matter to me if he were gay, would it? Since *I'm* gay."

Chrissie gasped. "What? *You*?"

Thom was too angry, too focused on Jim's smirking, Neanderthal face to notice Abby's reaction.

Jim was shaking his head, as though disgusted. "I shouldda known. Well move your car, faggot, because I'm outta here."

"Jim, wait, don't *leave*!" Chrissie pleaded.

"You know what they say about homophobes," Thom said, in that same rigid, disembodied voice. Whose voice was that? "The ones who make a big deal about hating gay guys are usually closet cases—didn't you know?"

Jim's reaction was visceral, so rapid that Thom didn't have time to raise his arms in self-defense. Not that it would have done any good. Jim lunged toward Thom and slammed his big-knuckled fist into his jaw. In the first instant Thom was too numbed to feel the pain, but he heard the sickening crunch of his teeth breaking, tasted the wet salty blood filling his mouth. He'd bitten his own tongue, hard. The next blow—he heard Jim's low, guttural voice just before it hit, "You fucking faggot"—went to Thom's gut, doubling him over. His arms crossed his stomach. He'd fallen sideways, his arm scraping the concrete, his head thudding onto the bed of pine straw lining the driveway. Later people would say there was that to be thankful for, at least: his skull hadn't slammed against the cement. Curled in a fetal position, he endured Jim's rapid, methodical kicks against his rib cage, his kidneys, even up the crack of his buttocks, and somewhere beyond the pain he heard Chrissie and Abby shrieking, "No! Stop! My God, you'll kill him!" Or maybe he only imagined this, for later—the next night, in fact, when he woke bleary-eyed in Piedmont Hospital—the memory seemed vague, improbable.

He did remember, with an almost surreal clarity, the drive to the hospital. Abby and Chrissie had gotten him into the passenger seat of his car, and maybe Jim had even helped (Jim was said, later, to be "really sorry" about what happened, and Thom supposed he was worried Thom would press assault charges: Thom hadn't, of course), and he recalled how Abby had leaned into the steering wheel, tears streaming down her face, but her chin jutted forward, determined, carefully navigating the traffic and looking both ways before running red lights, clearly hell-bent on getting her brother to Piedmont Hospital as quickly and safely as possible. That image was imprinted in his memory forever. His throat knotted with tears whenever he thought about it.

Another memory from that wild car ride troubled him even more. Pressed against the door, panting, the pain shooting through him with each pulse of his blood, Thom wanted to say something: had wanted to speak, to tell Abby that yes, goddamnit, he was gay. Back in Chrissie's driveway, after all, he'd been speaking to Jim, and it was somehow shameful that he'd told that stupid football player what he'd never said to *her*, the one person he might have told and bridged his way out of the loneliness in which he'd dwelled for all these years. So he ignored the pain, cleared his aching throat, opened his mouth, but it kept filling with blood, and he had to clamp it shut. He pawed at his chin and the front of his shirt where the blood gushed so freely from his broken teeth, his bitten tongue.

So he'd hoped, yearned, tried: but still he could not speak.

• • •

That had been the only hospital stay of Thom's adult life, and these days, whenever he'd visited Carter or another friend in the hospital, his mind had reeled back to that long-ago incident, Abby's panicked drive to Piedmont, the atmosphere of rush and emergency that had shoved away the huge unspoken truth hovering between them. During these past four years that truth had become a gulf, a chasm, separating them, and he'd thought more than once how the current phrase, *don't tell,* had been his family's motto for decades. You focused on minutiae and ignored the larger truths, except at crisis moments like his bashing, like his father's illness and death, but at such times the crushing weight of the unspoken bore down on everyone, swift and merciless, like a bomb exploding into bits whatever wasn't firmly joined, secured.

Bombs, minefields, why was he thinking of these things? he wondered. When he was eleven, at a Fourth of July barbecue next door, a firecracker had exploded in his hand, and that incident now seemed meaningful, too, if he stopped to ponder what had happened. But instead of pondering, he tended to plod along with a kind of grim hopefulness, keeping everything together as best he could. What was that quote that had grabbed his attention one time, during a college English class? People lived in *silent desperation*—no, in *quiet desperation,* that was it. Almost everyone he knew lived this way, not just his mother and sister. Carter's family, Connie's family, his friends themselves—almost everyone he knew was in therapy or taking Prozac or reading New Age books or self-help articles. Nothing really worked, of course, but they tried; like him, everyone else was more or less plodding along, enduring the same mapless journey, the same grief and befuddlement. This was living, and had always been; would always be. To expect more was pointless, wasn't it?

Such thoughts consoled him, a little.

Carter had died on Wednesday, and by Friday his friends had decided the memorial service should be postponed until after New Year's. Too many people were leaving town for the holidays, there were too many distractions, and they all agreed there was no hurry, after all. Mr. and Mrs. Dawes had taken the body to Charleston, and though Mrs. Dawes invited Thom and a few others to the funeral, they'd decided not to attend. Carter's will adamantly stated that he preferred cremation, with no religious service of any kind (Thom knew the stipulations, since he'd gone with Carter to his lawyer's office), but although Carter had sent his parents a copy of the will, they were busy planning a traditional, rather showy funeral at the same Episcopal church where they'd been married in 1959.

Guiltily, wondering if Carter would have minded, Thom decided not to argue with Mr. and Mrs. Dawes over the issue; he didn't see the point. Dead was dead, he'd always believed, and what remained was for the living. Thom did explain to Mrs. Dawes that he and Carter's other friends preferred their own service here in Atlanta, where they had known him, and she had seemed to understand. Of course, Thom told her, she and her husband were welcome, but she'd said without hesitating that one service was all she could take. Thom didn't blame her, and once that topic was exhausted he'd found himself prolonging the conversation, knowing that most likely he would never see or speak to Mrs. Dawes again. The idea saddened him. Before they hung up she said, in a low, husky murmur, "Thank you, darling Thom, for being such a good friend to our son." Taken aback, Thom could only say, his own voice lowered, "You're welcome."

Later that same day Thom and Connie decided to postpone the trip to Key West, too. Christmas was practically here, and they'd made no plans; Thom had been correct in assuming Connie hadn't booked reservations but had merely "intended to." Key West would be jammed with revelers during the holidays and none of Carter's friends were in the mood for that. "Let's wait until January," Connie said. "The town will be quieter, and we can just relax."

Thom had agreed, though the postponement meant Abby could not join them. She'd scheduled a new flight for her return to Philadelphia: she had to leave the day after New Year's, since her classes started the following Monday. She'd made a reservation for him, too, and gave him the flight number so he could call and buy his ticket. Thom had thanked her and said he would call, but of course he hadn't. The agent, Abby had remarked, glancing off, had said the flights were filling up quickly, since people were returning home after the holidays, so of course Thom was procrastinating with the idea that no seat would be available. Or so he imagined, for he didn't understand his own inertia. Actually, he did want to return with Abby, make amends, see his mother; now that they'd talked on the phone, their reunion no longer loomed as such an ordeal. Yes, he told himself, he wanted to go back. But still he had not bought the ticket.

Watching Abby fly off without him held no appeal, either. He would drive home from the airport alone, and his normal routine would resume, his life continuing except his best friend would not be here. This nearly intolerable idea darkened his mind on these already dark and insomniac nights.

One good thing: his new boyfriend from Athens, whom Thom had all but written off, had started phoning again. The fall semester was over for him, and he apologized profusely for being "dilatory," as he put it—he'd had papers to write, he was student-teaching; he knew these were just excuses, but he'd really like to see more of Thom during the holiday break. Would that be all right? he'd asked. And Thom said, yes, that would be all right.

The next Saturday, he and Chip shopped all day at Lenox Square. Since they'd both been so busy the past few weeks they hadn't given a thought to Christmas. Since Thom planned to shop mostly for Abby, he'd felt relieved that she had other plans. In recent days, she often had other plans, a fact that intrigued and perplexed him. She'd begun calling up old friends from high school and having dinner out, as she put it, "with the girls," though her reports of these evenings, when Thom quizzed her the next day, were oddly vague.

"We just went out for dinner and then a movie…"

"Which restaurant?" Thom asked.

"Oh, that place up on Peachtree, I can't remember the name…"

Thom laughed. "There are dozens of places 'up on Peachtree,'" he said. "Half the restaurants in Atlanta are 'up on Peachtree.' And which movie?"

"Oh, I can't remember the title, some silly comedy Amber wanted to see, one of those movies you forget the minute you leave the theater…"

The next evening, he'd come home and find her dressed in one of her familiar outfits, her hair and makeup carefully done; she'd started painting her nails, too, which she hadn't done even back in high school.

"Wow, jungle red," he said, laughing.

"What?"

"Your nail polish, is that new?"

"Oh, I guess so, it matches the lipstick…"

Evidently she'd bought new perfume, too, a heady, almost cloying scent that didn't seem quite like Abby. After they chatted for a while, Abby would grab the keys to her newly rented car—an extravagance that seemed unlike her, he'd thought, but she'd insisted on getting it—and would hurry out the front door.

"Shall I wait up?" he called after her, with an ironic smile, but Abby left the cloud of her perfume for a reply.

He and Chip spent hours at Lenox Square. Chip shopped for his large, extended family, which included many nephews and nieces; tomorrow he was leaving to spend Christmas down in Albany. Thom had snooped in Abby's closet the night before to find out her sizes, deciding that more than anything his sister needed clothes. These past few weeks she'd been recycling the same four or five outfits, and when she'd decided to prolong her stay and Thom had suggested that Lucille could ship more of her clothes down, she'd laughed. "Except for some jeans and a tired old bathrobe, what I've been wearing is it." So he bought a diamond-patterned silver and blue sweater at Neiman-Marcus, and in Rich's he found an ice-blue silk blouse to go with the sweater. He chose a few more casual blouses and, aided by young salesgirl who had begun flirting with him when she learned he was shopping for his sister, he bought some wool slacks that contrasted with the blouses, and a couple of scarves, and some pieces of costume jewelry. When he saw the total—more than $600—he felt a little faint, but he handed over the charge card without hesitation.

"You and your sister must be close," Chip said, as they reentered the mall. His tone was almost reverent. Chip had spent less than twenty dollars apiece on his eight or nine gifts.

"This year, we are," Thom said. "This year is kind of special."

Only a few days later, on the twenty-fourth, as he and Abby were getting the condo ready for his cocktail party, did the idea occur to him that he should have bought something for his mother. Abby, who stood near the fireplace decorating the six-foot Douglas fir Thom had gotten around to buying yesterday, said casually that she'd Fed-Exed a package to Lucille a few days earlier. In the dining nook, arranging stacks of plates and napkins, Thom went pale and stopped his work; he took a deep breath. Mitzi and Chloe, who had been troubling Abby's ankles as she circled the tree, had followed Thom over here; the clink of silverware always attracted them. Every few seconds Chloe gave a soft, interrogative whimper.

"I guess I should have, too," he said, uncertainly.

Abby looked over. "Oh, I didn't mean that," she said. "I know the two of you haven't…well, I don't think she'd bought a gift for you. I mean, the two of you haven't settled anything."

"I know," Thom said guiltily. "But that might have been a start." He joined her next to the tree, reaching into the battered Macy's shopping bag full of ornaments he'd hauled out of his storage bin down in the basement. He added, with the same casualness Abby had affected, "Have you spoken to her lately?"

"Not in a while," Abby said.

Then what were all the phone calls she kept scurrying into his room to make, closing the door behind her?

"Really?" Thom said.

"The last time we talked, I did ask her to ship some things down— some shoes and gloves, a few other things I was tired of doing without. We had kind of an argument over that."

Thom strained to imagine this. His sister, "arguing."

"Guess I'm really a persona non grata now," Thom said. "On top of everything, I've lured you down here and kept you all to myself."

Abby stared. "It wasn't that. She's angrier at me, I think, than she ever was at you."

She'd lifted one of the angel ornaments out of the tree, a dark-tressed figurine swathed in white, blowing a tiny trumpet. A few years ago, an ephemeral boyfriend Thom happened to be dating around Christmas had given him the ornament, saying with a twinkling smile that it reminded him of Thom. Abby's hand paused at several branches and finally hung the angel just beneath the treetop ornament they'd bought at Lenox, an enormous gold star that Thom, sock-footed on a kitchen chair, had put there the night before.

Abby said, "Sometimes I think she knows me better than—than I know myself."

Alarmed, Thom saw that her eyes had filled, her lower lip starting to quiver. What on earth was she talking about? He was still wondering how to reply when the doorbell rang.

Mitzi and Chloe shifted into attack mode, barking hysterically as they stampeded toward the door.

Thom glanced at his watch: quarter till six. He'd asked Connie to bring Warren and Pace around six o'clock, an hour before the other guests were due. Whenever Thom gave a party he liked a few close friends to arrive early so they'd have a chance to talk. Connie, for all his habitual lateness, was seldom late for parties.

"Listen, I made that reservation," he told Abby. He would call the airlines first thing in the morning. "As for Mom, I'll stress that none of this is your fault. Please don't worry, honey. I'll explain everything."

Abby touched at her eyes with the fingertips of both hands. "You probably should," she said, "but I don't think I want to."

"Want to…?"

"I don't think I want to go back, at all."

Too shocked to respond, Thom merely stared. After the bell rang a second time, inspiring a new volley of ear-piercing yelps from the dogs, the unlocked door swung open and Connie stepped inside, shivering, straight-armed with gift-wrapped packages stacked to his chin. Warren and Pace followed close behind. As usual, Mitzi and Chloe swirled minnow-like among the perplexed human legs, almost bringing down Warren as he quick-stepped to avoid Mitzi; the others laughed.

"The dachshund trot!" Connie cried. "I'd think you'd have learned it by now, Warren."

With the swish of one hip Connie slammed the door, fanning a blast of frigid air through the room. He dropped the packages onto the coffee table, then stooped to greet the dogs.

"My little precious babies, yes they are, all ready for Santa Claus to come, yes they are, *yes they are,*" he cooed.

He'd been drinking, Thom thought. He watched with mingled pleasure and alarm as Connie punctuated the dogs' excited yips with air kisses, rubbing his gloved hands along the quivering lengths of their bodies as they competed, leaping and cavorting, to lick his face.

Awkwardly, the others stood gazing down at this display. When the silence finally registered Connie glanced up, with a tilted smirk.

"Hey there, you two! Merry Christmas and all that!"

"Yeah, Merry Christmas!" Warren said happily. His boyish cheeks were flushed from the cold, or perhaps he'd been drinking, too; he seemed unusually cheerful.

"Ditto!" Pace grinned.

So their celebration began, as Connie chattered to Abby about the tree, saying how pretty it was, and they all traded the wry remarks people made this time of year about the traffic, the weather, how impossible it was to get everything done. Beneath their talk, which was forgettable enough, there was a heightened excitement, a childlike anticipation, that even Carter's death and their array of other problems had not repressed. Thom had gone back to the kitchen to uncork the first bottle of champagne, chiding himself. This was Christmas, after all, so why shouldn't everyone feel cheerful, or at least behave as if they did? They deserved a little reprieve, didn't they?

I don't think I want to go back, at all.

Abby's extraordinary confession puzzled and excited him, and of course tomorrow they would talk, and plan, and figure out everything—or so Thom told himself, halfway through the second glass of Perrier-Jouët. Abby's mood had changed as well, her delicate cheekbones flushed pink, her eyes bright with laughter. For a while they stood around the tree, drinking and sampling the hors d'oeuvres ordered from An Affair to Remember (what a rip-off, he thought, but 'twas the season), and then they lounged around the living room, laughing as the dogs jumped from chair to sofa, lap to lap. Eventually they ended up in the kitchen, as party guests must, waiting idly for the others to arrive and watching as Thom heated a new batch of hors d'oeuvres and opened another bottle of champagne. They debated whether they should exchange gifts as soon as their cocktail guests departed and then venture out for dinner, or should they leave for dinner immediately—not that they'd begun the arduous process of selecting the restaurant—and open gifts as the *pièce de résistance* (as Connie exclaimed, his French pronunciation comically exaggerated) of the evening?

They couldn't decide; they considered one plan, then someone suggested another; and as they talked Mitzi and Chloe's toenails clicked along the kitchen tiles in frantic rhythms, eager for the warming focaccia and Cajun chicken wings. A few minutes later, with nothing decided, they returned to the living room to sample more appetizers and down another flute of champagne.

Thom stood near the fireplace, which he'd stoked for the third or fourth time, and smiled down at Abby, who sat slumped in the middle of the sofa—jammed between Connie on one side, Pace and Warren on the other—holding her empty glass cocked at a strange angle.

Thom laughed. "You look like a corrupt sorority girl."

Abby said, "Hah. Is there any other kind?"

Pace narrowed his eyes in a villainous leer. "Yeah, ready to give the drunken frat boys a good time."

"Pace, you bitch!" Connie cried, delighted. "That's a case of projection if I ever heard one!"

"Where *are* those drunken frat boys when we need them?" Warren asked, smiling.

Connie cleared his throat. "OK, enough of this palaver. Let's make a toast," he said.

Abby lifted her glass. "To Christmases past, and passing, and to come," she announced.

"Honey, that's *so* poetic," Connie said, in a marveling voice. He thrust his own glass into the air, sloshing a few drops onto the carpet. "And to our friends, the ones we have and the ones we've lost."

A brief silence. Thom felt a warm sheen of moisture stinging his eyes. At last year's Christmas party, of course, Carter had been with them.

"That's it—to friendship," Pace said.

"Absolutely," said Warren.

They leaned forward, clinking glasses. Thom couldn't quite meet the others' eyes; he was afraid he might get silly, make a fool of himself. He edged closer to the fire; relished its warmth caressing his back, his legs. He sipped the champagne, keeping his eyes cast down, holding inside his chest a cauldron of emotion, a swirling of intense grief, intenser joy.

I don't think I want to go back, at all.

And neither did he.

Chapter 5 .....

"Is this love?" she kept asking.

She'd decided it had little to do with sex. The sex was wonderful, he was the most efficient and considerate of lovers, yet her emotions rose above the physical snarls of their lovemaking in the way the soul—as the nuns at St. Jude's had insisted—transcended the body after death.

During the act itself she could not, did not want to "think" at all. But in the moments before their passion gathered force and especially during the long moony afterglow as they traced fingertip lines along an arm or rib cage, or down a still trembling, heated thigh, her awareness hovered above his carved rosewood four-poster, an antique inherited from his grand-mother, gazing down upon them with the questions *Is it? Could it be? After so many years? When she had resigned herself even before Graham, even before she and her mother had moved to Philadelphia, to the role of Good Daughter, if not the cliché of Good Daughter as Dried-up Catholic Spinster, rosary beads melding to her chilled bony fingers?* Those questions and more, so many more, she could scarcely acknowledge, much less answer.

A few mornings after they'd met at Pace's party, he had telephoned, the pleasantly stilted British accent recognizable at once, though not the low-ered, chastened voice.

"Abby, *can* you forgive me?"

It was ten-thirty in the morning; Thom had left for work an hour before; she was alone in the condo, feeling unmoored and disconsolate, no longer quite sure what she was doing in Atlanta. She hadn't known how to answer Philip's question. He had humiliated her, yes, but she considered that her own fault. She'd been credulous, naive. She'd been a little drunk. Why should she have trusted an impossibly handsome stranger dressed in black, a man who had flattered her absurdly? Lying sleepless that night she had punished herself with masochistic notions: a straight man at a gay party, what options did he have? At another party, one populated with beautiful, laughing women, he'd never have glanced her way. She'd been a moment's whim, a way of passing the time. She'd been presentable, but not beautiful. She hadn't been laughing.

"Of course," she breathed into the phone, aware that her heart was racing. "Of course, but where did you go...?"

His tone changed, his vast relief audible in his abrupt exhalation of breath and sudden laugh. She heard herself laugh, too, as though listening to some other woman.

Together for several hours each afternoon, they talked with the harassed urgency of lovers from whom everything is about to be snatched away. They went everywhere, the Botanical Gardens and the High Museum and the symphony, to Lenox Square and Phipps Plaza and the Galleria where they didn't "shop," exactly, but simply wandered through the vast open spaces thronged with holiday crowds. Holding hands. Letting the window displays and the horde of shoppers blur to a brightly hued insignificance. They seldom released their attention, even their vision, past one another. They walked and talked in a sphere of imperturbable quiet where they focused on each other's words and, as though some invisible glass shield had encircled them, stayed deaf to everything else.

"I can't understand what you're telling me," he said, frowning, as they sat in a little coffee shop near the museum. "How can you not have boyfriends back home? Surely they must queue up outside your door."

She laughed a girlish, disbelieving laugh, the one she had not used since high school. Something about his gentle British puzzlement, the quizzical frowns he was always giving her, amused her, for matinee-idol handsome as he was, nonetheless he seemed uncertain, stymied by his boyish, romantic notions. Such as the foolish idea that she outranked him in physical beauty, which had become almost a refrain. He talked constantly of her skin, her hair; he noticed the molding of her ears, her throat, her collarbone; when they were alone, he bent to kiss each item in his catalogue of marvels, and it was her wisdom at such moments to fall silent and no longer feel tempted to laugh but instead to allow this elegant, rather eccentric man to feel whatever he wanted to feel, give what he wanted to give.

In public she ridiculed him, gently. "Yes, each man takes a ticket," she said. "We ask them to please not clog the sidewalks."

"No, I'm serious," he said, fixing her with his intent, black-eyed stare. His eyes were his most striking feature: thickly lashed, so dark as to seem all pupil. At such times, he refused to laugh. After a moment she would grow uncomfortable and change the subject.

All the while, she clung fast to her sense of irony: an alternate vision of herself as Miss Abigail Sadler the veteran schoolmarm presided over their clandestine meetings, their hushed conversations, even their frantic lovemaking in that elaborately carved bed in his oversized house in Druid Hills. A month from now, she supposed, her soul would reenter Miss Sadler's body and recall this affair with the same sense of inconsequence and wry disbelief one felt after watching an intensely romantic film. All that passion, all those emotions, had happened to someone else.

Even as she lay next to Philip caressing his sleek, well-muscled thigh, her fingers tracing the etched lines along his flat stomach and the firm curve of his breastbone, she would allow Miss Sadler a little smirk at such frank enjoyment of this man's body, his physical near-perfection. Philip's skin—olive-pale and unblemished, smoother and silkier than her own yet firm to the touch, undeniably male in its layered girding of muscle— brought a literal itch to the ends of her fingers, each caress inspiring another as she explored his body in a way she'd never dreamed of touching a man before. He would lie still for these appreciative caresses, his eyes closed, an artwork passively accepting the admirer's tribute, but gradually his uncircumcised penis (a novelty she found pleasing: very pleasing) stiffened as her caresses grew bolder, franker, and at some point he would seize her hand abruptly and bring it to his lips, the signal that their lovemaking would begin in earnest. He kept his eyes closed, the lids just perceptibly fluttering, yet through all this Abby allowed Miss Sadler to hover somewhere above them, an eyebrow quirked in condescending bemusement, her ghostly, faintly mocking laughter filling the room. Abby's enjoyment of their passion was oddly enhanced by this flouting of Miss Sadler's arch disapproval, and by the thought of the ancient nuns from grade school who now lay smirking in their graves. She could not relinquish this ironic vision of their affair, keeping it clearly focused in her mind's eye even as her body surrendered to the sweat and toil of a passion she'd never believed might be hers.

During the weeks between their first meeting and Christmas, they met every few days for lunch at one of the restaurants Philip favored: settling into a darkened booth at the rear of Houston's, where he would reach across the table to stroke her hand, sometimes gently, sometimes a bit harder than she liked; or at small, out-of-the-way places in Brookhaven or Decatur, restaurants Abby had never visited before. One day she'd said, with a thoughtless laugh, "My brother and his friends wouldn't be caught dead in here" (they were in a seafood place, a chain restaurant whose menu featured special meals for children), and though Philip gave a tic-like smile he was clearly hurt.

"Sorry if you don't like it," he said, snapping open his menu.

This time it was Abby who reached across the table; she gave his hand a brief squeeze.

"No, I do like it," she said, truthfully. "It's just that some of Thom's friends—like Connie, for instance—"

"Oh, of course," Philip said shortly, "this place doesn't have a bar."

He'd given Abby a quick amused glance over his menu, and they broke into laughter.

She'd learned soon enough to avoid mentioning Thom and his friends, since her lover seemed jealous over the time Abby spent with them. One Saturday she'd declined to see Philip because Thom had asked her to lunch with Pace, who had a new boyfriend he wanted Abby and Thom to meet. There had been a long pause over the phone line. Then Philip released his breath, an exasperated sigh.

"Well, blood is thicker, etcetera," he said. She waited but he said nothing more.

"How about Monday? At lunchtime?" she had asked, troubled by his sudden change of mood.

"I hope so," Philip said. And hung up.

Nor did Philip want anyone, including her brother, to know that he and Abby had started…dating, was that the correct term? For the first few days, Abby herself had enjoyed the secret, not quite examining her own motive in sneaking off to meet Philip, even when this involved blatantly lying to Thom. Somehow she shared Philip's inclination, at least for now, to keep their relationship to themselves. Their passion was so raw, so new; it was purely *theirs*. A few days ago she couldn't have imagined lying so profusely to her brother, the one person she'd grown up trusting more than any other. Of course, she hadn't really phoned Amber or her other high school friends. She marveled at her own daring, putting forth such a preposterous idea. What if Thom should run into Amber, by chance? How would Abby explain the lie to him? She couldn't quite explain it to herself.

Inevitably, though, she tried. It was her job, explaining things, and not only in the classroom. Growing up, Abby had been the conduit between her brother and their parents, especially Lucille, serving habitually as the smoother of ruffled feathers, bearer of messages, interpreter and apologist. She hadn't minded serving as peacemaker, really, for some quality of hers reassured other people ("Your company is so soothing," Graham had told her, perhaps the only thing he'd said that had genuinely touched her) and somehow calmed their fears, softened their emotional rough edges. Back at school, lonely or bewildered students would sidle into Miss Sadler's office for tearful conferences about family problems, romantic unhappiness, various other teenage miseries. Among her colleagues Abby was known as one who refused to play politics or be drawn into factions, treating her friends and people she disliked with equal tact and fair-mindedness. And she told herself she didn't mind. In the argot of the times, she liked herself. She reflected that against the odds, she had grown up more or less successfully, and there was satisfaction in that.

Only at home with her mother had she come to chafe inside her role as Miss Sadler, the levelheaded schoolmarm whose ethics were as impeccable as the high-necked white blouses she often wore to teach her classes. She had grown tired of gently correcting the exaggerated stories that her mother, for no particular reason, conveyed to other people—especially family members to whom Abby found herself speaking often on the phone, putting out little fires her mother had started. Even when she and her mother were alone, she served as Lucille's buffer of common sense, her reality principle, her foil. Not long before Abby sent him packing, poor Graham Northwood had commented on how honest and straightforward she was, and how much that attracted him. He'd encountered a number of "flighty" girls in the past, he'd said somberly, unaware that while the stolid Abigail Sadler sat there listening sympathetically another woman, the Abby he'd never known, had already taken flight.

So she shouldn't have been surprised at the pleasurable abandon with which she hurried off, these past few days, in her rented bright-red Altima, which she drove much faster than Miss Sadler drove the clunky, dented Buick she'd bought straight off a used car lot in South Philly. Impulsively, she'd rented the car one day, asking Philip to drop her at the rental agency instead of taking her home. She'd grown tired of depending on other people—her brother, her lover—to get around town. Thom had been appalled when she rented the car, insisting it was a needless expense, he'd take her anywhere, anytime, but she'd laughed at him. "We aren't an old married couple, you know," she said. This newly discovered kernel of stubbornness, the need to preserve her own secrets, prevailed over her conscience and common sense, the twin beacons which, like dependable headlights, had guided Abby's course through her adult life.

Perhaps there was something deeper than mere stubbornness. One day, driving down Ponce de Leon Avenue toward one of her lunches with Philip, swift and easy as a serpent's whisper a single word glided into her hearing. *Payback.* She'd allowed herself no particular resentment toward her brother during their estrangement yet at once she felt a shimmer of assent even as Miss Sadler dismissed the notion with a curt shake of her head. *But yes. Payback.* Her palms sweating, Abby stopped for a red light at Highland Avenue, peering around at the other cars with the furtive quickness of a criminal who feared she might be recognized. No one glanced her way. She sat flexing her fingers on the wheel until she heard a horn's toot and, imagining Thom's grinning face, glanced fearfully into the rearview mirror. Of course, the driver was a stranger, his impatient hand raised sideways. The light had flashed green.

Each day she sped along in her new-smelling red car, her pulse racing as she followed her lover's carefully dictated directions to this or that restaurant. Instinctively, she refused to come directly to his house, just as she'd ignored his complaint that he should pick her up, that she needn't drive at all. She liked the feeling of autonomy and daring, hurrying to meet her lover. She slid into her seat across from him with the awareness that no one on earth knew where she was at that moment, or with whom. She kept telling herself that she would tell Thom, in a few days; she expected a fair amount of ribbing but she hoped he would approve. He and Philip were friendly acquaintances, after all, weren't they? There was no logical reason not to tell him. What disturbed her was Philip's suspicion, his jealousy; and the impression he gave, once or twice, that he could read her thoughts.

"You haven't told anyone, have you?" he said in a level, grim voice.

On that day, they'd bought a deli lunch and were sitting in the open-air courtyard at Ansley Mall. After a cool, cloudy morning the day had turned brilliantly sunny, almost unpleasantly warm for mid-December. It had been Abby's idea to meet here, and it had taken some persuading. At first, she hadn't recognized her lover where he'd been sitting by himself with a cup of Caribou's coffee, pawing through a newspaper. Whereas normally Philip favored dark, dressy clothes—shirts of black silk or thick

cotton, perfectly creased dark slacks, an expensive-looking charcoal over-
coat that might have been cashmere—today he'd surprised her by wearing
sneakers and blue jeans, and a rumpled white oxford-cloth shirt under a
nylon windbreaker. Seeing him, Abby had thought immediately they were
clothes her brother might wear, making Philip look younger than his age;
he might have passed for a college student.

Thom had said he'd be showing houses to some out-of-town clients all
day in the Gwinnett County suburbs, but what if he should appear unexpectedly, hurrying down the sidewalk in his long, loping strides? The
Ansley area was his stomping ground, after all; she'd felt a bit reckless,
insisting that Philip meet her here. After they'd bought their food and
found a table, Philip rushed through the meal, keeping his head lowered,
muttering that he felt "on display" among the ceaseless stream of shoppers
out strolling in this unseasonable weather. When she put down her half-
eaten sandwich and said wearily, "All right, then, let's go," he stood at once.
They dropped their leftovers in a trash barrel and joined the other shoppers crisscrossing the sunlit mall.

That's when he'd asked his question, apropos of nothing. And it was
true: she'd been thinking exactly that.

"Have you?" Philip repeated. "Have you told anyone?"

"No," she said slowly, deliberately not glancing at Philip. She didn't
want to see the expression on his face, that bereft unhappy look. Whenever
Philip became jealous or momentarily displeased, his eyes would narrow,
retreating beneath the unbroken dark line of his brow. His lips tightened,
stubbornly; the handsome olive gloss of his skin vanished, mirage-like,
leaving his face a mottled, ashen gray. "No, but in fact I was planning...I
was thinking of having you over, next week. Thom is planning a get-
together on Christmas Eve, and I thought—"

"As I mentioned before, I don't celebrate Christmas," Philip said
shortly. He spat the words out one side of his mouth. His gait had quickened so that Abby struggled to keep up with him. Though they'd been
headed toward Pier One—she needed to get something to send her Aunt
Millicent—Philip passed by the entrance and headed for the parking lot.

He paused at the curb. "Maybe you could shop for your aunt later—
would you mind?"

"No, of course not." She'd assumed that when they got into Philip's
black Jaguar they'd return to his house, his upstairs bedroom with its tall
evergreen-shaded windows—so far, that was how they concluded each of
their afternoons together. Each day, she relished the muted excitement of

their drive back to that old, ramshackle house on Clifton Road. She loved the twists and turns along Clifton—a classic example of Atlanta's nonsensical street patterns—almost as if the road, as they snaked along, mimicked her unpredictable, swiftly changing emotions since the night she met Philip. But now she'd annoyed him and she imagined, for the first time, how bereft she might feel if her lover, angry and disgusted, decided not to drive her there. That would mean their intense but peculiar affair was over. Her pulse raced, thinking this. Some wayward, unnamed emotion caught in her throat, fluttering.

She said: "I don't have to tell him right now. If you'd rather I didn't."

They'd reached the car, and instead of getting inside Philip leaned against the driver's door, pulling her close. He bent down, nuzzled one side of her face.

"I want everything to be just ours, at least for a while," he whispered. "Let's keep it this way another week or two, all right? Until after the holidays, maybe. Then we can—" He'd paused, perhaps remembering that Abby would return to Philadelphia just after New Year's. "But not now," he said.

Her answer was simple: "All right. That's fine."

She told herself they'd been thinking along parallel lines, and that *she* might feel jealous in his position. If he had a sister, for instance, with whom he lived and to whom he seemed close, confiding, she'd worry that the sister might judge her—might find her not good enough, as Abby supposed she might consider Thom's new friend Chip, once she met him, not good enough for her irreplaceable Thom.

Yes, she understood her lover's need for privacy, his near paranoia; she told herself she understood.

So they got into the car and returned to Philip's where he made love to her with a silent, almost grim efficiency, to which her body responded helplessly, wave after wave of shuddering pleasure, a new one beginning even before the previous one had ended. His skill astonished her: there was none of the sweaty groping she'd endured with the handful of men she'd dated in her twenties, or more recently with Graham Northwood, who fumbled his way through elaborate precautions (in addition to donning two condoms, made of two different materials, he daubed himself with various gels and lubricants, which had the benefit at least of masking her own dryness) before venturing into their three or four minutes of actual intercourse, which often ended with a husky-voiced "Oof—sorry, I couldn't hold back" muttered into her hair.

Philip was practiced and confident and graceful. She scarcely noticed when his hand slipped away quietly to extract the tiny packet from the top drawer of his bedside table, then with the same hand—distracting her with the other—unwrapping and donning the condom and entering her in one seamless, luxurious shifting of their limbs. After just a few of his deft slow lunges, she was coming the first time, her bent legs tensed with expectation against his smoothly muscled hips. He whispered something into her hair, he released his warm breath in another of his deep lovely moans against her throat, and already another hot shuddering wave had formed as the core of her being opened to him, halved by him, welcoming his quicker, faster lunges as he, too, neared climax, and by the time he came she was there again, for the third time—or was it the fifth. Afterward he lay quiet, as always, not simply rolling off like other men she had known but lingering with his parted lips against her breast that was flushed and a little sore from the friction of his skin against hers. He said nothing for several long minutes but kept his cheek pressed along her pale, cooling flesh. Then they rose silently and dressed, interrupting the procedure every few moments for a brief, wordless hug as he pulled her against him, decisively, then released her. In her dazed abandon she finished dressing, and he delivered her back to her car, and she drove home in her usual erotic befuddlement, aware that she'd angered him earlier that afternoon, a tiny lifetime ago, but not quite certain what the problem had been—or not quite caring.

It occurred to Abby that despite her few earlier affairs and her several months of dry, antiseptic couplings with Graham Northwood, she'd remained a virgin until she met Philip. The question kept pestering her awareness: *Is this love?* And one day she understood, suddenly but without regret, that Miss Sadler had abandoned her watch from that cleared-out mental space Abby had preserved so carefully in the first days of their affair. Abigail Sadler with her high-necked blouse and her arched, ironic brow—she was gone.

"Abby, *can* you forgive me?" Philip had asked, that first time he'd phoned Abby.

They'd been giddy, almost childlike with relief; with an electric sense of anticipation, excitement.

"Of course, but where did you go...?"

Of course, as she recollected later, the question had gone unanswered.

• • •

Every few days Abby called her mother, once or twice with her face still flushed from the passion, or was it the shame, of her hours with Philip. She sat on the side of Thom's bed, which was always neatly made (just for her?—in high school, he hadn't been particularly tidy) and let her eyes roam across the now-familiar objects in her brother's room. The TV stand in one corner, with its stacks of videotapes on a lower shelf. The cherry-wood dresser with its jewelry box of jade-colored stone (a long-ago gift from Lucille) and a vase of tiny purple dried flowers. There were few personal touches: some childhood photos on his bureau along with a framed snapshot of grinning, raffishly handsome Carter; Abby's own framed photo on the night table, at which she cast only the briefest glance.

"Have you changed your mind about coming home for Christmas?" her mother asked. The question had become a refrain, beginning each of their conversations.

"Mom, I don't think so. You know that friend of Thom's we mentioned, the one who was ill? Thom's best friend, actually. He died a few days ago, and I don't think Thom is in the mood for a trip right now."

"His best…friend?" her mother said, awkwardly.

"Yes, a friend," Abby said, wishing she hadn't mentioned Carter. This wasn't the time to start explicating Thom's relationships for their mother. "He lived here in the same complex. They've been buddies for years."

"Oh, buddies," Lucille said, relieved. "Goodness. Tell him I'm sorry to hear it—I mean, don't tell him I said to tell him, it's just that I *am* sorry to hear it, so if you want to—I'm just telling *you* that I'm sorry, but if you—"

Her mother broke off, perplexed.

"But I wondered, Mom, would you mind sending me some things?" She read off the mental list she'd composed, thinking it was modest enough: a few pieces of jewelry she missed, some jeans and sweaters. And a few of her summer clothes, she added quickly. Her shorts, her short-sleeve tops.

"But why—"

"I'm sick of doing laundry every couple of days," Abby laughed, trying to keep it light. "*Please*, Mom, will you? And I'm sure the mail has been piling up, just dump all that in the box, too, will you? I gave you Thom's address last week, do you still have it?"

A long pause. "Is it *that* warm down there, honey? That you need your summer things?"

Abby said quickly, "Well, I was thinking—Thom and a couple of his friends are planning a trip, right after Christmas. You know, to get away? I was thinking of joining them."

"A trip? A trip where?"

"Um, to Florida. Down to Key West, I think."

"OK, fine," her mother snapped. "You two have a great time down there sunning yourselves, while I explain everything to your aunt and cousins and try to entertain them by myself. I'll finish all the shopping, I'll try to find someone to shovel the snow out of the driveway, I'll do everything. You kids have fun and send me a postcard, all right?"

To Abby's great shock, her mother hung up.

Her mother had never hung up on her before. In fact, no one had hung up on her before. Hang up on Abby Sadler? Why would they?

She began to cry. Her insides ached, and she drew one arm across her abdomen as though the pain, so massive and somehow old, even ancient, were merely physical. Ancient, yes, but she'd never allowed herself to feel whatever it was that now welled inside her like a pooling of blood. A hemorrhage. Tears snaked along her cheeks, and she wiped them with two flat palms, and instantly more tears took their place.

That's when she knew: she would make another phone call, too. It was time.

During the last days before Christmas, she recalled Philip's insistence they not exchange gifts—for he truly despised the holiday, he repeated, not only for the usual reasons of disliking its near-hysterical commercialism but because he despised Christianity itself. Like her, he'd been brought up Catholic, even more of a minority in his "boxed-up London suburb," as he called it, than in Atlanta. But the catechism was the same, he said, the nuns and priests were the same, and he'd come away with the same seething resentment toward Catholic orthodoxy and authoritarianism that most intelligent, imaginative people of his generation had felt. He complained that most of his friends went along with the gift giving and party-going even though they'd long ago jettisoned any pretense of belief, but he couldn't stomach any of it. Checking Abby's reaction, he looked almost sheepish.

"I hope you don't mind," he said. "I do want to get you something, a piece of jewelry, maybe…. How about your birthday? When is that?"

"In August," she'd said, smiling. He looked pensive.

"Perhaps for New Year's, then. We'll celebrate the start of our first year together."

"All right," she said.

There had been a long pause. He'd given her an earnest pained stare. "But don't buy me anything, promise?" he said. "I'm uncomfortable with gifts, somehow."

She was uncomfortable with the request, but she didn't care to argue. "All right," she said.

Yet on the morning of the twenty-second, she gave Mitzi and Chloe their bacon-flavored treats (what Thom called their "guilt cookies," doled out whenever he was about to leave them alone) and slipped out the front door and drove to an expensive jewelry store in Buckhead, Maier & Berkele, where she bought Philip an elegant Rolex watch. It was one of the less expensive Rolexes but nonetheless far more than she'd ever spent on a gift for anyone. More, in fact, than she earned in an entire month. As she emerged from the store with the gift-wrapped box in her hand, her face burned with her own daring, an eerie scalp-tingling excitement she'd never felt before. Within an hour she'd come to her senses: she imagined the moment when she presented the watch to him, saw the clouded look in his eyes and his pale, cemented lips, and knew it was impossible. Somehow she'd had to buy the watch, but she knew better than to give it to Philip. So she put the tiny silver-wrapped package in the glove compartment of the Altima, promising herself she would return it the following day. Was there anything more foolish than giving an unwanted gift? Her face burned and burned.

During that same week, Abby began mentioning to Philip that she might move back to Atlanta. She'd voiced the idea several times, at first tentatively, then with more conviction. She'd always had the fantasy of coming back to Emory, she said, and getting her doctorate. She was tired of teaching *Jane Eyre* to silly high school girls. She didn't really care for Philadelphia, she told him—subtly monitoring the look on his face, the light in his eyes—and she probably shouldn't be living with her mother. Getting away, staying here with Thom for the past few weeks, had made her realize that.

Yet it was such a major decision, of course. Moving to Atlanta. Changing her life.

His gaze would fall to the table, or if they were walking along he would give her hand a brief but desperate squeeze.

"I don't know what to say. I can't ask you to do that."

"I'd been thinking of it, anyway. For the past few months..."

But she was a terrible liar, so she went silent.

She hadn't told him about the argument with her mother, or that half an hour later, waiting only until she had composed herself, she'd gotten the home number of her principal at West Chester Academy and had called him and resigned. She was sorry to leave between semesters, she told him, rather than completing the year. She'd intended to return, of course, but here in Atlanta there were family problems—and there were personal problems, she added, hoping to forestall any discussion, any awkward questions. She was sorry, sorry, she said quickly, and she hoped he understood. Numbed by her own daring, her breath coming fast, she'd scarcely listened to his reply. Within two minutes the phone call was over. It was done.

"Maybe I should wait," she told Philip, "and finish out this year, at least." But then she stopped herself—they were standing on the second-floor balcony of symphony hall, at intermission, gazing at the swarm of well-dressed people down below—for she'd heard the wheedling tone in her voice, and felt herself waiting with a feminine desperation for him to say the magic words, the empowering words. Behavior she despised in other women but here she stood, craven as the worst of them, her limbs seized with an age-old paralysis and longing, her very eyesight glazed and fixed. She wanted to glance at Philip, but as in a bad dream she could not. "Never mind," she added, hastily. "It's something I have to decide on my own."

He let out his breath, relieved. "I'm pleased to hear you say that. It's exactly what I was thinking."

Back in their seats, scarcely hearing the music inside their glass shield, she sat awash in shame, her eyes burning.

It had happened too quickly, she supposed, but didn't it always happen quickly? In life, as in books? She had studied all the books, but they had not prepared her for this.

Each of their outings led to the muted excitement of their drive back to that lovely old house Philip had inherited, he'd told Abby, from his grandmother, the bequest that had brought him to Atlanta almost a decade ago.

"Tell me about her," Abby had said. "How did she come to live here?"

During their long, languorous afternoons together in Philip's bedroom, they would make love several times, slowly, luxuriously, and in between their bouts of passion, they would discuss their families, backgrounds, histories, in the seemingly haphazard but selective way in which new lovers come to know one another.

Startled, Philip made an exaggerated gesture of slapping his forehead. He laughed. Yes, he said, he'd forgotten to tell Abby that his father was an American—he'd met his mother while stationed in London during World War II. He'd brought her here to Atlanta shortly after the war (they'd been married in St. Philip's, in fact, right on Peachtree, and years later, when her son was born, his mother remembered that beautiful church, and thus she found her baby's name), but after a few years she grew homesick and "fretful," as Philip's father later told his son. So the couple had moved back to London, where Everett DeMunn went to work for his father-in-law's insurance firm, acquitting himself quite well, and where his wife was happy again among her family and friends, which in turn made Everett happy. ("My father was a somewhat uxorious fellow," Philip told Abby, with an indulgent grimace.) And there they'd lived until that night in December 1989 when both his parents had died in a head-on collision while driving home from a Boxing Day party.

Philip delivered this information in a light, almost jocular tone that left Abby uncertain of how to respond.

She began, in a tentative whisper, "I'm sorry to hear—" but he interrupted with an abrupt, barking laugh.

"I've never been sure that it wasn't my father's fault," he said. "He always claimed that after thirty years, he still couldn't get used to driving on the wrong side of the road."

Abby stayed silent. Much to her relief, Philip's defensive, almost hostile smirk had vanished, replaced by a look of dreamy reminiscence. They lay in their usual posture after lovemaking, cuddled in one corner of his overlarge but wonderfully cozy bed, shielded from the chill of this dusky high-ceilinged room by the quilt they'd drawn across their shoulders, both reclining against a bank of thick pillows. Philip began stroking her side absently as he continued with his story.

When his parents died, he'd been only twenty-one, a few months away from graduation at the University of London, and by the time he did finish school his grandmother, too, had died. Since the accident Grandma had been inconsolable, Philip whispered, for Philip's father had been her only child. Her grief was such that she hadn't been well enough to fly over for the funeral. Within months her heart had failed. Having no serious ties in England, Philip had decided with a young man's impulsiveness to sell his parents' house and move to Atlanta. He'd visited his grandmother several times as a boy, then as a teenager, and had loved Atlanta—the climate, the lovely trees and vegetation, the friendly people. So he'd started work on his MBA at Emory, and here he'd stayed.

"After a while, I saw that almost everyone in Atlanta was from somewhere else, like me," he said. "Somehow I found that appealing, along with the newness of everything, the energy."

Abby said nothing. As a native, she saw the city differently.

"So you moved in here—" she said, breaking off. She'd had the sudden thought that this might have been his grandmother's room; perhaps even this bed, this quilt, had been hers. She decided not to ask.

Philip resumed his story, as though she had not spoken.

Deciding to pursue a business degree had been difficult, he said, for he'd wanted to study acting after graduation. The freelance securities work he did—he'd gestured toward his laptop, on a cluttered table near the door—was just to pay the bills, and frankly bored him silly. In London, he'd planned to attend the Royal Academy, but then, after moving here, he'd gotten involved in Atlanta's lively theater scene, where he'd found his niche fairly easily in the annual Shakespeare Festival and in the many classic plays mounted by various small theaters around the city. He'd done Shaw, he'd done Wilde. He'd done Molière and Chekhov and Ibsen. Abby might think it odd, Philip said, his lips creased in a wry smile, but actually he preferred American roles, American playwrights—Tennessee Williams was his favorite, and he loved O'Neill, Miller, Mamet—but despite his ability to mimic a flawless American accent, the local directors seldom cast him in the parts he longed to play. A classic case of typecasting, Philip said, with a rueful laugh.

"They think of me as the local Brit, period. Ironically, the actors who grew up in the South are jealous of me. They're all dying to play Hamlet, whereas I've done all the major roles so many times I'm thoroughly sick of Shakespeare."

Abby said, "I can understand that. Growing up, I read Austen, Dickens, the Brontës. Even now I read Martin Amis or Anita Brookner—never the Americans. Believe it or not, I've never read *Gone with the Wind*," Abby said, feeling unaccountably pleased with herself.

"Abigail Sadler," he said in a severe, censorious tone, propping one arm against his naked hip—the quilt had fallen away, exposing his smooth olive skin that looked so pale, ghostly in the half-light—"and you call yourself a Southerner? Well, let's see if you recognize this: 'Sick people form such deep, *sincere* attachments.'"

The line sounded vaguely familiar, she thought, but it had the ring of the kind of Southern Gothic claptrap she couldn't abide.

"Sorry, no," she said. "Who is it?"

Philip gave a mysterious smile, his eyes narrowed. "*I'll* never tell." He moved closer, bringing his mouth to her vaguely parted lips. Her body had tensed, as always, but then relaxed as his hand caressed her side, the outside curve of her thigh. Then the inside curve, gently parting her legs. Already her breath came quickly. For another long while, she said nothing at all.

When Abby arrived home she went to her bedroom dresser and without thinking took the letter from its hiding place among her underclothes. She went into Thom's room and dialed the memorized number. Mitzi and Chloe, accustomed to her routine, had rushed ahead, yipping frantically, and had leapt onto the bed, positioning themselves so there was exactly enough room for Abby to sit between them. The manic Chloe flopped eagerly onto her side, and with her long black tail thumping the bed, she whimpered softly until Abby, shaking her head, placed the letter on her lap and rubbed the dog's soft, plump belly; on Abby's other side, the more sedate Mitzi contented herself with burying her pointed snout into the crook of Abby's arm, snuggling into the warm folds of her fluffy pink wool sweater.

"You two girls aren't spoiled, are you?" Abby asked, as she half-listened to the ringing phone.

After that embarrassing earlier attempt when she'd hung up, panicked, at the sound of Valerie Patten's voice, Abby had waited several days and then, steeling herself, had tried again. But Valerie had not answered. Nor had the machine picked up. Almost every day she'd tried again, wanting not to interpret the shrilling phone as a sign that something was wrong. If anything had happened to Marty Luttrell, after all, wouldn't the line have been disconnected? Yet each time her heart skittered as the phone rang ten times, twelve times. Why did this faceless stranger matter so much? Why couldn't she simply toss the letter away and be done with it? She hadn't really thought about what she would say if Marty himself answered the phone. *Hello, you don't know me, but I've got your suicide note here, and I just wondered if you were still alive.* But the next day she'd be back again, dialing the number, not smiling, holding the letter in her trembling hand. The telephone rang and rang.

Now it was the twenty-third of December, almost a month since that airplane flight from Philadelphia, and it seemed unlikely, Abby thought, that Valerie was still in town. Whatever had happened between her and her husband had happened, and by now Valerie had resigned herself to having lost the letter. At the moment Abby decided to give up, to throw the letter away and forget all about Valerie Patten and Marty Luttrell, there was a click on the line, and the sound of a woman's hoarse, sleepy voice.

"Yes? H-hello?"

"Valerie?" said Abby, startled. "I mean—is this Valerie Patten?"

"Y-yes. What time is it? Who's this?"

Abby glanced at her bedside clock. "It's a little after three. I'm sorry if I woke you, but—"

"Three o'clock? Good grief."

Abby recognized now the good-natured ruefulness of Valerie Patten's voice.

She apologized again, and explained to Valerie who she was. This took a minute. Laughing, Valerie admitted she'd been fast asleep and was "out of it." Finally she coughed, cleared her throat, and said, "But sure, hon. I remember you. Flying home to visit your brother, right?"

"That's right," Abby said, taking a deep breath.

There was an awkward pause, then Valerie's offhand, throaty laugh. "How on earth did you find me?"

Another breath, and Abby plunged ahead. "I have your husband's letter," she said. "You—you left it behind on the seat, so I picked it up. Remember, you'd been planning to show me the letter, before we ran into that turbulence? Anyway, when I got inside the gate, I looked around but I couldn't find you."

"Sure, I remember," Valerie said, sounding amused. "That's funny, because I saw *you*. I saw you talking to your brother and hugging him when I came out of the ladies' room. Sorry we missed each other, hon. I had no idea you were looking for me. I *did* wonder what the heck I'd done with Marty's letter."

Abby's heart raced; she felt encouraged by Valerie's pert, cheerful voice.

She said, timidly, "Then he's—he's all right? I hope you don't mind my asking, but—"

"Oh yes!" Valerie cried. "In fact, we're thinking of getting back together! I was just intending to stay a few days, you know, but it's the strangest thing...I realized I still care about the guy, I guess. I'm not getting any younger, either...but my Lord, you don't want to hear all this."

"No, it's fine. Really." Abby felt relieved, and strangely pleased. "I'll just—shall I mail the letter back to you? The return address is here on the envelope. Or would you rather I throw it away?"

"God, yes, just toss it," Valerie laughed. "I sure don't want it. It would be like saving my gallstones or something."

Abby laughed, too, though she felt eager to get off the phone. This little drama had a happy ending: Valerie and her husband would live happily ever after. She didn't need to hear any more.

But Valerie said, "So what is your phone number, Abby? We ought to get together, have lunch or something. It was so sweet of you to call me about that letter! You know, I don't really have any girlfriends here in town. What about tomorrow? Want to have lunch?"

At the same moment, both Mitzi and Chloe raised their heads and glanced to the doorway; Chloe, still on her side, gave a sharp little yip, her tail skittering lightly atop the bed. Abby had heard nothing, but it must be Thom's key in the front door.

"What was that?" Valerie asked. "Does your brother have a dog?"

"Can I call you back?" said Abby, relieved for this excuse not to give out Thom's number. "Someone's at the door."

Without quite knowing why, she didn't want to have lunch with Valerie Patten. Once they hung up, Abby would not have to think about that plane ride, or the embarrassing way she'd hidden Valerie's letter, or about the letter itself. She would throw it away and that would be that.

"Sure, Abby. I promise not to be napping, next time," she laughed.

"Goodbye, Valerie," Abby said.

"Bye, hon."

Abby waited until she heard the pleasant click, breaking their connection.

Later that evening, Abby went shopping with Thom for his Christmas Eve party. Connie and Warren were coming, and Pace had said he would try to make it; he'd been invited to several other parties. Thom had also asked some of Carter's friends, thinking they might be lonely or in need of cheering up, but he kept assuring Abby it would be a small gathering.

"I specifically said 'for cocktails,' so everyone's clear we won't be feeding them," Thom said, as they drove toward Lenox Square. "Otherwise, some people will stay all night. We'll just have a couple of drinks, exchange a few gifts, and when the others leave we'll go out for dinner somewhere with Pace and Connie and Warren. Do you think most places are open on Christmas Eve? I can't even remember what I did last year."

Their shopping would have taken less time but for Thom's habit of chatting with salespeople, clerks at the registers, grim-faced shoppers waiting in line. Abby had her old sense of pride in accompanying her handsome, likable brother, seeing how people glowed and smiled as they basked in his casual but friendly attention. Old men, teenage girls, small children—all responded to his smiling banter about the Christmas traffic, the mall crowds, the high prices of everything, ordinary conversation he managed to personalize just enough to make anyone feel singled out, pleased by the unexpected approach of this tall, brightly talkative, but easygoing man. At such moments Abby would see her brother from a stranger's perspective—his genial, angular face with its deep-set, amused blue eyes; his glossy dark hair, wet-looking as though he'd just stepped from the shower; his lanky, long-limbed build; his rumpled clothes. Handsome in a friendly, anonymous way, Thom Sadler was someone you might not notice until you felt the pleasurable warmth of his grinning, gently flattering conversation. Abby remembered that in high school one of Thom's girlfriends said laughingly he was "comfortable as an old shoe," a remark that had gratified Abby though the girl hadn't intended a compliment, exactly; underneath the laughter, there had been an edge to her voice. Now as they walked through the mall Abby supposed anyone to whom Thom had spoken must assume she was Thom's girlfriend, and once or twice Abby suppressed the odd impulse to slip her arm through her brother's. After several weeks of living together, he treated her with the same careful attentiveness he'd given to girls he dated in high school.

After they'd left the mall and were driving back down Peachtree through the gathering dusk, Abby felt mildly elated without quite knowing why. Earlier that day, she'd felt troubled at the prospect of not seeing Philip until after Christmas; he'd insisted he had no plans, and no intention of making any. Christmas was just another day to him, he'd said, and he would probably use the holiday to get some reading done, or catch a new movie. She shouldn't worry about him, he said, giving her a peck on the cheek; Abby should just have fun with her brother and not think about anything else. She'd felt hurt by this remark, but now she decided the advice was easy enough to follow, since during this shopping expedition with Thom she hadn't, in fact, given her lover a moment's thought. Or her mother. Or the job she had resigned so impulsively, abandoning her colleagues and her students, those bewildered needy adolescent girls who all adored "Miss Sadler." This morning she'd indulged in some guilty moping at the idea of her and Thom enjoying their party while Philip sat home alone, reading; and of her and Thom sipping champagne with their friends while their mother endured a dull holiday dinner at Millicent's town house. But, Abby thought, didn't everyone choose how they would spend the holiday? Lucille had made her choice, hadn't she?

Abby stared ahead at the lovely skyline of midtown Atlanta, shrouded this evening in a kind of foggy glamour, the faraway glimmering of the downtown hotels overshadowed by these soaring, stately midtown build-ings: the elegant conelike structures built in the booming '80s by Coca Cola and BellSouth, glowing eerily in their complex swathings of multi-colored wreaths and winking "stars"; the splendid obelisk of the IBM building with its crisp geometric outline of red and green lights. These opulent towers thrust skyward into the mist, basking in the homage-like illumination cast up from the hunched, shoulder-like masses of the smaller buildings below.

Abby remembered driving along the interstate with Lucille the night before they'd left for Philadelphia, those few but impossibly long years ago, and how tears had pricked her eyes at the thought *Home. This is home.* Lucille had been chatting busily, her clipped northern vowels returned in self-conscious force; she was reverting into the Yankee she'd always claimed to be. All through Thom and Abby's childhood, their mother had made the tired joke that Atlanta "might be a nice city, once they get it fin-ished." How energetically she'd decried the never-ending construction, the traffic detours, the startling blend of preserved antebellum glamour and spit-polished urban sheen you could witness along any single block of Peachtree Road. Yes, her mother allowed, Philadelphia might be gritty and glowering; you may not want to dip your little toe into the Schuylkill River, or drive into Center City after dark, or venture into South Philly at any time; but she'd insisted fervently those last few days how she couldn't wait to get back.

Abby, sitting next to her in the car, or across from her during dinner, or in the den watching television at night, had not made so much as a gri-mace of protest, even as her heart throbbed with longing that Thom might call. Surely, at the last minute, he would call and apologize and coax his mother into staying here, for they could be a family only if they lived here together, now that Daddy was gone they *had* to stay here, didn't they...? These sentimental notions had evaporated as the final slowed days of their Atlanta lives ticked past. Against Abby's will her heart had hardened. Even her mind had hardened, for she had stopped thinking about what was happening, what she was allowing to happen. And so these past few years Abby, too, had chosen how to spend her holidays, and the long stretches in between, inhabiting her life as a kind of ideal tenant, she thought, someone who made no noise or trouble, left no impression on her surroundings. Yes, *the mere tenant of her own life,* and she forced these words through her mind slowly, as if to insist she would not forget them, not stopping to consider that if she was the tenant, then who was the owner? Self-pitying tears no longer threatened her now, but her sense of home, no less of herself, seemed as foggy and unformed as that skyline glimmering in the distance.

The next evening as they prepared for the party, she felt a moment's shock, but no real surprise, when she blurted to Thom that she'd wanted to stay here, move back here. When the doorbell rang, precluding his reply—except for the deft instinctive curl of his arm around her waist as they turned to greet Connie and the others—she knew that beneath the surface hilarity of the evening ahead she and her brother would be acclimating to a new togetherness, an alliance she had sealed with as unilateral a stroke as Thom's when he'd seceded from the Sadlers' broken, bewildered family union in the aftermath of their father's death. During the party Thom met her eyes every few minutes with a sad-looking smile, or an amused-looking frown, as the others sipped and munched and chattered all around them. Somehow Abby couldn't bear these moments and had to glance away.

Yet Thom and Abby—as Connie declared after they'd all drunk several glasses of champagne, and had resettled in the living room awaiting the seven o'clock guests—were the "perfect hosts," and despite his many invitations to other parties he could think of nowhere else he'd rather be. He added, "You really *are.* Now, I'm sure Abby did most of the work, as I've never seen this place so tidy and so nicely decorated for Christmas, but you two make a great team. I wish you'd just chuck it all and *move* here, Abby"—this was a moment when she'd glanced at Thom, then had to look away—"since it's silly for poor Thom to be all alone. And now that Carter's gone..."

"It really *is* better to live with someone," Warren said, with his genial smile. Like the others, Warren looked his best tonight, his bushy swatch of reddish-brown hair elaborately combed and parted, his face shiny as a choirboy's; even his pleated navy corduroys and wool shirt of red and green plaid looked boyish, like a set of school clothes from which the tags had just been removed. "People who live with someone tend to have a longer life expectancy, you know, than—"

"Come on, Warren, no psychobabble tonight," Connie said teasingly, but then he leaned across and pecked him on the cheek. "This is what we get for inviting a shrink," Connie told the others, rolling his eyes.

"I need one, goddamn it!" said Pace, with his affable bark of a laugh. Tonight even Pace, who normally wore what he called his "uniform"—flannel shirt, faded blue jeans, a pair of ancient, battered moccasins with thick white socks—wore a dress shirt. His mop of dark brown hair—even more copious than Warren's—was neatly brushed; his sharp-boned face with its rimless spectacles looked alert and curious, like the straight-A prep school student he'd once been. Now his chin jutted forward as he exclaimed with a pained grin, "The traffic is driving me crazy! Usually, I get out of town during Christmas, but this year it slipped up on me."

"I'm glad you stayed," Abby said, touching his forearm. She understood why everyone liked Pace so well. Despite his incessant complaining, and his overloud voice, and her own disinclination to admire a man in his forties who lived off his "investments," there was a kindliness to Pace, for all his world-weary bravado, that tugged at her sympathy. Often he snarled half-jokingly about his "goddamn stockbroker" and his "goddamn lawyers" and his "goddamn accountant, stealing me blind," and about the service he'd hired for his housework, whose employees didn't "clean worth a damn," but even during these tirades his sky-blue eyes, slightly enlarged by his thick glasses, seemed unsullied and expectant, like a small boy's.

Abby thought: Were all gay men essentially childlike, even in middle age?

"I'm sure your other friends are glad, too," she told Pace. "I heard you've gotten plenty of invitations."

Pace shrugged. "Social obligations. It's a vicious circle—I give a big party, then I get invited to three-dozen smaller parties. And they feed me dinner, some of them, so then I feel I've got to reciprocate, so I throw another big party. I think I'll move to New York, so I won't have to see any people!"

He laughed and took another swallow of champagne. As his head tilted back, his glasses became small octagons of reflected light.

"Where were *you* invited tonight?" Connie demanded of Pace. "I was asked to five other parties, but I'm staying right here!"

"Your parties are terrific, Pace," Warren said quickly. "I wish you had one every week."

"Then I'd be one of your patients, for sure!" Pace shouted.

Around seven-thirty, shortly after Thom's remark that after two flutes of champagne Abby resembled a "corrupt sorority girl," the other guests began to arrive, each exclaiming over the tree ornaments, the "almost obscene"—as Pace had observed—heaps of brightly wrapped packages underneath it, and the fireplace mantel decorated with holly and candles and braided strands of red and silver tinsel. During the next hour Thom's living room became a scene of constant commotion—shrill talk and laughter, exclamations of pleasure over small gifts (mostly bottles of wine) passed from hand to hand, and over the trays of pungent-smelling party food Thom kept bringing out from the kitchen. New arrivals called to friends across the room, waving excitedly and shouting "Happy holidays!" as, at shin level, the black-and-red blurs of Mitzi and Chloe raced among the guests, begging shamelessly for bits of food and racing off again, barking hysterically with each new ring of the doorbell.

Abby had intended to help Thom, but Connie kept hold of her elbow and involved her in conversation with the new arrivals, most of whom she remembered from the gathering after Carter died. But she couldn't recall their names or think of much to say, so she simply smiled and shook her head and took another swallow of champagne. Thom carried the food trays back and forth, and managed to dart into the room every few minutes and refill his guests' glasses; Abby had stopped after her third, her head reeling. She attributed Connie's almost obnoxious ebullience to the champagne, too, though she'd seen him consume large quantities of alcohol before without becoming quite so agitated. There had been a degree of frankness—and occasional vulgarity, too—to his incessant chattering tonight, including several jokes about Monica Lewinsky and Clinton (she gathered that Connie despised Clinton) that Abby thought especially jejune. Lockerroom jokes, sniggering double entendres lacking in Connie's usual wit and playfulness. She found herself watching him and wondering if something might be wrong. (Nor did Warren seem quite himself: he stayed close to Connie but had gotten quiet, his forehead creased in what might have been chagrin, or simple embarrassment.) Connie's aqua-blue eyes glittered as he spoke, his attention flitting from one person to another; his talk seemed oddly random, disconnected.

During a rare moment of quiet, when the others were focused on some picture-taking next to the Christmas tree, Abby leaned to Connie and whispered, smiling, "Are you feeling OK? You seem—I don't know, a little jittery?"

His eyelids fluttered, taking in this unexpected query, but he gave his theatrical smile, his cheeks flushing, and gestured broadly.

"It's the company, sweetheart, and the occasion! I always get hyped up at Christmas time…"

His attention veered off, as though Abby had not spoken.

By eight o'clock, more than a dozen guests had arrived, and the talk had gotten louder, the bursts of laughter more raucous. Although Connie downed each glass of champagne swiftly, Abby noticed the others drank at the same accelerated pace, leaving her to imagine, with a schoolteacher's anxiety, their cars weaving off drunkenly into the night. She and Connie found themselves talking to Alex and his lover, the two physicians they'd seen during lunch at Agnes & Muriel's, whom Connie had disliked so intensely, but tonight he joked and bantered happily with both of them, though allowing himself a perfunctory, offhand bit of malice.

"I thought you two would be jetting off to Rio or something!" he cried, greeting them both with air kisses.

The four of them chatted for a while, though Alex's cell phone kept beeping—"the hospital, sorry!"—and Alex, frowning, sank into the sofa and gave medical advice in his authoritative mutter, as if oblivious to the chatter and hilarity swirling around him.

Again the doorbell rang and they greeted the new arrivals, a lesbian couple with whom Connie seemed to have a close but teasing friendship.

"Patsy!" he cried, hugging a heavyset woman with short-cropped gray hair and a round, pudgy face that reminded Abby of Roger Ebert's. "Patsy, it's *you!* I should have known—I thought someone had just opened a can of tuna fish in here!"

Receiving Connie's embrace, Patsy said, "Shut up, you overdressed old queen," winking to Abby over Connie's shoulder.

Resuming his usual, elaborate courtesy, Connie presented his friends to Abby. Patsy's lover, whom Connie introduced as "Miriam—isn't she sweet? And isn't that the sweetest *name*?"—was a petite woman in a tight-fitting black leather jacket and skirt and matching knee-high boots. Despite her boyish haircut (virtually identical to Patsy's, though Miriam's darker, finer hair was more sleekly combed, and severely parted on one side) and what appeared to be flowery tendrils of a tattoo between her small breasts, Miriam was pretty in a waif-like, big-eyed way. After Connie and Abby had chatted with the two women, Connie grasped Abby's shoulders, turned her sideways and introduced her to another couple, a handsome blond man in his forties with a receding hairline and hawk-like nose, and his much younger, exotic-looking lover.

"James is an architect, and Reginald is an interior designer, though I keep telling him he could make lots more money as a model."

Reginald had slipped an arm around James's waist: "Thanks, but we enjoy working together," he said. "James has taught me so much."

"And I'll bet you've taught *him* a thing or two," Connie said, with a mischievous leer.

Abby, exchanging smiles with Reginald, saw that he was indeed spectacularly good-looking: close-cropped dark hair, enormous fawn-like brown eyes with impossibly long lashes, a strong nose and square-cut jaw that saved him from effeminacy. His skin, a glimmering-pale sienna, made Abby wonder…but what was the point in wondering, she thought, chastising herself. He was a beautiful young man, easily the most attractive man at this party: wondering about his "background" was a vestige of her Southern upbringing she hoped she had outgrown.

Connie, keeping hold of Abby's arm, chatted amiably with James and Reginald for a while, until the inevitable moment when Connie's eye wandered, and he called across the room to someone else.

Another hour had passed, and by now Abby supposed they wouldn't be going out to dinner, after all, though Thom had stopped refilling his guests' champagne flutes, and had asked here and there if anyone wanted coffee.

"*Coffee!*" Connie protested, wrinkling his nose. "What kind of scrooge are you, Thom Sadler!"

Thom gave a slight smile as he turned away. "I'm your host, not your enabler," he said.

Warren gave a melancholy laugh. "Thank you!" he called out.

Connie said, pettishly, "If you can't get blitzed on Christmas, when *can* you?"

At last came the moment she'd been awaiting. Alex and Randy deposited their empty flutes on the coffee table and approached Abby, glancing at their watches.

"Got to be going—"

"Had a lovely time—"

They'd spoken at the same moment; they laughed.

"Wait a second, I'll get Thom," Abby said. "He'll want to say goodbye."

As if the gesture were contagious, the other guests glanced at their watches, too, and there were histrionic sighs and exclamations as if they'd all lost track of time, and a few moments later Thom and Abby stood by the door as people filed out, buttoning jackets and drawing on gloves, offering last hugs and pleasantries and "Happy holidays!" while those staying behind shouted "Happy holidays!" in reply. When the door had closed and Abby, shivering, turned back into the room, she saw Pace and Warren slumped on the sofa, each with a dachshund on his lap, while Connie hovered near the fireplace with his coffee mug, looking displeased.

"What's the deal with 'Happy holidays'?" he said, with mocking emphasis on the phrase. "Why don't people say 'Merry Christmas' any more? Nobody at this party was Jewish, were they?"

Thom shrugged. "Might as well play it safe," he said. He glanced around with the successful host's smile of satisfaction; the room looked as if a friendly cyclone had blown through. "I think everybody had a good time, don't you?"

"Yes, but next time let's chat about your guest list beforehand," Connie said, with his mischievous grin. "I mean, honestly...Alex and Randy?"

"I thought I should," Thom said. "Alex called to invite Abby and me to their big New Year's Eve party. He specifically mentioned Abby, which I thought was nice, since he only met her that once."

"You're going, then?" Pace said, morosely. "That's good, there'll be *somebody* there I want to see."

Connie's face had blanched; he and Warren exchanged a sudden, communicative look. It took Abby a moment to understand that Connie and Warren hadn't been invited to the party. But Connie recovered within seconds.

"I wouldn't attend one of their pretentious soirees if you begged me," he said. "I'll curtsy for the queen, but not *those* queens."

"I guess James and Reginald won't be going, either," Warren said, his head tilted sideways as Chloe licked his earlobe.

Abby said, "Why not?"

Connie finished his coffee in a long swallow and set the cup on the mantel. "A few weeks ago," he said, "there was a little get-together at Craig Black's to start planning the Human Rights Campaign Fund dinner next spring. When someone mentioned James's name, I heard Alex bend to Randy and sort of stage-whisper, 'Oh, God. Don't tell me James and his little slave boy are on this committee.'"

Thom stared. "Alex said that? Really?"

"In case you were wondering, Abby," Connie said, fixing her with his intent, glassy stare, "Reginald is a mulatto. But isn't he gorgeous? I've never been with a black man, but I'd gladly spend a few hours with *him*."

"I doubt the reverse would be true," Warren said tartly.

Everyone laughed, Connie most of all. "Touché!" he cried. "But then everybody is crazy about Reginald. My friend Keith goes to his gym and says he's *hung.* Of course, that's no surprise, since his daddy's the black one. And I heard—"

Thom and Abby had stayed by the door, but now Thom stepped forward quickly, waving one hand as though dispelling imaginary smoke. "Connie, please don't pollute the atmosphere," he said.

Abby saw from the clench of her brother's jaw that he wasn't quite joking.

Connie rolled his eyes; he bowed magisterially to Thom. "My apologies, O Enlightened One," he said, but he gave Abby an anxious look. "You'll have to excuse me, sugar. I'm just an old Southern queen. I'm really *not* prejudiced. My cleaning lady is black, you know, and I just love her to death."

"Yes," Warren said, looking chagrined. "She gets all of Connie's best castoffs."

"Well, she *does,*" Connie protested. "What's wrong with that? She has two sons in high school, and they're thrilled to have my clothes. Some of the stuff has been worn only once or twice. You know, Abby, I could sell my things in consignment shops, but Ruby is one of those good churchgoing types. Her sons don't belong to gangs or anything. *Those* are the ones you want to reward, you know?"

"Can we please change the subject?" Thom said.

Connie waited by the fireplace, his arms crossed.

"All right, on one condition," he said, in a mock-demanding tone. "That we all have *one* more glass of champagne, before we toddle off to dinner."

Pace glanced at his watch. "Dinner? My God, I forgot about dinner!"

"It's only 10:15," Warren said. "We could go to Mick's or something."

"Or Terra Cotta," Thom said. "Their crowd should have died down by now."

"What about Tiburon Grille?" Connie said. "They've redecorated the place, you know, and the food is *fabu.*"

Abby felt how swiftly the atmosphere had changed: again they were a close group of friends, deciding where to have dinner on Christmas Eve.

Pace said, "Has anybody tried Luna Si lately? It used to be so pretentious, but I heard they have a new chef."

"Veto, veto!" Connie cried. "Luna Si is the *worst* restaurant in Atlanta, bar none! I'd rather eat at Pittypat's Porch than that place!"

They laughed. It had been years since Abby had even thought of Pittypat's Porch. Noted for its bad food and worse service, it was one of Atlanta's premier tourist traps, a Southern cliché jammed nightly with camera-toting vacationers from Kansas and Wisconsin.

"I vote with Thom," Pace said. "I've never had a bad meal at Terra Cotta."

"Fine with me," said Warren. "Abby?"

"Four gay men agreeing on the same restaurant for dinner," Thom said, smiling. "Amazing."

Abby helped Thom carry plates and glasses to the kitchen, and she was about to hurry back to her room for her coat when the doorbell rang.

Thom glanced at his watch. "Who could that be?"

Abby said, "Did one of your friends leave something behind?"

"Quick, look between the sofa cushions," Connie said gleefully. "Maybe Alex left his cell phone. We'll pretend we can't find it, then later we can drown it in the bathtub."

Warren said, smiling, "Maybe it's Santa Claus!"

But when Thom opened the front door, he and the other four—Abby most of all—stood gaping.

On Thom's cement stoop waited a petite, dark-haired woman with mascara-stained tears running down her face. She wore a stylish red wool suit, but the jacket hung askew; she held a wet-looking, much-shredded kleenex in her fist; her face wore an expression of adult embarrassment mixed with childlike uncertainty, almost an orphan's look of pleading.

"Hel-hello," she began. "I'm so sorry to disturb you, but—" Her words gave way to a new bout of tears, which she tried to daub away with the overused tissue.

Abby stepped forward. She put her arm around the woman's shoulders and coaxed her inside. Thom closed the door and joined his three staring friends while Abby, hugging the woman's narrow, trembling shoulders, made the introduction.

"Everybody, I want you to meet a friend of mine," she said. "This is Valerie Patten."

In this abrupt way the course of their evening changed: instead of leaving for Terra Cotta, Thom insisted on making them an impromptu dinner—and a delicious dinner it was—of fruit and cheese and sourdough rolls, along with the plentiful leftover hors d'oeuvres reheated in the oven.

Valerie Patten insisted she could not eat, but she did accept a glass of champagne, from which she took ladylike sips as she told them about the ruination of her Christmas Eve.

After apologizing repeatedly for foisting her troubles on them—apologies they all dismissed energetically, especially Connie, who seemed rapturously fascinated by Valerie Patten from the first moment he saw her—Valerie haltingly told them about her revived marriage to her fourth husband, Marty, and how they'd planned a "special" evening together: a sumptuous dinner at the Hedgerose Heights Inn, followed by dancing at the Biltmore Room, and then a night at the Ritz-Carlton, where Marty had booked the twenty-second-floor Presidential Suite with its breathtaking view of the city. Around six o'clock she'd returned home from some last-minute shopping; Marty was not there, so she'd gone ahead and put on the new dress she'd bought at Parisian and had gone into the living room to slip under the tree yet another gift she'd bought him, a pair of cuff links from Tiffany's. Then she'd wandered into the kitchen to pour herself a glass of wine and sipped at that while she waited. By then, it was past seven and she'd begun to worry: their dinner reservation was for eight. She'd started on her second glass of wine before she found the envelope.

Here Valerie succumbed to a fresh assault of tears, while the others made supportive, sympathetic noises. On the sofa, Abby and Warren sat on either side of Valerie (Warren was in his element, and Abby noticed how several times he had touched her hand and asked skillful, gently leading questions), while Thom and Connie listened intently, perched on dining room chairs pulled close to the sofa. Only Pace looked uncomfortable, cracking his knuckles in an armchair near the fireplace. But he listened, too, as Valerie told them what Marty's note had said: that he'd gone to the airport, that he was flying home to Minneapolis to spend Christmas with his mother, that he couldn't explain why but he felt their relationship could not work out, after all. He would call in a few days, he said. Unless she decided to leave for Philadelphia, which he would certainly understand. He hoped she didn't hate him, he said. Goodbye.

"That was the last word. Goodbye," Valerie sobbed. "Then just his name—not even 'Love.' Just…'Marty.'"

Abby wanted to criticize Marty's behavior, but this wasn't the moment for that; and Warren, who urged Valerie back to talking about how she felt, rather than about what Marty had done, seemed to confirm her instinct. As Valerie glanced around at the others, as if seeing them as individuals for the first time, she gave a tentative smile.

"Thank you all for being so nice," she said, huskily. "I just didn't know what to do, or who to call. Abby may have told you guys that we met on the plane, and then we talked on the phone the other day.... Anyway, Marty has this newfangled caller ID, and the name 'Thomas J. Sadler' had appeared on the screen, and that had stuck in my head so I looked up the address in the phone book. I should have called first, I know, but—but I guess I thought if I showed up in person, it would be harder to turn me away!"

She gave a feeble laugh, and Abby smiled back at her. "We don't mind. Really."

"When I got here and saw it was a complex, my heart sank," Valerie said. "Then I looked on the mailboxes, and sure enough, there was your brother's name and the unit number. So here I am!"

Connie said, brightly, "And we're glad you are! We really *are!*"

He was drinking champagne, too, and sat with a paper plate perched on his knees, munching on cheese and blackened chicken while Valerie talked. Mitzi and Chloe were having a field day, making the rounds and begging piteously for bits of food that Connie and the others, absorbed in Valerie's story, absently handed them.

When Valerie stopped talking, it was Warren again who took the lead, telling her they'd just been having an informal get-together and repeating that she was perfectly welcome.

Then another idea seemed to dawn on Thom; he looked at Abby, then back at Valerie.

"There's a place called Blake's not far from here," he said. "But it's a gay bar. I mean, I wasn't sure if you realized—"

Connie laughed. "Valerie is upset, Thom honey, but she isn't brain-dead."

Yet Valerie, her smile faltering, did seem perplexed. She took another— and slower—look around the room. "I guess I didn't...I mean, it doesn't matter in the least to... The lovely man who does my hair, you know... What I mean is..."

Warren laughed gently, patting her hand. "We know what you mean."

"You'll get used to them," Abby said. "They're basically harmless."

"But wait, I want to hear more about Valerie!" Connie said. Again his eyes had that glassy sheen. "How about one more glass of champagne before we leave? What do you all think? Valerie?"

There was a polite silence while the others gazed at their new guest.

Again Valerie smiled, more broadly this time, her hand fluttering to her throat as if she'd been paid an extravagant compliment.

"Why, thank you," she said. "Another glass of champagne would be lovely."

Chapter 6

"Tell me about the others," Chip said.

"The others?"

Thom looked up from the yearbook, dazed. The twenty-year-old photographs from St. Jude's had plunged him into the usual bittersweet reverie that came when he remembered his teenage years.

He and Chip sat on the edge of Thom's bed, the 1979-80 edition of *The Torchlight* spread open on their laps. Thom had lured his boyfriend back here allegedly to show him a crimson-red sweater from Neiman Marcus (one Connie had given him, several birthdays ago) he was thinking of wearing for the small dinner party he was giving tonight, but despite Chip's youth and occasional naïveté he knew better, surely. He knew Thom didn't care about clothes and that whenever they ended up in the bedroom together—even in the middle of the afternoon, like this, Thom still wearing the jacket and tie he'd donned for his two o'clock closing—it was because Thom wanted to undress Chip and undress himself and make love in their slow, languorous way for as long as possible. But when Thom had slid his arm around Chip's waist and kissed him, his other hand tugging at the tie, Chip had glanced down at his feet, distracted.

"What's this?" His shoe knocked against an edge of the yearbook, and before Thom could protest his boyfriend had retrieved the book from under the bed (Thom had forgotten he'd kept the yearbooks under there, along with God knew what other detritus from the past) and with a delighted air of discovery sat on the bed and started flipping through it.

"...You know," Chip answered. "Your other boyfriends."

Thom had shown him the square-jawed, grinning Lawton Williams, two years ahead of him in school, whom he'd described to Chip as his first "great love." The year these pictures were taken—he'd only glanced at his own photograph, though Chip made the obligatory noises over how cute it was—Thom's crush on Lawton had been so intense as to cause him a physical pain whose ghostly throbbing he could feel even now, with Chip, both of them staring at Lawton's big, bony, handsome face with its longish mane of glossy blond hair brushed sideways along his forehead in vintage 1970s style. Those deep-set, long-lashed blue eyes had sent Thom into an inward swoon every time he'd passed Lawton in the hall, but staring at the photo he recognized the eyes looked fairly vacuous, and he remembered with satisfaction that Lawton had been a straight-C student and later had flunked out of Georgia State in his freshman year.

But yes, he'd confessed to Chip: "My first great love. He and Abby were both on the senior prom committee, and they met at my house a couple of times. They'd gather in the den, and Thom the dorky little tenth grader kept dreaming up reasons to go in there, pretending he was looking for something, passing *very slowly* through to the kitchen."

Chip laughed. "Did he notice you?"

"Not even a glance. I was a piece of furniture. An eye mote. The funny thing was, Abby knew I was up to something, but she thought I had a crush on her best friend, Marilyn Freeman."

"You mean she didn't know?"

"That I was gay? Not back then. I barely knew myself."

That's when Chip had paused, cleared his throat, and asked about the "others."

Thom shrugged, ran the tip of his finger along Chip's jawline. "That's a tall order," he said, grinning. "We don't have time." His fingers itched to remove Chip's glasses, gently, and lay them on the bedside table; this had become the signal their lovemaking would begin, no more talking for a while. But something in Chip's eyes prevented him.

His boyfriend's placid gray gaze, which just now had seemed tinged with sorrow—the residue, Thom assumed, from the long talk they'd had last night—had fallen back to the yearbook.

Chip said, brushing his fingertips against the opened pages, "It's amazing, I was five years old when you were having your first great love."

"Oh, thanks a lot," Thom said.

Chip grinned, shaking his head. "Sorry." He kept staring down at the book, but Thom could tell that he wasn't seeing, really; that he wasn't quite comfortable. In the past month, spending every weekend together—and even some weeknights when Thom had driven impulsively to Athens just to enjoy a few hours with him—Thom had grown more attuned to his boyfriend's subtle changes of mood. Though Chip was twenty-five, and looked younger, with his sand-colored mop of hair, his glowing skin, the taut lines of his lean, muscular body, Thom had become aware that Chip lacked the impermeable, cheery optimism he often sensed in younger men; in fact, Chip often had quiet spells, when the gray eyes would turn opaque, as if clouded with some obscure hurt. When asked, he would insist he was fine, fine; no, of course Thom hadn't said anything; he just wasn't feeling that well.... The next day he would be his affectionate, wryly humorous self, a graduate student in marine biology who planned to get a Ph.D., become a researcher, teach in a university, his career fully mapped out in his logical, tidy mind. Thom sensed that Chip hadn't necessarily welcomed Thom's two or three impulsive visits to Athens, that his life was scheduled and regimented in a way that Thom's never had been; but he had been the first, a couple of weeks ago (on Friday, January 29th, as Thom remembered well: just before midnight, as they lay together in this very bed) to say "I love you," and without hesitation Thom had said "I love you" back. The days since then had been among the happiest of Thom's life.

He took a deep breath. "OK, then," he murmured. "What did you mean..."

"Just that you've had these other experiences—other relationships," Chip said. "And I haven't."

"It doesn't matter, does it?" Thom said. "I mean, except for Roy, none of the others really mattered."

"No, but last night you said it wasn't Roy who—" Chip broke off, embarrassed. He'd folded his hands on top of the yearbook and started methodically cracking his knuckles.

Who infected you, Thom thought but didn't say.

Last night, as they lay bathed in the flickering light of several candles on Thom's nightstand, the moment had come: Thom had finally told Chip about his condition. He knew Chip was negative and they should talk, but he'd told himself he was waiting for the right moment. As long as they were fastidious about safe sex—Chip, with his researcher's mentality and cautious disposition, wouldn't have wanted any other kind—Thom had supposed there was no hurry. But last night the "right moment" had come unexpectedly when Chip, just as Thom was about to enter him, his eyes half-closed in a passionate tremor of longing, had said, running a finger slowly along the underside of Thom's sheathed penis, "It would be nice if we didn't have to use these things...."

Startled, Thom had drawn back; had given his quick, instinctive grin. "Yeah, but..." His erection had faltered; he felt the blood draining from his face, as well.

As he'd done today, Chip had looked off, leaving Thom to stare at his lover's handsome, finely etched profile in the flickering dark.

"I've gotten tested twice in the past four months," Chip had said. "The second time was three weeks ago. Both were negative. I haven't been with anybody else."

"I know that, but..."

Then Chip did turn to him; Thom was startled by the look of urgency in his face, a sheen of moisture in his eyes. "I mean, we've been monogamous for a couple of months now, and I'd like to stay that way. So I was thinking...."

For a moment, Thom could not speak.

Chip said, a slight edge to his voice, "You do trust me, don't you? I mean, I don't even know any gay guys in Athens. I've been totally buried in work."

Thom had shaken his head, sadly; he'd run the back of his hand along Chip's side, his smooth taut skin more wonderful to the touch than anything he could imagine. Then he'd told Chip the details of his condition. He'd tested negative for several years after Roy's death, and through process of elimination—for there hadn't been *that* many others—he'd discovered that a guy named Edward had infected him. A boyfriend he'd been passionate about and who hadn't wanted to use condoms. Very foolishly, Thom had trusted him.

Only a few months ago, Thom learned that Edward had spent some time last summer in the intensive care ward at Crawford Long; with all his other lovers Thom had used condoms, every single time, and so... He hadn't told Chip, however, that not only had Edward knowingly infected him; after a few months, he'd also gotten irrationally possessive about Thom, resenting his friendships with Pace and Connie, and especially with Carter, with whom he imagined Thom was having an affair. Finally, Thom had listened to his friends—"That queen is a psycho!" Connie had exclaimed, more than once—and had broken off the romance. Then, for a brief, anxious period, Edward had kept calling, left ominous messages on his voice mail, made vaguely threatening remarks to mutual friends;

then he'd simply vanished. But to Thom's chagrin he'd begun glimpsing Edward lately around town—gay Atlanta was a small town, after all—but so far Edward had kept his distance, and for that Thom was grateful. He avoided sharing with Chip the more embarrassing recollections of what had happened between him and Edward; everyone had one lunatic passion in his life, Thom supposed, but broadcasting the details was another matter. Chip's questions naturally had focused on Thom's condition, and his medications, and he'd seemed relieved that Thom had suffered no symptoms. In fact, he'd seemed to take the news better than Thom could have hoped.

Finally Thom had asked, "Well, does it matter?" and Chip had said quickly that he loved Thom, of course, and these days HIV was far from a death sentence, and in fact Chip had an art history professor he'd befriended in college who had been diagnosed fifteen years ago and was still doing fine. Living with AIDS these days is like living with diabetes so long as you take your medication and watch your diet and stress, and of course, practice safe sex, so there's no reason you can't—

"Whoa, slow down," Thom had said, laughing. He'd reached across and given Chip a quick, dry kiss. "I believe you, okay?"

They'd talked for another hour, or maybe two hours, and one by one the candles had guttered out, and of course they were too exhausted, emotionally—and physically, for it was almost four A.M. when they said good night—to make love. But on the whole, Thom thought, the discussion he'd been dreading for weeks had gone well. In his darkest fantasies, Chip had drawn back in horror, had run out the door and driven back to Athens and Thom had never heard from him again. Instead, Chip had given him a long hug good night, massaging his shoulders. "I love you, I'm glad you told me," he'd said, and Thom had fallen asleep with his lover's quiet, consoling words echoing in his mind.

Now Thom said, laying his hand gently over Chip's, "Roy was a real lover, we lived together for several years. Edward was more of an obsession, a fatal attraction." He gave a rueful laugh. "Literally."

"Don't say that," Chip said with a wounded look.

"Sorry, but when I think about Edward, I can either laugh or start tearing the furniture apart." Despite himself, he laughed again. "I mean, Edward was far and away the best-looking man I'd ever dated. I went around in a kind of daze, wondering what this GQ-type saw in me. Have you ever dated somebody like that, somebody so stunning that you just lost your senses?"

Chip smiled. "You," he said.

Thom rolled his eyes. "Funny."

"Well, I guess I did, actually," Chip said. "When I was still a sopho-more, an undergrad, I had this English prof. Or I thought he was a prof—turned out he was a T.A. and hadn't even finished his doctorate. But he was gorgeous, so I kept stopping by his office for 'help' with Emily Dickinson's poetry." Chip laughed. "He wasn't stupid, so after the third or fourth time he invited me back to his place, and within half an hour he was fucking me like a wild man. I did make him use a condom, though," Chip said, looking anxiously at Thom as though afraid he'd spoken too frankly. "I don't know what I'd have done if he'd refused. I was pretty young, and totally infatuated."

"You were still in his class?" Thom asked, amazed.

"Yeah," Chip said with his mischievous grin. "And I got an A, though I never did understand a line Emily Dickinson wrote."

Thom shook his head. "So how did it end?"

"Badly. One Saturday night he wanted to visit Atlanta—to go dancing at Back Street, or so he said. That's when I discovered he was a raving alco-holic. He must have started drinking long before he picked me up, because he kept running his little Hyundai a few feet off the road, saying 'oops,' then overcompensating and coming pretty close to head-on collisions in the opposite lane. By the time we got to a restaurant in Atlanta I needed a few drinks myself."

While Chip talked Thom's mind drifted to Connie, whom he'd never seen as drunk as the man Chip was describing but who'd been drinking more lately; and taking a lot of prescription pills. Medication for depres-sion, for anxiety, for sleep, for his "headaches"…Thom hoped Warren was keeping an eye on him, but Connie was both stubborn and crafty, he was always slipping off "to the bathroom," where Thom suspected he was rifling through the assortment of pharmaceuticals he kept in his pant pock-ets like loose change. The last time they'd gone to Key West together, Connie was getting dressed for dinner and had tossed his walking shorts on the bed: a spray of pink, green, and white pills had cascaded onto the bedspread.

"I trust that was your last date with your English teacher," Thom said. Idly he began stroking Chip's arm, remembering why he'd maneuvered them in here.

"No, but it was the last time I let him drive me anywhere." He tossed the yearbook aside. As it hit the bed, Thom saw something slip out, what looked like a newspaper clipping. Chip didn't notice. He glanced at his watch. "Gosh, it's past six," he said. "Wasn't Abby coming at six?"

He stood and stretched his arms. Thom stayed on the bed, crestfallen. Mitzi and Chloe, hearing the louder tone of Chip's voice, had raced inside the room and were scampering around them.

"Hey, girls," Chip said, bending down to them.

The doorbell rang, and Thom supposed it was Abby. He glanced at his own watch and saw that yes, it was later than he thought. As though she'd caught the disease from Connie, his sister was late for everything these days. The punctual schoolteacher had turned into a rushed, somewhat impulsive Abby Sadler who seemed always out of breath, arriving with a flurry of apologies and explanations, most of which sounded as flimsy as Connie's. Was she mimicking him, unconsciously?—during the past few weeks she and Connie had grown closer than ever, along with their new pal, Valerie Patten. The three hung out together so much, Connie had become fond of saying, "Hi, we're the three Mouseketeers—my name is Annette!" But Abby spent much of her time on her own, too, seeing various "new friends" she'd made at Emory. Now that she'd decided to pursue her doctorate she'd begun hanging around the English department, she said, getting to know the graduate students and the newer professors hired since she'd gotten her master's. And she socialized with other, unnamed old friends from high school, and went shopping for clothes and books and for the minimally furnished condo she'd rented here in Thom's own complex.

That news had surprised and displeased Thom, though he'd tried to disguise his reaction. Within just a few days she'd signed the lease and had bought a red Altima that was nearly identical to the one she'd been renting, and she had asked one of her former colleagues in Bucks County, an older woman she'd once introduced to Lucille in the hope they might become friends, to box up some of her belongings and ship them down. Their mother had made surprisingly little fuss, Abby told him, and had even helped Mrs. Pargiter pack the boxes. Abby added that when she and Thom flew to Philadelphia, they could drive back in Abby's old Buick, and then she could sell the car.... He'd felt bereft that she was moving out, and so abruptly. Living with him, she'd helped to compensate for the gaping absence in his life left by Carter.

Tonight she seemed in her usual high spirits. Even her walk seemed different now, Thom noticed. These days she practically bounced into a room, and with her new clothes and hairstyle (the cut was shorter but wavier, the honey-tinted auburn a shade lighter) she appeared younger by eight or ten years than she'd looked a few weeks ago. The other night, over dinner at Babette's with Valerie and Connie, Valerie had bent toward Thom and made a joke about "keeping your sister in line"—Connie had been insisting absurdly that Abby was making eyes at the waiter, and that the waiter was leering back at her—and Thom hadn't even bothered to correct her. He *did* feel like Abby's older, somewhat stolid big brother, these days.

"You look nice," she said, greeting Thom as he shuffled behind Chip into the living room. She stood on tiptoes to kiss his cheek.

"Come on, I just got home," he said. "Had a closing that sort of went haywire. I haven't even showered and changed."

"Oh, the five o'clock shadow looks handsome on you," Abby said. "What do you think, Chip?"

Chip tilted his head in mock appraisal. "Yes, and the mussed hair is a nice touch, too. He looks raffish—like he might be dangerous."

Abby and Chip laughed while Thom stared back at them, smiling. Their hair and faces shone. His sister and boyfriend looked ready for the choir, whereas he felt old and jaded. And tired.

"I should make the two of you cook dinner, then," he said.

They did follow him into the kitchen and helped as much as he allowed. Cooking soothed his nerves; he really preferred to be alone while making dinner, letting his mind relax and expand into a state of meditative calm as he chopped, boiled, poured, and diced, ambling peaceably about the room searching out utensils and ingredients, dropping an occasional tidbit into the dogs' eager mouths and jerking his fingertips clear, just in time, from the alligator-like snap of their jaws. Tonight, just to keep the others involved, he'd say, "Abby, would you check the spice rack for the oregano?" or "Chip, honey, want to hunt down the salad bowl for me, the wooden one?—I think it's in that big drawer under the oven." But mostly Abby and Chip leaned back against the opposite counter, sipping their glasses of Merlot, chatting and laughing as Thom worked.

To Thom's surprise, Abby brought up a normally avoided topic: their mother.

"We had a great talk today," she said, airily. "She said to tell you happy Valentine's."

"Really?" The usual stab of guilt. "I should have sent her a card."

"Don't worry, I did—and I signed your name," Abby said.

"You did? You forgot to tell me."

"I know—sorry." She laughed. "I even changed the handwriting, so it looked like you really signed it."

Thom looked over, startled. "Are you serious?"

She gave a brief, chagrined smile. "It was just an impulse. You don't mind, do you? She's been so friendly lately on the phone and has kept asking about you, so I thought..."

Thom stared down at the chicken breasts, coating them with a mix of oregano and fresh ground pepper. "I'd have signed it myself, if you'd just asked me."

"I know, I should have," Abby said, "but it was Wednesday, and I wanted it to get there today, so I just went ahead."

"OK, it doesn't matter. As long as the card makes her happy."

"I think it will," Abby said. "And you know, she actually said she was happy for *me*—you know, about my going back to school, and that you and I were living in the same complex. She might come to visit sometime soon."

"That's good, maybe she—" Thom broke off. He hadn't been listening closely, but now he heard. How smoothly Abby had brought the information out.

"What did you say? She might what?"

"She's not sure," Abby said quickly. "Maybe sometime in the spring. She said something about the azaleas. The dogwood festival."

Thom laughed angrily. "Since when did she care about that stuff? That was Daddy's interest, not hers."

"Well, Thom..."

The doorbell rang, and Abby brought Connie, Warren, and Valerie back to the kitchen, where they sipped wine and talked brightly while Thom put the finishing touches on the meal. Finally he herded them into the dining nook, asked Chip and Abby to set the table, and got the others working on the salad, the Italian garlic bread. Normally there would be an hour for cocktails, but tonight they'd gathered specifically to plan their trip to Key West—which they'd plotted, and delayed, and plotted again for weeks—and Thom didn't want the others, particularly Connie, to drink too much, or for the party to drag much past ten o'clock. These past few months Thom had felt his energy eroding, day by day, and lately he'd gotten more possessive of his time. Especially when Chip was around.

If Thom stayed quieter than usual during the meal, the others didn't seem to notice—not even Abby. By nine-thirty they were finishing their third bottle of wine, and the conversation had been so avid that Connie and Valerie—the most energetic talkers—hadn't finished their main course. The raspberry cheesecake Thom had bought at Alon's still waited in the refrigerator. Just as he was wondering if it would be rude to start the coffee, Valerie put down her fork and sat back with a small, apologetic smile.

"I hope you guys don't mind, but I've *got* to dash out to the porch."

This was her third dash out to the porch since they'd sat down. Again Thom said he didn't care if she smoked in the house, and again she exclaimed she wouldn't dream of such a thing.

"You know, I sort of miss smoke-filled rooms," Connie said with a sigh, as Valerie hurried out. He lifted his wineglass and downed his last swallow with a ceremonial flourish. "It added atmosphere to a dinner party, you know? I miss all the little gestures—the way people lit the things, and crimped their lips, and waved the smoke away so you could see each other. And the different ways people stubbed them out. And how you would watch someone's ash getting longer, wondering if they'd notice before it fell."

"Yeah," Warren said. "And the coughing. And the irritated eyes."

"And the way your shirt would smell the next morning," Thom said.

Abby laughed, while Chip looked blankly around at the others.

"You guys used to smoke?" he said.

Connie gave the raspy bark he'd perfected as a response to Chip's remarks. These past few months, Connie hadn't done much to disguise the fact that he had little use for Thom's boyfriend. Before Christmas, when they'd first discussed the Key West trip, Chip had said with boyish enthusiasm that he'd done a graduate project on marine life in south Florida and was looking forward to inspecting the area firsthand; Connie had laughed acidly, saying he'd been to Key West a dozen times and had never gone near the beach. The other day on the phone, Connie had drawled, "Thom, your inamorata *is* coming with us, isn't he? We'll all *so* want to hear a lecture on the local flora and fauna."

Now Connie said, "Yes, Chip dear, we all smoked back in the olden days, while we watched our porn on eight-millimeter projectors, and discussed whether we liked Greek or French."

"Greek or French?" Chip said, glancing around.

Connie tittered brightly and rolled his eyes.

"Behave yourself," Abby said, in the light, scolding tone she often used with Connie.

"Yes, teacher," Connie said. He gazed plaintively across at Thom, holding out his glass. "Please, sir, may I have a little more?"

Thom smiled noncommittally; he saw how quietly Warren sat next to Connie, staring down at his plate.

"I was just going to ask about coffee," Thom said.

"You and your coffee!" Connie cried. "You'd think you'd been raised by Mrs. Olsen. Chip, do you know who Mrs. Olsen was?"

Before he could answer, the front door slammed shut and Valerie rushed inside, flapping her arms. Thom blinked: it always seemed odd to him that Valerie was here. Tonight she wore a fawn-colored wool suit, and as usual her glossy dark hair and heavy makeup were as carefully tended as any Buckhead matron's. A stranger might think she was a visiting aunt, though she was probably in her mid forties, not much older than Connie. She had melded into their little group easily, though repeating often that the only gay man she'd known before was her hairdresser. "Possibly also the man who does my taxes," she would add. And maybe one of her nephews, as well, a sweet college-age boy—her favorite nephew, in fact. The other night Connie had told Valerie she'd had a misspent youth as a closeted fag hag, but she'd found herself at last.

It amazed Thom that Valerie had changed so much in the weeks since she'd appeared on his doorstep, mascara-stained tears running down her cheeks. Barging into their Christmas Eve party. It wasn't like Abby to befriend someone so quickly, he'd thought, especially on an airplane, but these days Abby often surprised him. That night, after everyone had left, he'd suggested that her own kindness might have misled her, and had even wondered aloud if Valerie Patten was unstable, possibly even mentally ill...?

Abby had laughed. "It's her ex-husband who's unstable," she said. He'd thought he detected a note of asperity in her voice. "Valerie is very sweet, I think—very vulnerable," she'd added, and though it struck him that Abby protested too much, he'd said nothing.

Nor had he objected when she'd invited Valerie over again for dinner the following week. By then, Marty had returned from the visit to his mother and was "a changed man," Valerie reported, with an odd mix of girlish happiness and ironic disbelief. He'd apologized profusely for ditching her on Christmas Eve, blaming some new medication his psychiatrist had prescribed that caused him to do random, impulsive things, to run away from his problems instead of confronting them.

"It was so nice to hear myself described as a 'problem'!" Valerie had said giddily, sipping at her wine. Then her voice lowered, and in a husky murmur she added, "Still, we're very hopeful this time. We really *have* made a new start, I think… He even hinted about joining me tonight—and it was sweet of you to include him in the invitation, Abby—but I said no, these are *my* friends, and my not having any life or friends of my own, apart from you, was one of the problems in our marriage to begin with." Valerie had nodded vigorously and gazed across the table at Abby with glistening eyes. "I really owe you so much, Abby," she'd said, reaching again for her wine. "If I hadn't met you on that airplane, what would I…I mean, on Christmas Eve I was at my wit's end, and—" She'd paused, closing her eyes.

When she opened them again, it seemed she had recovered. She had an odd, childlike resilience, this Valerie Patten; Thom couldn't deny that she was enormously likable. Before Abby or Thom could respond, she'd tilted her head, as though struck by a new idea.

"Isn't it amazing, how big a role pure *chance* plays in our lives? I mean, what if we hadn't happened to be seated together in that airplane? For that matter, I met at least a couple of my husbands in odd circumstances—with Marty, it was a taxi shelter in Center City where we'd huddled together because it had started to pour down rain and neither of us had our umbrellas. Just like in a movie! We'd been walking down Walnut Street—he was in town on business, I was out shopping or something—and we both ran under this shelter and we got to talking—" She'd stopped, glancing self-consciously at Thom and Abby. "I'm sorry, I'm talking *way* too much," she said. "It's just that I feel so comfortable with you guys…and things are so much better now in my life, and I feel like I owe you, somehow, both of you…."

Thom and Abby told her not to be silly: they were glad they'd met her too.

"You can never have too many friends," Abby said, and Thom grinned, nodding.

"Never," he said.

He'd refilled their wineglasses, and they'd sat discussing all the chance encounters in their lives and how important they'd been and how no one had much control, really, over whom they would meet, over whom they would love and befriend or where they would live or what they would ultimately make of their lives…. It was all chance, really. Pure blind chance. They'd all agreed on that.

"Whoosh, it's chilly out there!" Valerie said now, settling back into her seat.

"Just think," Abby said, "in a couple of weeks we'll be down in Florida, lying by the pool."

"I hope I'm lying next to more than the pool," Connie said. He directed an abrupt, imperious glance across at Thom. "How about some champagne with dessert? I mean, it *is* Valentine's Day. Aren't we supposed to celebrate or something?"

"Celebrate what?" Warren said.

These were the first words he'd spoken in quite a while.

Half an hour later they'd gathered in the living room, dessert plates perched on their laps, champagne flutes and coffee cups scattered about the room. Exhausted, Thom had taken the chair near the darkened fireplace—last week he'd run out of logs and had forgotten to buy more—and he stayed quiet, letting the others enjoy themselves. Even Chip had drunk more than usual tonight. He'd focused most of his attention on the high-spirited banter from the sofa, where Connie sat in the middle with Abby and Valerie on either side. Thom's gaze kept straying to Chip, but his boyfriend seldom looked at him.

Every few minutes, though, Abby did glance over, and they exchanged their companionable smiles. She'd worn one of the blouses he gave her for Christmas—wide red and black stripes, with a snugly fitting black wool skirt—and of course he was wearing the Rolex watch she'd bought him at Maier & Berkele, an extravagant gift that had moved him almost to tears. The watch was slender and elegant, with a silver mesh band—the kind of thing he'd never have bought for himself. He supposed it clashed with his casual, cheerfully mismatched wardrobe, but he didn't care. He would wear the watch for the rest of his life.

He sat peaceably as the others' alcohol-fueled chatter filled the room, listening vaguely. For some reason he thought of his father: his gentle, quiet-mannered father, who had often sat like this in their den after dinner, while Lucille and Thom and Abby would laugh and exclaim over family and neighborhood news, over some silly program they were watching on television. Thom would glimpse the meditative contentment in his father's eyes as he rested in his overstuffed wingback, usually with a newspaper on his lap but seldom reading it, simply enjoying his family's company, and Thom had hoped he might achieve a similar contentment when he was older. The other night, on the way home from dinner at Bacchanalia with Connie and Warren—Abby having gone out with one of her "old friends"—

they were stopped at a red light when impulsively Connie had bent over and had given Thom a quick, embarrassed hug, offering one of those touching remarks Connie made sometimes that redeemed all his silly behavior, his tireless self-absorption.

"You know," he'd said, apropos of nothing, "*you guys* are my family. I don't know what I'd do without you two, and Abby and Pace, and now cute little Valerie. And God, how I miss Carter."

Thom had shot a quick look in the rearview mirror; Warren sat looking small and alone in the backseat, his eyes stricken with emotion.

"That's sweet," Thom had said. "Thanks, Connie. I feel the same way."

They'd said nothing else for the rest of the drive.

Thom was worried about Connie. Tonight he'd launched into one of his favorite monologues, the others' laughter washing around him as he described some of his high jinks on his and Warren's last trip to Key West, where Connie claimed he'd had a hot-tub encounter with a tall Swedish college student late one night, then the next day found out that "Jakob" was fifteen and had sneaked away from the Pier House, where he was staying with his parents. In previous versions Thom had heard Jakob was thirteen and staying at the Marriott with his divorced gay father; or sixteen and staying at Lighthouse Court with his gay older brother. The variations depended, Thom believed, on how many cocktails Connie had consumed when he told the story, and as Thom listened he wondered if the others noticed the exaggerated dartings of Connie's hands, the squeak of desperation in his ribald, high-pitched laugh.

"And there he was, my young Swedish Tadzio, sitting with his gorgeous blond mother who looked about thirty-five, and his father who looked like a handsome Nazi, and what does he do when I walk into the restaurant but *wave* at me, and motion me over to the table! He's going to introduce me to Mom and Dad! Connie Lefcourt, meet my *volks*! *Volks*, meet the American queen who blew me last night in the hot tub! My God, I high-tailed it out of there like my shorts were on fire."

Valerie had bent over double, giving her throaty, croaking laugh. "Oh, Connie, that's too much!"

Abby and Chip were laughing, too, though more at Connie's animation, Thom supposed, than at the story itself. Only Warren seemed unimpressed; he sat slumped in his chair, staring glumly down into his coffee. What worried Thom was that Warren no longer bothered to gently mock or contradict Connie's outrageous recollections (for surely Warren had been there, and knew what had really happened). Thom knew that if he was worried about Connie, then Warren must be scared to death, and several times in the past few weeks, after getting one of Connie's frantic phone calls, Thom had thought of calling Warren at his office. They ought to compare notes, really, and figure out what was going on between Connie and his father. Only this morning Connie had phoned Thom at work, insisting tearfully that his father kept calling him up, drunk, and threatening him.

"He's just blowing off steam," Thom had said. "Don't let him get to you."

"I know, I know—it's just that he always calls first thing in the morning, and then the rest of my day is shot."

"Well, he's having a hard time," Thom said. "Remember, this is his second—" He broke off, wincing.

"I know, and they are both *my fault*," Connie had said, laughing bitterly.

"I didn't mean that," Thom said.

These conversations with Connie were like tiptoeing through a minefield. Only last week, Connie had hung up on him, exclaiming that Thom was "defending" Connie's father. Now that Mr. Lefcourt's second wife had been diagnosed with breast cancer, Thom speculated that he was reliving the death of his great love, Connie's mother, whose uterine cancer Mr. Lefcourt had somehow attributed to her difficult pregnancy with Connie.

Unlike Connie, who had a few cocktails every evening but seldom became severely intoxicated, Mr. Lefcourt was a binge drinker: he could go years without touching a drop, then he'd have episodes of near-ceaseless drinking that resulted in irrational, wildly abusive behavior. After years of little communication, he'd kept phoning Connie and lambasting him for a variety of crimes, especially his "faggotry," as Mr. Lefcourt called it, and his inability to "make something" of himself. Since Connie's trust fund, established by his mother shortly before her death, enabled him to live comfortably without regular employment, Thom supposed that was the core of the problem. To a man like Mr. Lefcourt, money equaled love, so Connie had benefited all his life from the stream of his mother's love that had been diverted from his father. It was the ancient drama of a mother transferring her affection from her husband to her child, though Thom knew there was no point in trying to explain this to Connie. He would be accused again of "defending" his abusive, drunken father. Instead, he'd done as Connie seemed to require, offering sympathy but not advice—certainly not advice that might be difficult to follow.

When Connie had called this morning, Thom had bent his own rule a little when Connie had mentioned his stepmother's impending death.

"Daddy dearest says she'll die within the next few days. What I'm really worried about, Thom, is the funeral. I don't dare go, in case he's drunk and makes a scene with me right in front of the woman's casket. But I don't dare *not* go, either."

"You'll have to go," Thom said gently. "I mean, she *is* your stepmother."

"That's easy for you to say!" Connie cried.

Thom had paused, not sure if Connie was being sarcastic; of course, he knew that Thom had not attended his own father's funeral. He'd said, "Look, Connie, it's not going to be an easy few days, but you'll have to go through with it. Your father is a big shot in Oklahoma City, isn't he? All his friends and associates will be at that funeral. He's not going to make a scene. The rest of the time, you can avoid him if you have to."

Connie had exhaled, noisily. "You're right, Thom honey, I'm sorry. My nerves are just frazzled, I guess. I hope I'm not miserable company at your dinner party tonight."

But now the party was winding down—it was almost eleven, Valerie had been the first to glance at her watch and say she'd better get going—and Connie seemed as bubbly and energetic as always.

"Must you, Val?" he said, disappointed. "Give Marty hell, now, for not taking you out on Valentine's Day."

"Well, his mom is sick again," Valerie said. "He couldn't help it, he said he really ought to stay by the phone. And he *did* bring me two dozen red roses this morning."

Everyone gave the obligatory "Oooh." Connie added, "I can't remember the last time a man brought me flowers."

"I sent you pink glads last year on your birthday," Warren said. He sounded hurt. "Pink glads are your favorite."

Thom knew Connie so well, he could hear the phrase fully formed on Connie's tongue: *But you don't count, Warren honey. I meant flowers from a boyfriend.* As Connie's lips parted, Thom said quickly, "OK, did we decide everything?"

"Decide?" Valerie said blankly.

Abby said, smiling, "About Key West. I guess we did, didn't we? Valerie and I will stay at Pier House, and the rest of you...what was it, the Brass Door? Warren is making the reservations and ordering the tickets."

"The Brass Key," Thom said. "Thanks for doing that, Warren. Put my ticket and Abby's on my credit card. I'll call you tomorrow with the number."

"Me, too," Valerie said. She stood, smoothing out her skirt. "Thanks for the lovely dinner, Thom! I really need to skeedaddle."

"Skeedaddle!" Connie cried. "Did you hear that? You're too much, Dorothy."

Earlier in the evening Connie had announced, as if he'd invented the phrase, that they were all friends of Dorothy; and that Valerie Patten *was*, in fact, Dorothy.

"Now, you'd better behave, or I'm going to start calling you Constance," Valerie said with a little moue.

Warren had risen, too. "That would be a misnomer, wouldn't it?" he said. "Come on, Connie, we'd better get home, too."

Connie stood and stretched his arms, sighing. He laughed abruptly. "Remember that Lucy episode, where she got drunk doing the commercial for that vitamin tonic—what was it? Wait, I remember—Vita...meata...vegamin! My favorite line in all of television: 'Do you pop out at parties?'"

"Come on, Connie, let's go," Warren said. He stood at the door, jingling his keys.

"Well! You guys are party poppers if I ever saw one!" Connie cried.

After everyone had left, Thom and Chip started cleaning up. Chatting idly, they straightened the living and dining rooms, then worked a while in the kitchen, putting things away, rinsing plates and glasses. When Chip started wiping the counter, Thom came up behind him and ran a finger along his neck.

"Hey," he said. "Enough scullery work for one night."

Chip turned, and before he could speak Thom kissed him lightly on the mouth.

He said, "Happy Valentine's Day."

Chip smiled. "Same to you."

Thom took his hand and led him back to the bedroom, flipping off lights as he went. Mitzi and Chloe raced ahead: by the time Thom and Chip got to the room, the dogs had hopped into their fleece-lined beds and begun the nightly dachshund ritual of padding slowly in a circle, three or four times. Eyelids drooping and paws tucked under their haunches, they settled and were quiet.

Unbuttoning his shirt, Chip said, "I wish I could get to sleep that easily."

Several times, Chip had mentioned his insomnia; Thom always fell asleep first, he said. Thom's deep, regular breathing helped lull him to sleep, too.

"How about a massage?" Thom suggested. He turned off the bedside lamp and lit a new candle.

Thom always slept nude, but tonight Chip got into bed wearing his briefs. And his glasses. When Thom took his hand, Chip said, "Can I ask you something?"

"Sure," Thom said.

"Have you—have you ever really trusted somebody? You know, somebody you felt you could tell *anything*, and it wouldn't go any further?"

Thom thought a moment, and he supposed Chip expected him to mention Roy, or perhaps Abby, but Thom decided to tell the truth. He wanted to start this relationship fresh and clean, steering clear of all those old bugbears from the past: the small evasions, the untold stories. The outright lies.

"No," he said.

Chip's response was unexpected: he hiccuped. Then he laughed and Thom laughed, too.

"Sorry," Chip said. "Too much champagne."

Idly, Thom stroked his boyfriend's thigh. "Why did you ask that?"

Chip took a deep breath. Exhaling, he said in a jocular, almost offhand way, "My work is research, and I'm always looking for the 'truth,' because in science that's the goal. Factual truth. Empirical truth. But where people are concerned, I'm not sure it's always a good idea."

Gently, Thom squeezed Chip's leg and felt his muscle tighten in response. "Really? Why is that?"

"Because people can't take it," he said. "Like my parents, for instance, down in Albany. They were both raised on farms, you know, in rural south Georgia in the 1940s. They go to church on Sunday and on Wednesday nights. They hardly ever watch television because the preacher tells them how corrupt it is, and they haven't gone to a movie since Liz and Dick made *Cleopatra*. The only things they read are the Bible and *Reader's Digest*."

He stopped, as if he'd answered Thom's question.

"So?" Thom said. "A lot of guys in Atlanta have parents like that."

"My point is they grew up thinking homosexuals were three-headed monsters from hell. They still hear that at church. I'm their only kid, and if they found out I was gay, it would practically kill them."

Thom thought a moment. "Don't be too sure. Sometimes people like your parents...they can surprise you. I'm not saying they'd be thrilled, but—"

"It would kill them," Chip said flatly. He hiccuped.

Thom opened his mouth to speak but he could not. He'd given Chip a selective version of his own coming-out story, that memorable Sunday afternoon when he'd lowered the boom during a Falcons game. Chip knew that Thom's mother lived in Philadelphia and that he hadn't seen her lately, but he didn't know the details. Nor had he seemed curious.

Thom remembered something Chip had said earlier. Now he asked, "You don't know any gay men in Athens, really? It might help if you joined the campus gay group or something, you know. It's important to have support."

Chip looked over with one side of his mouth raised, almost a snarl.

"Are you serious?" he said. "I'm a graduate student in biology, Thom. If they knew they had a flaming queen alongside them in the lab...my God." He shook his head.

"You're not a flaming queen," Thom said. The comment was inane, but he couldn't help adding, "You're *not.*"

When he'd first gotten into bed, Thom had felt the familiar stirring fullness in his groin, his automatic response to Chip's body. His anticipation of their lovemaking was no less keen than it had been on their first night together. But now he felt chilled, shriveled; his hand had retreated from Chip's leg, and Chip had raised to a sitting position, arms folded across his chest.

"What about that alcoholic English teacher?" Thom said. "What happened to him?"

"Oh, he's still there. He's one of those losers who take a decade to finish their dissertation. He's probably still banging his undergraduates."

"I thought you didn't know any gay guys in Athens," Thom said.

Chip laughed shortly. "See what I mean? You can't trust a thing I say."

"That's not what I—"

"I didn't think of *him,*" Chip said. "Haven't talked to him in a long, long time."

For several minutes, neither of them spoke. Thom had propped a pillow behind his head, and both he and Chip stared out into the room's shadowy, shifting darkness, the illumination from their one candle now seeming less romantic than menacing, forbidding. Thom lay engulfed in a memory from his and Roy's last vacation before Roy became ill: they'd gone to Provincetown and then Boston, where Roy wanted to visit some old friends from his Harvard days. Thom had never visited Boston, and he'd picked up a "gay guide" at the bookstore. They'd read descriptions of

Boston's gay coffee shops, the dance clubs, a bathhouse described as "wonderfully seedy."

"Oooh, the baths—that's where we should go, Thom," Roy had said, poking him in the side.

"Ha ha," Thom had said.

Their second day in Boston, over lunch, Roy had said he wanted to visit some of the local gardens—his grand passion was landscaping, and at home he usually puttered out in the yard from the minute he got home until the last shreds of daylight were gone.

"But you don't care about visiting gardens, do you, hon?" he'd asked. "You want to go shopping or something, while I do that?"

This had been the last afternoon of an eight-day trip, and Thom was exhausted.

"I may just stay in the room and read, write some cards," he said.

After Roy left, Thom had gotten in the shower and simply let the hot water run over him, glad he'd decided to take a break from their relentless sightseeing. (For Roy, vacations were always rigidly scheduled, every hour of the day accounted for; downtime had been an alien concept to him.) Thom remembered the exact moment the truth had struck him: his head had been tilted back as he rinsed shampoo from his hair. He saw Roy walking out the door of their room, a map of the gardens he'd gotten from the hotel clerk in his hand, along with the gay guide.

You didn't need a gay guide to visit the gardens, did you?

Calmly, methodically, he'd shaved, gotten dressed, and decided what he would do. It was 5:15, and Roy had said he'd be back around six, when they'd decide where to go for dinner. Thom looked up the address of the bathhouse in the phone book, called for directions, found it was a ten-minute walk. Half a block down there was a small café, and Thom sat there with a Diet Coke, remembering that today Roy had worn a brightly flowered shirt Thom had bought him the year before on their trip to Maui. He sat sipping the Coke and glancing every few minutes at his watch. It was 5:30. It was 5:35. He decided that at 5:50 he would leave, hoping he'd find Roy back in the room, happily clutching brochures from the gardens and maybe a little souvenir for Thom. That didn't happen. At 5:47 the bathhouse door opened, and there was damp-haired Roy in his flowered shirt— the shirt Thom had bought him, an extra twist of the knife—and Thom merely watched as Roy, disoriented for a moment, looked down at his map, then took off down the sidewalk in the direction of their hotel.

Thom left the café and caught up to Roy in the next block.

"Hey there," he'd said.

Roy looked around, startled. He gave his handsome, tilted grin. "Guess what. I've managed to get *lost*."

"Are the gardens around here?" Thom asked.

"Well, yeah," Roy said, stammering, pointing vaguely down the street, "but I—somehow I took a wrong turn, I guess."

Thom was tempted to play out the charade: ask how the gardens were, were they crowded, what had he liked best, endless questions leading his lover into a forest of lies. But he didn't have the heart for that.

Instead he asked, "How were the baths?"

On their way back to the hotel, they'd had the worst argument of their lives. On public streets. In lowered, hissing voices.

"You fucking *lied* to me. Looked me right in the face and *lied*."

Roy was walking fast, head ducked. "Sometimes that's easier," he said. "What did you do, follow me? Stalk me?"

"I didn't have to follow you. Do you think I'm stupid? I knew you were trying to get rid of me earlier—suggesting I wouldn't enjoy the gardens. How considerate!"

"You know, this isn't the first time you've been really intrusive," Roy said. "Sometimes you really intrude into my life."

"You're trying to make *me* into the bad guy? You just fucked your brains out in a bathhouse, and I'm the bad guy?"

"Look, sometimes I need a quick release like that—I did invite you, and you just laughed."

"You fucking liar! That wasn't an invitation—you wouldn't have taken me there in a million years."

Roy walked faster. "I'm really pissed that you followed me."

"No, you're really pissed that you got caught. If you'd just told me where you were going and why, I could have dealt with that. It's your streak of dishonesty that drives me up the wall."

"What you did was worse. You followed me all the way here, just to embarrass me."

"You've been prancing around nude in a bathhouse. I don't think you're that easily embarrassed."

And so on. Yes, by far the worst argument of their four-year relationship, but although things had been strained for a while, and they hadn't really talked out the matter to Thom's satisfaction (a few days later, Roy had sent a card apologizing for the "dishonesty incident," saying he hoped it hadn't ruined the trip for Thom) their relationship had not only survived, it had thrived. Somehow their ability to have a no-holds-barred verbal fight and stay together had strengthened their rapport, and in the months afterward, and especially after Roy fell ill, Thom had never felt closer to him.

Yet he'd had to answer Chip's question truthfully and say no, there was no one in whom he could place full, unquestioning trust. Chip said nothing.

Finally, Thom broke their silence. "I still don't understand why you asked me that."

"Oh, I was just curious."

Thom turned on his side and reached out. Brushed his fingertips along Chip's bare stomach.

"Are you OK?" Thom asked.

"Sure," Chip said. Now he did remove his glasses, carefully placing them on the bedside table. He moved away from Thom and closed his eyes.

"I'm really bushed," he said. "Too much food and liquor. Sleep tight, OK?"

Thom lay there, stunned. Again they would sleep together without making love. Recovering, he said, "OK. Good night." He leaned over and gave Chip the same peck he'd given earlier to his sister.

Chip kissed him back, then pulled the sheet up to his shoulder and turned his back to Thom. Thom raised on one elbow to blow out the candle, then paused. His eye had caught on the old newspaper clipping that had fallen out of the yearbook. He'd dropped the clipping in the nightstand drawer, and now the drawer was partway open, as if taunting him. He remembered vaguely that the article had something to do with the Atlanta child murders in the early 1980s, but he couldn't remember the details. He wondered why he'd saved it, and why his stomach churned with anxiety at the mere sight of the yellowed clipping, so neatly folded into squares almost twenty years ago by his teenage hands. Probably he shouldn't touch the clipping; it would be like unfolding the past. The present was difficult enough, wasn't it, without going back, remembering?

He hesitated, waffled, changed his mind. After all, he had nothing better to do.

When Thom had turned sixteen and gotten his license, he'd gone with his father to pick up the '74 Ford Torino he bought with his life savings, literally, of $2,450.

From the sidewalk, his mother had watched their homecoming,

Thom's father inching his year-old gray Chrysler up the street as though proudly escorting his son, who'd been delirious with joy throughout this first solo drive in his first car. The trip home had been marred only by frustration at his father's stubborn adherence to the speed limit. Thom's fingers itched to swerve the wheel and pass the Chrysler, his foot itched to floor the pedal and drive off by himself, get onto some back road and do eighty, a hundred, all the windows down and the clean May wind riffling his hair in an ecstatic frenzy. But they'd promised his mother they'd come directly home, and she'd promised to be waiting outside with her camera to snap a picture of her handsome son in his handsome new car.

And there she was. Easing into the driveway behind his father, Thom saw that she looked worried, fretful. She stood wringing her hands, and there was no camera in sight.

"I was just watching the news!" she called out the instant they emerged from their cars. "Another boy disappeared. Only fourteen, poor thing, and he's the seventh one—imagine that, the *seventh*!"

It was 6:30 P.M., May 18, 1980. If you believed the police and an increasingly hysterical media, there was a serial killer loose in Atlanta. Since the previous summer, a series of bodies—all black, all children or teenagers, and all boys except for one twelve-year-old named Angel—had been found shot, bludgeoned, or stabbed to death. The girl had been tied to a tree, sexually molested, and strangled with an electric cord; a pair of panties had been stuffed down her throat. Television and newspaper reports insisted that Atlanta's black population now lived in a "vise of terror." There was speculation that the killings were being systematically planned and carried out by the Ku Klux Klan; or by a radical black group trying to fuel hatred toward Atlanta's white minority in the hope of starting a race war; or by some lunatic pedophile, a Southern version of John Wayne Gacy. Whenever there was a new murder, Thom's mother suffered throes of anxiety, worrying aloud that Thom could be snatched off his bicycle, or kidnapped from the high school grounds. She'd even complained to Thom's father that they ought to leave Atlanta and move to Philadelphia, where she'd grown up and where some of her relatives still lived. Philadelphia was the city of brotherly love, she insisted, while Atlanta had become the murder capital of the U.S., a place where innocent kids were no longer safe.

Half-listening, Thom and his father would point out, yet another time, that all the victims were black, all the killings in black neighborhoods; the situation was horrible, of course, but neither Thom nor Abby was in any personal danger, and it was the kind of thing that could happen anywhere. You couldn't blame Atlanta.

After Thom had returned home with his car, his mother spent the rest of the evening begging him not to drive it. What if the killer spotted Thom driving alone and decided to follow him, and attack him the moment he opened the door! What if Thom was stopped at a red light and the killer simply pulled alongside and shot him, right through the window! What if—

In his quiet but decisive way, Thom's father put an end to his wife's overblown speculations. He held up one hand (the family was eating dinner, Thom and Abby chewing busily on their fried chicken and corn on the cob in an effort to ignore their mother) and said, "Lucille, enough. That killer isn't interested in a goddamned white boy."

Thom looked over, startled. He could count on one hand the times he'd heard his father swear. Even Lucille glanced sideways at her husband, abashed.

"All right, then," she said to Thom. Her voice had lowered to a stubborn whine that abraded Thom's nerves far more than her usual shrillness. "But promise me, honey, that you'll drive with the doors locked? And you'll look around you before you leave the car?"

Thom nodded, eager to break the tension. "Sure, no problem. I'll just be going to school and back, mainly. And I'll be giving Andrew Jeter a ride every morning, remember? So there'll be two of us."

"There you go, Mom," Abby said, smiling. "No psychopath in his right mind is going to approach *two* overgrown kids like Thom and Andrew."

Thom laughed. He and his sister shared a droll, irreverent sense of humor, but usually Abby was more circumspect than he was.

"No psychopath in his right mind—very funny, Abigail," their mother said. She gave a droopy smile that tugged at Thom's sympathy; she looked so bedraggled, her wispy reddish hair plastered along her temples after her sweaty work in the kitchen. She turned to Thom. "That does relieve my mind a little, honey. But don't forget, the first two bodies were found together—"

"Lucille?" Thom's father said. He was picking among the platter of chicken pieces. "Is there any more white meat?"

His wife stared. One hand flew to her mouth as she exclaimed there had been two platters, but she'd been so upset and distracted that she'd brought out only one. Muttering crossly to herself, she jumped up and hurried back to the kitchen. There was no more talk of the Atlanta child murders for the rest of that evening.

• • •

The fourteen-year-old black boy was found dead, his head bludgeoned with a blunt instrument, but Thom paid little attention to the news reports, which had become routine. Now that he could drive, he could not think of anything else. He loved everything about his car!—its deep burgundy color and black vinyl roof, its black leather bucket seats and sleek dashboard whose controls he eyed so fondly he'd almost rear-ended several cars in his first week of driving. He loved zooming along Rock Springs Road or Morningside Drive, switching radio stations every few seconds, smiling at the way the burgeoning oak trees dappled his hood and windshield with quick-darting shadows, as if teasing him. He was always heading somewhere; now that he owned a car he was volunteering happily to do errands for everybody.

As he drove, his heart throbbed with an almost uncontainable joy.

For his birthday a couple of weeks earlier, Abby had given him a silver key chain with his initials engraved in fancy Gothic script on a small disk, and though he'd gotten kidded for this "faggy" item (boys' new keys were always inspected minutely by their high school peers) the gift had touched him. Now that he had a car, Abby had followed through on her months-long threat and had fixed him up with an "older woman": one of her senior friends, a shy white-blond girl named Melissa Hayes who was new this year at St. Jude's.

During the next few weeks, his mother kidded Thom, calling after him, "I guess I won't wait up for you, Casanova!" as he walked out the door wearing a starched dress shirt and reeking of cologne. He left around seven every Friday and Saturday night, and sometimes Sunday night, too. His family seemed mildly but pleasantly surprised that he dated so much. Of course, he didn't really have dates on most of those nights (why had lying come so easily to him, from the moment he'd gotten his car?) and he suspected that Abby, who was good friends with Melissa Hayes, knew the truth. But somehow that didn't matter, either. Once he got into the Torino and drove off, he forgot about his parents and his sister, as though he'd turned into someone else. Someone who could lie smoothly to his family and feel not a twinge of remorse.

He drove all through Atlanta, marveling at its steep hills and crazily twisting streets and lush foliage as if he were new to the city and hadn't lived here all his life. He puttered through his own neighborhood, Sherwood Forest, with boyish vanity, hoping kids he knew might see him, and he drove through Ansley Park and Garden Hills, through Buckhead and Druid Hills and Brookhaven, looping and twisting and occasionally getting lost but again finding his way. They called Atlanta *the city of neighborhoods*, after all. Or *the capital of the new south*. Or, most famously, *the city too busy to hate*.

Would the Atlanta child murders put an end to that?

Thom gave little thought to the matter, though he'd frowned at the image of Ronald Reagan he'd seen the other night on television, a clip from one of his campaign speeches insisting that *his* America would become "a shining city on a hill." Thom had watched dully, thinking, *What an old fool—does anybody really believe this guy?* And he wondered how anybody imagined that a doddering actor with dyed hair and one foot in the grave could get elected. For some reason Thom had thought of Oz and had a fleeting image of Reagan as the wizard they discovered behind the curtain, a charlatan with reddish hair dye oozing down the sides of his face. Yet the local Republicans had taken up Reagan's buzz words and claimed the candidate ought to come down to Atlanta, his shining city on a hill was right here, just waiting! As though the city needed another nickname, Thom thought. The politicians never mentioned the fact his mother had cited: that Atlanta was "the murder capital of America," too, where a serial killer was slaughtering black kids and the local police literally didn't have a clue. In early June another boy, twelve years old, disappeared on his way to a neighborhood swimming pool, and soon there were more killings: a girl snatched from her bedroom the night before her seventh birthday, a ten-year-old boy found with his neck broken beside some railroad tracks. Punching buttons on his car radio, Thom heard a report that Mayor Jackson—a portly, smiling black man, charismatic and fairly popular—had been asked what the murders suggested about race relations in Atlanta, but the normally loquacious mayor had no comment.

The summer advanced, the hysteria mounted, and Thom drove. Though he'd promised his parents he would stay off the interstate, he drove along I-75, keeping his eye out for patrol cars as he inched the speedometer to eighty, even ninety. He would exit at random, turn around, and head back toward the city, glorying in the fact he could take any exit he wanted, do anything he wanted. Back in town, he drove up and down Peachtree, the city's most famous street, one he'd traversed hundreds of times in the backseat of his parents' car. There Thom and Abby would have their own quiet, murmured conversations, and in the months before Thom got his car, one of their favorite topics had been a blond-haired senior boy named Lawton Williams, a hunky football player on whom Abby had a desperate crush. Or so Abby's little brother insisted. There was no real evidence for this, since Abby was dating Justin, a nice-looking but boring math whiz, and Lawton had been dating one of the school cheerleaders, Ashley Blaylock, since their sophomore year. But Abby and Lawton were both on the yearbook committee and the senior prom committee and the debate team, so Thom claimed that Abby had joined these groups just to be near *Lawton,* a name he pronounced with an exaggerated Southern drawl, batting his eyes.

After the prom committee had met at the Sadler house, Thom ribbed her about how "cozy" they'd looked, there on the sofa. Abby just laughed at him, asked what he was talking about, insisting *she* had no interest in Lawton Williams—he wasn't even very bright.

"Well," Thom said, one eyebrow cocked in a conspiring leer, "he doesn't need to be bright, does he?"

Abby laughed again. "Oh, he's gorgeous, I'll give you that." She frowned in disbelief. "But I can't believe you seriously think I *like* him."

Thom had given a little grimace, turning away. "I know what I know," he said.

One midsummer day Thom drove slowly through Ansley Park, one of the city's oldest and most elite neighborhoods—clean, winding streets; towering oaks and magnolias; aging homes set far back from the road; red-brick mansions and spectacular white-painted colonials with pristine columns, verandas, porches. The other day a nine-year-old black boy had been found dead of multiple stab wounds in west Atlanta—but you would never know it in Ansley Park, and certainly not on Westminster Drive where Lawton's family, descendants of plantation owners who now made their money in real estate development and a design firm run by Mrs. Williams, lived in an ochre-colored brick estate originally built by Lawton's great-grandfather. Thom drove along Westminster first thing every morning, no matter where he was headed, and again on his way back home. That day his vigilance bore fruit. He slowed at the sight of Lawton's white Porsche in the circular driveway, the soapy water snaking its way down to the street. He'd been waiting for this, he supposed: a summertime glimpse of Lawton Williams. He parked across the wide street, under the shade of a huge magnolia, not feeling at all like one of those movie detectives who did stakeouts, waiting for endless hours in their cars. Though later, much later, he supposed he must have looked like one.

The afternoon was still, cloudless, and very hot, the temperature in the high nineties. Typical July afternoon in Atlanta. Like a mirage there Lawton Williams appeared beside his car, an orange bucket in one hand and a spurting garden hose in the other. He sprayed the driver's side and then, taking an oversized sponge from the bucket, began soaping the door, working slowly, meticulously, his big sunburned face stilled in the meditative frown of a teenage boy alone and thinking of nothing in particular. He wore a pair of denim cutoffs and some bedraggled sneakers. That was all. Shirtless, his muscular smooth chest and arms gleamed, his skin gently stippled by sunlight filtering through the ancient oaks and elms. His tanned legs shimmered in their coating of pale blond hair. His body seemed almost too smooth and hard to be flesh, the rippling muscle beneath the skin perhaps a trick of the light, and even the shadowy armpits, revealed as he scrubbed the hood in a dreamy circular motion, seeming smooth and sculpted with only a suggestion of silky hair, itself part of the universal blondness of Lawton's physical being at which Thom simply and endlessly stared in the way of homely gawkers at a museum.

The only disruptive moment came when Lawton dropped his sponge and, bending to pick it up, seemed to glance in Thom's direction, so that Thom lunged to the floorboard as if urgently looking for something. When he inched his head upwards, peering out the bottom part of his window, he saw to his relief that Lawton had gone about his work, unbothered. He'd picked up the hose and stepped back a few feet. Idly, he sprayed the car, gripping the hose a few inches from its tip as he moved it along with a frantic, shaking motion, Thom watching enraptured, his mouth ajar, until he blinked and came to his senses and, covering the exposed side of his face with one hand in case his car's movement should catch Lawton's eye, cranked his engine and pulled away. In his side mirror, he caught a last glance of Lawton's bare back, the arching muscle of a brawny damp shoulder gleaming in sunlight as he lifted the hose and continued rinsing the car.

That evening Thom had one of his infrequent but friendly dates with Melissa Hayes, who seemed to understand and not to mind that they were "just friends," though she waited patiently each time he escorted her to the door for her good-night kiss, which was also friendly and which Thom enjoyed as much as she did, since clearly she did not expect anything more. That week Thom had made several hundred dollars helping landscape a big place near the Ansley Golf Club, working eight or ten hours each day, so feeling flush he took Melissa to the Pleasant Peasant, where the older patrons beamed at this handsome teenage couple: the amiable, dark-haired, sunburnt boy with his angular face and ready smile, the frag-ile sweet-looking girl with her delicate chalk-white skin and straight whitish-blond hair reaching past her shoulders. Then they went to a movie at the Tara, and afterward stopped at the Dessert Place in Virginia-Highland where they shared a huge chunk of triple-layer double-Dutch chocolate cake, Melissa allowing herself only a few tiny bites but chatter-ing happily to Thom, looking around constantly as though pleased to be seen here with this handsome, popular boy. But even as he talked with Melissa, joking and smirking and ducking his head in laughter when one of them made a joke, every few seconds he thought about Lawton Williams.

The brawny-smooth cut of his chest.

The sinewy twists and turns of his arms in the leaf-dappled sunlight.

The salty glisten of sweat along his biceps, his back....

Thom could feel droplets of his own ignoble, ordinary sweat running down his sides, causing him to twitch one wrist sideways and glance at his watch.

"Gosh, it's almost twelve," he said.

Midnight was Melissa's curfew, though usually he'd gotten her home not much past eleven.

"We can be a few minutes late," she said, smiling. "My parents really like you, Thom."

Thom looked slightly to one side and narrowed his eyes—meant to express friendly skepticism, the gesture was popular with boys at St. Jude's, that year.

"They don't know the *real* me," he said.

Melissa gave her vague, misty smile. Often Thom had thought she looked like one of the young girls in those Renaissance paintings from their art-appreciation text; she had the same pinkish-white skin, the overlarge, slightly protuberant eyes.

"Maybe I don't, either," she said.

For some reason Thom was in a jaunty, jokey mood; maybe it was the late hour or the long days he'd spent this week out in the sun. He bared his teeth and made his eyes round, like someone in a loony bin. He stage-whispered, "Who knows, maybe I'm the Atlanta child killer! Watch for my mug shot on the eleven o'clock news!"

They laughed. They finished eating their chocolate cake.

On their way back to Melissa's, they listened to an old Stones tape, "Satisfaction," the volume up high, and at a red light he reached over impulsively and took her hand, their fingers interlacing, squeezing, and Thom wondered idly how many times Lawton and Ashley had gone out before they'd had sex for the first time, and whether they now had sex on every date. Was it the natural, expected conclusion of every evening they spent together, and was it Lawton who always initiated their lovemaking, and were they limited to fugitive couplings inside his car? Thom couldn't imagine how they accomplished it, in that tiny Porsche. Maybe Lawton had college-age friends who loaned him their apartment, or did they rent a motel room? Thom had no idea. This was 1980 and Thom had turned sixteen, but he was still a virgin. He was fairly sure that Melissa Hayes was a virgin, too.

By the time Thom parked in front of her house, not only their hands but their forearms were linked, Melissa having scooted as close to Thom as she could get in bucket seats, the console between them. He switched off the ignition, turned, and brought his mouth to Melissa's; her lips were already parted, her big magnolia-petal eyelids closed and trembling. Thom supposed that Lawton Williams kissed his girlfriend like this, and that she probed Lawton's mouth now gently, now boldly with her tongue, as Melissa was doing, and he supposed all boys instinctively cupped their hands to a girl's breast in this way, to which Melissa seemed to respond eagerly, inching closer to Thom as if somehow she wanted to squeeze her way over the console and into the seat beside him.

Before he was quite aware of it, she was gently massaging the wobbly erection inside his khakis and then—was it possible?—she began unzipping him. Sweet angel-faced Melissa Hayes with her little-girl's pale blue eyes reached deftly inside his pants and grasped his warm, bobbing penis that was now fully erect: for imprinted on Thom's eyelids so vividly that not only his penis but his whole body ached with longing there was Lawton Williams, finished washing his car and lying with his brawny naked limbs flung along the backseat, crooking one finger to Thom. Blinking his eyes open, Thom resisted the urge to glance behind him. With a few more strokes of Melissa's thin, bony fingers, he felt the familiar heated anticipation and his breath came heavy and Melissa stroked harder, their mouths still locked and tongues probing wildly, but then Thom had to pull away, his head tilted back, as he spurted all over his cordovan leather belt and starched blue shirt. He stayed still a moment, breathless. When he opened his eyes, Melissa was digging in her handbag. Efficient as a nurse, she daubed at his clothes with a Kleenex, then reached over and kissed him on the cheek. She allowed herself a smile.

"Feel better?" she said.

He couldn't speak. His head was reeling.

"You don't need to walk me to the door. G'night, Thom," she said.

He shook himself and smiled sleepily and had enough presence of mind to kiss her, the same friendly good night kiss from their half-dozen previous dates, and then she was out the door and hurrying up the sidewalk.

Thom sat there awhile, inhaling, exhaling.

The next morning, Sunday, Thom skipped mass for the first time in his life. He stood at the sink rinsing his cereal bowl, staring at his face vaguely reflected in the window and thinking he looked like a criminal.

He hadn't shaved. He hadn't bathed. Strands of dark hair sleep-plastered along his forehead gave him the look of a mental patient. He had thrown on a T-shirt and blue jeans and had no idea what he would do with the rest of the day. That's when his mother came up behind him, clicking her tongue.

"Thom Sadler, it's almost ten! Hurry and splash some water on your face, honey, and change clothes—we need to leave in five minutes!"

Self-consciously, Thom rubbed one bare foot with the other as he leaned back against the counter. He let his shoulders slump a little, feeling the lie already forming on his lips.

"I'm not feeling so great—I think it's the flu or something. Maybe I'll go to evening mass."

She hurried forward, laying her palm against his forehead. "But you're not hot, honey—if anything you feel chilly. Why aren't you wearing your sandals? Why haven't you shaved?" She fondly brushed his jawline with the backs of her gloved fingers. "You always shower and shave before you come to breakfast."

He stared at the floor, not daring to meet her eyes. "Think I'll just go back to bed," he muttered. "I feel like I might throw up or something."

Thom had no history of feigning illness. He'd always loved school and had missed only four or five days in his life. His mother had no reason to doubt him.

"OK, honey," she called as he shuffled out of the kitchen. "We'll be back about twelve—I'll peek in and see how you are. If you're asleep, I'll make you a plate for later."

"OK. Thanks, Mom."

On the stairs he met Abby, who was wearing his favorite outfit of hers: a pink silk blouse dotted with tiny white flowers, white pleated skirt, white sheer stockings and shoes. Her light-auburn hair shone; it smelled fresh and lemony.

"Thom? Are you OK?" she said, tilting her head sideways.

"Feel sick," he said, hurrying past.

He went into his room and shut the door. He sat on the side of his bed and stared at his longish, bony feet. Along the tops of his big toes were tiny dark hairs; he hadn't really noticed that before. A few years ago, he had thrilled at the sudden growth of hair on various parts of his body, but now he felt something akin to disgust. His toenails could stand a clipping, he thought. It occurred to him that his body was gross. *He* was gross. He closed his eyes, feeling suddenly drowsy.

From downstairs, he heard the slam of the door to the garage, then the tedious grinding of the garage door as it shuddered open. He waited with his eyes closed, and after a minute or two the grinding noise came again. His family was gone and it was official: he was deliberately flouting his holy obligation to attend mass on Sunday, which was a mortal sin that would condemn him to eternal damnation if he should die before going to confession. Even if the Atlanta child murderer got him, he would go to the same hell where the murderer himself would end up!—a mortal sin was a mortal sin, after all. Once in theology class, in fourth or fifth grade, a girl had asked Sister Barbara—a slender, ivory-pale nun with a thin bitter line of a mouth—why there weren't different hells for different sins. Robbing a bank and killing somebody were both mortal sins, but shouldn't hell be hotter for the murderer than for the guy who just stole some money? A wave of giggling had shimmered through the room, but Sister Barbara, who seemed oddly pleased by the question, shook her head.

"No, not at all," she said. "Hell is hell. Burning is burning."

The girl had frowned, dissatisfied, but had not asked anything else. For years, the nun's words had pestered Thom's memory at random moments. *Hell is hell. Burning is burning.* Now he let out his breath, exhausted. He realized he didn't care. A dozen years of daily religious training leaked out of him in a few seconds, like water from an overturned glass. He lay down and felt a heaviness to his eyelids like the weight of damnation itself.

When he woke, the light in his room looked funny. He felt groggy and bewildered—he almost never took naps—and eased up to a sitting position. That's when he glanced at the bedside clock: 3:20. He couldn't believe he'd slept for so many hours. Maybe he *was* sick, after all?

Bumbling around his room, he gathered fresh underwear and a clean T-shirt; he understood that he was fine. He was hungry, and he longed for a glass of ice water, but otherwise he felt normal. Only when he glanced into the wood-framed mirror hanging over his dresser did he understand how bad he looked. The faint reflection he'd glimpsed in the kitchen window earlier had been too kind: his stubbled face looked gaunt, sinister. He pawed at his hair with splayed fingers, then rubbed briefly at his eyes, but he didn't look any better. He decided there was no point in shaving. He didn't feel like the usual ritual of taking a shower, using his razor, brushing and flossing, blow-drying his hair…the hell with all of that. He did put on the fresh T-shirt and underwear, but then slipped back into his cut-offs and dug his sandals out from under the bed. He lifted his car keys quietly off his nightstand and slipped them into his pocket, then edged to the door.

He heard the distant noise of the television from the den. His parents would be in there, probably watching a baseball game, and he imagined Abby had driven off somewhere. Stealthy as a burglar, he opened the door and slid into the hall. Fortunately, he had parked his car out front last night instead of in the driveway, which was visible from the French doors off the den. He was able to tread soundlessly from the hall to the foyer and out the front door; he slipped into his car and sped off.

He drove. On auto pilot, his car went directly to Lawton Williams's house, where there were several cars in the driveway: a Chrysler New Yorker, a lipstick-red El Dorado, and an ancient-looking Fleetwood the size of a small battleship. But no Porsche. Often Thom glimpsed Lawton and Ashley together at 10:30 mass, where they sat in one of the back pews presumably so that the instant mass ended they could make their escape and hurry off to fuck somewhere. Or so Thom thought, morosely. He gave a small laugh, but it sounded more like a croak. His voice felt rusty from disuse. Was it only last night that he'd been an ordinary teenage boy, chatting with his cute blond-haired date over a piece of chocolate cake at the Dessert Place? Now he drove through the winding streets of Ansley Park aimlessly, as though waiting for the siren to blare up behind him, the authorities to shackle his unwashed limbs and haul him off to jail. Or for the road itself to end abruptly, his car to spin along a wild tumbling descent into the fiery pits of hell. He gave another croaking laugh as he slowed for a red light at Peachtree. He looked both ways, then took a quick left not waiting for the light to change. Why bother? he thought. There was no point in following the rules. If you broke one, you might as well break them all.

He was not attracted to girls. Never had been. He held this thought in his mind for five seconds, maybe ten, then looked around him.

Another red light, but there was a car ahead of him so he had to wait. The car had an old bumper sticker that read SAVE THE FOX, and up ahead in full sight was the Fox Theatre itself, an Atlanta landmark that had been scheduled for demolition last year but had been saved by a vocal citizens group disgusted by this city's willingness to achieve "progress" at any cost. Thom had mixed feelings about all this. He liked old buildings like the Fox and the Georgian Terrace hotel and the ancient downtown Rich's, but he liked the towering new skyscrapers, too, especially the sparkling glass cone of the Peachtree Plaza Hotel. For a while in sixth grade, he'd thought he might like to be an architect one day, though math was his worst subject; lately he'd thought he might build houses, though he supposed you had to have plenty of money to get started. He had no idea what he would do, or even what he wanted to study in college, which was only two years away. The thought of college scared him, these days. At St. Jude's he was popular because the kids had always known him and they had no idea he was slowly (or was it quickly?) turning into another person. A stranger. A criminal. A boy who would no longer date Melissa Hayes but might continue to pretend he did, who might in fact be willing to break almost any rule if he could get away with it. Open rebellion was not his style; he would be sneaky, sly. No one would suspect him because he had no history of being sneaky or sly. It was like that story they'd read in English last year, as if he'd always been Dr. Jekyll, but now the spirit of Mr. Hyde had infected his limbs, his swirling brain.

Later he would arrive home, shave and shower, make up some story for his parents about where he'd been, and somehow he knew the lie would be good enough; they would believe him because he could impersonate the boy they knew yesterday. Thom Sadler, their son. Their good son. He would lie smoothly and watch television with them for a while and then go back to his room and plot his next horrendous crime.

He turned off Peachtree at North Avenue, headed for the expressway. He wanted to drive—and to drive fast. Taking I-75 northbound, he grew frustrated at the slower cars, but he resisted the urge to honk or to swerve from lane to lane. He hated people who drove like that. Out past the perimeter the traffic would be lighter, he reasoned. For now he was content to drive sixty, sixty-five. He could stand being good, he thought, so long as a bit of criminal pleasure hovered ahead of him, like a glistening red apple on a branch when he was so hungry, so thirsty. He could wait.

Yesterday he had read a longish story in the newspaper about the Atlanta child killer and had trouble keeping it from his mind in idle moments like this. The story was written by a psychologist who claimed the killer was probably not the KKK, as many people thought, but rather a "sadistic pedophile." Thom usually flipped through the newspaper quickly, if he bothered at all, but the word *pedophile* in the headline had caught his attention. It was one of those expressions that gave a twist to his insides whenever he read or heard them—like *sexual inversion,* or *sodomite,* or the word *homosexual* itself. He didn't care for *gay,* either. There was no good word, he thought. In the past few years, since Anita Bryant had her crusade, he saw the word in the newspaper a lot, or maybe he just noticed it more. Gay rights, gay marches. Gay men rounded up in local parks, or in highway rest stops. A couple of weeks ago, there was even a Gay Pride celebration in Piedmont Park, and a march down Peachtree Street, which the mayor and other officials had supported. If the Atlanta child murderer turned out to be a pedophile, the psychologist had written, would the city continue to be tolerant of the "homosexual lifestyle"? Thom noticed that the psychologist posed a lot of questions, rhetorical questions, but never answered them. Thom read the article twice but couldn't tell if she approved of homosexuality or not. He wondered if either of his parents or Abby had read it; somehow he doubted it. He couldn't remember a single instance of any member of his family referring to the "gay" issue, even indirectly. It was in a category, he thought, with masturbation and menstruation and bowel movements: something that polite Southern white-bread families like the Sadlers wouldn't dream of mentioning.

Outside the perimeter, traffic did begin to thin out. Thom eased into the farthest left lane and pressed the accelerator. He was going seventy-five, then eighty. Though the sun glinted fiercely from the hood, Thom switched off the air conditioning and cracked his front windows, letting the warm wind funnel through the car. Excited, he punched radio buttons until he found some nameless hard rock song and twisted the volume upward as high as he could stand. He increased his speed steadily. To ninety. Ninety-five. He had never driven even close to one hundred miles per hour but today he would. As he zoomed past, a station wagon in the next lane honked at him, and Thom glanced over. A dark-haired man of about forty with a fleshy, angry face. He was mouthing something at Thom, who glimpsed a vague-looking wife in the front seat and several small children in the back, their faces like pressed flowers against the windows. The man wanted him to slow down, of course. If Thom had been another sort of

teenager, he might have made a rude face or stuck his middle finger bluntly up in the air. Instead, he lowered his head and kept driving, a few seconds later noting in his rearview mirror that the wood-paneled station
wagon had become a tiny speck in the distance behind him.

He was driving a hundred miles an hour. He felt a surge of intense
choking emotion that must have been joy, and then he slowed the car. Back
to eighty-five. Eighty. He took a few deep breaths. It was only a matter of
time, he supposed, before he passed a patrol car and received his first ticket. Maybe he would lead the cop on a high-speed chase? Maybe he would
run his car off the road into a deep ravine, killing himself? He slowed the
car to seventy, then noticed a sign: REST STOP – ONE MILE. He needed to
urinate, and his tongue was parched with thirst. Lane by lane, he eased to
the right side of the interstate and exited, gliding down the long ramp and
into the parking lot. There were several cars, a couple of pickup trucks, and
to the far left in a reserved lot, a few freight trucks. The rest stop had a row
of vending machines, an area with raggedy grass and a couple of picnic
tables, and two brick buildings marked MEN and WOMEN. People trailed
back and forth between the restrooms and the cars, children tugging away
from their parents and pointing at the vending machines. Thom dug in his
jeans and was pleased to find plenty of change; he was dying for a Coke.
He got out of the car, locked it, and hurried into the men's room.

The air was dank and smelly. Poor ventilation, and a fly buzzed around
slowly as if dazed. There was a long row of stained urinals, none in use.
Out of habit Thom went to the one on the far right, next to the toilet stalls.
He stood there letting his mind wander, only half reading the familiar graffiti on the walls. It was the same graffiti he saw everywhere, though now
striking his eye with the force of a personal affront.

"I give great BJ, be here 6/22 10 A.M. Truckers welcome!"

"I'm jacking my big dick while you read this, homo."

"Fuck me HARD, white dudes, ev'ry night. 10 to 11. No niggers!"

Thom made a whistling noise of disgust. Idly, he looked down, adjusting himself, and saw that someone had carved a golfball-sized hole through
the metal stall door. His face reddened. Had someone been watching him?
Inside the stall there was sudden movement. The toilet flushed. Behind
him, a man had emerged from the stall, his feet shuffling against the damp,
gritty floor. Thom felt the back of his neck burning. He wanted to turn
around but didn't dare. His shoulders and back felt petrified as the man
came up to the next urinal. Thom glanced aside and met the man's narrowed eyes for the briefest instant. Tall, skinny, in his late twenties.

Neither handsome nor homely. Blue jeans and a brown leather vest with
no shirt.

"Hey," the man said. "Hot day, ain't it?"

Thom had zipped his jeans. He made a show of turning away from the
man as he flushed the urinal.

"Yeah, sure is," Thom said.

He fled, blindly.

Outside, his breath came quickly, his heart hammering. Fumbling with
his keys, he managed to unlock the car door and start the engine, turning
the air-conditioning on high. He glanced in the rearview mirror and saw
that his face was brick-red. His eyes looked pinched and scared. Almost as
quickly as he'd started the engine, he turned it off again. When he saw the
man emerge from the men's room, Thom glanced in another direction. He
waited until the man got in his battered red pickup and drove off. Exhaling,
Thom grabbed his keys and opened his door.

He bought a Coke and went to one of the picnic tables, where he sat
for a long time. People came and went. Single men, married couples.
Families. Fathers took their squirming little boys toward the men's room,
mothers took their squirming little girls toward the women's room; people
drifted in and out, chatting or not chatting, looking tired or happy, pale or
sunburned, a ceaseless flow of people, a ceaseless noise of slamming doors
and cars revving their engines and driving off. Thom sat there quietly. An
hour passed, or two hours. Afternoon shaded into evening. What was happening to him? That scared, almost wounded pair of eyes he'd glimpsed in
his rearview mirror—who was that? These questions flitted through his
mind every few minutes, but mostly he thought of nothing. Every once in
a while he glanced at his watch. It was 6:30, it was 7:10. His parents would
be worried about him, he supposed. He noticed how there were busy times
and lulls at the rest stop; there would be several trucks and eight or nine
cars, then only a couple of trucks and one or two cars. Then the cycle
would all start again. A kind of rhythm was established, soothing his
nerves. He felt that he'd become part of the landscape, that he belonged
here. Almost nobody noticed him. When he finished his Coke, he bought
another, then returned and sat down in exactly the same spot as though
he'd never left.

Around eight o'clock, as the sky began turning a rosy deep violet in the
west, a black hearse-like car drove up. An ancient Olds 98, '64 or '65. It
sat there for a moment, and Thom watched it idly. Maybe the Atlanta child
killer waited inside that car, deciding whether to strangle Thom or stab him

or shoot him. Thom smiled, taking the last warm sip of his second Coke, or was it his third. Well, he thought with an odd thrill of satisfaction, he wouldn't even put up a fight. Here he was.

After a few seconds the front doors opened. The driver was a teenage boy who looked even younger than Thom. He was slight and blond-haired but with sharp-chiseled, handsome nose and mouth and chin. The passenger was surely his mother, a petite woman in her thirties with an oversize blond perm and the same small, careful features as the boy's. Then a back door opened and an older woman got out heavily. She must have weighed three hundred pounds. Her face looked doughy and unformed, her mouth puckered into a grimace of tired effort as she struggled from the car. The boy's grandmother, Thom thought. Despite her weight, she had the same coloring and thinning blond hair as the younger woman, who now took hold of her mother's flabby upper arm and led her off toward the women's room. The boy said something to them and headed to the men's.

Thom felt an urgent need to pee. He rose and stalked toward the men's room and took the first urinal he saw and relieved himself. The blond boy was already washing his hands. When Thom approached the sink, he met the boy's glance in the mirror.

"Hi," Thom said. "That your mom and grandmother you're with?"

The boy looked startled, but then he gave a quick, thin-lipped smile. He was wiping his hands slowly and methodically with the brown paper towels. They were the same towels Thom had used for years in parochial school: their damp, yeasty, terrible yet half-pleasant smell assaulted his nostrils.

"Yeah," the boy said. "We're going up to Chattanooga. My older brother got in a wreck, so we're going up there."

"Sorry to hear that. Is it bad?"

Thom kept drying his hands, though they were already dry.

"Broke his collarbone, cut up his face pretty bad. He's not gonna die or anything."

In the mirror, they watched each other. The boy had clear, almost translucent pale-blue eyes, like glittering marbles. So pretty. He had an innocent look about him, his skin smooth as a baby's.

"You old enough to drive that car?" Thom said, with a tilted smile.

The boy ducked his head, grinning. "Nearly. I'm fourteen, but I'll be fifteen next month. Then I can get a learner's permit. My mom hates to drive on the highway, and Grandma's scared to."

"Bet you're a good driver," Thom said quickly. The remark was stupid, but he didn't care. His eyes stayed locked onto the boy's, and the boy gazed back at him steadily. It was almost like those jokey staring contests Thom used to have with his sister back in grade school, a game they played when there was nothing better to do. But this was not a joke.

Finally, the boy said with a lazy blink of his pretty eyes, "Where you headed?"

"Me? Oh, back to Atlanta. I'm just riding around, sort of. Just got my license."

"Yeah, I wish I could do that. By myself, I mean."

"It's great," Thom said. "Nobody knows where you are, you know? That's the best part."

The boy stared at him, not smiling but not unfriendly, either. They'd both discarded their towels, and there was no reason to keep standing here. Yet Thom longed to touch the boy's cheek, just once. Just with the tips of his fingers.

From outside, they heard a woman's voice. "Meredith? You in there? Mer-e-dith!"

The boy turned his head sharply. "Yeah, I'm here!" he called. "Just a second!"

"Come on, baby, we got to go!"

All at once the boy crumpled forward, as if collapsing into Thom's startled embrace.

They hugged awkwardly for a second, maybe two.

The boy pulled back. "You're nice," he said. He was looking down. "Bye."

He turned and hurried out.

Thom said, but not very loud, "Bye...Meredith."

The boy had not heard. He was gone.

Dazed, Thom emerged from the men's room a few seconds later. The black Olds was pulling out of the lot, and by the time Thom reached his own car it had merged with the stream of traffic heading north on I-75. Thom started his engine and got onto the other ramp, heading in the opposite direction, toward Atlanta. It was getting dark, so he turned on his lights, careful to drive fifty-five miles an hour. There was no reason to hurry.

He drove. He kept the windows cracked open and enjoyed the fresh warm air swirling through the car. He had no thoughts about anything for a while but then, as he approached the perimeter, he became aware that his heart was beating lightly, quickly. His limbs, his chest, his mood itself felt light and airy. He took slow, deep breaths, resisting as he exhaled the urge to release a bright rippling laugh. Why should he feel so happy all of a sudden? What had happened? His hands flexed on the wheel, his fingers spreading, then gripping tight and spreading open again, as if they would like to be wings and fly.

Hill by dreamy hill, he approached the city. As he passed the West Paces exit, he crested one of the steeper grades, still going the speed limit and in no hurry, no hurry at all, and then the skyline of Atlanta rose through the dusk before him. The vault of sky beyond had darkened to a bruised violet, a plush background for the bejeweled cones and spires wavering in Thom's vision like a mirage. The magical city beckoned to him, glimmering. Shining. He would keep driving, he thought, until the city embraced him, absorbed him, and there was nothing left. He felt something in his throat, a stinging in his eyes. What is wrong? he wondered. Nothing was wrong, or maybe everything. He had no way of knowing, but he supposed that was all right. He was sixteen. He would find out soon enough.

When you're in love, Thom thought, smiling, everything looks beautiful. Even Cobb County.

He'd gotten a call at eight this morning, a referral from Metro Brokers; a longtime agent there, an acquaintance of Thom's, had died a couple of months ago. He'd stopped all his medications and in the weeks before he died apportioned out his clients—"bequeathed them," as he'd put it— among his agent friends. Thom's appointment this morning was with a young couple from South Carolina who wanted new construction north of the city in the mid $200s, so Thom planned to show them some of the subdivisions a few miles beyond the perimeter. For the most part he avoided Cobb County, which was Newt Gingrich's home district and, more infamously for Atlanta's gay population, ground zero for Southern "religious" homophobia. In the early 1990s the county commissioners, prompted by a play presented in a Marietta theatre that had dared to mention gay people, had passed a resolution condemning the "homosexual lifestyle." The usual '90s-era controversy had followed: groups protesting the resolution, groups supporting the resolution, heated discussions on radio and TV talk shows, boycotts of Marietta businesses by gay groups, fiery sermons from conservative pulpits. The county had lost some convention business, and the '96 Olympics had rerouted the torch ceremony to avoid the Marietta square, but otherwise the turmoil had little effect on anybody. No gay people became ungay; no bigots became Christlike. Marching in the streets wasn't Thom's style, but he'd done his bit by steering clients away from Cobb into other suburbs where housing was relatively cheap: Gwinnett County, or Alpharetta. Thom knew that per capita there were just as many homophobes in those areas as in Marietta, but still these maneuvers made him feel better. Only when the infamous resolution had been quietly rescinded last year had he resumed occasional ventures north of the Chattahoochee River on I-75, into the heart of Gingrich country.

Yet Thom was in love, and even the bare trees gleamed on either side of the expressway, the evergreens bending gracefully in the February wind, as though welcoming him. It was one of those frigid but brightly sunny winter days that had forced Thom to dig his sunglasses out of the glove box. He had WABE on the radio—a Chopin prelude, he guessed, not that it really mattered—and he had his boyfriend to think about. In the days since their talk the previous weekend, Thom had berated himself for expecting too much: of course, learning that Thom was HIV-positive had been a blow for Chip. Thom had to keep reminding himself of that his boyfriend was only twenty-five. Their sexless Valentine's Day visit at first had assumed tragic proportions to Thom but now seemed a small milestone in their relationship (for certainly, people involved over long periods of time did not have sex *every* night: why was he still prey to the kind of gay romanticism he was quick to deride in others?) and he was pleased, overall, with the way the weekend had gone. The next morning Chip had kissed him sweetly on the cheek and given him a long, lingering hug, again murmuring "I love you" so that Thom, startled, again merely echoed the words. Then a touching thing had happened: Chip had stepped back, his sober gray eyes glistening with tears. Somehow Thom had never imagined such a moment: his level-headed, calm-voiced young boyfriend, a graduate student in biology with a methodical temperament and an eerie self-possession for one so young, abruptly overcome with emotion.

"Hey," Thom had said, touching his cheek. "Don't worry, I'm going to be fine. *We're* going to be fine."

Flushing, Chip had given an embarrassed smile, slung his backpack over one shoulder, and taken off. That was three days ago. Each night Thom had phoned him, and they had resumed easily their old camaraderie, carefully avoiding the topic of Thom's health. Chip had gotten excited about a new project his graduate adviser had proposed, asking Chip to help him read submissions to a prestigious journal for which the professor was a consulting editor, and he had chattered happily about that into Thom's indulgent ear. Each night, going to sleep, Thom felt his body weightless and insubstantial except for the red-hot core of tumbling, teeming emotion that was his heart. Yes, Thom Sadler was in love—it was official—and Cobb County this stark sunlit winter morning might have been paradise itself.

As he exited on Windy Hill Road, his pager buzzed at his side; he unlatched the big mosquito, as he not-fondly thought of it, and stared at the message: CALL OFFICE. He was only a mile from the subdivision where he'd agreed to meet his clients at ten o'clock. There was a new secretary at his office who paged him with annoyingly vague messages that might or might not be important. Had the clients canceled at the last minute? Was it a call about one of his listings he could easily return later? Was his condo on fire? Whatever the case, the secretary would merely enter CALL OFFICE, as if preferring to surprise him. He knew he was on the verge of breaking down and getting a cell phone but for now there was nothing to do but pull into this BP station and dig thirty-five cents out of his pocket.

"Jolene?" he said. "I'm out in Marietta, on my way to meet the McPhersons. What's this message about?"

"What? Oh, hold on, Thom..." Chattering in the background. Laughter. Shuffling of papers. Thom shivered in the frigid wind of paradise. "OK, here it is. Sorry. Um, you got a call from somebody named Chip Raines. Said you had his number. Said it was urgent and call right away."

"OK, thanks." He hung up.

Urgent? Call right away? The words took the wind out of him, they were so unlike Chip. Instantly, Thom pictured an accident, a death in Chip's family, some horror he couldn't imagine.... His fingers were shaking as he started the ignition, trying to think where his nearest branch office was. He couldn't call Chip from that phone niche outside of a BP station in Cobb County.

Thom drove, blindly. Somehow he had turned onto Cobb Parkway; he knew there was a branch office along here, but he might be headed the wrong way. Traffic was heavy, moving with a ponderous slowness. After a mile Thom forced himself to pull over, into a used car lot. He sat there, breathing heavily, forcing himself to think. After a few seconds his head did clear, and he understood the office was the other way, north of Windy Hill Road. He merged back into the parkway traffic, forcing himself to keep control. He drove.

A few minutes later, he blustered into the Marietta office and asked a startled-looking receptionist if there was a conference room not being used. She pointed vaguely. He rushed inside, shut the door, and grabbed the phone.

Chip answered on the first ring. "Thom? I've been sitting here waiting, I'm about to leave for my lab class...."

"What is it, honey?" Thom said. "The secretary said it was urgent. Or maybe she misunderstood, she isn't very—"

"No, I did say that. I guess I shouldn't have. I'm sorry."

There was a pause.

"Well?" Thom said. "Honey? What's wrong?"

Chip exhaled, a small whooshing sound. Exasperation? Helplessness? "You know, your calling me 'honey' doesn't make this any easier."

"What? What do you mean?" Thom gripped the receiver as though it might fly out of his hand.

"Listen, I've been doing a lot of thinking and here it is. I just can't be in a relationship like this. I can't spend the whole time worrying about when you'll get sick, and how bad it will be. I'm just not the sickroom type. I don't want to be a widow in my twenties."

He'd reeled out the words quickly, as though reading from a card. Thom supposed he'd been practicing them; that's why they sounded harsher than Chip intended.

Thom said, "My God, we need to *talk* about this. Of all people, you should know this isn't a death sentence anymore. I'm perfectly fine. I've got friends who were diagnosed ten years ago, and they're doing great. I have no symptoms, I... But you know all this. What's really going on here?"

He talked as though running blindly in a dark cave, not knowing if any moment he might hit a jagged wall. Why the hell couldn't Chip have come to Atlanta, at least, so they could talk face to face?

"I told you what's going on," Chip said coldly. "I can't handle it. I've thought out all the permutations, Thom. I've weighed everything out, and it just isn't going to work. I'm sorry."

Instinctively, Thom's free hand had extended, palm up, a gesture he used when trying to reason with someone. A salesman's gesture.

"But listen, honey, we've got to—"

He stopped. Chip had hung up.

Thom felt something along one side, a tingling sensation, and his first thought was that he was having a stroke. He was thirty-four and having a stroke. Then he understood the pager had buzzed.

He plucked the thing off his belt and stared dully at the message: CALL

OFFICE. He was going to fire that stupid bitch. He picked up the phone and dialed.

"It's Thom. Another message?"

"Oh yes, Thom, hold on a sec... Oh, here it is. A Mr. Lefcourt called. He says please call him right away."

Thom hung up. He dialed Connie's number.

"Thom? You're such a doll to call back so fast. I'm an emotional wreck here! Do you have a minute?"

"Sure," Thom said. "What is it?"

"You sound a bit short, Thom honey. Are you busy? You want to call back later?"

"No, sorry—I've just been dumped, that's all. So how is your morning going?"

Thom had heard a thickness in Connie's voice, as though he'd been crying.

"Dumped? By that—that boy over in Athens? Oh, sweetie, I'm so sorry...."

"Thanks, but I'm not ready to talk about it. It just happened five minutes ago. What's going on with you?"

Thom heard a snuffling, wheezing sound. He'd seen Connie cry only two or three times in the decade they'd known each other; but when Connie cried, he *cried*. Thom felt the dull pounding of his heart, a sore lump in his chest.

"What's wrong?" he said, gently.

"I shouldn't have bothered you with this. I just didn't know who else...it's just that my father called this morning, and I'm so upset...."

"Is it your stepmom? Did she pass away?"

"No, no, she's still in a coma. Nothing has changed. But Daddy is taking solace in the company of Mr. Daniels." Connie paused, gulped, then blew his nose. "Sorry about that, I've got a little mountain of used-up Kleenex here. Anyway, he called at eight-thirty this morning, drunk as shit, and started screaming at *me*."

"You've got to ignore him when he calls up drunk. I've told you that. Hang up if you have to."

"How can I do that? I mean, his wife *is* dying. I never thought he really loved her, or even liked her—maybe I was wrong. But this morning he starts screaming all sorts of *hor*rible things at me, Thom! That I'm his only child, and how could I turn out to be a worthless fag; how I have shamed him and the family so much, he should have strangled me when

I was eight years old and he first realized I was just a big sissy—stuff like that."

Thom stifled an angry laugh. How could Connie take his father's drunken ravings seriously? Why did he care? The two had never been close. Thom supposed Connie's father must be reliving the death of Connie's mother, his first great love, but at the moment Connie couldn't see that.

"That's just the liquor talking," Thom said. The comment sounded lame but he couldn't think of anything else.

Connie sniffed, then gave a timid laugh. "He said if Wilma weren't so sick, he'd fly out here tonight and slit my throat!"

"Jesus, Connie..."

"But I shouldn't have bothered you. You're not having such a great day yourself." Again Connie paused, sniffed, blew. "But you know, I never did trust that boy, somehow. He always seemed like a chilly customer to me, and I didn't understand how someone like you—"

"Let's not get into that, do you mind?"

"OK, I'm sorry."

"And it's fine that you called me. That's what I'm here for."

"You're so sweet. I do feel better already. Of course, my Xanax is kicking in, too."

Thom laughed. "That's good," he said.

"You know my motto!" Connie said, buoyed by his instinct to amuse. "What love cannot provide, your local pharmacy can!"

"I may come over and raid your supplies tonight," Thom said. "Listen, I'm late for a showing, but I'll call you this afternoon, OK?"

"Sure, stop by for a cocktail if you want. We'll drown our sorrows together."

"All right. Bye."

Thom stopped at the receptionist's desk on his way out, introducing himself and apologizing for his brusque entry into the office. "Having one of those mornings," he said, with a rueful smile.

"Oh, that's no problem!" she said. "We all have them!"

Outside, as he started his car, he felt that roiling heat in his chest that only an hour ago had felt like love. Now what was it? Rage? Sorrow? *Hell is hell. Burning is burning.* Poor Connie, to have his father speak to him like that. What an asshole. Thom had never understood why people became alcoholics. Genetic, the experts claimed. A disease. What bullshit. There were no more vices in America, only diseases. And victims of diseases. Was love a disease too? I don't feel like a victim, he thought. I just feel pissed.

He pulled out of the parking lot; the clock on his dashboard read 10:10, but he resisted the urge to slam on the accelerator. Chances were the clients would be late anyway. Waiting to merge onto the parkway, he took deep breaths and again oriented himself; the subdivision he wanted was on the other side of the interstate, so he'd cross on Windy Hill. He could be there in five to seven minutes, even in this traffic. He tried to ignore the heaving of his chest and the urgent need to cry. Come on, Thom, do this later. You've got to show this stupid listing. He turned up the radio but instead of music the announcer was muttering about something; he switched it off. He drove.

On the other side of I-75, less than a mile from his destination, a new-looking black Chevy Suburban changed lanes abruptly, cutting him off; Thom had been preparing to speed up, to make a light that was just changing to yellow. Cursing, Thom hit the brakes. The Suburban had stopped at the light, so Thom would have a minute or two to stare daggers into the back of the driver's head. But the headrest was too high, and Thom couldn't see the driver, so he passed the time imagining a jowly Republican fat cat, a cross between Jerry Falwell and Jesse Helms. That's when Thom noticed the row of bumper stickers along the Suburban's fender. ABORTION=MURDER. I LOVE NEWT. Thom gave an angry laugh. Typical Cobb County. He was enjoying his feeling of superiority to the man until he read the third bumper sticker, on the far right side of the fender. Thom blinked his eyes, incredulous. His heart convulsed. He took a breath, glanced away, and then looked back, as if the words had been an ugly trick of his vision. But no. There they were, perfectly legible red letters against a background of flag-striped white and blue.

THE MIRACLE OF AIDS: TURNING FRUITS INTO VEGETABLES.

Something had happened to Thom's body. It had turned cold, then hot. His chest seemed to constrict, and for a moment his vision blotched, then cleared again. He reread the bumper sticker, the letters so overbright and sharp they burned into his vision with a white-hot clarity. THE MIRACLE OF... He looked away. His chest ached. His skin tingled as though unable to contain his rage.

The light changed to green. The Suburban started forward with routine sluggishness, but Thom sat there. A few seconds passed. He was aware of honking sounds behind him. Then his foot of its own volition jammed the accelerator pedal to the floor, and he gripped the steering wheel in a white-knuckled vise. Thom aimed directly at the back of the Suburban, his car like a missile released from a slingshot. For a few seconds, he felt a G-force exhilaration, a sense of power sweeter and more violent than anything he'd felt in his life. And that was all.

Chapter 7.....

"I don't want you to go."

He stood next to the bed, naked, the evergreen-filtered light from his grandmother's bay window gently dappling his body. This late in the afternoon his room had a shadowed, undulating aura, in which she and Philip lay submerged, glimpsing one another through pleasing, rippling waves of erotic perception. Even his skin had a deep-olive, shadowy cast as though darkened by fathoms of silent water.

Abby lay in bed with the sheet demurely pulled to the tops of her breasts, like someone in a movie. Unlike Philip, she did not feel quite comfortable in her nakedness, despite the ardent praise her lover bestowed on her, head to toe.

"It's only four days, OK? Thom and his friends have been planning this for weeks. For months."

He stared down at her, eyes clouded by disappointment, his mouth twisted to one side in what she considered one of his cynical, British mannerisms.

"That doesn't mean you can't cancel. They'll have a fine time without you, I'm sure."

"But Valerie's going, too. We're staying in one hotel, like roommates, and the guys in another. It would be too awkward to back out."

"Not even if…it means so much to me?"

She tried not to smile, for his feelings were easily hurt; more than once, when she'd shown the barest sign of amusement, he claimed that she'd "laughed" at him. But his frowning look of disapproval did amuse her, for he stood there beside the night table holding a square of torn foil in one hand, an unspooled condom in the other. He'd lain alongside her for several minutes; they'd been kissing and murmuring and taking their time, but instead of reaching aside to slip the foil packet out of the drawer he'd drawn away and stood, taking his time with the condom while she lay there, waiting. She knew something was on his mind, but she thought he'd made peace with her trip to Key West. Several minutes had passed and his erection had drooped and he held the condom and wrapper as if no longer aware what was in his hands. He *did* look comical but no, she didn't want to wound him.

She raised on one elbow, patting the bed. "Come on."

He looked sulky, but he obeyed. He dropped the piece of foil into the drawer but held onto the condom with thumb and forefinger, then lay down beside her. Relieved, she began stroking his hip, and at once his eyes closed, and so she stroked the inside of his thighs, watching as he became aroused, his warm solid body edging toward hers and his stiffened penis grazing her thigh as if flirting, with a cleverness and will of its own. Despite her knowledge of him, despite their many passionate weeks together, she was surprised at the swiftness of his desire. Seconds later he had donned the condom and was probing her, his heated breath along her throat, her shoulders, her own breath coming fast, ragged. Often they made love for half an hour or longer, much longer, their memorized rhythm slow but rapt in a gathering intensity unlike anything Abby had imagined before, even in her teenage fantasies. But today he seemed fiercer, wilder, and once or twice she'd almost cried out in pain, but a pain so alloyed with pleasure that she bit her lip and stayed quiet so that when he finished with a few jamming lunges and quickly withdrew, dragging his damp limbs off to one side, a wounded animal, she felt torn and exposed and imagined she might be bleeding.

She glanced down the length of her own damp body, but no. Her fingers itched to pull the sheet back up, but she resisted; Philip would make a *tsk*-ing sound if she did that. He lay beside her, his breath easing as the moments ticked past.

"I really *don't* want you to go," he said.

His tone angered her; the assumption, perhaps, that what he wanted should be her first concern. Since they'd met, Philip had shown little interest in her family, though she often mentioned Thom; whenever she suggested introducing them, Philip insisted he wasn't "ready for that." Abby assumed her lover had felt the heterosexual male's discomfort with gay men, though surely in the theatre world Philip knew well, he must encounter gay men all the time. More recently, he'd confessed that what he really wasn't ready for was an encounter with someone else Abby loved.

"I do have a jealous streak," he'd admitted. "You two have such a long history together, and I—I'd feel like the odd man out. OK?"

No, it wasn't OK; it was absurd.

"But he's my brother," Abby had said. "You'll have to meet him eventually, and you'll *like* him, Phil. Everybody does."

"I know he's your brother, but I'm just not ready, all right? Please don't force the issue."

She'd had no choice but to let it drop. His possessiveness was flattering, she decided, and after a while she'd consciously avoided mentioning Thom, feeling drawn more deeply into Philip's hermetic, slightly paranoid world. (Yes, she thought, "paranoid" but somehow not off-putting; even sympathetic, in a way. After all, he'd admitted *her*.) Oddly his vulnerability only fueled her passion, her need to protect the boyish, wounded soul peering out from his lovely dark eyes.

She took a deep breath. She waited for the surge of annoyance to pass. I'm sorry if it makes you uncomfortable," she said. "But I have to go."

He sat up, hurling his legs over the bed. She stared at his back, waiting.

"What am I supposed to do, then? For four days?"

She allowed herself an audible expulsion of breath. "Come on, be fair. You went out of town last month, didn't you? For a week?"

"That was different. My aunt was sick, and she doesn't have anybody else. I told you that. You can't compare that with a vacation in Florida. In fucking Key West."

Now she did jerk the sheet toward her throat; she was aware that her hands were shaking. Ten minutes ago they were toiling in frantic, white-hot passion, and now this...this tawdry argument. She couldn't remember the last time she'd felt so angry.

"Well, I'm going," she said. "There's no point in arguing about it. I don't understand why—"

He stood, banged shut the nightstand drawer, stalked toward the bathroom.

"Get dressed," he said. "I want you to leave."

He slammed the door behind him and left her there, gaping. She felt the blood drain from her face.

She waited a few seconds, assuming he'd slip back out the door to apologize. But then she heard the familiar sound of the shower, the glass door clicking shut. She stood and got dressed, still trembling with anger. It was over.

It wasn't over. The next morning at eight-thirty, Abby stood with her suitcase opened on the bed, trying to decide between two pairs of walking shorts—a pretty, pleated white linen, a less pretty but more practical white cotton—when the phone rang. She started toward the phone, then stopped. Two rings. Three. Not long ago Valerie had expressed surprise that she didn't have caller ID, but Abby didn't see the point. There were only four people who called, for the most part: Philip, Thom, and Val—and Abby's mother. Sometimes it was Connie, a pleasant surprise, since lately she'd heard less from him. Now she stared at the ringing phone and wished she hadn't turned off the answering machine; she and Thom were leaving for the airport in half an hour. She decided the caller must be her brother, and she snatched up the phone on the sixth or seventh ring and of course it was Philip.

"I'm so glad I caught you," he said. He sounded panicked, out of breath. "I was afraid you'd already left."

She didn't know what to say. This morning it had crossed her mind that he might call and apologize, but she wasn't sure if she would accept the apology or not. After she'd returned home yesterday, straitjacketed by anger, Abby had decided it really *was* over. She'd thought she loved this man, but maybe that had been a romance-novel delusion. She'd lain awake with dry eyes gazing upward into darkness, wondering if she'd become temporarily deranged by her sudden lust, her shed repressions—the prim schoolmarm Abigail Sadler transformed into the naked Abby with her sweaty limbs and burning eyes. But it wasn't just that. Her heart had burned as well. Last night it had become a sore lump in her chest, bruised by longing and by the fear it was no longer needed. She did not know if she loved Phil DeMunn or not. Did that mean she did not, or was that idea the kind of psychobabble she and her mother had heard on talk shows? Weren't there borderline states? Wasn't there a period of transition when you might drift in and out of love from one day to the next? One hour to the next? She didn't know. She was glad to be going away for a few days to sort her thoughts. She was not glad to hear from Philip this morning.

"No, not yet," she said cautiously. She tried to sound neither distant nor encouraging. "I've still got some packing to do."

"I know, I just wanted to say that I'm sorry and that—well, I'll be counting the days until you get back. Your return flight is on Monday, right?"

"Monday, yes."

"In the afternoon? Evening?"

They returned to Atlanta at 2:40 P.M. on Monday but she said vaguely, "I'm not sure. Thom took care of the tickets."

He paused. "I don't blame you for being angry."

"You said some hurtful things. I'm not sure what I feel."

"But I hope you can understand," he said quickly. His voice lowered to a whisper. "It hurts *me*, you know, that you're going off like this."

"I'm sorry you feel that way," she said. Her hand gripping the receiver felt oddly numb and she resisted the urge to hang up.

"It's not too late, is it?" he asked, timidly. "To back out?"

The nice girl Abby Sadler wanted to apologize, she was afraid it *was* too late, she couldn't disappoint the others, but instead she said, truthfully, "I don't want to back out. I'm looking forward to this trip."

Another pause. Maybe Philip would be the one to hang up, and that would be that. She longed for this to happen.

No, she dreaded it. She waited.

But he said, "What time are you leaving for the airport? Let's see, it's quarter till nine…"

Her mind worked quickly, deftly. "Not until one o'clock," she said, "but I have a lot of packing to do."

She felt slightly breathless. Again she'd lied baldly to her lover.

"Oh, one o'clock," he said, relieved. "I thought—well, I'll let you finish packing, then." She couldn't quite read his tone of voice. "But will you do something for me?"

"What's that?" She sounded more agreeable, more pliable than she intended.

"Will you call right before you leave? To say goodbye?"

"All right. I will."

Did lying get easier each time, like murder?

They hung up. Though she was already taking too many clothes, she jammed both pairs of shorts onto the pile and with a grunt of effort closed and latched the suitcase. You couldn't have too many pairs of white shorts in Key West, could you?

• • •

When they stepped off the small plane they'd boarded in Miami, Connie declared the weather was a good omen. In Atlanta the day had been overcast, the temperature in the fifties; here in Key West the sky was a crisp, cloudless blue, the air at least twenty degrees warmer and not nearly as humid as she'd feared. As they hobbled along tourist-like, lugging their carry-ons from the plane to the little airport terminal, Abby tried not to think of her silent bedroom and her telephone ringing, ringing. It was just now one o'clock.

An hour later Thom and Connie had checked into the Brass Key and walked back to the Pier House, where Abby was sharing a room with Valerie, and the four of them left together and drifted onto Duval Street. They found a large café called Mangoes where, though it was past two o'clock, the outdoor eating area facing Duval still hummed with a lunchtime crowd. Once they were seated Abby marveled at her buoyed emotions: she'd rarely felt so elated, so free. Leaving Atlanta and Philip, she felt she had averted some unnamed but potent danger. In only a few hours, it had become clear that she did not love him. It had been an intense affair; in most respects it had been good for her, but it was over. There would be a few awkward phone conversations; perhaps she would have to hang up on him, finally. Yes, it was over. The bright, expectant faces of Connie, Valerie, and her dear brother Thom had never looked so appealing.

"I'm so glad we're here!" Abby exclaimed gratefully.

The others smiled back at her, surprised.

"And we're glad *you're* here," Thom said.

"Yes, you're looking really beautiful," Connie said, giving her a silly, infatuated stare. "Is that a new blouse? I think pink is your best color, honey. Have I told you that? Is it silk?"

These past few days Abby had gone shopping, a bit recklessly. She still had plenty of money saved, but until next fall, when her teaching fellowship began, she would have no income. She'd had no business buying new spring clothes but the thought of bringing to Key West the same ordinary cotton blouses she'd worn the past few summers had depressed her. She wanted bright colors, clingy fabrics; in the past few months she'd managed to gain ten pounds, and everyone marveled at how she'd "filled out" (as Philip had put it, running one hand along the curve of her hips, her thighs); she'd even visited a tanning salon, amazed at the improvement in her looks after a few sessions. No longer the pale schoolmarm, she had become prettier and more sensuous-looking, especially since she'd gotten her shorter haircut and experimented with a darker lipstick, a glossy mascara. Men noticed as she walked through the mall or along the campus sidewalks. She'd enjoyed moments of gratified vanity and pleasure in her physical being that she hadn't felt since high school.

Valerie touched her forearm. "See? I told you."

Abby smiled. "My big sister has been helping me," she said.

Often she and Valerie went shopping together; they were in similar situations, since Valerie had renewed her relationship (a fairly passionate one, Abby gathered) with her husband, but like Abby had no job and really should have been avoiding the malls entirely. The sense of daring, of the forbidden, had made their expeditions that much more enjoyable. The other day they'd spent a couple of hours in Nordstrom's, trying on swimsuits one after another, giggling like teenage girls. Both had spent more on their suits than Abby normally paid for an entire outfit.

"Wait till you see her bikini," Valerie said, as though reading her mind.

"I *can't* wait!" Connie cried.

"Oh, it's not a bikini," Abby said in mock reproof. "Just a two-piece."

"A bikini," Valerie insisted. "Abby has gorgeous legs, *so* long and sleek and tanned. Not doughy white and dimpled with cellulite, like mine."

The others made vague, demurring noises. Their champagne had arrived, and Valerie laughed giddily. All four lifted their flutes for the toast.

"To our first day in Key West!" Connie proclaimed.

"And to us," Abby added.

"To my three *wonderful* new friends!" Valerie cried.

They all looked at Thom, who hadn't said much since they sat down but who looked happy despite his evident tiredness, his pale, somewhat sunken cheeks. Since his accident, he hadn't quite been the same, though his injuries had been minor enough: one eye swollen for a week, an ugly bruise on his upper arm. Yet he looked unwell. Underfed. When had his cheekbones become so prominent? The other day he'd mentioned losing weight: he'd dropped to 150, he said, less than he'd weighed since high school.

Now Thom raised his glass, giving his tilted smile as he looked at Valerie, then Connie. Then his pleasant blue gaze settled on Abby.

"To friendship," he said quietly.

As if pulled by strings, the others' flutes rose to their lips; they drank.

• • •

A vacation in Key West, Connie and Thom had instructed her, should be haphazard and formless, strictly void of ambition, planning, or energy. The next afternoon, as they lounged beside the Pier House pool drinking mimosas, the men poked fun at Abby when she opened her "guidebook" to the city. She'd never been here before, she told them, and had thought to visit the Hemingway house, maybe, or the Lighthouse Museum. Connie stared at her the way he might regard a dim-witted child.

"Honey, I hope you don't think we're going to *do* things while we're here. That's really not the point."

He'd been thumbing through some magazines he bought at the airport—a *Southern Living,* a *People* with Monica Lewinsky on the cover. He seemed only to be glancing at the photographs, not reading anything.

"That's fine with me," Valerie said, her face tilted back to face the sun. She wore overlarge Jackie Onassis-style glasses and a short white sundress—or was it a tennis dress?—with blue piping; the others had sneaked glances at her legs, which were indeed pasty-white and plump, but not really fat. For a woman of forty-six, she was quite attractive and well-preserved, Abby thought. Her hair and makeup were perfectly done, as always. Her toenails were painted the same blaring fuchsia as her lipstick.

She added, "All I want to do is laze around, and pretend that I'm not married."

Connie laughed. "That's naughty," he said. "I like naughty."

"Don't get me wrong, I love Marty to death. I'm just sort of glad he's not here. He isn't good at relaxing."

"Then I'm glad he's not here, too," Connie said. He added, smartly, "And it's fine with me that Warren backed out. He can't stand it when I have *fun.*"

Thom glanced over, frowning, but said nothing.

Since they'd sat down, Abby had felt her gaze settling frequently on Connie, who looked remarkably tanned and fit. He'd mentioned visiting a tanning salon, too, but somehow she'd guessed that under his expensive tailored clothes there might lurk an imperfect middle-aged body going to fat. A few minutes ago, complaining of the heat, he'd removed his lime-green Nautica T-shirt to reveal a hairless, well-toned chest, muscular shoulders and biceps, long shapely legs. His voice and manner might seem effeminate at times, but his body was a man's body.

She told him, "You're looking well, Connie."

"Thank you, sweetheart," he said. "You know what they say—better to look good than to feel good."

He struck a fashion model's pose, his glittering blue-green eyes as fixed as a mannequin's.

Thom gave a brief, weary laugh. He'd put on sunglasses too, and now he glanced away. "Please, Connie," he said.

Connie's hand flew to his mouth. "Remember a few years ago, when we came with Warren and Pace? When I'd just had my lipo and had to sit around wearing those big, loose-fitting Hawaiian shirts? I was such a grouch."

"But they were such lovely shirts, Connie," Thom said, deadpan.

Connie considered this. "Yes, that's true. They were some gorgeous Tommy Bahamas I'd bought that time Warren and I went to St. Croix."

"You had lipo?" Valerie said. "Did it work?"

The others tittered, briefly.

"My dear, I'll ignore that somewhat tactless question," Connie said, with an airy wave of his hand.

"Oh, I didn't mean it that way." Valerie ran one hand along her thighs. "It's just that I've thought of getting it, too, for my legs. I hate my legs."

Connie said, "As it happened, my guy was a criminal. I had it for my tummy, but the swelling and bruising were so bad, I couldn't walk for three weeks. Of course, during that three weeks I did nothing but watch TV and eat ice cream, feeling sorry for myself, so I just put on more weight. And the pain pills!—they slow down your metabolism, you know, so you gain even more. The bruises were so bad, I couldn't take off my shirt for six months."

Valerie's immense sunglasses had turned in Connie's direction; she made a tsk-ing noise. "That's terrible, Connie. Did you confront the doctor?"

"Oh, he kept stuffing me with Percocet to keep me quiet. Eventually, I healed up, but I was no better off than before, and sayonara to 4,000 clams. Finally, I just started living at the gym. That's really the only way to slim down."

Thom was laughing to himself, gently. Connie's head jerked sideways to face him. "What?" he said.

Thom grinned. "I was just remembering what Pace said when you were recounting all your problems with that surgeon." He lowered his voice and barked out a perfect impression of Pace: "'Sue the bastard!'"

The others laughed, even Connie. "I should have, too," he said.

They were quiet for awhile. Connie returned to his *People*, Valerie to her sun worship. Thom sat looking pale but not unhappy behind his sunglasses. Across the pool, several middle-aged couples sat at tables sipping tropical drinks and reading.

Abby shut her guidebook and tossed it aside. The others were right; this wasn't a time for sight-seeing. She had no problem with the routine Thom and Connie apparently followed in Key West—sleeping late, lounging by the pool discussing where to go for lunch; then strolling up and down Duval with a bit of shopping here, a cocktail there; then more lounging by the pool and discussing where to go for dinner. In the evenings there were neighborhood bars and oversized dance clubs that began filling slowly around eleven o'clock and by one A.M. were packed with gay men and a few "fag hags," as Connie persisted in saying, with wry glances toward Valerie and Abby. Last night they'd stopped at Epoch after dinner, but they hadn't stayed long; Connie had danced with Abby, Thom with Valerie, but she noticed that the men hadn't danced together. She hoped Thom didn't feel constrained by her being there. She wanted him to be himself, didn't she? A younger man had come up to her brother while he was buying drinks, but Thom hadn't seemed receptive; was that because Abby stood next to him? Close as they were, they'd had so many secrets from each other. After all these months, she still hadn't told him about Philip; nor had they talked much about their mother, or about their long estrangement that had ended so abruptly last fall…. It might be too late, she thought. They might go forward and never "process," as Warren would put it, anything that had happened. A few months ago this idea would have bothered her much more than it did now. Had she become a less responsible, earnest person, or had she merely discovered that she was no more responsible or earnest than anyone else?

This laid-back, patternless vacation in Key West seemed the right time to have such thoughts, without pain. Even her life in Atlanta (much less her old, constricted life back in Pennsylvania, with her mother) seemed distant and unthreatening, its claims easily ignored. The image of Philip's lean, angry face and the jealous tone of his words over the phone seemed almost cartoonish, remembered here. She could not take them seriously. It seemed likely she would never tell her brother about that affair, for what was the point? And Thom had his secrets, too. Sitting there behind his dark glasses with his new wan smile and his old familiar, slumping posture, his way of hunkering down into a chair that their mother had scolded him about for years. "*Sit up straight, Thomas Sadler!*" But he never had.

The last thing Abby expected on this humid March afternoon in Key West was that Connie would toss down his copy of *People,* look over to Thom, and say something Abby found so startling her hands began to shake.

"I've meant to ask you, Thom honey—how are you feeling? Are you taking your medicine?"

Thom didn't seem unsettled by Connie's question. "Yeah, sure," he said.

Abby's body had tensed, partly because she feared what Valerie might say, or ask; sometimes Valerie was unpredictable, with a tendency to speak without thinking. Abby held her breath, but Valerie gave the impression of not having heard Connie's question. She'd stayed in the same sun-worshiping posture, her head tilted back and her mouth slightly ajar, so that Abby wondered if she'd gone to sleep.

"You know," Connie said, "I was reading in *Southern Voice* that lots of guys get sick because they get careless about their doses. With some of these new things, if you miss even one pill—"

"I know all about that, Connie," Thom said. He hadn't turned to face them, either, and Abby guessed that behind his glasses her brother's eyes were closed.

Shortly before Abby had moved out of her brother's condo, she'd been in the kitchen one morning after he'd left for work, hunting down his copy of the Yellow Pages. She was opening and closing drawers, and in a bottom drawer near the refrigerator she'd been startled to see a shoe box stuffed with amber-tinted plastic containers of various sizes. She'd lifted the box out of the drawer, careful not to disarrange the containers. They were alphabetized, she'd noticed, Acyclovir and Bactrim in the front of the box, Viracept and Ziagen in the back. Perhaps two dozen in all. The labels faced frontward, and carefully tucked into one side of the box was a folded sheet of notebook paper. Her hands had shaken as she'd gently unfolded the paper and read, in the small, precise handwriting Thom had learned in parochial school, a chart outlining the time of day and dose for each drug, and brief reminders about each: *Clarithromycin (suppresses MAC), Hydrea (suppresses T-cells but enhances effect of other drugs), Zerit (can cause neuropathy!)* One or two had been whited out, with new prescription names written over them.

Another language, she'd thought. Another world. The sheet was soft and crinkled, as if folded and unfolded countless times. Abby handled it with the care she would give to an artifact, a sacred relic. Her eyes had filled at the idea that Thom must be thinking about all these pills throughout each day and even at night (two of the drugs had 2 A.M. and 6 A.M. doses) without saying anything to her, perhaps to anyone. Except when he visited his doctor, he was alone with all this, wondering if these hundreds of pills would continue to work, if he would live or die. He was alone with all these thoughts.

Even today he seemed alone, and a little remote. But he was the polite Southern boy Thom Sadler, nonetheless, for now he did look over at Connie, offering his lazy curl of a smile. "But...thanks for asking," he said.

Over the next couple of days, as Connie said, they did all the things they were supposed to "do" in Key West. They bought silly T-shirts and postcards at shops along Duval Street; they shopped at Fast Buck Freddie's, the town's colorful department store where Connie treated himself to several designer shirts, and both Abby and Valerie shamelessly bought another new swimsuit apiece. On anyone's whim they all stopped for ice-cream cones or a round of tropical drinks at a sidewalk café. They rented bikes and rode lazily and aimlessly through the muggy, shade-dappled streets. Despite all the tourists with their multiple cameras, their inimitable mix of weariness and aggression, the fabled charm of this place worked its spell on Abby. She loved the dilapidated white-painted houses smothered in purple bougainvillea; the sudden glimpses of huge multi-colored parrots perched on a porch rail, or the handlebar of an abandoned bike; the weathered, zonked, but harmless-seeming druggies wandering the streets as though it were still 1968; the loud crowing of roosters at all hours, proclaiming an eternal dawn; the little tumbledown cafés where your sandals might push dead flies along the floor, but you'd be served key lime pie so cool, sweet, and smooth it felt like manna filling the desert of your mouth. She couldn't remember days when she'd eaten or drunk so much, yet she rationalized the excess by imagining their bicycle rides and hours of dancing each night worked off the calories. Even Thom seemed livelier by the end of their second day, and she was pleased when he and Connie finally did wander off to dance, while she and Valerie rested at their table in pleased, sweat-soaked exhaustion, sipping gin and tonics.

It was almost midnight, yet this was Saturday and the place was still filling up.

"I have an idea," Valerie whispered in Abby's ear.

Abby felt a lurch of panic—what if Valerie, as a lark, asked her to dance?

But Valerie said, "Let's just stay here in Key West. We'll open up one of those little shops, peddle seashell jewelry or something."

Relieved, Abby smiled. "If you've got the money..."

Valerie gave her throaty laugh. She seemed thoroughly at ease in this cavernous, smoky dance bar with its shirtless young men, some of them with pierced nipples, others with shaved heads and elaborate tattoos adorning their muscular arms, their sweating backs. She might have been frequenting gay bars all her life. Though the men smiled politely at Abby, they seemed more drawn to Valerie, who often blew them kisses or batted her eyes. With her makeup and perfect coif, Connie had remarked over dinner, Valerie had missed her true calling—she could have been a drag queen!

"That's the highest compliment I can offer," he'd insisted, with a wry little smirk.

It was past two A.M. before they left the club, unlocking their bicycles and meandering slowly down Duval. The air was still warm, but the street was darkened, everything closed, the sidewalks almost deserted.

Connie, in the lead, turned abruptly down a side street, calling back over his shoulder, "Let's take a little detour. I'll show you where Tennessee Williams used to live!"

But they made a turn, then another turn, and Connie's pace slowed; Abby could tell by his frequent head-craning that he'd gotten lost. Along here the streets were so poorly lit that Abby could barely make him out, but her brother was just a few yards ahead.

"Thom?" she called. "Are we going the right way?"

Thom shrugged, but Connie had overheard.

"Yes, dear!" he cried. "Just follow the yellow brick road!"

"Very funny!" came Valerie's small, winded voice, bringing up the rear. "This 'little detour' is wearing me out!"

As Connie turned them down another side street, Abby heard the squeal of tires and the loud twang of country music. She felt exposed in the sudden illumination of headlights. An old pickup truck approached them, slowing. The music switched off. Abby glanced over and saw three gawking heads inside the cab, all wearing cowboy hats. She heard an empty beer can hitting the street, close to Thom's bicycle.

"Hey fag!" one of the men called. The others laughed raucously.

Another can flew out, hitting Abby's calf; she winced and glanced down.

"Hey there, fag lady!" the voice cried.

More whoops and laughter, then the truck swerved toward the side-walk, behind Connie's slowed, weaving bicycle. Abby held her breath.

"Connie, watch out!" Thom called.

Abby heard a scream of the truck's brakes—or was it Connie's terrified voice?—and then the tires screeched away from the sidewalk and back onto the street. The cowboys' laughter was drowned in the loud farting of the truck's engine. The country music switched back up, loud, as the truck sped off.

Within seconds the others had reached Connie, who'd evidently pan-icked and run his bike into the red-brick wall facing the sidewalk. He got to his feet, brushing at his clothes.

"My, wasn't that fun!" he said, trying to sound unbothered. But his voice was shaky.

"Are you OK?" Thom asked.

"Yes, but I believe this darling Ron Chereskin has a rip on the sleeve," he said ruefully. "I just bought it this afternoon!"

"You're not hurt, are you?" Valerie asked. She added, indignantly, "Those stupid rednecks! But how did they—"

She broke off, but Connie was quick. "Know we weren't breeders, boy-girl-boy-girl? They probably saw us leaving the bar," he said, with a flutter of his hand.

"They followed us?" Valerie said.

"Things like that happen, even here," Connie said. "One time, when poor Tennessee was walking home..." He stopped and looked around him. "Wait a minute, now I know where we are." He pointed to the red-brick wall. "That's the Hemingway house!" He slapped his forehead. "Boy, did I get us lost."

From the thicket of vines along the wall, Abby thought she heard a muffled, plaintive mewing.

"One of Hemingway's cats!" Connie cried. "This block is overrun with cats, you know, and they're all descended from Hemingway's. They all have six toes. Or is it three toes? Anyway, some wrong number."

Thom laughed, wearily. "I vote that we head back." He pointed. "Come on, Duval is right up there."

"All right," Connie sighed, gazing up to the sky. "Maybe we'll see you tomorrow, Tennessee!"

When they returned to their room and the men had gone, Valerie said, "Wasn't that awful? Imagine having to put up with that kind of abuse all through your life!"

Abby said, quietly, "I can't imagine it."

"You know, hon," Valerie said, unscrewing an earring, "despite my advanced age, I never gave a thought to gay people before, one way or the other."

"Really?" But Abby was only half-listening. She'd noticed a folded square of paper that had been shoved under the door, and picking it up she saw her name—"Ms. Abby Sadler"—scrawled across it. She unfolded the sheet and read:

Hello, darling. Spending a lonely Saturday night and just wanted you to know I'm counting the hours until Monday. Call me when you get this? Sorry I was such a cad the other day. Love, Philip.

Watching Abby's face, Valerie said, "Is something wrong?"

Abby handed her the note.

"Oh. Isn't that sweet?" Valerie said, uncertainly.

"No, it's not sweet. It's annoying and intrusive."

Valerie said, "Oh, dear."

Abby went to the phone and dialed the concierge, who told her that Philip had called the message in around ten o'clock. Relieved, Abby hung up. She hadn't thought the handwriting was Philip's, but she had to be sure. She took the note firmly in both hands and ripped it into small pieces, then tossed them into the trash.

"Abby? It's not *that* bad, is it?"

"No," she said quickly. Why had she torn up the note? Melodrama wasn't her style. "It's from someone I used to know. The relationship is over, and he won't quite recognize it."

Valerie rolled her eyes. "Believe me, I know what that's like! We ought to introduce him to Marty—they'd have a lot in common!"

Abby smiled. "Let's get to bed. I'm exhausted."

The next morning, shortly after she and Valerie had gone out to the pool, Abby came back to the room: she'd forgotten her sunscreen. She stood in front of the bathroom mirror, applying the lotion and enjoying its rich coconut smell, the silken coolness along her arms, her abdomen.... One of the great pleasures of this vacation was the attention she gave her body, sunning herself, sleeping late, eating what she pleased; she couldn't remember having indulged herself in this way. She did recall, with a little shudder, the trip to Hilton Head she'd taken with Graham Northwood about this time last year. Graham, of course, had plotted out virtually every minute of their trip, wanting them to "get the most" from their first vacation together, not knowing, as Abby had known, that it would also be their last. On the plane Graham had shown her, proudly, a "log" he'd made in his neat printed script. Meals had been scheduled, reservations made weeks in advance; their tennis and swimming time had been scheduled, too, as had the various side trips, at least two each day, Graham had chosen from the countless brochures he'd ordered from the Hilton Head Chamber of Commerce. Once they arrived she did talk him into going dancing on their first evening—he'd bought tickets to a tennis exhibition, an idea that made her heart sink—but when Graham "danced" he resembled a man trying to operate an invisible jackhammer, his face scowling with effort, his fists pounding up and down in the air, feet jerking in spasms that bore no relation to the music. It was the hopeless dancing style that afflicts certain overeducated, uncoordinated white males, and after a few songs she'd suggested they go back to their hotel. Later that night his lovemaking—which she supposed he'd scheduled, too, though he'd had the tact not to write it down—had been awkward and uncomfortable. He'd had to approach her twin bed, since the management had failed to provide the king-size bed he claimed he'd reserved, but fortunately their coupling was brief (like a pair of sand crabs, she thought, dry and mechanical) and soon enough he'd retreated to his own bed, leaving her wide-eyed in the dark and counting the days before their return to Philadelphia.

Now as she gently rubbed lotion along her thighs, that memory, which would have struck her as comical if it had happened to someone else, seemed so distant it might have been a scene she recalled from a movie.... She was twisting the cap back onto the sunscreen when she heard a brief, polite knock. Valerie was always forgetting her key; Abby hurried to the door.

It was Philip. He held a dozen roses in his arms.

She gaped at him, too startled (as she would later think, furious at herself) to slam the door in his face. She must still have worn the pleased, dreamy expression she'd had before the mirror, enjoying the pure sensation of her own fingertips as they massaged her tender, sun-reddened skin. Philip pressed the advantage. He smiled, extending the bouquet.

"Special delivery," he said. "From an admirer."

She shook her head. "Philip..."

"May I come in?"

Later she would think, too, that he'd never looked more stunning: his dark hair combed back neatly, glistening; his black polo shirt accentuating his chest, his smooth biceps; his face tanned and gleaming. His broad forehead, the finely cut eye sockets, the prominent nose and thinly curved lips were so flawless in their masculine beauty they might have been drawn from an Italian sculpture. But he was very much here. Very much alive. Her confusion must have shown plainly in her eyes, her mottled skin. He cupped one of her cheeks in his warm, living hand.

She stepped back, looking around her, and not knowing what else to do with the roses, she dropped them on a nearby table.

"They're lovely," she said. "I guess they'll have a vase somewhere, I'll call the front desk…"

He came forward and kissed her, first gently, framing her face with both hands, and then less gently, massaging the small of her back as he pressed his mouth to hers, taking firm control of her limp, uncertain body. She closed her eyes, and with the same unresisting pleasure she'd felt when applying her lotion. She held him, too, first with a kind of tentative politeness, then with an urgency she did not question. Already his hands were undoing the thin strap between her shoulder blades.

He whispered, "This is a lovely swimsuit, but…"

She heard the flimsy shred of fabric drop to the floor. Even as they kissed hungrily Philip was easing them toward the bed. Step by step, urging her along. A kind of dance. He reached down with both hands, tugging his knit shirt upward along his smooth chest, and of course she helped him. They laughed briefly as they patted the standing dark quills of his hair back in place.

"You look so beautiful," he whispered. "Your skin is so rosy and warm, I hope you're not burned…" His jaw abraded that tenderest skin along the tops of her breasts, which indeed had gotten sunburned in the tiny new swimsuit, and though she winced, somehow the pain heightened her need for him, her hunger, her lust—whatever it was! Later she would decide it need not be named, merely avoided, but now she did not want to avoid it. When he'd dropped his khaki shorts and briefs to the floor, he knelt and tenderly lowered the bottom half of her suit, kissing her belly, her thighs, darting his tongue up between her legs so that her eyes closed and she parted her thighs, no shame, of course she wanted him, and then he rose and lifted Abby, and they both fell gently, again with a conspiring laugh, onto the bed, a tangle of dampened hair and heated, writhing limbs, mingled odors of her lotion and his cologne, muted groans and exhalations from their opened mouths when one drew away, only to be pulled back greedily by the other.

They fucked for half an hour, though it might have been half a day. Later she would tell herself yes, they had fucked, might as well use the plain, unvarnished term, they had not "made love," for she did not love this man. In fact, she felt alarmed and angry all over again, when she thought about what he'd done, showing up here. And what she had done. But she hadn't been able to deny him. Too much sun, too much self-indulgence, the easy formless atmosphere of Key West—she could blame all these things, or she could blame her own guilt-raddled soul. But did it matter? She had enjoyed that sex, that day, more than she'd ever enjoyed anything in her life.

Yet even in Key West pleasures come to an end, and after they'd lain side by side for several minutes, the sweat on their naked bodies slowly cooling, both of them staring up at the ceiling without saying a word, the nagging anxiety began to prod, like small but rude pokes at her abdomen, and she felt a renewed sense of alarm. By the time she rose and slipped into her swimsuit she was trying to keep the anger from showing in her narrowed eyes, her hard little smile.

She kept her back to him, pretending to fiddle with the roses. She said, "Come on, you'd better get dressed. Val could be coming in, you know. Any minute."

"I saw her when I was looking for the room," Philip said. "Out by the pool. She was conked out in one of the lounge chairs."

"But still…"

Something in Philip's voice caught her attention, made her frown briefly, but she couldn't place what it was. And his phrase "looking for the room" troubled her. How had he known which room?

She heard him leap up from the bed and start dressing. "I'll go and let another room, all right?" he said. "Your friend can have this one to herself."

Abby dropped the roses; a thorn had pricked her finger, and she glanced down. No blood. Now the very sight of the flowers enraged her. She turned to face him.

"You shouldn't have come, you know," she said. "You've got to leave, Phil. I'm on a vacation with my brother and our friends. You shouldn't be here."

Dressed, tall and lean, his thick wet hair combed back with his splayed fingers, he looked absurdly handsome; she glanced away.

"What do you mean? I love you, goddamn it. I belong where you are."

She felt a threat of tears bubbling up from somewhere, but she breathed deeply and kept them down. Frustration? Anger? Fear that she might love him, too, in spite of everything?

Could you love someone you hadn't quite managed to *like*?

She said, "We'll talk when I get back, all right? I—I guess I appreciate the gesture, the flowers, the trouble you took coming down here, but you shouldn't have done it. It really wasn't fair."

He ran his slender fingers back through his hair, this time in frustration. His mouth wore a boy's sneer of displeasure.

He said, "This is the thanks I get?"

She turned toward the door; she didn't want to argue. He rushed forward and grabbed her arm.

"Listen, goddamn you. What is it you're afraid of?"

She thought the threat of tears had subsided, but now they flooded her eyes and she tried to blink them out. She hated herself at this moment, but she hated him even more. Twisting her arm from his grip, she shoved at his chest with the heels of both hands.

"Get out!" she cried. "Get the hell out!"

She shut her eyes and wiped at her cheeks with her palms, like a child. She stood that way for several seconds after he'd slammed the door.

She hurried over and twisted the lock behind him, though knowing he wouldn't come back. It occurred to her that the day before she left Atlanta they'd argued and then had wonderful sex, while today they'd had even more wonderful sex and then had an even worse argument. The thought consoled her, briefly. They'd come full circle. Perhaps it really was over, this time. Then the tears came again, and she stood for a long time with both palms pressed against her eyes, feeling alone and stranded in a hotel room in Key West.

It was their last day, and as they sat over a late lunch Connie rattled off the things they ought to do.

"On Sundays, the tea dances are fabulous," he said. "First there's the Marina, and then the La Tee Da."

"The La Tee Da?" Valerie laughed. "That sounds festive!"

"My dear, it's *most* festive or we wouldn't be going. But somewhere in between we've got to dash back to the Pier House for the sunset—you girls must have the sunset deck experience, at least once. It's not the least bit gay, but it's fun all the same. We'll take pictures and have a couple of drinkies. Then I'm going to take you all someplace fabulous for dinner—my treat, I insist. I made a reservation at both Café des Artistes and La Trattoria Venezia because I can't decide which one. Then after dinner..."

They were happy to let Connie engineer their last evening in Key West. Throughout their trip Thom had kept his smiling but low-key demeanor, agreeing to anyone's idea of what to do, seeming pleased to be here but unusually quiet, as though conserving his energy. During their lunch Abby had felt a pang of recognition, for as the others chattered about nothing much, Thom had reminded her of their father, presiding over their lively dinner table when they were young. Thom, Abby, and their mother had all been talkative, sometimes contentious, sometimes too loud, and though their father had said little, he'd always seemed, like Thom these past few days, at peace, sometimes putting in a gentle correction, responding to some outrageous comment with a tilted, dubious smile, but largely content to let the others' talk and laughter wash around him. If Thom had turned into their father, would she turn into their mother eventually? This thought, coming to her shortly after they were seated at the sunset deck, struck her like a blow to the stomach.

"Shall we have one of those *huge* margaritas?" Connie said, pointing to a group at the next table.

Abby didn't need to look. "Yes," she said. "Definitely."

The others laughed. Signaling the waiter, Connie held up four fingers and pointed to the next table; the waiter hurried off.

"You know," Valerie said, reaching over to pat Abby's hand, "you look so much healthier than that first day we met on the plane. You looked pale that day, honey, and worried. Remember how awful the weather was? First a thunderstorm, then that crazy snowfall..."

They were silent for a moment, as if stunned by the thought of snow here in the early-evening placidity of the warm breeze, the cloudless deep-turquoise sky above the water.

"I'd had a rough semester," Abby said quickly, wanting to change the subject. She noticed how Thom's eyes had settled on her, assessing. She'd never liked being the focus of attention. Though she knew the gesture was obvious she pointed and said, "Oh, look at the sun! Over there!"

Obediently, the others turned and looked. People had begun to drift away from their tables, congregating along the deck railing with their cameras ready. Out on the horizon, the sun was a perfectly round orange ball poised a couple of hand widths above the water. The surrounding sky bore streaks of paler orange and gold, shading upward into gently bruised purples and deep blues that blended indistinguishably into the crisp blue-black of the sky with its early handful of winking stars. Abby breathed, deeply. She had not imagined the sunset would be so beautiful. She watched the stately movement of the sun as it descended, darkening now to a blood-ringed orange, staining the dark water where, near the deck, small triangular sails skimmed along lightly, as though innocent of the looming drama poised at the horizon.

"See what I mean?" Connie said proudly, as though he'd staged this event for his friends' enjoyment.

"You were *so* right," Valerie said. Her voice sounded dreamy and far-away. "Now I do sort of wish Marty were here…"

"And I wish—" Connie began. "Oh, never mind what I wish. Thom, what do you wish?"

Thom looked over, smiling. "I wish Carter were still here. And Roy. And about three dozen other people."

"Oh, gosh, let's don't get gloomy," Connie said. The enormous drinks had arrived, so he reached for his glass and took a long swallow. "What about you, Abby? Make a wish on the sunset."

She smiled, keeping her eyes on the horizon. She'd been sipping her drink, too, and imagined she could feel its first effect, seeming to buoy her and the others as if they were suspended in air these few feet above the water, not anchored here on this deck, in these chairs. Now the sun was a bloody orb poised just inches above the water; people along the railing were exclaiming over the sight, their cameras clicking.

"At this moment, I don't wish for anything," she lied, for of course she was thinking of Thom and hoping he might somehow outlive them all.

"Oh, *look!*" Valerie cried. They craned their necks and finally had to stand, for everyone had risen and pressed forward, watching as the sun descended majestically into the water. It moved with such precision, like a wafer of blood slowly tugged below the surface by an unseen hand. Abby felt the tendons in her neck and shoulders straining as she watched the final topmost sliver ease down and down until, at last, amid a chorus of groans and cries from the others on the deck, it dipped out of sight. The crowd began to clap, and to laugh. It was a delighted but nervous laughter, and the clapping seemed less celebratory than a way to cover the anxiety—but maybe she was imagining this? Looking around she saw that everyone was smiling and nodding happily. Connie, Thom, and Valerie were smiling as they settled back into their chairs and yes, Abby was smiling, too.

"Wasn't that *wonderful*?" Valerie sighed, her hand flying to her mouth.

"Oh dear, we forgot to bring our cameras!"

Connie pressed his lips together; it was clear that he'd meant to bring one. But he gave a dismissive wave. "Oh, who cares—we'll remember it forever, won't we?"

"Absolutely!" Valerie cried.

Neither Thom nor Abby spoke, but she knew her brother felt as she did. Connie was right, of course. They would never forget.

When the waiter approached and Connie smiled roguishly and again held up four fingers, no one protested.

They sipped the second enormous drink, and their conversation grew more general, disconnected. Abby felt her head spinning pleasantly, painlessly, and she was happy to sit here floating for a while and making forgettable conversation with Thom and the others. She noticed that the background music, some generic rock song she couldn't identify, had grown louder, and the talk and laughter at the other tables had intensified, too, as if competing. As the sky darkened, the deck lights had flashed on, then dimmed, casting everyone's face in a flattering rosy-pale glow. Connie looked lively and mischievous, Valerie was animated and laughing frequently, and even Thom looked better, as if invigorated by the alcohol, though he'd barely touched his second drink. He'd grown more talkative, however, and when Abby focused on the conversation she understood they were talking about one of Thom's old boyfriends.

"I could swear I saw him the other day," Connie said, "driving up Piedmont. Are you sure he's left town?"

"Not sure, no, but I hope to God he has," Thom said. Idly, he stirred the little straw through his slushy drink. "He supposedly went back to New York to live with one of his relatives—his aunt, I think, or maybe one of his cousins."

"Who are you talking about?" Abby asked, idly.

"Oh, Thom's evil boyfriend from last year—Edward," Connie said. "Such a con artist he was."

"Less a con artist than a psycho," Thom said.

"But a gorgeous psycho," Connie said, grinning sideways at Thom.

Thom nodded. "Yep. My own stupidity."

Valerie gasped, "Oh, you mean *he* was the one...?"

"Yes," Thom said. "He called and told me over the phone. 'You might want to get tested, Thom dear. I've gotten a bit of bad news.'"

"'Thom dear?'" Connie repeated. "What an asshole."

"I didn't believe his 'bit of bad news,' either," Thom said. "I think he knew all along."

Connie rolled his eyes. "Definitely a psycho. Too bad you can't prove he infected you deliberately—you could get his ass thrown in jail."

"Oh, this is awful," Valerie said. "Let's change the subject, please! Let's talk about pleasant things." She hiccuped; she'd slurred her words and actually said "theasant plings."

Connie laughed. "You're right," he said. "It's fun raking Edward over the coals, though." He shuddered, then sipped at his drink.

Abby said, knowing she must be drunk or she'd never have asked this, "But did you love him, Thom? I mean, before you knew—"

"Before I knew he was a psycho? I guess I did. I thought I did."

"I wonder if all actors are really that crazy," Connie said. "Is that how they manage to play other people so well?"

Thom shrugged. "I don't know. I don't care, at this point."

"I dated an actor once, in college," Valerie said. "Totally into himself—his looks, his own ideas. I could never get a word in edgewise."

"And I..."

But Abby had stopped listening. Now she remembered what had struck her odd yesterday when she'd been talking with Philip: *She was conked out in one of the lounge chairs,* he'd said. The words had sounded strange somehow, and now she knew: he'd used an American accent. Or had dropped his British accent. Just for that moment. She reached for her glass and took another sip, and her hand was not shaking.

"...last time I saw him was at that party Pace had, before Christmas. Remember that, Thom?" Connie was saying.

Thom laughed ruefully. "Yes, that doomed party. Poor Pace. And poor me—*every one* of my former boyfriends showed up. It was like they all had a conference call earlier that day and said, 'Let's spook the hell out of Thom!'"

"You poor baby!" Connie laughed.

The air around them had grown chill, and despite the alcohol coursing through her body, her dazed head, Abby's blood had chilled, too. The others' voices sounded distant, as though submerged—like the bleeding sun awhile earlier—under layers of water.

One day she and Philip had stopped at a bookstore where he'd bought several titles, and she'd stood watching idly as he signed his credit card receipt, "E. Philip DeMunn." He went by Philip always, and didn't encourage her to call him Phil. She'd asked what the *E* stood for, hadn't she? More than once? And he'd given some coy response. "You know how we actors are. We have lots of names."

Now she heard something. She felt something. Thom had leaned forward and touched her arm.

"Are you all right, honey? Did you drink too much?"

She regarded him through glassy eyes. Another odd thing had happened yesterday, but in their passion she hadn't noticed. For the first time, Philip had not reached aside to the nightstand and eased a condom out of the drawer. They'd literally fallen into bed—wild and thoughtless.

She smiled, weakly. "No, I'm fine... I was just thinking about that party. Which one was Edward, Thom? What did he look like?"

Thom watched her, puzzled; his features seemed blurred, as if she were seeing him through water, too.

Connie said quickly, "Oh, tall dark and handsome. Sort of exotic-looking, I guess you'd say."

Abby smiled vaguely. "Was he...British? I mean, did he come from England? You know, from—"

"Now, honey," Thom said, frowning, "I know what England is. No, he isn't British. Are you all right? You're pale, your skin looks clammy. Do you want to go back to your room and lie down? Or should we go on to dinner?"

"He wasn't from...England?" Abby murmured.

Now Valerie was leaning over, peering into her eyes. "Abby, why do you keep saying that? Thom said no, his boyfriend wasn't from England. What does that matter?"

Connie made a smacking noise; he must have slapped his forehead. "But you know what? He told me he was doing a Shakespeare play last fall out in Marietta, that little theater on the town square. He rattled off a few lines for me in his British accent. You must have talked to him that night, too. Did you, Abby?"

You know how we actors are. We have lots of names.

She let her eyes fall shut, knowing the others were watching her; she took a deep breath. She resolved not to think any more and to focus all her energy on keeping her composure.

When she opened her eyes, the other three were peering at her. She smiled at them vaguely.

Connie tried to make a joke. "Dottie, you're not in Kansas anymore!"

Valerie laughed; even Thom was smiling. Abby was smiling, too.

"Yes," she said, "I think the drinks got to me. I feel better now."

"You're sure?" Thom asked. "You looked so strange there for a minute."

"Yes," Abby said. "I'm sure."

Connie let out his breath, relieved. "You were in la-la-land for a minute there, Abby," he said gently. "'He wasn't from...England? He wasn't from...England?'"

Abby covered her eyes, as though embarrassed. The others kept kidding her, gently. The phrase *He wasn't from...England?* was to become a private joke among the four of them, whenever one was suspected of having had too much to drink.

They decided to have a quick dinner at the hotel, despite Connie's two sets of reservations. Later they would say it was a fortunate thing, too, for halfway through the meal Connie's name—*Mr. Lefcourt!*—came over the P.A. system. If Mr. Lefcourt was here, he had an important phone call.

Connie rushed off, then returned to the table looking pale and unhappy.

The caller had been Warren; Connie's stepmother had died, and his father wanted him to fly home to Oklahoma City right away. Connie was able to get a reservation for six-thirty the next morning, so they said their goodbyes to him after dinner, and the next morning around eleven Abby, Thom, and Valerie left for Atlanta as originally planned. Their vacation was over and Abby, gazing mindlessly out the small blurry window of the plane, supposed that her life was over, too.

Chapter 8 ....

Spring arrived in a yellow haze. Through the last days of March, the pine pollen swirled visibly through the air, and each morning Thom Sadler woke to find that its yellow dust, the color of egg yolks, had drifted against his exterior window sills, the white wooden railing around his front stoop, the windshield of his car. In early spring Thom kept a rag and bottle of Windex in his glove-box; he couldn't stand to drive any distance squinting through jaundiced glass, so he sprayed the windshield each morning before leaving for work. The effort winded him. After closing the glove box, he would sit there, catch his breath, then start the ignition with a hard twist of his fingers. So many things he once did thoughtlessly now took concentration and deliberate effort. Slowly, he navigated each day as if struggling through an element denser and more combative than ordinary time, ordinary air.

Ever since that stupid car wreck in February, which he refused to discuss with anyone—not even Abby—and which he tried to avoid thinking about, he hadn't felt quite the same. In whimsical moments he liked to think the ass-covering lies he'd told that day, and so fluently, had damaged his soul; somehow the weakness had spread through his body, enfeebling him. He had rammed the Suburban with its hateful bumper sticker so hard that the driver, a teenage girl who had borrowed her father's car for the day, had lain in the front seat, convulsing.

Thom had managed to struggle out of his car and hobble forward to see what damage he'd wrought. His air bag had inflated, preventing any serious injury, but he'd been badly shaken. His left shoulder had jammed so hard against the door it went numb. Peering through the driver's window of the Suburban—the door was locked—he saw the young girl sprawled along the seat, quivering horribly, her mouth contorted, eyes clenched in pain, and he'd felt the blood drain from his head. He slumped against the door, his breath ragged. His stomach lunged, and that unmistakable tingling in his throat told him he was about to throw up. Then another man, from the backed-up traffic behind him, ran up and took control. It was this man (whose name he could not remember) who had helped Thom to the side of the road, had called the police and an ambulance, had even started directing traffic around the accident. The man had been young, dark-haired, anonymous-looking. He had shown up in court and, to Thom's astonishment, had backed up Thom's blatant lie that the Suburban had braked abruptly, not giving Thom enough time to stop, though he also testified that Thom had been driving too fast. Thom, as the girl's father angrily insisted, got away with a "slap on the wrist": a ticket for following too closely and a stern admonition from a young, harried-looking black judge. The injured girl had arrived in court looking pale, wearing a neck brace; she had suffered no permanent damage, her father admitted, but she would wear the brace for three months, and the sight of her tore at Thom's heart. The image of her lying in that car seat trembling, convulsing, loomed in his nightmares for months to come.

Thom agreed with her father that the punishment had been too light, though a lawyer-friend Thom called had laughed that the girl had been wearing an "insurance brace" and probably wasn't hurt at all, that Thom shouldn't worry. Thom hadn't told the lawyer about the bumper sticker, or about the way his foot had seemed not his own but a mass of raging pitiless instinct when it stomped on the gas pedal. He would never tell anyone, he thought guiltily. *Never.*

Of course, no one had accused him of deliberately ramming the car. No one would have imagined that this polite, nice-looking young man, who had gone straight to the girl and her father and apologized, might have committed such a crime. The girl was only sixteen, a high school student, and she looked shy and fearful; she seemed even younger than her age, an innocent. *The Miracle of AIDS: Turning Fruits into Vegetables.* Yes, the infection in Thom's soul had spread to his body and brain so that he no longer felt well or thought clearly.

Maybe the punishment was about right, after all.

More than a month had passed and April was here, and Thom felt neither better nor worse. Since their vacation in Key West—which had been good for him, he supposed—he'd gotten busy again with work. The real-estate market was hotter than ever, and for the first time he'd actually begun turning away clients, referring them to younger brokers in his office. He now had few listings under $200,000, and those few sold quickly; almost everything sold quickly. Already he'd made more money this year than during all of last year, and even last year had been good. So had the year before that. Evidence of the Clinton prosperity was everywhere, though he didn't feel quite well enough to enjoy it. He ought to think about getting out of his condo and buying a house but couldn't imagine summoning the energy required to move, to buy furniture for a larger place, to shuttle forward into the next stage of his life the way his clients were eagerly doing. He was treading water, these days; he was maintaining. When the real estate market's spring fever had subsided, he thought he might take Abby and Connie on another vacation. To the Caribbean, maybe, or Costa Rica. Somewhere peaceful where the days were formless and he could read and rest and not have to think.

When he wasn't working he was usually helping Connie, who was having a rough time. There had been a predictable blowup when Connie went home for his stepmother's funeral, and as Thom had suspected, the main thing on Connie's father's mind was the money. His first wife's money. Connie's money. The first Mrs. Lefcourt had left behind a complicated, peculiar trust that seemed almost designed, Thom thought, to keep her memory omnipresent in the lives of her widower and only son. Though Mr. Lefcourt could not touch the money or control its disbursement, he was named as "trustee," and along with the estate lawyer he had to co-sign (Thom could imagine with what raging disgust) Connie's monthly checks. The checks increased in size through Connie's twenties and thirties, and only when he turned forty would the trust dissolve and his mother's estate become his alone. The intention, Connie's lawyer had explained, was that Connie not depend wholly on the estate and fail to make his own way in life; it was assumed that by the time he was forty, he would be established in his own career, be married and have a family, and be able, at last, to handle his inherited wealth responsibly.

In spite of everything, Connie and Thom could not help giggling as they discussed all this. By now Connie had given up even his occasional stabs at part-time jobs and no longer remarked that he hoped to "find something" soon; his mother's estate had prospered to the degree that the monthly checks, calculated according to some complex actuarial scheme that even the lawyer didn't seem to understand fully, had increased far beyond what his mother might have imagined thirty years ago. Thom learned for the first time that during Connie's teenage years, when Connie and his father had begun to have serious arguments, Mr. Lefcourt had launched the first of several legal challenges against the will; but these efforts had failed. The will had been airtight, Connie boasted: every *t* crossed, every *i* dotted. So it wasn't surprising that his recent visit home had not gone well. Connie had turned forty in March, a fact that had no doubt loomed unspoken between Connie and his father during the four stressful days Connie spent in Oklahoma City. His father had managed to control his drinking for the most part, but virtually every remark he directed at Connie had been laced with sarcasm, and since Connie was no slouch in that department either, they'd had several shouting matches, one in the funeral home parking lot within earshot of people arriving to pay Wilma Lefcourt their last respects. After the second day, Connie told Thom, he left the house and stayed in a hotel for the rest of his visit. Connie spent most of his time with the estate lawyers, discussing the transfer of assets.

"Now that your birthday's passed, do you have to go back there? You know, to sign papers and so forth?" Thom had asked.

Connie shook his head. "No, thank God. Daddy's lawyer—or the estate's lawyer, I should say—said everything is in stocks, bonds, and cash, plus some jewelry in a safety deposit box. All the assets can simply be transferred into my name. And after all these years of my father signing the checks, he's totally out of the picture once I turn forty. Not even his signature is required. He's out in the cold."

Thom blinked, hearing the note of triumph in Connie's voice, then said, "It's not surprising he's angry, then."

"Why should he be angry? He's known how the trust was set up ever since I was a kid. The stock market has been like a fever chart these past few years, so there's more money now than we'd ever imagined. I'm going to be filthy rich, and he can't stand it."

Thom thought a moment. "Your dad isn't exactly poor, is he?"

"Oh, no, he's done well enough. And poor dim Wilma left him a nice bundle too, I think. But it's like my mother has finally made this grand, posthumous choice—me over him, you know?"

A sly little smile had come across Connie's face. Thom glanced away, and at that moment an idea struck him.

"Connie, you said your mother left behind some jewelry?"

"Oh yes, I've seen it—I don't think it's all that much. A few rings, one or two necklaces. Probably worth fifty or a hundred thousand, but I'll never sell it." His voice had turned dreamy, his eyes softening. "I can remember my mother wearing every piece of that jewelry. I have pictures of her wearing it."

"I was just thinking...was any of the jewelry from your father? You know, something he gave her?"

Connie stared at Thom. "Most of it, probably. Why?"

"Maybe it would help mend fences," Thom said quickly, "and make him feel better if...well, if you offered him one of the rings, or whatever he wanted of the jewelry. You know, as a keepsake."

Connie had kept staring. He blinked. He opened his mouth to speak but then seemed to think again. He nodded.

"That's a good idea, Thom. I'll think about that. My father and I haven't been in the habit of...I mean, we've never exchanged gifts, you know. We haven't communicated much at all. But yes, now that he's so hot and bothered, maybe that *would* help."

"It might smooth the waters, you know, take the wind out of his sails— that's really what I meant."

"Thom, you're so metaphorical! But you're right. I shouldn't think of myself as engaged in some kind of war with him. That's *his* sickness, not mine." He was nodding eagerly. "Yes, there was this big opal ring with little diamonds around it that he gave her for an anniversary present. Frankly, it was an ugly ring, an old lady's ring, but she wore it to please him, and I suppose I could give him that." He'd clearly warmed to the idea. "Yes, maybe with a picture of her wearing it too."

By then Thom had felt more, rather than less uneasy. He'd said nothing.

Connie's birthday in early March had come and gone with surprisingly little fanfare. Warren had wanted to throw him a dinner party, but Connie had forbidden it; he'd allowed Thom and Abby to take him to dinner at Ciboulette, his favorite restaurant, and then a group of his male friends—Thom hadn't been able to make it—had taken him out to Swinging Richard's for a night of acting silly with the male strippers. Connie, Thom had heard, tipped the strippers so extravagantly that they'd practically fought each other for the privilege of giving him table dances. Thom was glad that Connie had enjoyed his birthday, but he was worried about him. He was still taking too many tranquilizers and "muscle relaxants" and sleeping pills, complaining constantly of anxiety and insomnia. He insisted that already people liked him for his money—news of his inheritance traveled with electric speed among Atlanta's gossip queens—and didn't care about *him*. Thom knew Connie well enough to discount most of these complaints (Connie loved being gossiped about, he loved attention of any kind) but the pills did worry him, as did the abusive, late-night phone calls Connie still received from his drunken father ("Of course, he always calls during the one night when I manage to get into a nice, deep sleep," Connie said), and the general formlessness of his life. Connie insisted he was in a "transitional phase" and was trying to think of a small business he might enjoy running, but for now he rose at ten or eleven, piddled around the house, spent the afternoon at the gym and the pool, then beginning around five o'clock—"my cocktail hour"—he socialized with his friends and also, Thom had gathered, with a few hustlers he'd met around town.

"I'm glad you're enjoying yourself, but I hope you're being safe," Thom had told him.

"Yes, Mama," Connie said, rolling his eyes. "First, I mummify the darling boys in Saran Wrap, and with *really* dubious-looking trade, I scrutinize their privates with a magnifying glass. They seem to enjoy that."

"Seriously, Connie," Thom said.

"I am serious!" Connie cried.

Every few days Thom vowed to stop meddling in other people's lives and tend to his own. Look at *you*, he told himself in his best scolding, big-brother's inner voice; who are you to tell other people how to live? He tried to avoid giving brotherly advice to Abby, too, since after all she was older, and smarter, and plainly resented any attempt to interfere with her life. A couple of weeks ago he'd made the mistake of offering her some money to "tide her over" until her teaching fellowship began, but she'd bristled at his assumption that she needed any help. She still had plenty of money saved, she told him; back in Philadelphia their mother had refused to accept rent or grocery money from her, so she'd spent practically nothing for the past few years. Thom shouldn't worry about *her*... He'd grasped the implication of that remark and had said nothing else. Abby was right, of course; though she'd seemed not quite herself lately (she was quiet, secretive, and also a bit irritable, which wasn't like her) he knew that Abby was worried about him, too. These days she asked probing questions about his condition, his medications. Did he take vitamins, had he tried "alternative therapies"; did he stay on top of the research; did he really trust his doctor...? The questions dizzied Thom. He supposed he did trust his doctor—the same nice, no-nonsense woman who had treated Carter—and he simply did whatever she told him to do. He did no reading about HIV; he attended no support meetings; certainly he joined no protests, wrote no letters to politicians or drug companies. He supposed he was too passive about his illness, but the shrill activism in which some of his friends engaged simply wasn't his style. Just doing his job and maintaining the semblance of a personal life were all he could manage.

His energy seemed to be seeping out of him, day by day. Occasionally, he felt overwarm, a bit dizzy, and would take his temperature and discover that it was 100, or even close to 101. He meant to start keeping a record, taking his temperature each day and writing it down, but he kept forgetting. He tried not to berate himself any more than was necessary or to indulge in the silly idea that this was a punishment of any kind. Didn't everyone lose control at least once in his life? Didn't everyone harbor at least one personal crime he had never confessed to anybody? Life meandered along through this yellow-hazy spring, and Thom sneezed, yawned, did his job, took his medicine, checked his temperature, and in general did the best he could.

One balmy morning Thom approached his car with a stack of manila file folders and bulging envelopes—he was dropping off tax records at his accountant's office on the way to work—and after he'd maneuvered himself into the car he noticed there was almost no pollen on the windshield. Good. That was something, at least. Yet he felt winded and overwarm. He put one hand to his forehead, a habitual gesture though it hardly ever told him anything. His forehead always felt warm, even when he wasn't running a fever. He sat there for a moment and considered going back inside to take his temperature and pop a couple of Motrin, but he was running late and this was an important day. He kept going.

That afternoon Abby paged him. The new Infiniti Thom had leased after he'd crumpled the fender of his Accord (he hadn't wanted to see the car again after that day) had a built-in cell phone, and now that Thom had the phone he didn't know how he'd lived without it. He was on his way from a closing in Norcross to meet a woman client in Ansley Park; this was the second time he'd shown her the listing, which at $1.2 million would be the most expensive house he'd ever sold. She seemed on the verge of making an offer, and he was a little excited; he didn't know if his flushed cheeks and aching eyes were due to a fever or merely his giddiness over the likely sale. He punched Abby's number and immediately started babbling about the house, a restored brick Colonial on Westminster Drive.

"Hey," he said, grinning, "remember that hunk we both had a crush on in high school, Lawton Williams? The house is right across the street from where he used to live."

"Lawton Williams?" Abby said. He could imagine her crinkled nose, her look of mild impatience. "That was *your* crush, Thom. I never went out with that dope."

"Hah, but you would have," Thom said. "I never told you this, but in high school I used to drive by his house all the time." He laughed. "I was a stalker before they even had stalking."

Silence on the line. Abby was seldom in the mood for joking these days. They'd had dinner at Camille's the other night, and Thom had noticed her features were sharper, more defined; there was a new vividness to her eyes, a quickness to her speech and even her walk, as though she were energized by some emotion akin to anger. Thom didn't understand. She'd begun spending most of her time in the library and going to grad student functions at Emory, even though she wouldn't enroll officially until summer school began. He supposed that he'd expected her to become the quiet, studious Abby he remembered from the time when she'd been working on her master's. During those months her skin had turned parchment-pale from her hours in the stacks, and she'd gotten a bit dowdy, paying little attention to her clothes and makeup. But these days, though she kept going on shopping sprees with Valerie—her new clothes accented her trim figure, her hair was always shining—the excitement over her "new life" in Atlanta had dissolved. She no longer seemed quite content. There was a displeasing edge to her manner, her voice.

"Listen, Thom," Abby said. "I just talked to Mom last night."

"Really? How's she doing?" he said eagerly. He'd brought up their mother several times recently, but Abby had always changed the subject.

"She's all right, but she's upset that we haven't kept in touch. She wants us to fly up there for Easter. You know how she is about holidays, and ever since Christmas—"

"That's a great idea!" Thom said. He'd turned onto Westminster and glided to a stop in front of the house, under the shade of a battered old elm; he glanced around but didn't see his client's car. "But wait, isn't Easter—"

"Yes, that's the problem," Abby said. "It's this weekend."

Today was Wednesday. Thom reached aside for his appointment book and flipped through the messy pages, sending yellow Post-it notes flying.

"Let's see…I have something Friday morning, but I could leave after that. Easter weekend, you know, the real estate market pretty much shuts down."

Another silence. "You mean—you're willing to go?"

Thom closed his eyes; a wave of heat had prickled his scalp, the back of his head. He thought of those films about Death Valley he'd seen as a kid, the air so hot you could see its shimmering waves along the scorched earth, blurring the landscape like a fever dream. His eyes were moist. The idea of going somewhere, even Philadelphia, held a strange appeal.

"Sure, why not!" he said. Then he wondered if he'd spoken too loudly; had he shouted the words?

Abby said, slowly, "All right, I'll see out about reservations. We could leave Friday evening, I guess, and come back Monday or Tuesday."

Now he understood, or thought he did. She'd been counting on him to decline the invitation; it was Abby who didn't want to go.

"Is that OK with you?" he said. He glimpsed something in his rearview, a bright-crimson flash of color. For a moment he thought his feverish brain had begun to hallucinate, but of course it was his client's lipstick-red Mercedes.

"Sure, fine, I'll call you tonight, OK? After I call the airlines."

"OK, I should be home around—"

But Abby had hung up.

He sat there a long moment, steeling himself for this showing. He must do well. The client was already "in love" with the house, and in fact the place was so fabulous it had practically sold itself; but still he had to be careful. Sometimes if you said the wrong thing, took the wrong approach, a client's enthusiasm could unravel quickly. You had to be a psychologist in this business. You had to stay on your toes. Thom took a deep breath. His head swam with heat, and now there was a dull, throbbing ache at his forehead, too. But he felt all right. He would do fine. He inhaled again, grabbed the door handle, and sprang from the car, smiling his eager salesman's smile.

Lying awake at night, he suffered not only the fevers, sometimes changing the sheets two or three times before he drifted off, but feverish memories, too, that reclaimed him with a hallucinatory power.

Rarely had he been sick, even as a child. Rarely had he missed school. But when he was eleven years old, he'd suffered another fever—or a fever dream—and had stayed in bed for days. Lately he'd been recalling that long-ago incident, though like certain other memories it was something he'd discussed with no one, not even Abby. Especially not Abby.

He was eleven years old. It was the day after he'd gotten hurt next door, after all the commotion died down.

Because it was summertime he'd usually slept late, but that morning his eyelids had felt tissue-thin, and they trembled open at first light, the faintly dawning rectangles of his window shades searing his vision as he blinked his aching eyes. He understood his room was all but dark and that everything around him was heavy, solid, in place, but that wasn't what he saw. His vision seemed coated with a warm mist, and his skinny kid's body had felt heavy and tangled in the sweat-dampened sheets. He saw things he knew, he *knew*, he wasn't really seeing. Amber-pale sheets of light throbbing on, off, on, off, with each beat of his heart; white-hot arcs of light shooting like stars from one corner of his room to another; countless pinpricks of neon reds, greens, yellows like dyed sugar sprinkled on cookies yet substanceless, elusive, dissolving if he tried to focus, but when he closed his eyes they reappeared, and again the sheets of amber light, and again the shooting stars. His eyes ached. His forehead burned. His tongue had felt dry, and he raised up feebly to call for his mother, for Abby, for anyone, but he had sunk too deeply into the fever and his head swam, falling back to the pillow.

The day before he'd gone next door for Fourth of July. He'd gotten to know his neighbors quickly, but already they seemed like a second family since at that age time yawned, especially in summer, and your frame of reference lasted only a few days. You didn't think much beyond that, forward or backward. So he'd hurried next door at the appointed time—half an hour early, in fact—in the loping kid's way he used in his own house, rushing from one room to another.

Only two weeks before, the Carsons had moved in, and it turned out they had a boy his age. The boy's name was Kenneth, but he had a nickname, "Kit." He'd told Thom to call him that. Even his parents called him that. Kit was a little red-haired kid, wiry and freckle-faced, always grinning; Thom's mother and sister had commented on how "cute" he was. They'd all been peeking out the living room drapes, which they kept closed against the heat, on the day the Carsons' moving van arrived—"all" meaning Thom and Abby, their mother, and Verna, the Sadler family maid since Thom and Abby were babies. Their mother stood at one window and Verna at the other, Thom and Abby kneeling on the floor on either side of Verna's knees.

"Mmm-*hmm*," Verna said, in her most emphatic negative. "That be some kinda ugly funniture."

Thom and Abby tittered, mostly to be polite; Thom hadn't noticed the furniture.

"But the wife is pleasant-looking, don't you think?" Thom's mother said, doubtfully.

"Guess they have just one kid," Abby said, poking Thom absentmindedly in the side.

"He's a cute thing, ain't he?" Verna said.

"He looks like Huck Finn," said Thom, with a small laugh. He thought of the big illustrated book of his sister's he'd thumbed through one day when it was raining.

"He looks like he doesn't eat enough," Abby said.

"They's all skinny, the mama and daddy too," Verna said.

That's when Thom's mother had put an end to their spying. She'd stepped back from the curtain and put her hands on her hips, as if she'd just entered the room and discovered them.

"Now, that's enough," she said. "What if they look over and see you children peeking out like that? They'll think they've got lunatics for neighbors."

Abby sat back on her heels and laughed. "They wouldn't be too far off."

Copying Abby, Thom laughed and sat on his heels, too, but lost his balance and fell backward. He wiggled his bare legs in the air, clowning, as though he'd fallen on purpose.

His mother said, "Now Thom Sadler, I want you to go over there and introduce yourself to that little boy. You want to be neighborly, don't you?"

Only Verna had continued her lookout between the curtains, which she held cleverly pinned together with thumb and forefinger just beneath her unblinking eye.

"Lawsy me, that's summa the nastiest funniture I ever *did* see."

Abby said, "Yeah, you could go help them, Thom. Carry some boxes and build up these gigantic muscles even more."

She pinched her brother's skinny upper arm.

"Ha ha," Thom said. He told his mother, "I don't want to."

"Do it anyway," she said briskly. "Meeting new people is like jumping into a pool. The water's cold at first, but ten seconds later you're glad you did it."

"Then why don't *you* go over and meet them?" Thom said.

"I don't have time," his mother said, turning away. "I've got a house to run, and so does Verna."

Verna took the hint and stepped back from the window. She looked down at Thom, who sat with his knees crossed, rocking back and forth like a much smaller child. He wore cut-offs and a T-shirt, and he hadn't combed his thatch of dark hair this morning (lately he'd started to feel self-conscious about how he looked, though not self-conscious enough to do much about it) and the last thing he wanted was to trudge next door, shame-faced, and introduce himself to the neighbors.

The look he gave Abby must have been more pained than he knew, for her eyes softened and she said, "OK, come on. I'll go with you."

So they went next door and met the Carsons. The mother was friendly in a vague way, her attention focused on the movers—"That's marked fragile!" she kept saying—while the father seemed outgoing and energetic, helping the two uniformed men and often winking at the children.

"If you kids feel like pitching in, don't be shy," he grinned, backing through the front door holding one end of a sofa. "I'm paying these gentlemen by the hour!"

Abby went immediately to the truck and began struggling with a small box perched on the edge, but Thom just laughed; he could tell that Mr. Carson hadn't been serious.

"No, sweetheart, I was just teasing," he called as the shadowy living room swallowed him and, foot by foot, the long bruise-colored sofa. "Ask Kit to get you a Coke or someth…" but the rest of his sentence trailed off.

Kit wasn't much of a host and didn't follow through with the Coke, but Thom liked him. Within the first five minutes, he'd told Thom and Abby that he was almost twelve he was in fifth grade they'd moved here from New Jersey his grandmother in Trenton had told them there were nothing but hicks in Georgia he wanted to play basketball when he got to junior high he wasn't very tall now but his father and both his grandfathers were and that was a good sign, right?

Thom and Abby smiled awkwardly, fidgeting like the polite Southern children they were and trying not to look like hicks.

"What does your daddy do?" Abby asked.

Kit's daddy was an engineer!—he helped design engines for Lockheed if Kit didn't become a professional basketball player he was going to be a pilot (his skinny arms shot straight out from his sides and he made cartoon airplane noises like a much smaller kid) or maybe an astronaut he hadn't decided yet maybe he would go to West Point what school did Thom and Abby go to did they like it were the teachers nice how long was recess maybe they could all carpool or was it close enough that they could ride their bikes?

If Thom had been there alone he would have changed the subject, but Abby always told the truth without thinking.

"We go to Catholic school," she said. "Sacred Heart. But this year I'm transferring to St. Jude's—that's the junior high and high school," she added, proudly.

Thom looked down, kicking at the gravel along the driveway. Then Kit had said something that surprised him.

"Sure thing, I'm going to Sacred Heart too, my dad already went down and talked to the principal when he was here last week meeting with his boss, he said the school was brand-new and the nuns wore short dresses and nothing on their heads, and you could see their hair! He said a couple of them didn't even shave their legs!"

He curled both sets of his skinny fingers around his bottom lip and pulled down like somebody watching a horror movie. Thom and Abby laughed.

Without warning Kit took off running toward the side of the house. He was such a bundle of manic energy that he made Thom feel old and tired, but instinctively he and Abby followed.

"Come on back!" Kit called over his shoulder, and then came another stream of words about his stash of fireworks for the Fourth of July they were going to have a barbecue out on their patio every year they had gobs of sparklers and firecrackers and Roman candles it was going to be super Thom and Abby should invite the other kids around here back in their old neighborhood everybody came to their house on the Fourth nobody could do fireworks like his dad, so come on, come on!

Neither Thom nor Abby had told Kit that setting off fireworks inside the city limits was illegal, and almost everyone went to the big displays in the Lenox Square parking lot unless they left town altogether. But a few evenings later, as Kit and Thom were fiddling in the Carsons' backyard with an old bicycle Kit was trying to repair, "just for practice" for when he was an astronaut and might need to repair rocket engines on Mars, the subject came up again. Mr. Carson was a few feet away, affixing a hummingbird feeder to a pine branch. At first Thom hesitated when Mr. Carson asked, mumbling between the nails he held in his mouth, if Thom and Abby were coming to help them celebrate the Fourth.

Thom said tactfully, "If our parents will let us. Sometimes we go to Lenox Square."

Mr. Carson looked over, grinning; he pulled the last nail from between his lips, casually as though it were a toothpick.

"I hope they will," he said. "I bought some extra stuff the other day, thinking you would join us."

Thom liked Kit's dad so much that he decided then and there he wouldn't tell him their fireworks plans were illegal. Maybe they would all get arrested and that would be part of the fun.

Then Mr. Carson said, slowly, "Since the lots are so big in this neighborhood, I'm hoping nobody will mind. There aren't any grouches living around here who'd tell on us, are there?"

Thom smiled nervously, thinking of his mother, who wasn't a grouch, exactly, but who did like to complain. And she hated loud noises.

"Nah," Thom said, placing a wrench in the wiggling hand Kit had held up.

Thom didn't understand why, but he felt so happy just being here. It was one of those long summer evenings when the sun is already down but there's plenty of light, the big trees turning a dim, lush green, the air crisp and dry, fresh-smelling. In the distance, along the dark line of trees bordering the Carsons' property, fireflies had started winking. Though he was supposedly helping Kit, his attention stayed on Mr. Carson, who was so different from the other men in this neighborhood. Like Thom's father, who was a banker, most of the men got home around seven o'clock in their wrinkled coats and ties, gave their families a weary smile, mixed themselves a drink and settled down to read the paper, staying in their office clothes until bedtime. Thom's father would unbutton his top button and loosen his tie, but that was all. Already his hair was mostly silver, his kindly but abstracted face often seeming ashen gray when he sat reading the paper at the kitchen table under the harsh fluorescent lights. He read in there to appease his wife, who liked to chatter about her day while she finished preparing dinner, but Thom's father said little. Thom and Abby would greet him and receive his quick, automatic hug and maybe pick at his clothes, like younger children, for a few minutes while he mixed his whiskey sour and rifled through the paper until he'd found the sections he wanted. After that, they went their own ways until dinner.

Kit's dad was different. Though Thom guessed he wasn't much younger than his own father, Mr. Carson had the lithe, lanky build of a high school athlete (Thom knew from Kit that Mr. Carson had been a teenage basketball star), and he sprang up the sidewalk after work with the same eager, loping gait he'd used leaving home that morning. Then he changed into a T-shirt and blue jeans, or sometimes shorts if the day was really hot, and worked on projects around the house or out back. He liked shooting baskets with Kit and Thom in the driveway, and he didn't ask boring grown-up questions like what grade was Thom in, or what he wanted to be when he grew up. They talked about the Hawks and the Braves, about movies they'd all seen like *Airport* and *Earthquake* and *The Towering Inferno*, and about expeditions Mr. Carson wanted to take later in the summer to Stone Mountain and Six Flags. He wanted to go backpacking in the north Georgia mountains and go fishing on Lake Lanier and visit the Cyclorama and some of the battlefields outside the city. He said he was a Civil War buff, and though Thom's father read books on the Civil War, too, somehow Thom didn't think his father and Mr. Carson would become friends. (Mr. Sadler had read lots of books, in fact, but Thom didn't think he'd visited any battlefields.) Mr. Carson was like an overgrown boy, sometimes seizing Kit or Thom by the waist and hauling them into the air or shouting "Heads up" seconds before lobbing a basketball in their direction. Whenever Thom came over to Kit's house, which was often, one of his first questions was, "Where's your dad?"

Although Mr. Carson urged Thom to invite his friends over the evening of July Fourth, it turned out that every kid he knew would be gone somewhere with his family. The neighborhood hadn't been very welcoming to the Carsons, so far; there had been a few polite knocks at the front door once they'd had a chance to "settle in," as Thom's mother put it—of course, she'd been one of the callers, bringing over one of her cherry pies—but most of the neighbors were put off by the Carsons' harsh Jersey accents, or by Mrs. Carson's shyness and incomprehension in the face of elaborate Southern manners, or by the way Kit and his parents were always outside, darting this way and that, yelling and laughing to each other like they were all kids with no grown-ups in charge. Verna and Mrs. Sadler had kept up their spying off and on, shaking their heads over Mrs. Carson's "get-ups" (she favored shorts and tennis shoes and often tied her plain flyaway hair with a bandanna) and all the Carsons' loud, high voices. Sherwood Forest was a quiet older neighborhood with large manicured front lawns, but the Carsons ran around theirs "like a bunch of monkeys," Verna said. Since Thom's mother was a "Yankee," too, and since the Sadlers were the only other Catholic family on the block, Thom had thought she might warm to them, but she'd quickly grown jealous of the many hours Thom spent next door.

"Are the Carsons *that* fascinating?" she would say, when he edged away from the table the minute dinner was over.

He didn't answer. But to Thom, who often felt lonely during the summer, the answer was simple: Yes, they were. He felt happier next door than he'd ever felt at home, he told himself. Already he'd begun to have treacherous fantasies of being Kit's brother, Mr. Carson's second son.

Though he reminded his parents every couple of days that he'd been invited next door for barbecue on the fourth, he almost didn't get to go. The night before, watching the six o'clock news about the celebration in Lenox Square, Thom's mother had abruptly decided they should have a family outing: they could have an early dinner at Houston's, then see the display at Lenox. Mr. Sadler said something vaguely negative about the crowds, but Thom knew he would agree if his wife insisted. Abby had been the one to save the day.

"But I'm spending the night at Jennifer Treadway's—remember, Mom? Her mother is taking a bunch of us girls to Stone Mountain."

"Oh, that's right," her mother fretted. Then she said, "Still, I suppose the three of us could..." But she glanced at Thom, who wore such a long face that she relented. Her lips made a little twist. "Oh, that's right, you're going next door again, aren't you? It's a wonder they don't start making you pay room and board, you're over there so much."

Thom hadn't said anything. He'd felt his heart pounding, his hands sweating. The idea of missing the barbecue and fireworks at the Carsons' had the potentially tragic impact you can suffer that keenly only when you are eleven years old. His intense feelings of relief had left him winded.

Mr. Carson had said the "festivities" would start around seven, but by 5:30 Thom was ready, fidgeting in front of the TV set and waiting for time to pass. His father was catching up on work at the office (he loved going in on Sundays and holidays, he said, claiming he got much more work done when it was quiet), and Verna was off and Thom's mother had just left with Abby for the Treadways'. Since he'd turned eleven in May, his mother sometimes left him alone for brief periods, having decided he was "responsible," but only during the day and seldom for more than a couple of hours. Normally, he relished these times and would walk around the empty house proudly, feeling grown-up but also giddy, sometimes shouting out "Hallo-o-o!" and listening with a pleased smile to the echo of his voice, at other times singing some goofy song from the radio and flailing his arms and legs in a little dance, or a parody of dance, then laughing at himself. He liked being alone and was never afraid. He imagined what it would be like if Mr. Carson pulled into his driveway early and Thom went to the front door, as if impersonating his own father, and called out an invitation to come over for a "cocktail." That's what his parents called Mr. Sadler's whiskey sours; Thom's mother no longer drank but she used the word, too. Thom thought it sounded silly. Now it was July Fourth, and he went over and snapped off the TV set, where there was some boring "bulletin" about President Ford, and in the sudden silence Thom smiled and said aloud, to his dim reflection in the TV screen, "Would you care for *a cocktail*?"

He glanced hopefully at the brass clock on the fireplace mantel, expecting it must be past six o'clock. Only 5:45. Why was time so *slow* when you wanted it to hurry?

The idea and its execution came at about the same moment. He went into the dining room, opened the buffet cabinet, found the whiskey bottle and prepared liquid mix (greenish and hideous, Thom always thought) his mother bought each week at Kroger's. As he'd seen his father do countless times, he poured one inch of the bourbon and two inches of the mix, then took the glass into the kitchen and added ice cubes until the glass was full. His father used a spoon, but Thom stuck his forefinger in and stirred, then touched his fingertip to his tongue. He wrinkled his nose.

"Would you care for one of our *disgusting* cocktails?" he said aloud, in imitation of a mincing Southern hostess. He put the glass to his mouth, his nose touching an ice cube, and stuck his tongue doglike into the drink for a taste.

It was pretty awful, but tolerable. He sat at the kitchen table, where he had a view of the driveway through a side window. If he saw his mother's car or, less likely, his father's, he could pour the drink down the drain and rinse the glass and stick it in the dishwasher before the car had even stopped. He'd remembered to put the two bottles back in the cabinet, even turning the labels to face exactly as he'd found them. He hadn't thought of himself as sneaky, but he guessed he was. The thought pleased him.

He took a second sip and a third. He didn't feel anything. He'd seen adults get loud and boisterous when they drank—especially his father's younger brother, Joel, who stopped by sometimes to complain how much money his wife spent for clothes—and though his father had only one or two drinks by himself in the evening, he sometimes had more when company came, and even he would get livelier, his cheeks flushing. Lately when Thom went next door, he felt tongue-tied, especially when Mr. Carson focused his grinning attention directly on him, saying he bet Thom was "a lady-killer" at school and making Thom blush. He wished he could act suave and sophisticated like the actors he saw on TV or try to be funny like Mr. Carson himself. *Yes, I've killed a few ladies in my day,* he'd thought later, in bed, but at the time he'd just grinned a lopsided silly

kid's grin and looked down. He knew that Mr. Carson liked him and probably appreciated that he wasn't a motor-mouth like Kit, but Thom knew
he wasn't really *impressive,* which was what he most wanted to be. Abby
had gone next door with him one day and had bragged that Thom made
all A's in school the previous term, and Mr. Carson had looked at him in
a new way, as if surprised, and had said, "That's impressive, Thom."
Thom's blood had glowed and his heart had convulsed with pleasure. Yet
he knew from Mr. Carson's surprised reaction that he must not *look*
impressive, which pained him.

He thought about these things idly as he sat at the kitchen table sipping his whiskey sour, his bare legs dangling from the chair.

He couldn't finish the drink; it was just too foul-tasting. He poured the
rest out and put away the glass, glancing at the oven clock—only 6:10, he'd
thought it must be 6:30 at least!—and said, "Thanks so much for the
delightful *cocktail,* Mr. Sadler!" "Why don't mention it, Mr. Carson," he
answered. "We don't see nearly enough of you. Please *do* come back."

He wandered into the bathroom and stared for a minute at his face in
the mirror. The same bony, ordinary kid's face with its bush of dark hair,
but he took his comb from his back pocket, wet it, and combed his hair
again. Tonight he wanted to look nice. He'd put on a clean pair of khaki
shorts, not cut-offs, and the red knit shirt his Aunt Millicent in
Philadelphia had sent him, with the little alligator sewn onto the chest.
This was the first time he had worn it. He guessed he looked all right. Tired
of worrying about it, he raised his eyebrows and said, again in that silly
voice, "Why, you're looking well this evening, Mr. Sadler!" "Why thank you,
I've just combed my hair for the fifth time, and I'm so glad you noticed. Do
you like it?" "Oh yes, I do. It's most becoming."

That's when he felt a little dizzy. He grabbed the edge of the sink and
noticed in the mirror he looked pale. Then the wave of dizziness passed.
He felt OK. He knew he couldn't be drunk because he'd had only a few
sips, but his stomach did feel queasy. Once when he'd gotten sick, his
mother had said to put his head between his legs and to take deep breaths,
so now he sat on the toilet and tried it, then stood back up. It seemed to
work. He felt fine.

Next door, the Carsons were putting paper plates and napkins on the
picnic table, and near the back door Thom saw that the silver-painted grill,
made out of a barrel, had wisps of smoke fuming out the sides. Mr. Carson
wore a long red-stained apron that had "Kiss the Cook" written across the
front. The smell of the cooking meat gave Thom another wave of dizziness,

and he felt an unpleasant tingling at the back of his throat; the last thing he wanted was to eat, but he'd smiled and opened his mouth to compliment Mr. Carson on the aroma when Kit came whirring out the back door carrying a plastic bag.

"Hey, Thom, wait'll you see these firecrackers, they're twice as big as the ones we used last year! We've got three different kinds of Roman and we bought these humongous sparklers, too, come see, come see!"

Kit's parents looked over at Thom, smiling; Mrs. Carson had glanced at her watch.

"But not until after dinner, guys," Kit's father said. "It's still too light." He pointed up to the sky. "You want that pretty deep-blue dusk for fireworks, don't you?"

"God, I can hardly wait!" Kit said.

Thom felt awkward standing there with his hands in his pockets. His stomach was aching a little. He wished he'd worn his usual summertime T-shirt and cut-offs, since that's what Kit was wearing, and even his parents had on shorts and sandals. All dressed up, he felt like a geek.

Mrs. Carson smiled her shy, crinkly smile. "You look nice, Thom. Did you and your family go visiting today?"

"No ma'am," Thom said. He hoped Mr. Carson wouldn't say anything about Thom's being a lady-killer.

For the next half-hour, Kit showed him the fireworks and reminisced about last year's July Fourth back in Jersey. They had big-ass Roman candles but one went over into this shitty neighbor's yard and he called the police who came out but when Dad was talking to them you could tell they were on Dad's side and not the old neighbor's, it was really super, and then Dad invited the neighbor over for some barbecue and at first he said no but Dad kept talking and then he came over and turned out to be nice after all, and he even helped set off a few more Roman candles after that! Thom was shocked by some of Kit's language, but it didn't seem to faze his parents, who seldom reprimanded him for anything except once in a while to "settle down" when he talked too fast, little red streaks glowing along his cheeks.

"You and your dad ever do fireworks, Thom?" Mr. Carson asked. Holding a long pair of tongs in one hand, he'd lifted the top half of the silver barrel and instantly was swathed in billows of whitish smoke.

Thom started to lie because he didn't want his father to sound boring, but he said, "No, sir, never. We've watched the displays, though."

Mr. Carson laughed. "Well, we won't have much of a display, but at least we'll get to set them off ourselves. That sounds like more fun, doesn't it?"

"Yes, sir," Thom said. "I'm looking forward to it."

Finally, Mrs. Carson brought out a jug of sweet tea and said everything was ready whenever "the cook" was finished with the barbecue, and a few minutes later the four of them were sitting at the picnic table, Kit and Thom on one side and Kit's parents on the other, just as if Thom were a member of the family. The only problem was that Thom's stomach was cramping a little, nothing he couldn't handle, but he was afraid if he took one bite of food he would throw up, and the Carsons would send him home to bed and he would miss the fireworks. But Mr. Carson was so animated, talking and gesturing, and Mrs. Carson stayed so busy going in and out of the house fetching things and taking things back again, that neither noticed that Thom was only pretending to eat, picking at the bun with his fingers, lifting the sandwich to his mouth (holding his breath to avoid the smell of cooked meat which he was afraid might be enough to make him puke) and making chewing motions, smiling if anyone glanced his way. He shoved the baked beans and potato salad around with his plastic fork to give the illusion he was eating. Once when the adults' attention was on Kit—he'd spilled some barbecue sauce onto his shirt—Thom took half his sandwich and swiftly tossed it into the bag Mrs. Carson was using for trash.

After twenty minutes of noisy conversation the meal was concluded, and Thom had successfully avoided eating a single bite. Thom was relieved when Mrs. Carson said the dessert she'd prepared—peach pie with ice cream—could wait until after they'd finished with the fireworks, and he'd felt grateful that Mrs. Carson, unlike other women he knew, hadn't pestered him with complaints that he didn't eat enough. She'd simply taken his plate and tossed it with the others into the trash. Thom's stomach had settled, too. He felt a little warm, but the temperature had reached the nineties that day and the air was still muggy. There wasn't much of a breeze.

Before they did the fireworks, Mr. Carson said, Thom needed to come inside a minute. He had already put mosquito repellent on himself and Kit, but Thom was getting bitten. It was true: he'd been scratching absent-mindedly at the back of his knee, his earlobe. Thom followed Mr. Carson into the kitchen and down a dimmed hallway and through the big bedroom where he and his wife slept; the spray was in the "master bathroom," he said. Thom went inside, and Mr. Carson shut the door and sprayed both his arms, slowly lifting up his shirt and spraying his back and stomach, too. The spray felt cool and pleasant. It smelled like pine needles.

"You like that?" Mr. Carson said. Slowly, he rubbed the spray into Thom's skin.

Thom nodded, his head swimming. He liked anything Mr. Carson did, didn't he?

When they came back outside awhile later, Kit was sitting on the porch step, his arms folded; he looked grumpy. But when Mr. Carson said, "All right, all right then—let's do it," he jumped up. Kit's father made the "festivities," as he kept calling them, even more exciting than Thom might have thought. First, he sat on the back porch with one of the boys on each side and went through the bag, explaining the fireworks one by one, and how to use them safely. The rhythm of Mr. Carson's voice was deep-pitched yet boyish. He talked to them as if he were a boy, too, not in the half-scolding, know-it-all way some of the fathers of Thom's friends used when they spoke to kids. Thom didn't really focus on Mr. Carson's words but on his voice, and his strong fingers with their freckles and small reddish hairs, and his long arms with their ropy muscle, the biceps rippling smoothly beneath the skin as he handled the fireworks. When he clapped his hands and said, "So, you boys ready?" Thom understood that he hadn't listened to a word Mr. Carson said.

He decided just to watch Kit, who wanted to do most of the fireworks anyway. Mr. Carson admonished him to let Thom have his turns, but Thom said quickly he didn't mind, he'd rather just watch. He kept his eyes on Mr. Carson's as he spoke, but the man's grinning, crinkling eyes didn't quite meet his. Kit was digging eagerly through the plastic bag and pulling out fireworks of all shapes and sizes, some evidently left over from last year, some new in clear cellophane wrappers. There were Sonic Screamers and Glow Worms and Ribbon Rockets; there were plain Black Jack firecrackers and extra-large crimson Red Devils the size of Mr. Carson's thumb; there were Shooting Star Rockets and Glowing Candles and Golden Showers and Screaming Meemies. They laughed at the silly names, but Kit was too eager to play around for long, and once Mr. Carson had performed the "safety procedures"—a phrase he intoned with an ironic twist of his lips—of filling a bucket with sand and insisting the boys not forget "the way to hold a firecracker or any other type of—" his son interrupted, "All right, Dad, we *got* it!"

Mr. Carson laughed and handed Kit a long yellow tube and seconds later Thom's face was lifted skyward, watching in a warm dazed stupor as

Kit and his dad began shooting the sparkling rockets and bursting candles, exclaiming at the showering cones and blossoms of neon yellow and phosphorescent cobalt and searing bright green, the fierce bullets of light arcing and whistling and exploding and then shimmering down before the hunched acquiescent ridge of massed and darkened trees.

Kit's high yipping cries filled the air—"Look at that one, Dad, look at that. Hey, Mom, did you *see!*"—but Thom watched in silence, his tongue dry, his head swimming in a feverish joy and his vision swathed in hot mist. Ten minutes passed, or half an hour, or a small lifetime as Thom watched and watched, his head and body aching, his heart bursting upward like these explosions of light in a trance of yearning.

Only later would he ask what was wrong: had the fever overtaken him, had he stopped being fifth grader Thom Sadler of 156 Friar Tuck Road and become someone else? And who would that be? But only much, much later. After everyone had forgotten and even Thom thought he had healed.

The accident happened quickly and stupidly, as accidents do. Ordinary night had fallen, the fireworks were over. Mrs. Carson went inside to wash dishes, and Mr. Carson was cleaning out the barbecue barrel. There were only some plain firecrackers left—Red Devils and Black Devils—and even Kit was quieting down, lighting the fuses one by one and flicking them into the dark reaches of the yard.

"Come on," he said, "dontcha even want to do some of these?"

Earlier Thom had asked for a glass of ice water, and now he didn't seem as overheated, though he felt a layer of clammy sweat under his clothes, and his head still throbbed. He'd caught the disappointed whine in Kit's voice, so he set the empty plastic cup down in the grass and came forward, shyly.

"OK," he said.

For a while they stood there, Kit lighting a firecracker and tossing it out, Thom lighting his and doing the same, back and forth, a companionable rhythm, like two boys pitching a baseball from glove to glove. They didn't talk but just watched the momentary flash against the darkness and winced slightly in anticipation of the loud pop and then automatically reached for another. There were twenty or thirty left. Thom kept glancing over to Mr. Carson whose back was to them, faintly outlined in the light from the back windows of the house, and he felt a vague hollow ache he couldn't understand that had nothing to do with his fever, and that's when Kit laughed and said, "Well, hurry up, throw the thing," and Thom looked down and saw the little Red Devil in his hand, the fuse crackling, and for some reason he didn't toss it forward as he'd been doing but reared back as if throwing a football, and the instant before it would have left his hand the thing exploded and there was a piercing scream that must have been his own.

The next couple of hours would be a blur in Thom's memory for as long as he lived, but there was a brief remembered time at the Carsons' kitchen table, Thom sobbing as he held the shaking wrist of his bleeding hand with his good one. He sat on Mr. Carson's lap while Mrs. Carson held a cold compress around his burning thumb and forefinger, and then there was the ride to the emergency room and the tetanus shot and his glimpse of the swollen thumb with its nail torn away, exposing a pulp of hideous purple flesh oozing blood, and the smiling words of the doctor—"You're young, you'll heal fast"—and then they bandaged him up and sent him home.

Of course, his mother was furious, blaming those "darn people" next door and vowing to march over there and give them a piece of her mind, but Thom's father and Abby calmed her down, and he basked in the sympathy that came mostly from his sister, who asked shyly whether it still hurt and later brought him a Dr. Pepper float, his favorite treat, once they'd all calmed down and sat in the den watching television. But it was the day after the accident when he woke with his fever returned and worsened, feeling he was beyond all help, beyond all sympathy, and he had his feverish waking dream that Mr. Carson had entered the room and lifted him out of bed and settled him onto his lap. Thom was crying out, bawling like a much smaller child, and Mr. Carson was trying to hush him, his long naked arms held close around Thom, whose body felt suspended in this adult male embrace that felt so powerful and complete he thought he might have died from the fever—it might be Jesus holding him—and then he heard the disembodied voice whispering in his ear, *Don't worry, honey, just give it to the man upstairs, that's what we always has to do,* and that's when he understood he wasn't dreaming any longer and that the voice was Verna's.

She was sitting on the side of his bed, and yes, he sat in her big soft lap, and floating above him Thom saw the dim worried faces of his mother and Abby, and he supposed he would be all right. His face was wet with tears and he held up his bandaged, throbbing hand as if this were an explanation. He didn't say anything, he didn't tell about his fever dream or any of that but just kept listening as Verna repeated, "Just give it to the man upstairs, honey, you hear me? He won't let it hurt too bad or too long. You just quiet down now, you hear? I promise, honey, it ain't gonna hurt for long...."

In the months and years that followed, as his voice deepened and his body grew rapidly, Thom would occasionally think of Mr. Carson and dry-eyed, hard-hearted, he would study his right thumb and thumbnail. There was no sign of the injury, not even the tiniest scar. After living next door for a year, the Carsons had moved away, transferred to another city, and though Thom was relieved rather than saddened, he couldn't quite forget in the way everyone else had forgotten, *You're young, you'll heal fast,* and so he repeated to himself what the doctor had said, and Verna, whenever he did remember.

He thought how kind and hopeful were such words and he'd decided, through his life, to believe them.

Thom woke, dry-mouthed. Blinked his eyes. He recognized but did not recognize this room. Looked to the left, wearily, and saw the familiar but not-familiar IV stand with its clear bag of whatever and the narrow tube descending out of sight. He turned his left wrist and felt the heaviness of the bandage, the little twinge of the needle in his arm. Slowly, everything came back to him as happened each morning he woke in this place, but he didn't want to remember so he closed his eyes, thinking he might sleep again. But no. Once his brain clicked on, it stayed on, so he decided he would think of pleasant things and not remember what happened that day in that oversized house on Westminster Drive in lovely tree-shaded Ansley Park. As Connie had remarked last night, he and Abby sitting on either side of the bed, Thom should remember he'd displayed the good taste to collapse inside a million-dollar showplace. That was something, at least.

A little smile had creased Thom's lips, and now he heard a sly male voice.

"So what are you grinning about this morning?"

He opened his eyes, and there was one of the most beautiful sights of his life: a tall smiling man in his thirties who might have posed for one of Raphael's angels. Dark, close-cropped hair; eyes a pellucid green, like water cooled in an ancient fountain; strong nose and chin; exquisite thin-lipped mouth curved slightly in amusement. *Yes,* Thom thought, *an angel.* As Connie might say, he'd died and gone to heaven. But instead of wings the man wore blaring bright-green scrubs.

"Was I...smiling?"

"Looked that way to me." His tone almost flirtatious as he turned Thom's wrist gently and felt his pulse. Kept those cool green eyes, the color of just-emerged spring leaves, on his watch as he said, "Must have been thinking pleasant thoughts. In this place, that's a good idea."

"Are you—are you my doctor?"

The angel laughed as he tucked Thom's hand back beneath the covers. Now he laid his palm on Thom's forehead, then along his cheek. Kept it there for several long seconds.

My God, Thom thought. That feels so wonderful.

"You don't feel warm at all. I wasn't working the past two days, but they said you had a pretty vicious fever." He brought the thermometer probe to Thom's lips. "OK, open wide."

Thom knew his eyes must look desperate, but he kept his mouth clamped shut and stared at this vision, his heart convulsed in longing. He said, "Would you mind...doing that again?"

The angel in green scrubs looked perplexed but friendly. "I'm sorry? Do what again?"

"Your hand...you had your hand against my face..."

The angel blinked. Guiltily, Thom knew that his flesh felt clammy, cool, unpleasant; yes, the fever had broken, and now he lay here sodden, uncharming. He didn't even want to think about his sleep-plastered hair, his stubbly jaw. Probably smelled, too. This lovely man at whom he stared unashamedly wore a brisk-smelling cologne, his dark hair glistened with gel, his skin glowed with health and youth. But he didn't look displeased. He might even have been pleased, a little.

"It made you feel better?" he said, his voice fallen to a murmur, and the instant his hand cupped Thom's face—this time more intimately, closely— Thom could feel the cool fingertips along his temple, the smooth heel of his hand along Thom's jaw, and in between, pressed close against his cheek, the warm balm-like flesh of the angel's palm, and again Thom closed his eyes, and before he drifted off came the thought *yes*, he was healed; yes, he would be all right.

That afternoon, when Abby and Connie arrived, Thom was sitting up in bed, sipping a Diet Coke and watching *Oprah*.

Connie said, "My God, did you see that gorgeous nurse?"

Thom shrugged. "Already had him."

"Ha, I'll be glad to take sloppy seconds!" Connie laughed. "Or thirds— or fourths!"

Abby came to the side of the bed and pressed Thom's hand. "Hey, guys, there's a lady in the room." She gave her usual searching look into his eyes. "You look great. You really do."

Thom set the Coke on the bedside table and gave her a tilted smile. "My nurse gave me a shave," he said. "And a sponge bath."

Connie put one hand to his forehead, an operatic gesture. "I think I feel a fever coming on."

Thom said, "He just came on duty today, but I've already learned to discipline myself. Only three calls per hour, max. That's every twenty minutes. It's been eleven minutes now, and I'm already having symptoms of withdrawal."

Connie put his hands on his hips. "No, you're having symptoms of male lust. Which means they have to let you out of this place."

In truth, he'd shaved himself, and a diminutive male orderly from Pakistan had bathed him. But he couldn't tell Connie or even Abby about earlier this morning—those long healing moments, the smooth long-fingered hand caressing his cheek. That was sacred.

"I get out tomorrow," Thom said. Oprah had said something witty, and the audience roared with laughter, so he grabbed the remote control and flicked off the set.

Connie said, "Tomorrow? Oh, my God, that's *perfect*." He was looking at Abby, wide-eyed, as Thom glanced back and forth between them. He knew Connie well: something was up.

"What do you mean?"

"Nothing," Abby said. "He means we're glad you're coming home. Connie and I just gave your place the once-over."

"You didn't have to do that..." Now he knew why Abby wore a plain blouse and jeans today; her hair could use a brushing.

"I helped, too," Connie said. "I did the vacuuming, and I put some fabulous pink glads in your bedroom."

Thom smiled. "Thanks, Connie. But something's up, and I want you to tell—"

"Oh, Thom, guess what!" Abby said. Again she pressed his hand. "Mike called, from your office? That woman made an offer on the Westminster house."

Despite everything, he felt a surge of his salesman's adrenaline. "Really? For how much?"

Earlier today he'd been thinking morosely that he'd jinxed the sale. After all, if the agent collapses during a showing and a client has to call an ambulance, maybe the client would take this for a sign. Not today. Not this house. He remembered little from that afternoon except the intense heat flushing his cheeks, temples, ears, and how his eyes had ached. Then his vision blotched, and in dreamlike fast-forward he was lying on the living room sofa, then the paramedics were loading him onto a stretcher.

All that had happened day before yesterday, but it might have been last month, last year.

"One point one, I think he said. If you feel up to it, he said to give him a call, but he spoke to the owner and the owner said OK."

Connie said, "You're really going home tomorrow? For sure?"

"Almost sure. My doctor left town for the holiday, so one of the residents is going to check me. They said if I'm still 98.6 in the morning, I'm gone."

Connie gave an impish smile. "I'll bet you're in good hands. It's Easter, so the docs on duty are probably Jewish, and everybody knows they're the best doctors. If they don't have 'man' or 'stein' on the ends of their names, I won't go to them."

Thom rolled his eyes. "Great, Connie. I'll remember that."

He hoped Connie's buoyant mood wasn't chemically induced. He'd noticed a glassy sheen to those bright blue-green eyes, and there was a manic exuberance to Connie's remarks that bothered him. But he was hardly in a position to judge; which one had ended up in the hospital, after all?

"What about dinner?" Abby asked. "Want us to bring takeout? We could go down to Rocky's Pizza or—"

The door opened, and the three of them looked over: a small-framed man with dark hair and rimless glasses stepped inside. He wore a white coat over his crisp shirt and tie, and he was reading from a chart. Finally he glanced up, flashed a professional smile.

"Hello, I'm Dr. Friedman—I'm doing rounds for Dr. McIlhaney?"

Connie sputtered with laughter but managed to contain himself. Embarrassed, Thom said, "Sorry, we were just trading jokes. Stupid jokes."

Dr. Friedman's smile had become a little forced. "No problem, jokes are good. Jokes are good."

Once Abby had steered Connie out of the room, Dr. Friedman examined Thom and said yes, he could go home the next day. But when Thom asked what had caused the fever, and whether it would recur, he hesitated.

"Hard to say. With your—your condition, it could be lots of things. A random virus, or maybe CMV." He was flipping through the chart. "What tests did they run? I'm sure Dr. McIlhaney will go over it with you when she gets back."

He was edging away from the bed. Thom suspected he didn't often deal with HIV patients.

"Sure thing, doctor," he said. "Just thought I'd ask."

"No problem," Dr. Friedman said, the smile back in place. From the door he added, "That's what we're here for." He was gone.

The next morning Abby and Connie arrived promptly at nine o'clock to take him home. On the way down Peachtree, Connie chattered brightly. Thom sat feeling stiff, wooden, his discharge papers and sack of medications on his lap. Abby leaned forward from the backseat. The Saturday morning traffic was light, and Thom told himself there was no real danger, even if Connie was taking something. If anything he drove too slowly, more interested in talking than getting Thom home.

"...so it's a good thing you got sick now instead of during Freaknik. Can you imagine trying to navigate Peachtree with all that nonsense going on? We really ought to go somewhere that weekend, Thom honey, if you're feeling better by then. How about St. Bart's? We could just laze on the beach and do nothing. My father was threatening to come 'visit' sometime soon—of course he's decided to cozy up to me now, and you know why— but when I told him about Freaknik, he seemed to change his mind rather abruptly! Not that I blame him, really. I'm not a racist, you know, but sharing the city with 50,000 black college students, all with their rap music blaring at high volume, isn't my idea of fun."

Thom said, "I don't want to go anywhere. I'll just lie low that weekend, I imagine. Stay home and read."

"That sounds good," Abby said.

Connie glanced sideways at Thom. "By the way, I took your advice about the jewelry."

"The jewelry?"

"My mother's stuff. I sent Daddy a letter and told him he could keep it, if he wanted to. You know, for sentimental reasons. That's when he called about coming for a visit, so I think it really helped."

"That's good," Thom said.

"I just can't figure out why he wants to come, unless it's about the money. I mean, that scene after Wilma's funeral was *so* awful..."

"Maybe you should avoid him," Thom said, wishing they could change the subject. "Say it's not a good time or whatever."

Connie nodded vehemently. "Yeah, that's what I think. Warren, being Warren, thinks Daddy and I should *process* everything, of course, but I say leave well enough alone."

When Connie turned off Peachtree, he glanced at his watch and stage-whispered to Abby, as though Thom couldn't hear, "Should we run an errand or something? We're a little early…"

"No, it's fine," Abby said quickly.

Thom said, "Early for what?"

"Oh, I told Warren we'd get back around ten, but it's a quarter till," Connie said, glancing at Abby.

Yes, something was up; Connie was the worst person in the world for keeping secrets. Thom saw how he fidgeted in the seat, his fingers flexing on the wheel. He could hardly contain himself.

"Just watch your driving, OK?" Thom said. He smiled. "Remember, I'm an invalid."

By the time they arrived home, Thom bending to acknowledge Mitzi and Chloe's ecstatic yips and twirls, he wasn't exactly surprised when he heard a sudden commotion and several voices loudly proclaiming: "Surprise!" What did astonish him, after Valerie and Warren burst from the coat closet, waving and smiling, and Pace rose with a sheepish grin from his hiding place behind the sofa, was the fourth person who emerged shyly, awkwardly, from the kitchen. There, next to the dining room table heaped with gift bags, a decorated cake, and stacks of plates, silverware, and napkins, stood his mother.

"Hi, Thom," she said. "Welcome home."

His face had contorted into what looked, he hoped, like an expression of pleased surprise.

"Mom, what an amazing…I mean, I knew there was something, but I didn't expect…"

Both he and his mother stepped forward as if pushed, and as the others watched, they exchanged a long, ceremonious hug. Pulling back, he saw that his mother's pale-blue eyes were damp with tears. He inhaled the long-familiar scents of her skin lotion, her hair spray, and though he felt almost nothing, not yet, he was glad she was here. At his side he was aware of Abby, hovering anxiously.

"Since we couldn't make it for Easter," she said, "Mom and I decided—well, we thought she could come here."

"It was all my idea," Lucille said, "and don't worry, I'm not staying long." She sounded plaintive, as usual, but she smiled as though she had not heard herself. "I got here yesterday, and I wanted to come to the hospital, but the others thought—"

"We cooked up the idea of a surprise party," Valerie put in. "To celebrate your homecoming, you know?"

Thom grinned, embarrassed. "I've only been gone for two days."

"It's almost Easter, too," his mother said. She gestured toward the table. "See, I found a cake in the shape of an egg." For a moment they dutifully admired the cake, a pink-and-green confection that read "Happy Easter, Happy Birthday, and Welcome Home, Thom!" The dogs were swirling madly around Thom's ankles, whimpering.

"They're dying for some of that cake," Warren laughed.

"So am I!" Connie proclaimed. He grabbed Thom's arm. "Come on, honey, you need to sit down. And you've got some presents to open!"

"I know your birthday's three weeks away," Abby said, with an apologetic smile, "but since Mom is flying back so soon, we decided to celebrate that, too."

Thom shook his head. "This is amazing. Really."

"And don't forget your mom's visit—that's worth a celebration in itself!" Connie said. "I'd planned to have her get inside a *giant* cake and spring out like a dancing girl, but Miss Abby decided that was a bit much. Lucille was game, though."

"Oh, Connie," Thom's mother said. She waved one hand in his direction, a shooing motion.

Amazed, Thom looked from his mother to Connie. She'd arrived only yesterday, and already she was being ribbed by Connie? Called by her first name?

He said, "I see everyone's gotten acquainted while I've been gone."

With a flourishing gesture, Warren had pulled out a chair for him at the head of the table. Thom sat, and the others quickly took their chairs. Begging energetically, Mitzi had contrived to get lifted into Thom's arms, Chloe into Warren's, and now the dogs were sniffing energetically toward the cake.

"Girls, settle down," Thom said. "Hasn't anyone been feeding them while I was gone?"

Abby laughed. "We've all been spoiling them."

And so it went, a couple hours of chit-chat, laughter, their usual hilarity tempered by Lucille's presence but not much, Thom thought, and what surprised him was how readily his mother laughed at his friends' jokes, even Connie's ribald quips, and how shyly she kept stealing glances in Thom's direction when she thought he wouldn't notice. The four years had been kind, at least to her appearance: she wore her red-tinted hair short and pixie-like, and her silk floral-print dress (an Easter dress? or one bought especially for this reunion?) accentuated her trim figure. When she laughed, her hand went to her mouth, a girlish gesture he found endearing, but so far she'd exhibited no sign of her childish stubbornness, the readiness to criticize or complain. It wasn't, Thom thought, as if she were ignoring the sizable elephants in the room—their long estrangement, the unspooling bad memories that preceded it, the complex and forbidding details of Thom's illness—but more as if she'd dismissed or forgotten them. He hoped this wasn't just for his friends' benefit; he hoped harder that the moment they left and it was just he and Abby and their mother, the old threesome, she wouldn't instantly revert (he was ashamed of the thought) to Mother Hyde. He didn't have the energy for that.

For the moment he laughed and joked along with the others. Whenever his mother's eyes met his, he sent back a big, ready smile. He would do whatever she wanted, so long as it would be easy and would not hurt.

This reunion was so amazingly painless, he thought. They talked about random things—movies they'd seen recently, how little the city was doing to prepare for Freaknik—but no one asked about Thom's health, and before long Thom understood the elephants somehow had lumbered out of the room altogether. He took sips of the potent but delicious rum punch Valerie had made. He ate the cake and Häagen-Dazs, which Abby served deftly to everyone, easily resuming her old, familiar role. He opened the gift bags and exclaimed over the wallet and CDs and cologne. His mother's gift was a pair of gold cuff links, and though he never wore cuff links the gift pleased him. She had wrapped the box herself—he could recognize those awkward handmade bows at a hundred paces—and that touched him as much as the gift itself.

"These are great," he kept saying, holding the cuff links up to the light.

"They're 18-karat, I believe," his mother said shyly.

"Oh, Lucille, they're lovely!" Valerie cried. "I gave Marty cuff links for our anniversary one year, but they weren't half as nice as these."

Pace, who in deference to Thom's mother hadn't shouted "goddamn" a single time, said in his gruff voice, "I'm lousy at shopping, I never buy gifts. I wish I did, but I don't. So dinner's on me tonight, OK?"

Thom laughed; he reached across and squeezed Pace's wrist. Pace was well known among his friends for "ignoring" Christmas and birthdays, and he liked receiving gifts even less than giving them. His friends understood and didn't mind. Pace was generous in other ways.

"You don't have to do that," Thom said.

"But I want to, god—" He broke off, blinking behind his rimless spectacles. The others laughed.

Abby said, "Mom, weren't you going to...?"

"Oh, yes!" Lucille cried. "I almost forgot. Thom, I've got something else for you."

She hurried out to the kitchen and returned with another small box wrapped in the same pink-and-green paper. Embarrassed, Thom opened it quickly. "Mom, this is too much..."

"Oh, it's nothing, really," Lucille said, glancing down.

It was an ordinary videotape, the label inscribed in his mother's distinctive left-slanting caps: EASTER MORNING, 1971.

"At Christmas time," she said, with no guilt-inducing inflection in her voice, though Thom listened for one, "Millicent showed us a video she'd had made from her old home movies? You know, the girls opening their Christmas presents, going off to their proms? So I thought: I ought to do that, too."

Connie grabbed the tape from Thom's weak grasp. "What a great idea! Let's all watch it right this minute!"

The tape went around the table, hand to hand.

"I love watching home movies," Warren said, glancing anxiously at Thom.

Pace, who handled the tape as though it were a hot coal, mumbled "Terrific idea" and passed it to Valerie.

"My God, it's from 1971!" she cried. "Thom, you must have been just a baby!"

The others laughed.

"He was a week shy of seven years old," Lucille said, with a touch of pedantry, "and Abby was nine. We had a big backyard, and their father used to get up at dawn and hide eggs all over the place. They're *so* cute in this movie—we took film for more than an hour, can you imagine?"

Thom rolled his eyes. "This is an edited version, I hope?"

"Yes, it's twenty minutes," Lucille said. "This nice man at the video place made us several tapes. He divided them up into holidays, so we have a few Christmases on one, a couple of Thanksgivings on another. But I thought I should bring the Easter one," she said, a little proudly. "I thought that would be appropriate."

Though Thom tried to dissuade them, everyone insisted they wanted to see the video at once. A few minutes later they'd gathered in Thom's bedroom—his only TV was in there—and sat watching an impossibly small

Thom and Abby, dressed for church in their Easter finery, as they ran wildly around the backyard with Easter baskets in tow, bending every few seconds and holding up an egg triumphantly for the camera.

"Thom, that Easter basket is bigger than you are," Warren laughed.

He remembered the basket, elaborately woven of tan straw and shaped like a cowboy hat turned upside-down. Each year, he would wake on Easter morning and find the basket just outside his bedroom door, stuffed with glossy artificial grass, pink and green, that felt silken when he pressed his face against it, and with brightly colored candy eggs. Blaring reds and yellows, pastel greens and blues. Some filled with marshmallow and others mostly sugar, so cloyingly sweet you winced as you ate them. And the basket always held an Easter bunny, made of pure chocolate, inside a box with a cellophane window; he and Abby would save the bunny for last, eating the smooth chocolate one body part at a time. This was usually after church and the big breakfast Lucille made when they got home, and the Easter egg hunt in the backyard. That's where their father had hidden the real eggs, carefully dyed and decorated by Lucille the night before, using little kits she bought at the supermarket. Thom watched as his seven-year-old self, long-limbed and gangly in a pale-blue jacket and matching clip-on tie, careened around the backyard, finding eggs hidden in pine-straw, tucked behind patio furniture cushions, nestled inside potted plants.

"I could never get them to eat the real eggs," Lucille said, sadly. "They just liked the candy ones."

Abby said, a smile in her voice, "I remember how we'd have this sugar high for the rest of the day."

"I know that feeling!" Connie cried. "Oh, look, Abby, you were such a *doll.*"

Thom watched as his nine-year-old sister in her frilly pink dress and petticoats and black patent-leather shoes bent daintily over the coiled-up garden hose, then reached down inside and drew up the "prize" egg. Always there was one egg Lucille had dyed bright gold, and whoever found the golden egg got a twenty dollar bill to buy whatever they wanted at Toys "R" Us. Abby held up the egg, dazzling in the sunlight, turning it in her hand as though following her father's instructions.

Then Thom rushed into camera range. He bent forward to sniff the golden egg and then laughed, putting one hand over his eyes as if embarrassed. Their mother, looking impossibly young and pretty in a pale yellow linen dress and white shoes, got into the picture, too, exchanging silent words with their father as she arranged the children on either side of her.

The three of them stood there motionless, squinting against the sun, as though forgetting this was a movie camera, not a still camera; and obediently they smiled; and obediently the children both held up their Easter baskets so the camera could zoom in for a close-up. In the background against the house, there were blooming crimson and pink azaleas. The glimpses of sky overhead were a bright ceramic blue. The grass about their feet looked so richly green that it might have been artificial, too.

Easter, 1971.

Unexpectedly, Thom felt an egg-sized lump at the base of his throat, so there was a catch in his voice as he said, "Abby always found the gold egg, and then she'd always buy me something at the toy store, too."

"I didn't *always* find it," Abby said, gently.

"Always. You always did," Thom said.

Everyone stared at the TV screen, none of them even glancing at one another. The room had filled with the kind of tension you feel in public when intimate matters are revealed. Thom lay in the center of the bed, propped against two pillows, with Abby and their mother sitting on either side of him. Connie, Pace, and Warren stood back near the headboard, while Valerie had taken the small chair against the wall, a chair Thom used for one purpose: putting on and taking off his shoes. They'd all indulged in the murmuring, cooing noises people made when confronted with pictures of cute children, but there was nothing much else to say.

Then something unexpected happened: the TV screen went black, and suddenly there between Thom and Abby wasn't their mother but their father. He remembered now that Lucille would always insist, near the end, that they trade places so her husband would be in the movie, too. Thom stared hungrily at his father, who had crouched down in his crisp gray suit, just like the ones he wore to the bank, and slung an arm around each of his children. Again Thom and Abby gave those fake toothy grins children use when ordered to smile by picture-taking adults. Clumsily, the camera zoomed in. Their faces blurred, but then they came into focus again. Thom saw that one of his lower teeth was missing. He saw how his father's wedding ring, on the hand depending from Thom's thin shoulder, glinted brightly in the sun. His father looked friendly and solid, but impenetrable. He was their father, but he could have been any man. Tall, dark-haired, smiling. About the same age then, Thom thought, as his son was now. Present and accounted-for in April 1971 but gone now, vanished, leaving behind three orphans watching helplessly from this bed.

Again the tape went black.

"The end!" their mother said, with forced cheerfulness. She rose as if to retrieve the tape but then stopped near Valerie's chair.

On his other side, Thom could feel the stiffness in Abby's body—her arm and leg were pressed against him, and he could feel how they'd tightened, tense as bowstrings. With a brother's privilege he squeezed her thigh through the blue jeans, startled by how thin she'd become.

"What do you think?" he asked. "Oscar performances or what?"

When she didn't answer, Thom looked up, then followed his sister's gaze across the room where Valerie sat slumped in the chair, Lucille bent down with an arm around her shoulder. Valerie was weeping. Quietly but seriously weeping, her shoulders shaking, one hand cupped across her eyes.

Connie crossed to them. "Val, honey, are you OK?"

Warren said, "Let her alone for a second, Connie. She needs to cry. I think I need to cry."

He gave a brief, strangled laugh.

Connie grabbed a few tissues from Thom's bedside table and handed them to Valerie. Wiping her eyes, she looked at Thom.

"I'm sorry," she said. "I don't mean to spoil your—your birthday party, or—"

"Don't worry about that," Thom said. "You're not spoiling anything."

Warren might know why she was crying, but the others did not. Lucille kept patting her shoulder, mechanically, for once in her life at a loss for words. None of the others spoke, either.

After a minute Valerie's crying fit seemed to pass. She kept wiping her eyes, glancing around at the others with a look of apologetic pleading.

"You know, I grew up in foster homes," she said suddenly, in a surprisingly husky, composed voice. "Shuttled from one to another, from the time I was five all the way through high school. So I'm a sucker for families— for families in movies or TV, or for *your* family. Any family. You guys know, I hope, how wonderful it is to have—to have a family."

Valerie blinked away the last of the tears and wiped her face again. Her skin was pale and clammy, her cheeks stained with mascara. Her eyes looked red and miserable.

She repeated, softly, "How wonderful it is." Then she went silent, too, and left them to think about that.

Chapter 9

"I'm worried about him," Abby's mother said. "I don't think he's *well*."

Valerie shook out her napkin, patted Lucille's arm. "I know you've been a big help," she said. "He's having a difficult time, I realize, but I'll just bet—"

"He's been *so* good to me—so sweet," Lucille said, gazing past Abby's shoulder. "But still, I can tell that something's not right."

Valerie began, "I certainly know the feeling. When Marty…"

Abby had tuned out. She sat by herself on this side of the table, facing the mirrored wall and banquette where the host had installed Valerie and Lucille, who had dressed the part for today's outing to the Peasant Uptown, the best restaurant in the city's ritziest mall. Entering, Abby had judged that this elegant light-filled space with its crisscrossing black-tied waiters and sumptuous décor—the gilt-trimmed mirrors, exotic plants and potted trees, crisp tablecloths and massive silver and one heavy-headed pink rose for each table—was about ninety percent women on this late-April afternoon. Near the entrance a tuxedo-clad pianist sent the cascading notes of a Mozart sonata back through the skylit room to mingle with the odors of warm spicy food borne among the tables by deft and smiling servers.

Every few minutes as Abby glanced over her shoulder, she regretted gesturing her mother and Valerie into the banquette seat, which forced her to face the mirrored wall behind them. For the first time in weeks, she had shed her blue jeans, reluctantly assembling the black-and-gold outfit she'd worn to that Christmas party with her brother all those months ago, and halfheartedly she'd applied lipstick and mascara. The results were not encouraging. Today her mother and Valerie wore new spring outfits (maybe they'd bought them together, for Lucille had become Valerie's new shopping partner after Abby lost interest), and Abby saw they'd both spent time recently in a beauty salon; her mother's makeup was softer and more flattering than usual, and her coral-pink nails looked freshly manicured. Abby thought, with the kind of grim humor she allowed herself these days, that she must resemble some black-clad retainer tagging along with these two elegant ladies; or some poor relation, maybe, brought along as a special treat. Smiling, she did allow her gaze to settle in the mirrored space between her mother's and Valerie's busily chatting heads, but the pale sharp-boned face hovering there was not smiling, after all. She looked haggard, careworn. In a face she'd always considered fairly ordinary but youthful, Abby was able to glimpse—and for the first time—the hardening lineaments of middle age.

"What do you think, Abby?" Valerie said. "Has he seemed that way to you?"

Startled, Abby focused on Valerie's pert triangular face with its puzzled little girl's blue eyes that brought Abby a spasm of guilt. Valerie was buying their lunch as a "thank you" for all the kindness Abby had shown her as she coped with her turbulent marriage. In short, for being such a good friend, for so many acts of kindness, consideration…. Valerie's gratitude could be overbearing at times, but Abby had agreed to this lunch excursion, though she'd insisted on meeting them here at Phipps Plaza since she had another Buckhead appointment at two o'clock. Yes, she would come to lunch, but Valerie didn't owe her anything, Abby had insisted. She really mustn't feel that way.

"I think—I think he's having a difficult time," Abby said carefully. "I haven't talked to him in a while. At least a week."

"He hasn't been returning my phone calls, either," Valerie said quickly. "And that's *not* like him. I think your mother is the only person he likes any more! He *does* adore you, Lucille!"

Abby's mother lowered her eyes in the bashful, pleased gesture she used often these days. As Thom had said recently, their mother had "found her element" in these surprising new friendships with Valerie and Connie. She seemed at least a decade younger; her fretting and complaining had all but ceased. She could still be forgetful, but since her amnesia seemed to encompass all the formidable sins she'd once charged against her children,

Thom and Abby were hardly in a mood to complain. Laughing, Thom had said that Valerie and Connie had become her "surrogate children," since they were so much needier and responsive than her real ones. Her brother's lighthearted remark had caused Abby an obscure, deep-cutting hurt, but she'd said nothing; she'd laughed along with his joke. Privately, she'd thought that Thom, as well, was doing so much better than she could have hoped, even a few weeks ago, that she dared not quibble with good fortune. Nor had she the time lately to give much thought to Connie, though she resisted Valerie's exaggerated assumptions.

"I think he's just busy," she said. "Hasn't he started working part-time with Warren? And I know the estate matters still aren't completely settled."

Lucille raised one eyebrow. "He needs to quit that job—it's silly for someone like him to be driving all the way to the suburbs, just to work as a glorified secretary. He's too smart for that, and he certainly doesn't need the money!"

"But I thought the point was to put some structure in his life," Abby said. "Isn't that what Warren—"

"And his father keeps threatening to visit!" Valerie cried. "Connie said that every day when he gets home, he's afraid the old man will be sitting there on the doorstep, waiting."

Lucille was shaking her head; her pale-blue eyes looked misty. The waiter had brought their lunch, but she hadn't touched her fork.

"I don't think the real problem is his father," she said. "It's that the boy lost his *mother*. It's so tragic."

Abby glanced at Valerie: sometimes Lucille, one of whose favorite topics was the importance of family, seemed to forget what she knew about Valerie's background, her early years spent as what Valerie called, with her hoarse laugh, "a sad little orphan." Her middle name, it turned out, was Ann, and when Valerie was seven or eight, a mean stepsister had called her "Orphan Annie." For a while Valerie had endured the nickname at school as well. But as usual it didn't seem to bother her when Lucille made insensitive remarks; she was nodding emphatically, her eyes squinched half-shut in sympathy with Connie's "tragic" past.

Valerie said, "He's so sweet-natured, really. It *is* like he's still just a boy sometimes."

"In more ways than one," Lucille laughed. "He's such a scamp. The other day, he was driving me down Peachtree..."

Picking at her salad, Abby again tuned out. She wasn't hungry; she was seldom hungry, these days. Since their trip to Key West she had lost ten pounds (or was it fifteen?) though Thom was the only one who noticed. He laughed that the extra weight had transferred onto him, by osmosis, and it was true that with the new drug "cocktail" he was using, he'd never looked better. Yet he was concerned about Abby. She'd told him nothing, of course, but since that rather embarrassing moment in Key West (*He wasn't from...England?*) she could feel his kindly, slightly oppressive attention, the way he surveyed her clothes, her body, her face each time they met. Only for him, she'd thought more than once, did she pay attention to her appearance at all.

She could imagine at this point in her life withdrawing to some private hermitage, a place without mirrors or other people where she might wear the same clothes every day and become lax about bathing and eat only what was required to stay alive. Or stop eating altogether, if she chose. Stop thinking, too. Days and nights bleeding one into the other without pattern so that really she might stop everything: stop altogether. There was a poem of Emily Dickinson's she'd taught every semester, *Because I could not stop for death, He kindly stopped for me,* and now she understood those words for the first time, in her blood and bones. She seldom indulged such morbid thinking, but when she did, her heart convulsed in such deep and thrilling pleasure that she drew back, afraid. The emotion was not unlike the most perilous depths of her passion with Philip DeMunn, who existed now only as an abstracted memory—a face wreathed in smoke or mist, an insidious voice in her ear—but one lacking the power to harm or even to trouble her attention for more than a moment or two. Her new thoughts were elsewhere.

Sitting numbed on the way back from Key West, she'd seen herself rushing into an emergency room and demanding the test, demanding to know, but by the time their plane touched the ground, she'd understood she was in no hurry. There was even a kind of pleasure in the waiting, which seemed an eerily miniature but heightened reflection of these months she'd spent in Atlanta, waiting for some new life to begin. Using the Yellow Pages, she had found the name of a woman gynecologist in Buckhead—the combination of the simple name "Dr. Kim Smith" and the expensive address were somehow reassuring—and had made the next available appointment, which was several weeks away. But Dr. Smith had turned out to be a tiny Korean woman who, glimpsing the involuntary look of surprise on Abby's face, had quickly explained (with an endearing, shut-eyed smile) that she'd married an Atlanta dermatologist while still in med school at Emory. Embarrassed, Abby said she was pleased to meet her, and in fact she liked the woman at once. When her feet were in the stirrups, she'd said casually, "Doctor, I think I may have been exposed—" but her throat went dry.

"Yes? Exposed?" Dr. Smith said, her head bent.

"Yes, I'd like the test. The HIV test."

Later they'd talked over the options in a calm, clinical way, as though discussing a third person not in the room, and then a nurse had drawn Abby's blood. That was last Friday, and today she was returning to discuss the test result and future options. Abby had hoped she might get a phone call from Dr. Smith's office, saying the test was negative and she needn't come in, after all. Spending so much time with Thom and his friends, she knew that did happen sometimes. There had been no call, but she tried not to read anything into that. She felt strangely calm.

She hadn't told her family or friends, because certainly they would not be calm; and everything was going so well, at least on the surface. Her mother's visit had dragged on, much as Abby's had when she first arrived, and in the past week Lucille had even stopped apologizing for "overstaying her welcome." It was strange: here they were again, mother and daughter sharing Abby's condo, while their more expensive town house outside Philadelphia, still crammed with their furniture and most of their belongings, sat empty and silent. Aunt Millicent had sent over her maid to gather and ship more of their clothes, along with a few personal items, and the other day her mother had remarked that she "didn't miss the rest." Abby knew the feeling: except for a few books and photographs, she didn't miss anything, either. Nor did she mind sharing with her mother this glorified apartment with its two tiny bedrooms and rented furniture, since the tension between them had lessened almost to nothing.

These days her mother claimed to be "excited" about Abby's enrollment in the doctoral program, and she spoke about Thom, whom they saw every day, so fondly that Abby sometimes wondered if their mother *had* forgotten the estrangement, the old snarls and resentments, the past itself—or at least had willed herself to forget. Shyly, Thom had asked Abby if she thought their mother should have some "memory tests" done—adding quickly that he didn't think she had Alzheimer's, not at all, but she did seem vague and fuzzy about some things, and repeated herself so often— but Abby had not answered except to give him a brief pained look that had translated, she supposed, into *Let's don't rock the boat. Not now.* He hadn't mentioned the idea again, though Abby supposed he was right. After her dealings with Dr. Smith were concluded, she imagined that was next:

focusing on their mother. Sorting out the details of their future, such as where everyone was going to live, and how. And why.

Somehow none of this seemed pressing, and Abby had the strange idea that it would fall easily into place. Eventually, they would traipse up to Philadelphia, collect all their things, and come back here. Last Sunday, the three of them and Connie were driving home from a movie at the Tara when Lucille had the sudden idea they should see their old place, so without a murmur Thom had driven them to Sherwood Forest: to Friar Tuck Road. Paused before the house, which looked exactly the same, Abby had felt little emotion; she had no idea what the others felt. Lucille had said in her airy voice that meant nothing, "Maybe we should try and buy it back!" Thom laughed. Driving home, he'd talked about the soaring real estate prices in this neighborhood.

"Still, you ought to buy it," Connie said. "It's such a pretty house!"

But none of the Sadlers had replied, and that had been that.

The waiter was saying, "Dessert, ma'am? Coffee?"

"Look, you hardly touched your chicken!" Valerie cried.

Abby pushed her plate away, trying to smile. "Sorry, wasn't hungry…it was delicious, though."

"We'll take the check," Lucille said. She turned to Abby. "Honey, we're going over to Lord & Taylor—you'll come with us, won't you?"

Valerie said, "Their spring stuff is on sale already, can you believe it?"

"No, I—I've got an appointment," she told them, for the second time, and for the second time she steeled herself for their inquiries, wondering what she would say. Why would Abby have an "appointment"? But again they didn't ask.

On their way out of the restaurant, she lagged behind her mother and Valerie, who were chatting busily about Connie's upcoming dinner party, where supposedly they would all meet his father. Possibly the dinner would not even take place. According to Thom, Mr. Lefcourt's visit to Atlanta was scheduled one day, canceled the next, then on again, then off again, all according to whether father and son had spoken peaceably or argued violently in their most recent phone conversation.

"Warren is moving out for a few days," Thom had told her, "since he thinks Connie and his dad need privacy, but Connie seems to think the opposite. He wants us around as a kind of buffer. There's safety in crowds, he said."

Abby wasn't looking forward to the dinner, whether Mr. Lefcourt was there or not, but she could think of no excuse not to come. When Connie phoned the previous week, he'd sounded shrill and enthusiastic, but there was a disconnected quality to his words, as though he might be talking to anyone. When she'd accepted the invitation, he'd said, as if consulting a list, "Fabulous! Now, let's see, I need to call Abby and Valerie—no, I mean—what did I say? Goodness, I don't think I was cut out to be a hostess!" Abby had given a dutiful laugh, issued her white lie about looking forward to the party.

"Me too—bye now!" Connie had cried. "See you Saturday! Bye, sweetheart!"

As the three women parted outside the restaurant, among the sparse traffic of well-dressed people drifting through the mall, Valerie said, "Bye, hon," and hugged Abby tightly. To Abby's surprise her mother followed suit, lunging forward with a quicker, more awkward hug. Such embraces were hardly her style. She was craning her head, eyes trained on the far distance as though seeking out Lord & Taylor. Abby knew that she and Valerie were dying for a cigarette, too; among Valerie's other attractions, Lucille now had a smoking buddy.

"Well, my car's the other way," Abby murmured, but the other two had already blended into the crowd, their heads bent close together, and in this way Abby's lunch obligation was concluded.

She glanced at her watch: 1:35. Her doctor's appointment was at two o'clock, so she reasoned that the timing had been perfect, at least.

Usually, Atlanta had an abbreviated spring, the cold weather lingering through most of March and the insufferable heat descending a few weeks later, but this year the late-April afternoons turned just warm enough to coax the trees to leaf out, the dogwoods and azaleas to display their full riot of color. The long evenings were crisp and cool. Joggers and dog walkers streamed along the winding sidewalks of Morningside and Virginia-Highland, the Midtown parks and outdoor cafés throbbed with conversation, laughter, and music in such a picturesque mingling of black and white—rollerbladers and the elderly, families with small children and gay couples holding hands—that it might have been staged by Atlanta boosters portraying the city's inclusive and harmonious spirit. Around six o'clock on the evening before Abby's doctor appointment, her brother had knocked at her door, but when she answered and motioned him inside, he shook his head. He'd brought the dogs along and held a leash in each hand; though they strained to race inside, lunging at Abby's legs, Thom scolded them.

"No, girls—back!" He looked up, grinning. "And as for *you* girls, come outside and take a walk with us?"

Abby had checked with her mother, who didn't want to go—she was afraid she'd miss *Wheel of Fortune*—but Abby welcomed the diversion. She slipped a nylon windbreaker over her sleeveless blouse and took one of the leashes Thom handed her; they started out.

"Let's head toward Wildwood," her brother said. "It's so pretty in there."

As they meandered north on Rock Springs toward Wildwood Drive, an older residential street divided by a deep ravine and dense lovely growths of water oak and magnolias, both Mitzi and Chloe raced ahead, enlivened by the crisp evening air and the rare thrill of an outing.

"I've been so busy at work," Thom said, "I haven't been walking them much. Outside to do their business, then right back in."

"I'm glad you thought of this," Abby said. She hadn't brooded over the next day's appointment with Dr. Smith, exactly, but she'd felt tense and out of sorts, especially after a conversation this morning with her graduate adviser at Emory; the man had seemed to be hinting, and not very subtly, that Abby ought to forget about graduate work and stick to high school teaching. And her mother had picked this day to quiz her about money: how could she make ends meet for three or four years, and what if she couldn't get a teaching job once she did get her doctorate? Abby had murmured something about fellowships and part-time teaching, but her mother's queries had been pertinent enough. "If you'd gone to Penn instead," Lucille said, "you could have lived at home for practically nothing, just like—" She'd stopped herself before finishing the phrase, *just like you've been doing.* "I mean, I don't like the idea of your paying rent, honey—you know that."

Again Abby had told her mother that she shouldn't worry—she had plenty of money saved. "Partly because you *have* been so generous," Abby said, and her mother had smiled, mollified. She was so easy to make happy, these days. Then the phone had rung, and Lucille answered—it was Valerie, but evidently she was calling for Lucille—and Abby was left again to her eerie mood of anxiety and resignation, hope and indifference. She didn't know what she felt but at least, she thought with a dim smile, she knew that she didn't know. That was progress.

She told Thom, "I've felt cooped inside all afternoon." Today her adviser, with an audible sigh, had handed her the formal reading list for the week-long written exams she'd take once her course work was completed, and though she'd read most of the titles, she knew she'd have to reread them. Even the books she'd taught many times had faded quickly from memory as if lost to a distant past, a long-ago self. After lunch she'd picked up a new paperback of Dickens' *Bleak House* and retreated to her bedroom, but her attention kept wandering. After an hour she saw that she'd read only twelve pages. The novel was nine hundred pages long and such an intense wave of lassitude and hopeless indifference had overwhelmed her that she'd shut the book and thrown it against the wall.

She'd sat waiting patiently for a fit of tears, but the tears did not come.

"How's Mom doing?" Thom had said. "Is she driving you crazy?"

"Oh, no—she was on the phone with Valerie a couple of times. They're like teenage girls, those two. Planning their shopping expeditions, talking endlessly about Marty as if he were Valerie's high school boyfriend instead of her fourth husband." Abby laughed. "Mom seems happy, though, even if she is more forgetful, a little confused sometimes...."

"Has she said anything about going home—back to Philly? Not that her being here is a problem," he added quickly.

"Every few days," Abby said, "especially after Aunt Millie calls, she'll say she ought to 'get out of our hair,' but she doesn't sound too convinced. Yesterday she asked if I wanted to go to the Botanical Gardens sometime. Everything is so much prettier here, she said, than in Philadelphia. I just about fell over."

For a minute or two, they walked along in silence. Mitzi and Chloe trotted eagerly, plunging ahead with new energy once they'd turned onto Wildwood with its dense shade and cooler air. Attracted to the foliage along the ravine, Chloe crossed in front of Mitzi, and the leashes got tangled, so they stopped while Thom patiently undid them. Abby shivered, gripping the windbreaker close against her throat.

"You wouldn't vote for her moving back here, would you," she said.

"Me?" He shrugged. "I wouldn't mind. What about you?"

Thom handed her Chloe's leash and they resumed their walk.

"I guess it wouldn't make sense," Abby said. "Her living up there alone."

Thom said with a chuckle, "I think it's great that she's getting along with Valerie so well—and Connie!"

She wanted to shift their talk away from their mother. "How is Connie? He hasn't phoned in a while."

Thom shook his head. "I'm not sure what's going on. Warren called the other day, said he had to send Connie home from the office. He'd shown up two hours late for work—it was almost lunchtime—and he'd been drinking. 'Only a couple of Bloody Marys with my breakfast!'" Thom gave a thin laugh. "But Warren thought he'd had a lot more than that, and he was furious that Connie had driven up I-75 that way. He sent him home in a taxi."

Puzzled, Abby glanced at her brother. "I thought this job was going to be good for him. Is his father coming to visit, or not?"

Thom had quickened his pace; trying to keep up, Abby felt a little out of breath.

"That's the mystery," Thom said. "Connie talks like he's a cross between Simon Legree and Charles Manson—he still claims they have these huge arguments and his father gets obnoxious, says he's going to sue him about the estate, even gets drunk and threatens him bodily harm. Yet Warren says he's heard Connie talking pleasantly and even laughing on the phone with him. That Connie has been urging him to come. The latest thing is some flap about that jewelry Connie sent back, telling his father he could keep it—evidently his father sent it back again, and they argued about that. I don't know why."

Abby shook her head. "Connie makes everything so complicated, doesn't he?"

"Chaos," Thom said. "Warren says he's addicted to chaos."

The dogs crisscrossed in their paths, reacting frantically to a woman walking a pair of white poodles across the street; again they stopped while Thom sorted out the leashes. "Girls, girls…" he muttered.

Abby was grateful for the chance to catch her breath. She said, "I feel that way about Valerie, sometimes. Her life is such a soap opera."

Thom raised up, his face reddened. "Who is this mystery husband of hers, anyway? Sometimes I wonder if he really exists."

Abby stared ahead as the dogs, back on track, led them briskly along the sidewalk. "I haven't met him, either, and I think Valerie likes it that way. According to her, he's a workaholic with a mother fixation, and he's commitment-phobic to boot."

Thom laughed. "Warren should be here," he said. "He loves to talk psychobabble."

She recounted to Thom the few details she'd gotten from Valerie these past few months; though Valerie often enjoyed complaining about Marty, she'd noticed that when Abby asked specific questions about him, Valerie would turn evasive and change the subject. On the one occasion when Abby had said bluntly that she and Thom would really like to meet him,

Valerie paled visibly. "Oh, hon," she'd said. "You really *don't.*" Abby knew only that he worked seventy-hour weeks as a regional manager for an insurance-industry trade association, and that the job required extensive travel. Valerie had shown her a photograph: a light-haired, pleasant-looking man in his forties with an uneasy grin, the kind a man wears when asked to smile for a photo. Snapped on a San Francisco street during their honeymoon, this was a rare shot, Valerie had laughed. He hated having his picture taken.

"Their big issue," Abby said, "is that when Marty travels he sometimes visits his mother on the weekend, in Minneapolis, instead of flying back home. That drives Valerie crazy."

"But I thought he was the one so smitten with her."

Abby shrugged. "When she threatens to leave him, he gets that way. Sends gifts and flowers, promises they'll take a second honeymoon to Paris or Hawaii. Even threatens suicide when Valerie really gets intent on leaving. So she relents, and then the cycle starts all over again."

They'd reached Wildwood Park, a leafy enclave with smooth dirt paths, picnic tables, scattered benches. They sat on the bench farthest from the swing-sets, where children shouted to each other as they pumped higher and higher on the swings; both the dogs had lunged in that direction, but Thom and Abby had coaxed them up to their laps.

"It sounds like she ought to dump him," Thom said bluntly.

"I think she will, eventually. She's trying to figure out what she wants to do."

Abby gazed out at the sidewalk where someone jogged or walked by every few seconds. In the park's dense shade the air was cooler, and Chloe's panting warmth felt wonderful on her lap; instinctively, she had edged a few inches closer to Thom. She glanced at him, smiling. "You're looking so well, these days. Like you've got everything figured out already."

"Me? Are you kidding?" She saw that his throat and cheeks had flushed, as if he were pleased by this compliment. Now that he'd gained some weight Thom looked younger, his skin fresh as a teenager's even with his end-of-day stubble, his thick dark hair gleaming above his prominent forehead. The deep-blue eyes held a mischievous self-deprecation, as always. The thin mouth had its ironic curl, as always. He still wore his work clothes but the khakis and cotton dress shirt were amiably rumpled, his top button undone and the tie hanging askew. Next to him, she felt pallid and insubstantial, like some ghostly sidekick next to this friendly, handsome man in his prime. No one would guess they were siblings.

He said, "I just got dumped, remember?"

This surprised her; or the "just" surprised her, at least. "I didn't—I didn't think it was that serious. It's been a couple of months, hasn't it?"

"I don't know. Yes, but it doesn't seem that long. He really got under my skin, that one did."

Suddenly, Mitzi lifted her red snout and gave Thom's nose a broad swipe of the tongue. "Thanks, honey," he laughed, massaging the dog's head as her eyes closed in bliss. "I needed that."

Abby watched them. "I'm sorry." She didn't know what else to say.

Thom turned, his blue-eyed gaze no longer smiling. "What about you?"

"What do you mean?"

"Before we went to Key West, I knew you were seeing someone." He spoke matter-of-factly. "I didn't want to pry, but I knew. Now I'm assuming you're single again. You want to talk about it?"

She caught her breath, so startled that she gave a quick, nervous laugh. She said, "You didn't want to pry?"

"Sorry," he said, glancing off.

"No, I—" She took a deep breath, then another. He'd said "someone"; he didn't know who the someone was. "I'm just surprised, that's all. I thought I'd been so clever."

Thom rolled his eyes. "Honey, please. All that scurrying into my room to use the phone? The new clothes, the makeup? The long evenings out with 'old friends' doing vague things you could never quite describe? You're a very bad liar, you know."

He'd softened this with a quick squeeze of her forearm.

She didn't want to lie, so she chose her words carefully. "It was someone I met by chance, but I'd rather not go into it."

"OK. I don't mind."

"It's still too—too recent."

"I understand."

They sat staring out toward the street.

"I do wish you could meet someone, though," Thom said. "That guy up in Philly was really a bust? Ginger didn't say much, when she told me about it, but she seemed to think you were seeing a lot of him."

The image of poor Graham Northwood's pale, wounded face floated into her mind's eye, a ghost from an improbable past.

"I was, but it was just for something to do. It wasn't ever serious. He was nice in his way, but very 'safe.' Kind of boring, to be honest. He didn't count."

Thom made a clicking noise with his tongue. "I wouldn't mind someone safe," he said softly. "I'm tired of always being the one who's more vulnerable, more attached—I'm in the mood to find a guy who's wild about *me*. That would be really nice, for a change."

Abby gave the neutral smile she wore whenever she thought about Phil DeMunn. She would have to remember this conversation—the phrase "a safe relationship"—when she finally told Thom what had happened. That would occur when she no longer thought of Phil daily; no longer took shallow breaths when she considered what he had done. The other day, against her own best instincts, she'd lifted the receiver and dialed his number, not to tear into him, nor even to mention her discovery, or any of that; but rather to force him back to their first meeting and ask the real reason he hadn't returned to her at Pace's party. Had he worried that Thom might see them together? Had he suffered a twinge of conscience? Why had he left her there after taking so much trouble, slipping into the night while upstairs her head swirled with champagne and the sight of eddying snow against the glass roof? It was important that she return to that moment somehow, important that she understand. Yet she hadn't been surprised, of course, when she heard the recorded announcement that his phone had been disconnected. She hadn't really been displeased.

"Someone wild about you? You think it would be nice, but it wouldn't," Abby said.

Instantly, she regretted the words. Abby Sadler as a source of advice about romance was a laughable idea, if she'd cared to laugh.

Instead, she turned to her brother; Mitzi had begun squirming, so he'd let her down and sat bent forward, elbows on his knees as he watched the dog edging from the bench, sniffing. Gazing at him, Abby endured a flood of nostalgic emotion as she recalled the companionable, even-tempered brother she'd adored since their earliest childhood. This recent estrangement—four years!—struck her now as something so idiotic that she could scarcely believe it had happened to them. She leaned down to him, catching the tangy scent of his hair gel, and slid an arm around his shoulder. She whispered, "Thanks for being such...an angel," and though she felt a flush of embarrassment she didn't care. He smiled, his eyelids drooping as they always did when he embraced someone, and they hugged a long moment.

"Same to you," Thom murmured, and as they broke apart his lips grazed her cheek.

Abby let her gaze wander back to the sidewalk, where she saw an elderly couple walking along slowly, holding hands; both were watching Thom and Abby, smiling. Thom waved at them, and they waved back and passed on.

Lovers, the old couple must have thought. *Lovers in springtime.*

Abby dismissed this notion as the dogs, attracted by a scurrying sound from a nearby hedge, charged away from the path, and of course they managed to get their leashes wound together within seconds. Thom called sternly for them to come back, and they obeyed, but they scampered excitedly around Thom and Abby's legs, as though deliberately entangling them. They circled frantically until they ran out of leash and stood there gridlocked, perplexed. Thom and Abby laughed, trying to extricate their ankles. Near Thom's shoe, Chloe panicked and began trying to wriggle out of her collar, but the more docile Mitzi simply flopped onto her back in the grass, waiting patiently for Thom to sort out this hopeless new tangle that was binding them all together.

She arrived at the doctors' building at 1:50 and sat in the parking garage, waiting. Either she felt nothing or she did not know what she felt. Anxiety, tension, thrumming heart and clammy palms—she had none of these. Her fate lay waiting upstairs in Dr. Kim Smith's office, no doubt folded neatly inside an envelope. The doctor knew, maybe her nurse, her entire staff—"That young woman who came in last week...really doesn't fit the profile, such a shame..." Soon enough, maybe others would know. She pondered this and wondered if she cared. Another of Atlanta's nicknames was "the world's largest small town"; though most people who lived here came from somewhere else (natives like Abby and Thom were a distinct minority), mostly they were from the South, and Southerners *talked.* One evening after they'd watched a video at Thom's place, Connie had remarked, "Well, there may be six degrees of separation in New York, but in Atlanta there's usually just one. Two at most."

It was true. Any stranger you met, it seemed, attended high school with your best friend, or dated your cousin, or went to AA with somebody who lived on your street. "I've heard *all about* you!" was the common phrase, stripped of its sinister implications by the delighted, impenetrable smile common to white Atlantans from the better neighborhoods. So Abby Sadler ("Really? My matron of honor went to St. Jude's!") would be that poor, dying girl, struggling to get her Ph.D. in spite of everything. Emitting a little *paugh* of disgust, Abby interrupted this train of thought. She grabbed her keys and purse, then made her way numbly to the doctor's office and gave the receptionist her name, not quite meeting the woman's eyes.

Abby had waited inside an examining room only a couple of minutes before Dr. Smith entered briskly. "Abby! Good to see you!" she exclaimed with her shut-eyed grin.

Abby sat shivering in her chair; the room was very cold. The glaring fluorescent lighting made even the petite but robust Dr. Smith look washed out. Here, at least, Abby did not sit facing a mirrored wall. She must resemble a scared little mouse.

Abby said, "Thanks, you too. The results?"

"Yes, the results!" Dr. Smith said, in her harshly accented English. She held a manila folder in one hand and waved it briefly. But then her tone changed; her voice lowered, her smile disappeared.

"The pap smear, everything," she said with a direct, professional gaze into Abby's widened eyes, "was fine. Everything was negative. But it's important, Abby, that you come back. For another HIV."

Only now did she understand that the anxiety, the suspense, had been there all along; she hadn't allowed herself to feel it. While Dr. Smith stared, Abby's eyes filled with tears and her throat knotted; she blinked her eyelids, letting the tears fall, and waited until she could breathe.

"Abby? You OK?" Dr. Smith held out a Kleenex and Abby pawed at her face, embarrassed.

"Sorry, I—I didn't know what to expect—"

"That's OK. Sometime good news gets more reaction than bad—I see it all the time! But remember, I want you back in two months. The antibody—they take a while to form. You're *prob*ably OK, especially with just one exposure, but we want to be one hundred percent sure. OK?"

Abby nodded, gratefully. She felt like one of the weepy high school girls who'd often visited her office, back at West Chester Academy.

Ten minutes later, she was back in the parking garage inside her car feeling as though she'd been run through a meat grinder. *Everything was fine. Everything was negative.* Half an hour ago her body had been numb, but now it seemed that every nerve throbbed dully with pain, something strangely akin to grief. She did not understand. If she'd slipped near the edge of a precipice and extended her arms for a flailing hopeless plunge to certain death, but at the last moment a strong arm had circled her waist, pulling her back, might she have felt like this? She did not understand, but whatever the case her peculiar reaction did not last. For a while she drove aimlessly up Peachtree in the wrong direction—she wasn't ready to go back home, pretend to her mother this was some ordinary day. By the time she reached Lenox Square, she understood that her reaction had subsided; she pulled into a parking space near Rich's and again sat for a few moments. The paroxysm of emotion had left her feeling calm and almost weightless, breathing lightly. She left the car and went inside the mall, whose broad main corridor held few shoppers on this weekday afternoon. She walked, feeling elated and even pleased with herself. She wandered aimlessly.

After a few minutes she paused out of habit in front of a bookstore, but decided not to go inside. Her condo was filled with books. Her life was filled with books. Slowly, the awareness had taken hold that a life, probably long, had unspooled before her, blank as paper. Hadn't there been a writer who had bought a roll of ordinary butcher paper and written an entire novel as the paper wound through his typewriter? She saw the paper as if she took the roll herself and sent it unwinding down the long corridor of Lenox Square mall, speeding far and fast and out of sight. She saw the paper but not the words. She turned from the bookstore and went along in her aimless pleased way, pausing at a music store but not going inside, pausing at a ladies' shoe store but not going inside. Then she remembered that the first of May was her brother's birthday. Next Saturday. They had celebrated when he'd gotten back from the hospital, but of course that was two weeks ago, and they would celebrate again. She would invite everyone to her place; she would get party decorations, and they would all buy more gifts, and Thom would look embarrassed and sheepish, but of course this would happen, only a few days from now. Why hadn't she thought of this before today? Why hadn't she planned anything? Her future might be shapeless as dough, blank as paper, but she knew what would happen next Saturday.

In the Polo Shop, she found a light-blue cotton dress shirt that would bring out her brother's pretty blue eyes, and she selected a diagonally striped tie that complemented the shirt; the unctuous salesman remarked that she had excellent taste. She handed him her credit card with a delighted, impenetrable smile. The total was over a hundred dollars, but she didn't blink. Soon enough she would stop buying him extravagant gifts. Soon enough she would put herself on a budget, become an impoverished graduate student. But not yet. Or maybe she would not become a graduate student at all. There were private academies around here, of course, like the one where she'd taught in Pennsylvania, so she could simply resume her high school teaching, if she wanted. She was tired of self-centered rich girls in uniforms, but she needn't teach in a private school, of course; she could get certified for public school teaching and try that. She could even seek out a school in south Atlanta, teach black kids to read Langston Hughes and Rita Dove. Why not?

Meandering through the mall with the Polo sack flapping against her leg, Abby smiled at herself, recognizing this idea as a version of her girlhood convent fantasies. No, she would not become Mother Abigail, ministering to the city's poor. Instead, she would go to Emory and pursue Bakhtinian readings of the novels of Charlotte Brontë and spend months or years writing a dissertation only three people—her graduate committee—would read, and only because they were paid handsomely to read it. Then, if she was lucky, she'd get a job teaching freshman comp in a community college somewhere, putting marks beside dangling participles with that memorized flick of Miss Sadler's wrist. And why not? Surely this was preferable, she thought, to getting literally fucked to death in a hotel room in Key West? She had evaded that fate, and would replace it with another. As she meandered through the dim open spaces of Lenox Square, she felt herself an alien arrived in a new world, permitted the surprising freedom to explore, improvise, make her own way. Here she was.

After about an hour of this, she saw the doors to the outside near Rich's where she'd entered, so she left the building and returned to her car. She made her way slowly down traffic-clogged Peachtree, then an even more congested Piedmont Avenue; it was just past five o'clock. But she didn't mind. There was no hurry. When she reached Rock Springs and turned into her complex a pleasant surprise awaited her, like a reward for her patient drive through rush hour. Outside on the sidewalk she glimpsed Thom, looking fit and handsome in a red T-shirt and jeans, his back to her: he was heading away from his unit and toward her own building. She moved to toot the horn but stopped: she always enjoyed these glimpses of her brother when he thought himself unobserved. His long strides. His inimitable boyish slouch. His habit of rubbing behind his ear with the curled fingers of one hand. Sweet Thom. Her brother. By the time she had parked and gotten out—she left her sack with its gift-wrapped box in the car—he was coming back the other way, and she saw that he was scowling. A dark, heavy-browed scowl that wasn't quite like him, but she supposed he'd had a rough day. A contract gone awry. A difficult client. She'd fix that, she thought, still buoyed by that queer limitless elation she'd felt at the mall. Yes, this news would surely change his mood: his birthday was next weekend, she'd remind him, and she was going to throw the biggest party of their lives.

"Thom," she cried out, with a facetious grin. "You can wipe that tragic frown off your face! I'm *home*!"

But then she felt ridiculous, inane, for he didn't return the smile. Approaching him, she saw that his skin looked pale, clammy, his eyes threaded with blood as if he'd been crying. He opened his mouth to speak but then seemed to change his mind and did something that shocked her: he turned and stalked off, head ducked, toward his own front door, leaving her no choice but to follow.

Chapter 10 . . . .

"A man wearing two diamond necklaces, a pair of ladies' diamond ear-rings, and several bracelets and rings was struck and killed by a speeding motorist on Tuesday evening at the corner of Piedmont and Tenth."

That was the way Monica Kaufman on Channel 2, with a sad, sympathetic gaze into the camera, reported Connie's death on the eleven o'clock news.

Along with Abby and their mother and a steady stream of friends drifting in and out of his apartment, Thom watched the news reports and read the papers. The Atlanta dailies gave featured coverage to the accident, and it made the front page of *Southern Voice*. People talked endlessly about what had happened, what might have happened, why it might have happened, but no answers satisfied Thom or did anything to shrink the mass of leaden grief that again had lodged inside him. Only a few weeks ago, he'd noticed that when he woke up in the morning, Carter's death wasn't the first thing he thought about, and guiltily but gladly he'd begun to breathe easier as if that mass of grief had eroded without his quite noticing, without his permission. But now it was back, and after the first few hours of stunned disbelieving tears, he sat weighted by it, unable to comfort himself or others, able only to talk pointlessly about what and why, what and why. He listened patiently to everyone because he had no choice, but there were no answers he wanted to hear.

There were a few facts on which everyone agreed. Connie had been drinking in Blake's, arriving about five o'clock and talking boisterously to the bartender and the after-work patrons clustered around him. (But with no mention of his father, who had flown to Atlanta that morning.) Nothing odd about his behavior—at least according to the bartender, interviewed for news reports, who had seen no reason to stop serving Connie the whiskey sours he kept ordering. Nothing odd, that is, until around seven o'clock, when he'd said to the group he'd been entertaining—he'd treated them, all strangers, to several rounds—that he wanted to show them something. That's when he'd reached into his pockets and started pulling out the necklaces, bracelets, rings. "Sometimes a girl's just got to show off, dontcha know!" Connie had cried, donning the jewelry. Everyone had laughed, assuming all the jewelry was fake. Connie minced and posed, observing that of course diamonds were *this* girl's best friend, and he'd laughed and the others had laughed, and Connie ordered them all another round. He hadn't taken off the jewelry. He'd kept drinking. Most of the patrons he'd entertained with his lively banter drifted off to home, to dinner, and Connie's voice had gotten louder and did have, the bartender admitted, an "edge of anger" to it; actually, he *was* thinking of cutting Connie off, when abruptly Connie lurched off his stool and plunged out of the bar onto Tenth Street.

The facts ended here, for Thom had heard and read so many differing reports of the accident, if it was an accident, that he no longer knew what to believe. It was around eight o'clock and dusk was falling, and there were dozens of witnesses: people in the cars on Piedmont and on Tenth, others having dinner in the outdoor cafés along Piedmont, pedestrians on all four sides of the intersection. One claimed Connie had crossed Tenth legally with the light, and that the man in his maroon Nissan barreled through the intersection, striking Connie head-on. Others claimed the Nissan was making a right turn on red, and that Connie had seen the car and stopped perversely in its path. There were reports that Connie was jaywalking or meandering aimlessly through the busy intersection against the light, looking disoriented, mumbling to himself. At least one insisted that Connie seemed to put himself deliberately into the Nissan's path, though everyone agreed the Nissan was making the turn much too fast and had not come to a complete stop. The driver, a thirty-something black man in a crisp white shirt and tie, had jumped out of the Nissan and begun shouting hysterically over Connie's prone, bleeding form, blaming Connie and blaming himself and blaming the traffic, making little sense, so that when the paramedics arrived, they'd put him on a stretcher, too. Later he'd been "sedated," Monica Kaufman had reported with her earnest expression, with no charges filed against him pending a full investigation.

Thom didn't care about a full investigation; after the first 24 hours of chaotic activity swirling through his apartment, he wasn't sure he even cared exactly what had happened. Connie was dead, and would be flown back to Oklahoma City for a funeral sometime next week. Connie's father, with whom Thom had several quiet, calm discussions, had accepted—to Thom's extreme surprise—Thom's invitation to the memorial service that Warren and a few others had planned for this coming Saturday, in a Midtown park where services for men dead of AIDS were often held. Mr. Lefcourt had sounded pleased, in his mild-voiced way, and said he would fly back to Oklahoma City on Sunday instead of Saturday morning, as he'd intended. The memorial service, which Warren and a few others had cooked up with Thom's reluctant cooperation, would be Saturday afternoon at four o'clock.

Mr. Lefcourt, again at Thom's invitation, had been among the dozens of people who dropped by Thom's place on Wednesday night, accompanied by Warren. Thom's rooms were so full of people, scattered food and drink, intent conversation in various groups, that almost no one knew who he was. Thom had been sitting slumped on the couch between Abby and their mother, talking idly about the news reports, when Warren introduced Mr. Lefcourt as "Connie's dad" and stepped back, leaving Thom and the others to fend for themselves.

Connie's father was a small-framed, handsome man in his sixties with short salt-and-pepper hair and startling blue-green eyes. Thom's first dismayed impression had been of Connie staring back at him, out of the older man's face. Mr. Lefcourt spoke in an undertone, had polite if rough-edged manners, and managed to say a few words to everyone without saying much of anything at all. His face was sharp-boned and appealing, especially when he offered a brief smile and displayed the even, white teeth of a much younger man. Yes, as Thom and Abby and Lucille later agreed, it was easy to see where Connie got his good looks; the only surprising difference was the older man's short stature and dapper thinness, bringing Thom the unwelcome thought that Connie had been an overgrown, overdone version of his father. Thom could imagine they'd had conflicts but there was no suggestion here of a man who drank (his skin and eyes were clear) or flew into rages (he was soft-spoken, a bit awkward as though unused to large groups). They made small talk for several minutes, they exchanged condolences, then Warren took him back to his hotel.

Two nights later, on the eve of the memorial service, Mr. Lefcourt returned, and this time only Thom, Abby, and Lucille were home. In his soft drawl Mr. Lefcourt told them of his plans for Connie's funeral, and emphasized that his son's friends were certainly welcome if they chose to come to Oklahoma City; he would call them later with the details. Thom told him about the memorial service on Saturday, and Mr. Lefcourt stunned them all by accepting the invitation.

"I always heard so much about Billy's friends, but I never got to meet any except Warren," he said. On the first evening, he'd explained that at home, Connie was known as Billy. Since both father and son were named Constantine, they'd decided to use Connie's middle name, William, to avoid confusion. Thom had gaped: Connie had never told him this. Thom apologized when he kept using the name Connie by mistake, but Mr. Lefcourt insisted that was fine; he knew that Warren and all his friends here called him that. He'd never used a nickname, himself, but he hoped they would drop the formality of saying "Mr. Lefcourt" and call him Constantine. Thom smiled and said he would try to remember.

Abby said, gently, "We were sorry to hear about your wife…"

Thom blanched: in his own grief, he'd forgotten about Connie's step-mother. "Yes," he said hastily, "Connie told us—I mean, Billy told us about it. I'm sorry."

Lucille, who sat between her children on Thom's sofa gazing balefully across at Mr. Lefcourt, pressed both hands to her cheeks. "Oh, my Lord!" she cried. "You lost your wife and child in the same month!"

Mr. Lefcourt looked embarrassed. Since arriving he'd stood with his back to the fireplace, though there was no fire burning. "I've been sitting all day," he told them. Now he rubbed his jaw absently with one hand, using the tips of his fingers as though massaging a tender spot. This took Thom's breath away: Connie had used precisely the same gesture, in moments of uncertainty or chagrin.

"Thank you," Mr. Lefcourt said quietly. "I appreciate that."

Thom tasted panic, for his mother had begun fidgeting and wringing her hands. An outburst of sympathetic tears might be next.

"I just can't imagine it!" she cried. "When I lost my husband, you know, it was so awful, but to think—" She glanced desperately at Thom, then at Abby. "I can't—I can't imagine," she repeated.

Mr. Lefcourt stared down at his shoes.

"Do you have someone back home," Abby said quickly, "to help with the arrangements and so forth?"

"Oh yeah," Mr. Lefcourt said. "My sister, Billy's Aunt Deborah—she handled everything with my wife's funeral, and she's doing the same for Billy." He gave a tight smile. "She's one of these super-organized folks."

Abby was smiling painfully; Thom saw the grim set of her jaw but knew that Mr. Lefcourt would not.

"That's good," Abby said. "Thank God for people like that."

"My sister Millicent is that way, sort of," Lucille said, distractedly. Thom knew she was still pondering the magnitude of Mr. Lefcourt's loss; every few seconds she glanced up at him, as if wondering how he managed even to stand there, alone and unsupported.

"Is there anything we can do?" Thom said. "I mean, I know that Warren is going to pack up Connie's things, but—"

"No, no," Mr. Lefcourt said. "Warren's a nice fellow, though. I told him he could keep the furniture and whatever else of Connie's he wanted. I hope he'll do that."

Thom had spoken to Warren on the phone, thinking the job of boxing Connie's possessions would be too much for him. But Warren had taken all this with remarkable calm. No, he'd said, he actually found it soothing to pack Connie's things; each piece of clothing, each knickknack and book had a memory attached. It was his form of therapy, he'd said. Thom had suspected there would be a delayed reaction, that Warren was still numb. Then Warren had told him about the service he and a few other friends were planning. Last year, Connie and Warren had attended a memorial for a very young man—he was only twenty, a Georgia Tech student Connie had flirted with at the gym—who'd died of AIDS. The boy's friends and family had gathered in John Howell Park, a minister had read a prayer, several of the boy's close friends had given brief, tear-choked eulogies. Everyone had been handed a bouquet of red balloons, and at the end of the service they'd released all their balloons into the air. To Warren's surprise, Connie had choked up at the sight of the balloons, dozens of them, wafting upwards and growing smaller, finally disappearing altogether. On their way home, Connie had said that when his time came, he hoped they'd do "the balloon thing" too. Warren had told Thom, "He kept repeating how moving it was, `how you held the balloons in your hand, and then seconds later they were far away, moving out of sight. Just like the boy had done. He said he kept his eyes fixed on one balloon and had the idea it was the boy's soul ascending out of sight. He started crying again, right there in the car."

Thom hadn't known what to say; Warren himself sounded on the verge of tears.

"That's a side of Connie we didn't see too often," Thom had said finally, hoping the words conveyed what he meant. To his relief Warren said quickly, "I know, I *know*," and they'd agreed that the memorial service, with balloons, was inevitable. "OK, Warren," Thom said, reluctant to break the connection. Warren had loved Connie so passionately, and Thom hated the thought of him alone in the condo they'd shared, packing boxes. "Just call if you need anything," he repeated. "OK, Thom. Bye," Warren said. The line went dead.

The faces of Connie and Carter and Thom's father and yes, of Chip Raines—alive and well in Athens, Georgia—floated through his mind balloon-like, bobbing. They vanished as he blinked his aching eyes.

His entire body ached as he told Mr. Lefcourt, "Yes, Warren's a terrific guy. I've been amazed by how strong he's been through all this."

Lucille patted Thom's knee, as though reproving him. "It's awful to lose a friend, honey," she said, "but poor Constantine has lost family members, *two* of them. There's really no comparison."

Thom knew there was no way to keep his mother quiet, so he decided not to try. At such times, you let people say what they had to say. He noticed that Mr. Lefcourt's eyes had stayed fastened on Lucille's flushed, carefully made-up face. One corner of the man's mouth seemed lifted in a smile, whether of amusement or derision Thom couldn't quite tell. Tonight, even more than during their first visit, there had seemed a measure of detachment, even of chilly reserve, in Mr. Lefcourt's demeanor that puzzled him, and not only because the man bore no resemblance to the drunken, cursing parent Connie had described. The man seemed entirely unfazed by his losses. Unshaken. And sober, too. Thom had offered him a glass of wine shortly after he'd arrived, but Mr. Lefcourt had shaken his head curtly. "No thanks," he'd said, looking off.

Now Thom said, "Mr. Lefcourt, you're sure I can't get you anything? A Coke or something?"

"And wouldn't you care to sit down?" Lucille added, though they'd had that exchange already.

Mr. Lefcourt gave his grim, polite smile. "Ought to be heading back to the hotel. In Oklahoma, we get to bed early."

Thom glanced at his watch, surprised that it was past ten o'clock. These last few days, he'd lost his sense of time.

They gathered at the door, enlivened by the rituals of leave-taking. Mr. Lefcourt had rented a car and insisted he didn't need directions back to the hotel; nor did he need a ride to the memorial service, since Warren had

given him one of the photocopied maps they were faxing to people—
Connie's few straight friends, mainly—who didn't know where Howell Park
was. Again Mr. Lefcourt struck Thom as amazingly contained and self-suf-
ficient; there was nothing you could do for him. Just as he'd turned to
leave, however, Lucille sprang forward and threw her arms around him.
She pressed her newly tinted red hair against the man's shoulder. "I hope—
I hope you sleep well," she murmured.

Mr. Lefcourt accepted the hug and even, in a measured, uneasy fashion, returned it. After a pause he said, "That's the tough part, when you've
lost your spouse. The going to bed, the going to sleep."

Thom and Abby gaped at this frank admission, but Lucille nodded as
though agreeing to an observation about the weather.

"Yes, I certainly remember that," she said. Oddly, the man's first intimate remark seemed to have calmed her down. "But *try* to sleep well," she
added, "and the children and I look forward to seeing you tomorrow."

Thom and Abby murmured their assent as Mr. Lefcourt disappeared
down the sidewalk, into the night.

"Isn't he a *nice* man," Lucille said, after Thom had closed the door. "Of
course, I'm not surprised. Connie was such a *nice* boy."

Thom and Abby exchanged a look that said clearly: Don't say a word.

It didn't surprise Thom the next afternoon that his mother had donned
her Easter outfit for Connie's service. A silk floral print, tiny white and pink
flowers on a navy background: he remembered that Connie had praised the
dress profusely. "I've never been one of those queens who wants to be a
woman," he'd said, "but when I see a dress like *this*!" To Thom's amaze-
ment his mother had laughed girlishly, thrilled by the compliment. Today
she looked pale and weakened beneath a too-heavy layer of makeup. Thom
had the fatherly impulse to order her back to the bathroom to wash her
face. As she raced around the condo in an overdone impersonation of her
motherly busyness from years ago—asking Thom if he'd had enough
lunch, if he had a freshly pressed shirt to wear to the service—he saw the
desperation in her quick-darting pale eyes and had an uneasy sense of the
general aimlessness of her anxiety, her inability to settle down.

"Mom?" he'd said finally, "I guess I don't have a shirt. Would you mind
ironing one for me?"

This kept her busy for the last hour. Abby had wisely stayed at her place
most of the day—he couldn't blame her, since after all she'd been dealing
with their mother full-time—but at 3:30 she rapped on Thom's front door.
Dressed as if reenacting a Sunday morning from twenty-five years ago,

when they'd don their church clothes and troop off to mass, the three of them left for Howell Park.

To Thom's relief, the weather had cooperated: it was a mild, windy Saturday, and though he'd expected a good turnout he was startled by the huge crowd that had assembled near a row of benches facing a large open area of the park. Thom remembered that the organizational skills of Warren and some of his friends—especially a lesbian couple, ubiquitous local activists whose Rolodex of Atlanta's gay "A-list" was second to none—were formidable. There were several rainbow-draped card tables where people were serving refreshments, taking donations for a Project Open Hand gift in Connie's memory, and handing out professionally printed "memorial cards" featuring a photo of Connie, a brief biographical sketch, and some of his favorite quotes from Dorothy Parker and Oscar Wilde. Under a spreading water oak squatted a young man busily inflating white balloons from a helium pump, tying them with string. There was even a Port-o-let, which made Thom's heart sink: how long a service had been planned? He knew that several of Connie's friends were going to speak, but he'd assumed their remarks would be brief; he'd heard that a couple of local writers, acquaintances of Connie's, were going to read poems they'd written about him. But Warren had insisted no one would use the occasion for fund-raising or speechifying. Past memorial services he'd attended had taught him, however, that people could seldom resist the temptation, once they were given the microphone, to depart from their prepared remarks and start rambling; that often people not scheduled to speak would decide they wanted a turn, after all; that there was a general reluctance to bring such services to an end, as if putting off the wrenching moment when the balloons were given up to the sky and the grief-stricken silence descended, and there was nothing left but to go home with a hole in your heart.

Self-conscious in his jacket and tie, his mother and sister in their pretty spring dresses on either side of him, Thom joined the crowd and found Warren chatting with Pace near the handsome caramel-colored boy who was filling the balloons and tying them in batches to several stakes in the ground. Warren and Pace were watching him, idly, while they talked, so they hadn't noticed Thom's arrival.

"Am I interrupting something?" he said, smiling.

Startled, they looked up. Pace grinned sheepishly, shaking his head, but Thom was startled by Warren's appearance: he was drawn and pale, his face creased with exhaustion.

While Pace chatted with Abby and Lucille, Thom said to Warren, "Hey, how are you doing. You don't look so good."

Warren kept staring at the guy squatting next to the pump, filling balloon after balloon. Warren's eyes weren't red from crying, which Thom would have preferred: instead they looked vacant, faraway.

"I'm all right," Warren said. "Still kind of numb, I guess."

"You don't look numb," Thom said. "You look like you're hurting. After this is over, why don't we—"

Warren put up a hand, as though to block Thom's words. "Thanks, but like I was just telling Pace, I need to be alone right now. If it weren't for all the work Patsy and Miriam put into this, I wouldn't have even come. I—I didn't want to come."

Thom said, feeling awkward, "I'm glad you did." He didn't know what else to say, so he was relieved when his mother stepped over and hugged Warren; he hugged her back, holding on for several seconds. Thom and Abby looked at each other, then glanced away.

Another group joined them, including one of the organizers, Patsy, with whom Connie had traded jibes at Thom's Christmas Eve party. She introduced the men she'd brought over to Lucille, who spoke to each of them graciously, holding out her white-gloved hand. One of the men was introduced as James, and now Thom glanced over to the handsome boy working on the balloons: of course, it was Reginald, whom Connie had identified as a "mulatto," peppering his monologue with those other insouciant, tactless remarks Thom wished he could not remember.

Thom was thinking of this, paying no attention to the conversation, when someone touched his arm. Abby was smiling. Today she wore a dress Thom hadn't seen before, a sleeveless pale-blue silk, plain but elegant; her short hair looked fuller, brushed and swept into dramatic curves behind her ears. She wore pearl earrings, necklace, bracelet—a matched set Thom thought he remembered from her college years. She might have been a college student, looking so young and untouched today with her shining hair and eyes, and this clever little smile, almost a smirk, she was giving him.

"I was asking the others," she said, "if they knew something else about today. Why it was a special day."

His mother was smiling cleverly, too, and only then did he remember. As did Warren, who managed a ghostly smile and put a weightless hand to Thom's shoulder.

He said, "Happy birthday, Thom."

Then came a general surprised chorus of "Happy Birthdays!" from the others gathered around—several people had joined them, young men who looked vaguely familiar though Thom couldn't place them—and Thom gave an embarrassed grin.

"Thanks, but this is Connie's day," he said.

Pace barked out, "Now Thom, you know I never remember people's birthdays. But happy birthday, goddamn it!"

The others laughed and moments later, once the conversation had shifted back to Connie, he felt Abby's warm breath close to his ear. He inhaled her faint but sweet perfume, which made him think of pink roses.

"Happy birthday, angel," she said, kissing his cheek. "I have something for you, when we get home."

"C'mon, we already celebrated," he said, pleased. "You already gave me something, back when Mom first got here."

"But today's *the day*," Abby said. "You're not getting off that easy."

Lucille stood close to them, eavesdropping. When Abby stepped away, his mother came forward, bringing with her the matronly scents familiar since his boyhood: the same harsh but oddly pleasant smell of her hair spray, the sweet odors of her skin cream, makeup, perfume. He'd thought she was about to say something, but instead she kissed him, too, a moist and breathy kiss she planted half on his cheek, half at the edge of his lips. "Happy birthday, honey," she whispered. "And I—I'm sorry about Connie. I know he was a wonderful friend." Startled, he resisted the urge to wipe his mouth; he assumed her lipstick had left a crimson smear. He knew from experience that Abby, or Lucille herself, would take a tissue from her purse and daub the blaring red mark away.

Yet how many years had passed since this had happened, his mother hovering suddenly close, bright-mouthed, unexpected—and then pressing her half-parted lips against his cheek? When he was a kid, her breath would be sickly-sweet from the gum she'd chewed constantly through those years: Juicy Fruit. Today her breath had been clean, minty. Now she stepped back, glancing up at him shyly, and he tried to compose his face into the semblance of a smile. A grateful smile. He could tell from her face, and Abby's, that he hadn't quite succeeded.

So he added, "Thanks, Mom," and gave his salesman's grin. Before she turned away her face softened, just perceptibly, as if she were satisfied with that.

One kiss had stayed with Thom Sadler throughout his life.

After three decades he could still recall the greasy surprise as he touched two fingers to his cheek—then the sight of them blood-smeared, a bright vivid red—then the stale heavy smell as of spoiled berries as he brought them to his nose.

Later he'd raced into the house, into his room. His cheek flaming, burning. Stopped breathless in front of the mirror where the smeared lipstick reminded him less of blood than war paint, his pale small-boy's face taking on a cockeyed glamour since the other cheek was white, untouched, giving him an unbalanced look. He turned sideways to see himself in profile, his eyes cutting sharply to the right until his eyes ached. No, not war paint, and not even a kiss any longer, just a smeary red stain that wasn't anything but itself. Opening his palm he'd rubbed savagely at the kiss, the mark, whatever it was, then he'd rushed into the bathroom and used a soap and washcloth until his skin stung.

His cheek felt aflame for the rest of the evening, but the kiss was gone.

That day had been his birthday, too, and it had begun as the most exciting of his life. For this was the first time he'd had a real party, one to which he'd been allowed to invite his friends. There were eighteen children in his kindergarten class, which was run by the nuns at Sacred Heart but taught by a lay teacher, Mrs. Simpson, a sweet pink-faced woman with upswept blond hair. For weeks he'd been pestering his classmates with reminders about the party. His previous birthday celebrations attended only by family members seemed to him babyish, something he'd left behind. Now he'd started school. Now he had friends, and they were coming to his party.

When he and his mother talked about the plans for his birthday (which he loved doing, darting moth-like around the kitchen while his mother tried to work) she would use the phrase "your friends" as though repeating a kind of mantra. He'd never thought about this word before. Two or three boys in the neighborhood had been his "little friends" (somehow they did not count, and he hadn't invited them to the party), but now there was a whole roomful, boys and girls, from school. All shapes and sizes. Even a black boy. Even a girl from Korea. All these were his "friends." (What about Abby, though? He played more with his sister than with anyone. But no, she was his *sister*, a word he didn't like because that's what the nuns were called, and Abby was nothing like the nuns, and because a fat third grader had shoved him one morning at recess, calling him "little sister," and Thom had fallen face first into the sandy mound of dirt near the merry-go-round. Still, he couldn't say "my friend Abby." She was his *sister*, a plain fact that would never change.) In the days before his party, that new word lived in his imagination, became palpable in his mind's eye, a solid and welcome shape on his tongue: *friend.* He tasted the word, heard its rich, full tones, even shut his eyes and saw the letters that had burned into his thinking in their unbreakable, changeless order.

Because his parents and Abby and sometimes even Verna read to him, and because Mrs. Simpson wrote words on the blackboard in kindergarten class, he already knew how to read, though not as well as his family bragged he did. To him, the words he did know were still new and exciting, like the faces or smells or colors of certain people. For him, *Verna* was a rich brown word, like her skin, the same color as the battered antique roll-top desk in the den, inherited from Thom's great-grandfather, where his mother sat to write the bills. He thought *Abby* was a sweet, girlish word, and once when they were talking about words in kindergarten class Mrs. Simpson had pointed out that his sister's name had the same letters as *baby* and said that was an *anagram*—-which was a word he didn't like, since it sounded mean and fussy. He'd told Abby that her name had the same letters as *baby,* but he supposed because she was older than Thom and in third grade she didn't seem to like the idea. Soon she'd figured out that his name had the same letters as *moth* and for a few days called him "Thom the Moth," and of course he fought back by chanting "Abby the Baby," and quickly enough by mutual unspoken consent they'd dropped the game. But he kept thinking about names, about words. His mother's name was *Lucille,* which sounded like breaking glass, and his father's was *George,* which made him think of a big comfortable dusty room. But as his birth-day party approached, he thought mostly about *friend* and how it was a solid, good word, full of ordinary letters that you used a lot. He'd told Mrs. Simpson about the party his mother was planning and that she'd called the other mothers to invite his "friends," and something about the careful way he'd said the words made her smile.

That day, she'd written the date of his upcoming birthday on the black-board—May 1, 1970—and said in other countries this was called "May Day" and it was a very special occasion. He liked the ring of "May Day," too, because it sounded important, and he liked words that rhymed. The day she wrote his birthday on the board was only the middle of April, and he felt the day would never come. He imagined the next two weeks as a sprawling desert of time across which he must crawl, going to sleep at night, waking in the morning, dressing and undressing, eating and drink-ing, going to kindergarten and coming home, doing all this patiently, impa-tiently, for days and days before his birthday and the party would finally happen. All this depressed him, so to distract himself he thought about words, and pestered his mother about the party and what they would do, what they would eat, what would happen, all to make the time pass more quickly.

His mother insisted they were going to have an old-fashioned birthday. They were going to have a big homemade chocolate cake (she hated those flat, white ones you got from the bakery) and six big blue candles that matched the color of Thom's eyes. They were going to play games like Pin the Tail on the Donkey. She'd dug an old watercolor of a donkey folded in quarters out from a dusty box in the tool shed, and she'd said it was the same one they used at her own parties when she was a little girl. The tail was missing, though, so Abby had made a new one out of brown construction paper, and the color wasn't even close to the faded brown of the original donkey but Thom said he didn't care. "It's just a game," he said, trying to sound nonchalant though his excitement made his voice squeak. He was thrilled by the idea of all his friends playing games at his party. His mother said they were also going to play "go fishing," which meant each child in turn would be handed a cane fishing pole with a string on the end, which would be lowered behind a tarp stretched across the swing-set in the backyard. On the other side of the tarp his father would crouch, invisible, and each time a new child "went fishing" Mr. Sadler would attach a party favor to the end of the line with a clothespin. And they would play musical chairs out on the patio, with his father playing his harmonica, and whoever was the last one sitting would win another favor. Then, around 5:15—his mother had written all this out, planning how long each event would take—his friends would don their paper hats and sing "Happy Birthday," and Thom would make his wish and blow out the candles, and then at long last, he would get to open all his gifts, and they'd all eat ice cream and cake, and Thom and all his friends would be happy, happy.

Beyond that moment, Thom hadn't given a thought.

On the morning of the party Thom was behaving, his father grumbled, as though he'd had ten cups of coffee, racing around the house, double-checking that everything was there for the games, asking his father if he was sure it wasn't going to rain (his father pointed up at the cloudless sky, not saying a word), asking his mother if they should call his friends and remind them (No, his mother had insisted, that wouldn't be polite—of course they would remember), and asking Verna if she'd remembered to make the punch. Had his mother bought enough ice cream, enough party favors? "Yes, child!" she'd cried, shaking her head. Verna worked for the

Sadlers from eight until noon, and Thom caught her watching the clock; though Thom's mother had offered her double her hourly wage to "work the party," Verna had claimed to have business in town; she'd slapped her man's felt hat over her sour-smelling black curls and left at twelve on the dot. When his mother called each of his classmates' mothers, she'd told them it would begin at four and end by six, and by 3:30 Thom was so frantic and darting from room to room so often, and so aimlessly, and asking so many questions he'd already asked that his mother ordered him to sit at the kitchen table and eat a cookie and drink a glass of milk.

"And take some deep breaths," she said, rolling her eyes.

When he heard the doorbell ring at ten minutes till four, of course he dropped the milk, and the glass shattered on the kitchen tiles, occasioning a deep groan from his mother—"Why couldn't Verna have stayed this *one* afternoon," she muttered—and half the milk had splashed onto his shirt and shorts, so he'd had to run up and change, and by the time he got to the den, sixteen of his friends were there. (Two of them never showed, a fact that later, whenever he thought about it, made his chest ache.) The mothers had conferred, and four of them had volunteered to carpool. The four cars had arrived in unison, like a funeral procession, each disgorging four children, and at six o'clock four different cars would arrive to pick them up again.

It was a perfect Saturday, a sunny May afternoon. His birthday.

When he came into the kitchen, though, dragging his feet out of shyness when he saw the brightly chattering kids, the breakfast room table piled with gifts, his sense of time shifted abruptly. The party careened along from the first moment his friend Danny saw him and shrieked "HAPPY BIRTHDAY!" and all the kids began circling him like bees, the boys punching his arm, the girls trying to kiss him, Thom giggling and fidgeting all the while, the back of his head tingling with nearly unbearable excitement, pleasure.

Happy birthday! Happy birthday!

The words flew at him like tossed flowers through the rest of the party even as his mother took control, informing the children of the activities she had planned and shepherding them along, first into the den for Pin the Tail on the Donkey, where Thom's parents handed out cloth napkins to use as blindfolds, summoning them one at a time ("In alphabetical order," Thom's mother insisted) to approach the wrinkled, melancholy-looking donkey profile tacked against a giant bulletin board, which Thom's father had brought home from his office. One by one, they approached blindfolded and tried to pin the tail (actually, thumbtack the tail) in the right place. The other children watched quietly for the first couple of tries, laughing uproariously when Susie Blanchard stuck the tail onto the donkey's rear hoof, shrieking with delight when Tim Daniels pinned it directly onto the animal's exposed, balefully staring eye (several of the children grabbed their own eyes, crying "Ouch, I can't see!" and "Oooh, where am I?"), but even as Thom's mother determinedly made her way through the alphabet, the children began to lose interest in watching, preferring instead to don their blindfolds and walk into walls, into each other, laughing and shoving, deliberately falling on the floor, so that Thom's mother announced anxiously (Thom's father and Abby had watched all this from the den sofa, smiling) that they should go outside for the next activity, and even Luther Washington and Amy Zins, who hadn't yet had their turn at the donkey, didn't seem to mind. So Mrs. Sadler corralled them all into the backyard, where Thom's father had already affixed an electric-blue tarp to the swing-set against which an impossibly long cane pole was leaning, prompting Kenny Martindale to shout, "Hey, Thom, is that the switch your dad uses on you?" More shrieks of laughter from the children. "Yeah, Thom's got to have his birth-day spanking!" one of them yelled. "Yay, Thom's going to get his birthday spanking, yay, yay!" the others cried.

"And now," Thom's mother announced, gesturing to her husband behind the tarp, "it's time to play Go Fishing!"

So it went, one game after another just as Thom's mother had planned, every child getting party favors and strawberry punch and cookies just as Thom's mother had planned, and before he was even quite ready, she'd brought the huge five-layer cake out onto the picnic table, its six big blue candles lighted, "Happy Birthday, Thom," written across the chocolate icing in pale-blue script. Then Mrs. Sadler and Abby brought the brightly wrapped packages out from the kitchen. Everyone donned their cone-shaped metallic-blue hats and sang the birthday song, which again made Thom feel bashful, with his parents and sister and all the children watching him while they sang (he felt an odd lunge in his stomach when they got to the verse "Happy Birth-day, dear Tho-om") but soon enough it was over, and Thom was summoned to make a wish and blow out the candles. The other children were giggling and shouting and shoving, but they receded in Thom's awareness as he approached the cake, trying to remember what he'd decided to wish for, but again his scalp was tingling, his head was spinning, he couldn't feel the ground underneath him as he approached the gigantic cake with its six candles lighted just for him. He couldn't remember, he could *not* remember, so he closed his eyes and pretended to wish and opened his mouth and pursed his lips—he'd practiced this, lying in bed last night—and blew.

Then the chaos of cake and ice cream, and one by one he opened the presents, always remembering to stare at the tag and say thanks to the person who'd brought it, remembering to look surprised and pleased even if it was something he already had (a Batman coloring book, a kaleidoscope from Toys "R" Us), and as he opened the presents Abby and his mother gathered the torn wrappings and folded them neatly into a garbage bag, his mother setting aside the store-bought bows for the box where she kept her Christmas ribbons. Before Thom had absorbed what had happened, and certainly before he was ready, it was six o'clock. The four mothers assigned to pick up the children arrived promptly: the sixteen children, shirttails and hair bows askew, mouths smeared with chocolate, cried "Happy Birthday!" a few more times as the six adults (talking forgettable grown-up chatter over the noise) coaxed them out the front door and down the sidewalk.

Thom, his vision still throbbing with the bright shrieking flame-like colors and the frantic happy cries and dizzying motion of the party, stared at the front door. It had closed a final time.

His parents and sister stood with him in the suddenly hushed foyer, like actors stranded on an unfamiliar, poorly lit stage.

His mother said, "Whew!" His father gave a gentle laugh, but Abby was staring at the door, too, her face a bit long, forlorn.

No one looked at Thom.

They spent the rest of the afternoon out back, Thom and Abby going through his gifts, playing briefly with the good ones and making fun of the bad ones (there was a cheap balsa-wood airplane: "That must have set the Vaughns back at least ninety-nine cents," Thom's mother laughed), and around seven o'clock his parents, after they'd finished the clean-up, had settled into their metal lounge chairs, his mother lighting one Bel-Air after another, occasionally giving out an exhausted sigh. Both his parents sipped leftover strawberry punch spiked with vodka. Thom's father made a face when he first tasted the drink—"This is too damned sweet, Loo; why don't you make me a real drink?"—but since Thom's mother seemed unwilling to move, he finished the punch, then poured them both more vodka, to which he added more punch from the plastic pitcher, and he drank that one, too. When they finished playing with the gifts, Abby went inside and made two more plates of ice cream and cake for her and Thom, and as their parents sipped their punches, Thom and Abby sat eating quietly on top of the picnic table, their feet planted on the bench side by side.

To Thom, everything felt different. Already when he thought about the party, he could not remember much of it, or else he remembered the parts he hadn't liked (the boring half-hour when the kids had lined up to go fishing; the embarrassing moment when everyone stared at him, singing the birthday song) instead of the parts that had excited him. He could remember the endless days when he'd looked forward to the party, his chest aching, his head reeling, but then the party had come, gone. So quickly. He had pestered his mother and Verna with questions, he'd lain awake at night, sleepless with longing, imagining the huge lighted birthday cake and the glossy, mysterious packages, he'd worried that his friends would forget to come or that it would rain or that his Grandma Sadler (who'd just gotten home from the hospital, after a gall bladder operation) would die and his parents would cancel the party altogether, but after all that fretting and wondering and thinking and dreaming and looking forward, looking *forward*, the party itself had glittered a moment and then passed, exactly like a candle so carefully lighted but then extinguished in one breath, and even as he sat beside his sister eating leftover ice cream and cake (which he'd forgotten to taste during the party, and which now that he was full tasted doughy and wet and sickly sweet) everything was sinking to normal, the afternoon was darkening; soon his mother would return to kitchen and start dinner, an ordinary dinner, and Thom would merely be a year older and nothing would have changed, except now there was nothing to look forward to; nothing to think about at night; no reason to count the days, wishing they would hurry past; no reason to think about much of anything, one way or the other.

It didn't seem fair.

Yet the afternoon waned and dusk began falling and no one seemed ready for the day to end. His parents sat on their patio chairs, gazing out into the woods behind the house, chatting idly. Thom's father kept pouring little dabs of the vodka in his glass, then refilling it with punch—he'd stopped complaining the drink was too sweet—and though his mother had stopped drinking, she kept lighting cigarettes one after another, her smoke fading upwards into the darkening air in a way Thom liked to watch, his eyes straining to separate the thinning smoke from the delusive blue-gray sky spreading above the roof of their house and visible in chinks through the trees, the stilled oak and magnolia leaves. After finishing their ice cream and cake, Thom and Abby had stayed at the picnic table, slapping at flies and mosquitoes, massaging their itchy bare legs, passing Thom's opened gifts back and forth for inspection and reinspection, until finally Abby got tired of the mosquito bites and went inside to do homework. So Thom took the balsa-wood plane Danny Vaughn had given him and, abruptly filled with energy, started running up and down the stretch of grass in front of the patio, making airplane noises—*"Rrrhmmmm, ssssstt!"*—and occasionally stopping to send the plane into the air for brief unsuccessful flights.

"Be sure you don't send it over the fence!" his mother called. "I'm not in the mood to go next door to the Hendersons and fetch that cheap little plane."

His father laughed, briefly. "Humph."

"...so, why *was* she crying?" his mother said.

Thom picked up the airplane from where it had crashed nose first into the azalea bush near the fence; he pretended to examine it, adjust the wing piece, but really he was eavesdropping. Halfway through Pin the Tail on the Donkey, the little Korean girl, Rita Kim, had plopped onto the den sofa, on the end opposite Mr. Sadler and Abby. Her face had crumpled, and she'd raised both hands to hide herself. Thom had glimpsed this from the sides of his eyes but had decided not to pay attention. Fortunately, Rita Kim was one of those noiseless criers; she would hang her head, and her shoulders would shake, her face cupped in both hands, but that was all. Abby had gone over and put her arm around Rita's shoulders, and they'd whispered for a few minutes, and the next time Thom noticed Rita, she was happily fishing in the backyard, giving her gap-toothed grin as she hauled in a tiny blond Miss America doll wrapped in plastic.

Thom's father shrugged. "Her dog died, Abby said. A few days ago. Little girl can't stop thinking about it."

"Aww. Poor thing," Thom's mother said.

So Rita Kim's dog had died. What kind was it? How old was it? Why did it die? Thom had many questions, but he kept fiddling with the plane, his head bowed. He didn't want to hear his mother's answers. Last Christmas he'd asked for a puppy, and that was exactly why his mother said no. Something would happen to the dog. It would get sick. It would get run over. It would die and break Thom's heart. "Dogs and cats," Thom's father had explained, gently, "don't live as long as we do."

Thom had trouble standing still—he had so much energy left over from the party, from all the ice cream and cake!—but he wanted to hear what his parents were saying. He started running again with the plane, making soft noises to himself, staying within a few feet of the patio where his mother and father had become shapeless blue-gray blurs in the dusk. The only lights were the soft-glowing yellow rectangles from the house, and the occasional flash of the fireflies that had invaded the yard, and at the patio table the bright crimson glow, every few seconds, of his mother's cigarette as she smoked.

"Well, it happens," his father said flatly. Thom heard the chink of his glass against the glass-topped table.

"What happens?" his mother said.

"Dogs *die*. That's what."

Again his father gave that mirthless laugh. Humph. Thom zoomed back and forth with the plane. *Rrrrhmmmm. Sssstt.* The fireflies winked on and off.

"Oh, that's nice," his mother said. "Such a nice thing to say."

A brief silence during which Thom listened hard, and then his father said, "Well, it's the goddamn truth. None of us gets out of this alive."

Thom wished Abby hadn't gone inside. They could get a Miracle Whip jar and catch fireflies like they did last summer, punching holes in the lid with an ice pick so the bugs could breathe. Soon it would be too dark for that.

"That's nice, too," his mother said. Her voice sounded damp, unhappy. "Why would you say such a thing?"

His father's glass clinked against the table.

"Why?" his mother asked. "Why would you?"

Thom started careening around the yard, directionless. Feeling dizzy, he stopped a few feet from his mother, lifted the plane, aimed, and threw it with all his strength. In the faint glow of moon-washed sky, he glimpsed the plane sailing over the fence into the Hendersons' yard.

Scraping of chair legs against the concrete patio.

"Thom?" his mother said. "What are you doing?"

Thom turned and ran to his mother; up close, he could see her face looking tired, confused. And frightened. Her eyes still moist. But her cheeks were dry, so impulsively he kissed them, first one and then the other. Then he laughed. But his mother didn't laugh. He felt the vague push of her palms against his shoulders.

"Stop being silly, Thom. Your mouth is all sticky from the ice cream."

She pressed one hand against her glass, then rubbed at her cheek with her wet palm; she dried it with the napkin.

Thom's father stayed silent.

Quickly, Thom retreated back into the yard, far enough that his parents could not see him. They'd started collecting their glasses and pitcher, the ashtray.

"I'm getting eaten alive out here," his mother said to no one in particular. But as she neared the back door she stopped and called out, "Thom?"

He didn't answer.

"Thom?" Her voice sounded wobbly, uncertain. "Happy birthday, honey..."

His father had gone inside.

"*Thom...?*"

He didn't answer.

That's when she came at him, her large blurry face floating dreamlike through the dark, her moist red lips puckered for a kiss, slightly parted. Just in time he turned his head, and the kiss landed on his cheek, not his lips, and it was a messy kiss.

A wet, greasy kiss. A sticky kiss.

His cheek tingled, the skin along his arms and neck seemed to crawl. The sweetish fruity odor of her breath filled his nostrils.

"Happy birthday, honey," she muttered again, vaguely, but he didn't answer, didn't even glance in her direction. He sensed her quick retreat, the absence of warmth. He let out his breath, relieved.

She'd stopped a few yards away. She cleared her throat. "Don't stay out much longer, you hear? And be sure to bring your presents inside."

He knew that in a few seconds she would think to turn on the backyard floodlights, so he could see to collect the gifts. He dreaded the moment when this would happen.

He stood quietly in the yard, his ankles itching from the mosquito bites. They were eating him alive. None of us gets out of this alive. Happy birthday, honey. He didn't yet know that words, even good strong words like *friends,* would never again have as much power to thrill, enliven, console him. He saw the reddish aureole of his mother's hair at the kitchen window; she was washing dishes, just as she had washed away his kiss.

Around him the fireflies were winking on, off; on and off. As if lighting his path to the future.

He longed to race inside the house and wash his face, but first he waited there in the yard until the darkness was complete and the fireflies had vanished. He turned from the house toward the black woods, and when he waved his hand before his face, Thom could see nothing. He wasn't even there.

• • •

After half an hour, as the crowd swelled and the buzz of conversation grew louder, Thom felt uneasy, for the atmosphere was that of a cocktail party, as though everyone had forgotten why they were here.

At least there wasn't the cheerful distraction of food, the lubrication of drinking; many of the clustered groups scattered through the park's worn grassy stretches had a subdued, earnest quality, though Thom suspected they weren't talking about Connie. Many were local activists who'd come here to network, to schmooze, having known Connie slightly, if at all; a few, he suspected, were "memorial service addicts," who simply showed up at any service like this. But Thom drew a deep breath. He tried not to feel judgmental. Around him a large group had gathered, so large that he'd been able to absent himself from the bright unruly recollections of Connie they'd begun swapping back and forth, as though competing to offer the most colorful memory, the most outrageous anecdote. Pace and Warren stood closest to Thom, and Reginald and James had joined the group, James's proprietary arm slipped around Reginald's waist; Alex and Randy had arrived with their usual airy greetings and air kisses, cell phones at-the-ready on their belts. To Thom's surprise Valerie Patten had come rushing up, too, effusive with relief that she wasn't late and introducing everyone—at long last—to her husband, "Martin Luttrell," a bashful sandy-haired man who shook hands vaguely, not meeting anyone's eyes. There were a few others, too, mostly friends Thom hadn't seen since his Christmas party. But everyone had a Connie story, and they traded them with a Connie-like zest, as if somehow they must compensate for his gaping, unaccountable absence.

Like Thom, Warren stayed abstracted from all this, though he laughed politely as Pace recalled one of Connie's doomed romances.

"Remember that kid he idolized from the gym, the one who had such an angel face?" Pace harrumphed. "A waiter at Mick's, but Connie said he had the body of a Greek boy by Michelangelo—said he was twenty-five but looked sixteen."

"Oh, I remember him," Reginald said. "*Andrew*. The one Connie was always following into the shower room, hoping to get a glimpse."

Pace said, "Right! But the boy was so modest, he wore his towel until the second he stepped behind the shower curtain, so poor Connie caught only the tantalizing flash of his buns!"

"I think I remember this story," Valerie said, seeming eager to say something. "I think he told me this one."

Beside her, Martin Luttrell wore a polite but vaguely constipated expression.

Pace said, "He told *you*, Val? About Connie finally getting himself invited over to the boy's place, and then when they got down to business, the boy pulled something out from under the bed...?"

"Um, maybe I'm thinking of a different story," Valerie said.

"Oh yeah, I remember!" Alex said, with his cackling laugh. "An economy-sized can of Crisco!"

The others laughed, shaking their heads.

"What's worse," Pace said, "the can was almost empty."

"*Quêl dommage!*" Alex cried, mimicking Connie's eye-rolling look of outrage. "So much for my choirboy! My Greek angel!"

Valerie thrust her pert head forward, eyes alight. "What about the turban story? Did he tell you all the turban story?"

Martin Luttrell threw her a startled glance but Valerie paid no attention.

"Yes, we've all heard that one," James laughed.

Alex and Randy exchanged glances and said in unison, "*We* didn't. Tell us!"

Reginald said, zestfully, "He'd met this hunk at the Armory, a real macho guy—six foot four, I think, in jeans and a leather vest. No shirt. Three days' growth of beard and cowboy boots. You guys remember, Connie could go for rough trade on occasion."

Thom said, smiling despite himself, "I remember this."

"Connie was *so* hilarious when he told this story," Valerie said. "He and this man—"

"The two of them went to the guy's place," Alex interrupted, "I think it was a little condo out in Decatur, and they decide to have some fun in the shower. By the time the hot water ran out, Connie is sure he's found his soul mate, and they're about to proceed to the bedroom. But after this macho guy dries himself off, he bends over and wraps the towel around his head! A flawless turban on the first try!"

Again, Alex mimicked Connie's high-pitched cry of horror: "Just like my mother used to do! God, I lost my erection in five seconds! Suddenly, this virile hunk had turned into Carmen Miranda!"

Laughing, Pace said, "I think they had some quick, obligatory sex and spent the rest of the night swapping tips on moisturizers."

Smiling vaguely, Thom looked toward the platform where a microphone, podium, and a couple of folding chairs had been set up. He wished the minister would get things started: it was twenty minutes past four. He caught sight of Abby, standing near the platform alongside their mother, who was talking earnestly with a short-statured man whose back faced Thom. Then, as if obeying Thom's mental summons, the man turned and Thom recognized Connie's father. He had the same look of defensive self-containment Thom had noticed the other night, almost as if he were one of those anonymous participants who hadn't really known Connie. He seemed to be listening appreciatively to Lucille, nodding, standing close beside her; clearly, she was pleased to have his attention. A cool shiver of apprehension passed through Thom.

He hadn't yet decided what to believe about Connie and his father. The man did not seem like a drinker, nor did he seem like a man who could lose his temper easily, much less indulge in the abusive tirades Connie had reported. At the same time, Thom could not imagine even Connie indulging himself with such extravagant, self-pitying lies. The truth lay somewhere in between, Thom surmised, dissatisfied with this idea but not knowing what else to think. Perhaps Connie's father had simply been jerked back to reality by the prolonged death of his wife, the sudden loss of his only child. Thom could not know; he would never know.

Every family, he thought, retreating from speculation, has its secrets. No end to them. Better to let them lie.

Abby had caught his miserable glance and now, having spoken a word to her mother—who scarcely paused in her involved conversation with Mr. Lefcourt—hurried over to Thom.

"Are you OK?" she asked, taking his arm. Lately she'd used this gesture more often, clinging to his arm affectionately, even possessively, at random moments. "You look so..."

She waited as if for Thom to complete the sentence.

He tried to smile. "I have no idea how I look."

She gazed at him. "So...bereft." She was whispering, so the busily chattering group could not hear. Thom was aware that one of the organizers had approached them and was handing out balloons. The minister (a woman Connie had not liked, Thom recalled) at last had ascended the podium.

Thom said, "I guess that's accurate enough."

Abby stood on tiptoe to kiss his cheek. His sweet, wounded sister, there to comfort him. He felt a constriction in his throat, but he turned aside and pretended to cough; the moment of intense, knotted emotion quickly passed.

"Thanks, honey," he told Abby. He turned his shoulders slightly, a signal they should join the group, shouldn't stand apart from the other mourners, and just then someone approached Thom, offering him a balloon. But instead of the ordinary white balloon everyone else was holding, this one was larger: a blaring, metallic turquoise. And instead of the organizer, who had left the group and begun distributing the white ones elsewhere in the park, the man who handed him the turquoise balloon was Warren.

"I—I just slipped over to the helium pump and filled this one—for you," Warren said. "This was his color, and he idolized you, Thom. Would you take it?"

In his other hand Warren held a white balloon, like everyone else. Before Thom could protest (of course, it should be Warren himself who released this one) Warren had stepped away, leaving Thom with this extravagant bobbing turquoise globe on a string. Several others in the group—Reginald, Valerie Patten—had glanced at the balloon and then at him, seeming puzzled. Thom stared at the balloon himself, unable to think of anything but Connie's bright blue-green eyes, his lush turquoise sweaters, his scalding laugh, his impish and impulsive soul that even now seemed here among them.

So Thom's thoughts ran. Abby tiptoed again to whisper in his ear.

"Poor Warren, he's so sweet," she said. Before he could answer, the minister began speaking through the microphone, welcoming them to this memorial service for "their beloved friend." Everyone turned to face her, all the eighty or a hundred people holding balloons like children temporarily quieted during a party; all looking wistful, subdued; all, it must be admitted, looking a bit ridiculous as they held fast to the string in one hand, their white balloons bobbing in the mild spring air.

The minister's remarks were brief, and only three of Connie's friends—all of them lesbians whom Connie had liked but to whom he hadn't felt close—made the usual attempts at poignancy blended with humor as they offered their memories, their consolations. Connie's closest friends were too bereaved to speak, a typical situation at services like this. The women did mention Thom, and Warren, and Pace, and even Abby in their remarks, and the dozens of others scattered around the park often glanced in Thom and Abby's direction. At one point, Thom himself glanced around, missing Warren, and noticed him sitting by himself on a park bench, separated from the crowd, the only person in the park who was not standing and paying attention to the speaker. Warren had tied his balloon to the bench's arm railing and sat with his arms on his knees, gazing down into the grass. Thom's heart convulsed in sympathy. Abby was looking at Warren, too. Her grip on Thom's arm had tightened.

"Poor Warren," she whispered. There was nothing else to say.

When the last speaker had finished, the minister came back to the podium and mumbled some words about "releasing Connie's spirit," though none of them would ever "release him from their memories," along with some other mumbo jumbo Thom didn't bother to hear.

Abby poked him in the side, gently. "Pay attention," she said, in a mock-scolding tone. "We've got to do this right."

Thom looked toward the podium and saw the minister holding her own white balloon aloft. Now everyone in the group, like obedient children, lifted their balloons in the same way, and Thom did, too. On the woman's cue, "Goodbye, Connie," everyone released them, Thom and Abby opening their hands at the same moment as everyone else. They all craned their necks, watching the swift ascent of the dozens of pale bobbing globes through the postcard-blue sky. They seemed a mass of white, a great silent cloud, but then as the balloons ascended they began to separate, tossed here and there by darting breezes, and it seemed only a few seconds before they were drifting off to the east, like small white bubbles arising from the brilliant spring afternoon.

Several people had pointed at the turquoise one Thom had released. "*That* one's Connie," someone said loudly. "Always had to be different!" A general tittering passed through the crowd.

Thom felt himself staring at the turquoise balloon, hard, as though willing it not to float out of sight. At first it seemed slow and contrary, taking its time, but finally it wafted upward, too, and in fact took a prominent position, the star of the show, rising into the middle distance and surrounded by the white balloons on all sides as though following an inevitable choreography. Thom thought for the first time that Warren's idea had been inspired, for the turquoise balloon drew everyone's eye, of course; it focused everyone's emotion. Already Thom could hear the muffled sobs here and there, and in the small sea of upturned faces he glimpsed a few people daubing their eyes with tissues, with the backs of their hands. Yet they refused to look away, keeping their gaze trained on the balloon that had grown so small, so distant, as it rushed upward among the others into the blue dome of sky. Beside him Thom could hear his sister's gentle sobbing, but even for Abby he didn't look away, not until the moment the speck of dazzling turquoise was lost amid the blizzard of white balloons.